Act

CW00376906

Michael Jecks

4948

Table of Contents

Tuesday 13th September

00.26 Whittier, Alaska; 09.26 London

Danny Lewin knew this nightmare only too well.

In the beginning he had feared it. He had dreaded closing his eyes because of the horror that he knew would immediately assault his mind. In those early days he had kept himself awake to avoid it, drinking heavily, until the day he found himself in a friend's sitting room, naked, shivering, sobbing, and incapable of clothing himself. His mate stood back and stared, uncomprehending and incapable of helping.

That sense of utter desperation, the complete futility of his wretchedness, which was so near to madness, bludgeoned him into submission. Eventually he agreed to visit the hospital again and, a while later, he started taking the little blue pills. The military psychiatrist told him they would give him peaceful, dreamless sleep, but now even their protection had eroded, and the dream returned to him every night. It was so familiar, he almost welcomed it. There was no need to avoid it: it was a small reminder of his humanity. It proved he still had a soul. That he was not completely lost.

*

It began.

At first, all was black. He could believe himself dreamlessly comfortable – but then the darkness faded, and he could see that the darkness all about him was a vast, gaping mouth, as broad as all sorrow, as deep as all pain, a bottomless pit of grief. And then he was moving backwards, out of it, until it took form: Edvard Munch's *The Scream*. Except as his view panned back, it gradually transformed. The eye-pits deepened, until the chalky face became a mask, and in those eye-holes were real eyes, terrified, anguished eyes, the eyes of the men he had helped to break. Those who had suffered the regime of *fear up harsh*. He could smell their terror. He could see their urine-stained trousers, their chafed wrists and ankles, the sudden eruption of bloody froth from their beaten mouths as the electrodes flashed, and the agonised strain of their bodies as water poured onto the cloths over their heads and they began to drown.

And Munch's hideous, primal scream became his own, Danny Lewin's, for all the pain, terror, anguish he had inflicted, and Lewin dreamed he saw himself in a mirror, seeing not his own face, but the mask of *The Scream* and, in his anguish, he began to tear at his own face to release himself from the enduring horror, until there was only blood, and then he saw his bloody hands reach out for his eyes, to pluck them out and save him from seeing any more.

That was when he woke, screaming, to the feel of the cold steel at his throat and knew he was about to die.

It was a relief.

*

06.34 George W Bush Building, Langley, Virginia; 11.34 England

The George W. Bush CIA Headquarters was already beginning to fill up, even though it was early. It was never empty – through the night there were agents, analysts, electronics specialists, and a few recuperating intelligence officers from abroad who would be listening, watching, assessing data as it streamed in. Last night, Peter Amiss knew there had been a team in the southern section of the building deep underground playing their war games. They'd been successful, too, from the whoops of glee he'd heard. One of their unmanned drones had hit a target with a hellfire missile.

He turned on his computer and leaned back in his chair as the screen flickered. He detested these things – better and safer to commit data that mattered to paper and nothing else. One copy held in his safe was secure. It was the old adage: a secret shared wasn't secret, and Peter Amiss despised computers for that very reason. When his grandson came and showed how information on his wireless computer could be sent across the world, Amiss was sickened at the thought of the myriad ways in which that data could be intercepted, stolen, copied, and disseminated.

He was a professional. He detested insecure communications.

Behind him, against the office wall, were two flags. Over his left shoulder was the CIA's own banner, while at his right was the stars and stripes, a slightly worn version, which he had liberated from his office in Saigon when he was forced out to the waiting Jolly Green Giant that was to take him and the last of the agents from the compound out to the sea. He was not going to leave it behind for the gooks to piss on or burn. His love of his country was as deep and committed as his religious belief. Which was why, behind Old Glory, there stood a crucifix – simple one, the cross itself carved from cedar, the figure in some darker wood. Some reckoned that when he turned

8

and bent his head, he was praying as much to the American flag as to the figure on the cross.

Others reckoned he was dozing.

He didn't care what they thought. Peter Amiss was Deputy Director of the CIA, an appointment he had held since two months post 9/11. Before that he had been working his way to retirement, but the sudden eruption of violence in New York had saved him. Younger, more senior agents had collapsed under the strain, the previous Deputy and Director had both resigned because of the shame heaped upon the Agency for failing to prevent the attack. He had been one of those tasked with leading the Agency against this new threat. His experience from Vietnam onwards made him the natural choice, as did his contacts with senior operatives in other agencies.

Taking a sheaf of papers from his desk, he tapped them square on the glass top, and placed them in a file. They were notes, for the most part handwritten. So much nowadays was held on the Agency's computers in their air-conditioned suites, or over at the NSA's buildings where their massive supercomputers sat silently consuming energy while they filtered the billions of messages that were fed into them each day. All general Agency work was computerised, and even certain details of the work that Amiss performed were sent off to be included on the main systems for archiving and even, occasionally, for analysis.

Every so often it was good to be in this early, to keep the others on their toes. Today, though, he was in for a different reason. He was waiting for the signal.

Knowing that others were out there doing his bidding made him want to take up smoking again. In the past he would have been out there with them – one of the shadows, a man in the darkness, his every cell alert and listening. Those were the days he had been most alive, when he was still out there in the field. He had known the thrill of the hunter – whereas now he was a puppet-master. Sitting here in his panelled office – with his desk, his flat screens and his comfortable chair – he felt pathetic. It was as though this comfortable existence was preparation for the day when he would be given the handshake from the director and a final ride from Langley.

But not yet. He had so much still to do.

The telephone rang. It was a muted sound, the volume turned as low as possible so it would not intrude upon his thoughts when he was busy. Picking up the receiver, he glanced around the room, at the framed photos of presidents, soldiers, agents, and one oil painting: a picture of the pyramids at Egypt – that was a never-ending source of inspiration for him.

'Amiss.'

'Sir.'

'Go secure,' Amiss said, pressing the button on his STU-III phone. It took fifteen seconds for the two government telephones to coordinate their encryption, and then he heard the slight hiss. 'Yes?'

'All done.'

'Good. Any witnesses?'

'No. We were careful. I'm sorry it's taken so long to get through to you, but it seemed sensible to make sure all was secure.'

'You were quite correct,' Amiss said and replaced the handset.

He sat there for a moment, utterly still, his palms on the desk's glass top. It was like this at the beginning of every operation, he knew. The moment when one word could launch the project. The moment of doubt.

No matter how long he had spent assessing risks and benefits, nor how much time had been spent viewing possible alternatives and the merits of each, it always came to this: to go ahead or to close down the operation now, before he was committed, before other men were thrown into it, some to die, many to be changed forever.

His eyes rose to the pyramids and he felt the calmness return to him – a calmness reinforced by the knowledge that God was with him. God and his nation. The two forces he most revered.

Taking up the handset again, he put a call through to another government building.

'Mister Tullman, we are going ahead.'

'May God be with us.'

Wednesday 14th September

09.12 Near Okehampton, Devon

He parked the car and climbed out – a scruffy man of forty-four, square in build, with grizzled hair and a face that seemed perpetually surprised, always on the brink of a smile that somehow never quite materialised. He had the look of an amiable bear: not the cleverest man, maybe, but stolid and reliable. A good middle-manager or salesman. And instantly forgettable. Jack Case had depended on that ability to fade into a crowd for most of his life.

The parking area was quiet here in the valley. The river foamed as it rushed down the rocky gulley, swollen after the night's rain. Only a year ago a man crossing the ford had fallen into the river, knocked his head on a rock, and drowned. No one should treat the moors lightly – they could be deadly.

There was another car. Empty, nothing to make it stand out, but Jack glanced at it quickly as he stepped round his own silver Vauxhall – not too new, slightly scuffed, like an old pair of shoes. It wasn't out of place here, with the old Peugeots and Citroëns that were the popular choice among the local folk. It had a scratched bumper, a dent in the rear door, and a filthy windscreen. But there was one thing that was out of place down here. He could see a circle of dirt, maybe two inches in diameter, not far from the rear-view mirror. It made his blood run cold. He almost wrenched open his driver's door to hurry away, but there was no point. They knew where he was. He'd known someone would come for him before long.

Stooping, Jack grunted to himself, sniffed the cold November air, and wandered to the hatchback. Popping it open, he stood back to let the dogs bound out, tails wagging furiously, two identical Springer Spaniels, who immediately bolted down towards the gate that gave access to the moor.

Jack knew his life was about to change again. He felt it as a thickening in his throat, the same as he always had. Not quite fear, not quite excitement, but a mixture of both.

The man was there beside the gate, waiting for him.

Paul Starck. His boss – or, his ex-boss

*.

11

Jack Case walked past Starck without breaking his stride until he reached the gate to Fatherford.

'I've nothing to say to you.'

'Really?'

Starck was a good half a head taller than Jack, but his hair was sleek, like a well-groomed colt's. He had sharp, aquiline features that always reminded Jack of Sherlock Holmes: a broad forehead, pointed nose, bloodless lips and a complexion that paid testament to his smoking. In an age when so many were giving up tobacco, Paul Starck was one of the few men Jack had ever met whose entire hand was stained yellow from nicotine. He smiled at Jack as he raised a cigarette, drew heavily, and spoke through a cloud of smoke.

'Did you know I was here? I saw you clock my car.'

'Clock it? Yes. I recognised it.'

The little mark on the screen was enough: the mark a suction cup would make. All the pool cars would have a spare rear-view that could be stuck on the windscreen so that a passenger could keep watch on people behind. It made Jack wonder just how long he had been under surveillance. He hadn't seen them, but that was the point. The 'watchers' were among the best in the business. Targets didn't see them.

'We would like to have you come to town. There's something you can help with.'

Jack reached a second gate. The two Spaniels had already wriggled their way beneath, and Jack lifted the heavy latch and walked through.

'I'm out, Paul. Gone.'

'You know what they say, old darling. Once in, never forgotten. You can't forget us, and we won't forget you.'

The ford was in front of them, the river calm and apparently idle in the wider, shallow bed. Jack turned away and walked to the left, past the ford, to where a small wooden bridge crossed the river just beyond a railway bridge of rough granite blocks. There was a steady rumble and thump from the next bridge, a two-lane road bridge taking traffic down to Cornwall and back. The noise precluded talk, which was a relief. It gave Jack a little time to gather his thoughts.

They walked on in silence for some while, Paul Starck treading with care on the muddy trail, his impeccable suit and black leather shoes already marked with mud, while Jack strode on carelessly, his brown shoes already liberally spattered as though it was his form of rebellion.

'Don't you want to know why?' Paul said.

'No.'

'You have such bad feelings about the Service?'

'Is that supposed to be a joke?' Jack said.

He thrust his hands into the pockets of his old Barbour, clenching his fists. The coat had served him well during many walks on the moors, but now it felt fragile, as though he could push his fists through the pockets. It was foolish. He had nothing to fear from Paul Starck; if anything, Paul was a messenger, nothing more.

'The Service left *me*. I was kicked out, remember? Almost year ago.'

'You killed a man.'

'Where's the proof? I never left London.'

'There were rather too many people who didn't believe you.'

'For God's sake, I'm innocent!'

'That may be true, old darling. But the powers-that-be assumed the worst, or that they couldn't trust you any more.'

'And that's all?'

'I think it is, actually,' Paul Starck said. He looked at his cigarette and flicked it away towards the river. 'Don't blame the Service.'

'That part of my life's over. I'm rebuilding my marriage here. So fuck off.'

'You remember the comms man?'

'Didn't you hear me? I'm out,' Jack said, and whirled to face him.

His fists were clenched, and he could anticipate the fierce joy of grasping Starck's throat and choking the life from him. It was hard not to submit to the urge, and Jack could feel his fingers uncurling at the thought, ready to grab him.

Starck's next words saved his life. They shattered the spell.

'The broken man. Remember him?'

'We had so many.'

'Don't be coy, Jacky,' Paul Starck said.

He cupped his hands around a fresh cigarette and flicked his brass Zippo. The tinny clatter and rough scrape of flint was as familiar to Jack as it had been three years ago when he finally packed in smoking for good.

Starck inhaled deeply, shutting away the flame and staring bleakly at Jack.

13

'You were good once, weren't you?'

'I read the runes like a good little priest. But someone switched them for a loaded set,' Jack said.

'You were a Cold Warrior when everyone wanted to trust the Bear. The masters didn't want to think our new friends could turn on us.'

'It was fucking stupid, and you know it,' Jack said evenly. 'And I don't care any more. I have a new life now.'

'Patching things up with Claire, yes. How is she?'

Jack felt a crawling sensation run along his back.

'Fuck off. She's fine and I want her to stay that way. Keep away from her.'

'So we heard. I'm glad she's getting better. Sorry, Jack, but you know how it is: no secrets among family. I'm glad you're making a go of it,' Paul Starck said, staring at Jack through slitted eyes as he took another drag. 'But it's not her we're interested in. It's you.'

'Why?'

'An old matter's come up. You do remember Danny boy, don't you, Jacky? The comms man who went to serve his queen and country. You remember Danny Lewin, don't you? The boy with the embarrassing conscience?'

'Yes, I remember him.'

'Yes, well, I'm afraid he's even more embarrassing now. He's gone and killed himself.'

*

09.19

There had been too many cases of burnout that year. One more was hardly a surprise.

Danny Lewin had been an exemplary officer. In 1992, he had been hired as a communications technician in GCHQ as soon as he left Cambridge. With his skills in Middle-Eastern languages and his flair for computers, he had been an asset to the international snoopers. Jack had seen the glowing reports from his supervisors and managers in his files. He was charming, intelligent, and a breath of fresh air to the team of staid petrochemical experts who spent their lives listening to lengthy telephone conversations about the misbehaviour of globetrotting sons of oil sheikhs. He was popular, and his team was sad when he announced he was applying for a transfer to Iraq. When asked, he said he wanted to help the war effort. 9/11 had shocked him. Anything he could do to help find the murderers, he said, was worth it. Better to be out working with soldiers and helping bring in

14

those who could dream up such a hideous attack than sitting on a comfy chair in Cheltenham.

After Lewin's breakdown, Jack met him to debrief him and assess his case, and concluded his was the clearest example of post-traumatic stress he had seen. Lewin had left England as an athletic thirty-one year-old in 2002, and returned three years later a shattered husk. He smoked constantly, shivered, and had lost the ability to concentrate. The language skills he had once possessed were gone, as though his mind was sub-consciously shutting off the one resource that made him attractive to the Service.

'The Service treated him shabbily,' Jack said.

'No need to be prim, Jacky. Human Resources did what they had to.'

'They dumped him, poor bastard.'

'He went potty, Jacky, you know that. Started seeing al-Qaeda under his bed. With our budgets we can't nursemaid tired-out officers.'

'After all he went through, it's not surprising he was knackered.'

'Others had similar experiences.'

'You think so? Maybe he wasn't so brainwashed as them, then?'

'No one was brainwashed, Jacky. He had a job to do, and he couldn't cope.'

The footpath led along the side of the river, the sound of traffic lost in the roar of the water. Jack looked over at the dogs. One was standing at the water's edge eating grass, while the other, tail madly wagging, was darting in and out of a patch of dead ferns and brambles nearby. In his mind, he could see Danny Lewin, a gaunt six feet two inches, with sunken eyes and cheeks. He looked older than Jack himself, and there was an unhealthy glimmer in his eyes.

It was 2005 when Jack had met him in a ground floor briefing room in Vauxhall Cross, the gleaming new centre for the British Secret Service. It had pale green walls, a harsh bottle green carpet, and an incongruous beech desk with metal-framed chairs opposite each other. Dan Lewin had sat huddled, as though feeling the cold, a cigarette gripped like a talisman, one hand cupping the other, his ciggy protruding like a gun.

'I can't go back,' he said in a rasping hiss. 'It'd kill me.'

Jack had believed him. As he left the room he was enveloped in a claustrophobic self-hatred that wouldn't leave him until he got home and stood under his shower, as if water could wash away the horror.

Danny had an intense self-loathing that others could feel. His revulsion at his work had turned inwards. He didn't blame others for his orders, or even politicians for taking him to war; he blamed himself for being weak. If he'd been stronger, he would have refused to collude.

'What is it?' Jack had asked at one point. 'Don't you like the work?'

It was a question he had asked many others, but the implied cowardice didn't bother Lewin.

He sat up, both his hand and cigarette shook with anger, and when he spoke his voice was low and ferocious. 'You think I'm some prick who whines when things go wrong? You think I volunteered because I was too thick to realise what it'd be like? You sit here in your cushy job and look down on me? I tell you, if there was a guaranteed terrorist, I'd rip his fingernails out one by one if it'd help catch his mates before they could blow up bloody London. Fuck you! I just don't like what I've become – a killer *myself*! They were innocent, almost all of them. I wanted to help the war effort, not create victims to motivate martyrs!'

It was that which told Jack he was worthless. Lewin was confused; he couldn't rationally discuss his concerns. He wanted certainty of guilt before he would work on his victims. That wasn't how it went. They were brought to him with the presumption of guilt, and it was Lewin's task to force their confessions. But the poor bastard got so confused, he'd killed himself. Pathetic. The ultimate cowardice.

*

'What's it got to do with me?' Jack asked.

Paul Starck drew on his cigarette and stared at the stub with distaste. 'Really should give up. You know how much these little death sticks cost? Bloody silly habit. If it wasn't for the duty free allowances and foreign agents who don't smoke, I'd stop like a shot.'

'You heard me,' Jack said.

He kept his eyes on the dogs, not Starck. Long ago, he had learned that it was easier to hear a lie when you didn't watch body language. With professionals, it was too easy to be fooled by a gesture or a twitch. They were trained in deceit.

'It's possible he left a journal.'

'Send someone to clean up.'

'We need a *real* scavenger, Jack. One who can search through the man's life. You knew him; you would be better than some young whippersnapper. No matter how keen, these youngsters…'

'I'm out.'

'Well, no, actually. You're on your way, of course, but you're not out yet. You're on gardening leave, old cock – on the payroll. Still an embarrassment, of course. No one really knows what to do with you. Can't put you in a court for murder, of course, not a fellow like you – that could be even more embarrassing. So we were leaving you to fade away quietly. Case not proven, as the Scottish would say. This little affair in Alaska could end your career with a high. But if you want to leave sooner…' Paul added mildly.

Yes, he spoke mildly, but Jack could hear the edge. This was a genuine threat. His pay-off was at risk, maybe his pension too. No one would speak up for him. They all thought he had killed a fellow officer, but there was no proof. They couldn't kick him out, they couldn't throw him in gaol, so here he was, a year later, still in limbo –

untrusted, disliked, but still being paid. But refuse a job, and he'd be out in moments. HR would be delighted to see him off their books.

'You can use one of the others, can't you? What of Broughton's Bullies?'

'Stevie Broughton's fallen under a bit of a cloud recently. His lads have been growing a little over-enthusiastic. They lost a couple of men they were trying to catch. Shootings in rural Surrey don't go down well with the rozzers; they think they have a monopoly on killing the public. It's all a little embarrassing. There were several names thrown into the hat, but yours was top. You have experience. And you did meet the fellow. It's felt you'd understand him better, with your background.'

'I met him for one hour-and-a-half meeting seven years ago, Paul. You know that, you've looked at the files. I've got nothing to do with him. Why me?'

Starck sighed.

'He's been running wild. We had to hush up a nasty incident last year when he was caught trying to buy a pistol. Would've been when you were down here. With Claire, I mean. Took a lot to keep it quiet, the bloody fool. The rozzers nobbled him immediately, of course.'

'What did he want with a gun?' Jack didn't need to ask. He could guess: the pressing guilt of torture committed against the innocent. A gun would be an easy way out.

Starck's answer surprised him.

'He was convinced he was going to be killed – thought the Taliban were coming to get him, or al-Qaeda, or the bloody Women's Institute. Christ knows what. He'd applied to us, but he wasn't on the payroll so we couldn't oblige. Pistols aren't allowed for the general public. Toys like that are for us alone.'

There was a sharpness to his tone that spoke of regret. It was rare for Paul Starck to show sympathy for operatives: he tended to the view that the brighter ones would soon ensure that they were promoted out of the field, while those who stayed there deserved all they got. Still, even Starck would have realised that a man like Dan Lewin deserved better treatment. If the Service treated the genuinely unwell shabbily, it wouldn't bear thinking about how it would treat older officers like Starck. And there were plenty of applicants for all jobs now. The Service had grown popular since 7/7.

'You told the police, though? About his PTS?'

Starck was silent, considering his reply.

'You *did* tell them he'd been in Iraq? The sort of work he was involved with?'

'We had no authority. You know how it is, Jack. Deniability. And thank God for it. Can you imagine the fuss if it got out that he'd been an interrogator in Iraq and Diego Garcia? God, the papers would have had a field day!'

Jack stopped. The dogs were a distance away in amongst the ferns at the foot of the cliff, and the water here was louder as it rushed along a narrow channel of granite washed into smooth shelves.

'You left him in the cold?'

'What else could we do? He was certifiable, just about. We nearly had him sectioned.'

'Then?'

'He saved us the trouble.'

'What's that supposed to mean?'

'He didn't top himself here, Jacky. He took himself off to America to do it. Got a one-way ticket to Alaska, to some dreadful sounding place in the middle of nowhere, and blew his brains all over the ceiling. We would like you to go and do your job.'

'The police'll have been all over the place by now, won't they? And the FBI, since he's a Brit.'

'Yes. But there have been no repercussions yet. No Feebies, only the local fellows, and you know what they'll be like in Hicksville-by-the-Sea. So you are to fly out there under cover of being his lawyer, and find anything you can about this blasted journal. We can't have things like that lying about.'

'What was this "journal"?' Jack was walking again.

Paul Starck muttered something under his breath, lighting a fresh cigarette. 'Wait a minute, for God's sake!'

'What was in it, Paul?'

Paul Starck flipped his Zippo shut again and blew out a long feather of smoke that was snatched away by a short gust of wind.

'Eh?'

'You're activating an old git the Service wants rid of, you're flying me halfway round the world, and you're risking embarrassment. For what?'

'Oh, there's no risk there,' Paul said.

He smiled, showing grey teeth, two fingers stabbing towards Jack with the cigarette held tight between them. 'You won't embarrass us, because that would risk your future. You understand that? Any problems, any cock-ups, and your financial security will be as rosy as a coal miner's in Nottingham. Yes? *Voom* – gone.'

It was tempting to push him. A shove, and Starck could topple into the river so easily. An accident, one of thousands over the years. So many men had died in little rivers like this. For a moment Jack could almost feel his hands thrusting against Paul Starck's soft woollen jacket, the expression of horror on his face as he felt himself tumbling into the freezing water...

'What did he have, Paul? What's in the journal?'

Starck turned away.

'He was seeing a shrink after his arrest and the fucking cretin told Lewin to note his experiences to help his recovery. All Lewin's memoirs of his time in Iraq and Afghanistan. *Terrorists I have Tortured.* It'd make a good film. I can see it now. We can't let the journal out, Jack. You have to retrieve it if it exists. If not, good. Just come back and all's fine and rosy. You wander down here, and while away your last weeks to retirement. Easy.'

Jack walked on in silence.

Lewin had written everything down. He was sure of it. And the thought that UK complicity in torture could be exposed on *Wikileaks* would be enough to give the Director General of the Secret Service a fit of the vapours.

'Why me, Paul?'

Starck looked at him and there was a great sadness in his eyes. 'Because you're like me, Jacky. Disposable. We're both going to be put out to grass soon, and that means we don't matter.'

*

09.59

Claire was in the kitchen when he returned.

He had left Paul Starck at the car park. The idea of inviting him into Claire's house was enough to make his stomach churn. He would not invite the snide bastard back here; he couldn't put Claire through that.

The house had been a farm a long time ago. Now it was a large building split in half, two bedrooms on this side, another four in the other wing. Quiet and secluded, it lay at the bottom of a half-mile lane, with trees on two sides to screen the place from a steam railway and the noise of the main road. He had been allowed to return here last year when Claire finally agreed to try to repair their marriage.

Jack walked into the scullery and took the towel, wiping the dogs' paws in turn until he was sure that the worst of the mud was rubbed off and that their coats were dry, before leaving them to their bed of wood shavings. They sat in their bed with tails still wagging, eyes fixed on him with serious demand until he relented and threw them each a small biscuit. Only then would they settle, curling up in the sawdust together.

'You took your time,' Claire said. 'Where did you go?'

She was taller than Jack, a slim, elegant woman in her mid-forties, with long dark hair that held no trace of grey. Her blue eyes were clear and serious always, as though she was testing him. God knew, she'd tested him often enough in the past.

'The usual – Fatherford.'

'It took a long time today. Did you go up on the moor?'

He didn't know how to answer. The wounds of the last year were still sore, and he didn't want to pick at the scabs.

She gave a smile that transformed her features and warmth came into her eyes again, just as it had when she was in her twenties, before the coldness, when she realised what he was.

'Come on, Pilgrim, tell me about it. You walked there with a lover, didn't you? You met her down there and walked with her until you...'

'Paul Starck.'

He sat at the old pine table, and looked up, pleading with her to understand, to see that he had to obey, but even as he spoke he saw the curtain falling across her eyes.

Her bantering tone was stilled. She retreated into herself again, just as she had before.

'And?'

'He says there's a job. Just the one.'

'Doing what?' she said quietly, then winced and closed her eyes as she turned from him. 'No! Don't tell me! You can't anyway, can you? And it'll only hurt me more to know you're lying.'

It was enough to make him want to run out and jump into the car, hurtle off along the road until he found Starck, beaten his face to a bloody pulp, and then shoved him through the windscreen, and cut his throat on the glass...

She was already sobbing as he went to her.

He hated Starck. His job. Himself. There was never any way to explain to her.

'It's just one last one,' he said. 'Not what you think.'

'There's always going to be just one more, isn't there? Always,' she said. Her bitterness made her face twist. 'And you'll go when they tell you.'

'No. When I am off the books, I'm free,' he said. He tentatively lifted his arms to her, but she pulled away.

'No! Not now! You promised me, and I let you come here to make it good again.'

'It will be, Claire. Honest. They want this one last job and then I'm free of them. We both are. They'll discharge me with a pension and we can forget all about them. The last years will be over, and we can do something new. I'll get a job in Okehampton, just a part-time thing, and we'll never have to go to London again.'

He wanted her to believe him – as though her trust could make it true. A vision of Starck's face sprang into his mind, and Jack knew in his heart it was a lie. But there was the beginning of a thrill at the thought of another job.

'Yes? Until the next job, you mean? It's just the same as before: waving you goodbye in the morning, never knowing if you were

21

going to… I hated you for that. The horror, all the time, it wore me out, Jack! I can't face that again. Not now. I'm too old for this shit! Look at me!'

'You're lovely, Claire,' he said, and this time he did put his arms around her. She stiffened, almost pulled away, but then she bent her head and began to sob, her brow resting on his shoulder, crying for the ordinary life she had craved. The one thing he could never give her.

'Just wait for me. I'll be back,' he promised. 'It's not what you think. A guy's died. That's all. And I have to clear up the mess.'

*

15.02 Lebanon Border; 13.02 London

Over the southern border of Lebanon, a long-legged buzzard glided quietly through the still air. It soared and rose on the thermals, and Uri Misrachi watched, wishing he was anywhere rather than here on the border.

Russian by birth, Uri had come out to Israel ten years ago, joyfully embracing the culture of his adopted country. He had thrown himself into his new life, gleeful to be away from the misery of the collapsed Soviet Union and determined to demonstrate his gratitude at every opportunity. He was happy to join the engineers, and glad that he could use his skills to the benefit of the defence forces. But he hadn't expected to be posted here – forced to stand in the baking heat, carrying a heavy Galil rifle, laden with packs and water, waiting for something to happen, guarding a Black Thunder remote-controlled bulldozer.

In Russia many had ostracized him because he was a Jew; he was hated. The only people he could meet were other Jews. That was why he had fled, why he had come to the Jewish homeland, changed his name from Yevgeny to Uriel, struggled to make a new life for himself, studied Hebrew, and put his hands to work. Yet, the others in his unit treated him as a stranger because of his accent, because he was different. They were all born in Israel, and he was a foreigner.

He wondered whether any of them had the same commitment as him. They were born here so it took little effort to buy into the struggle for Israel's security; but he came here out of conviction. He had invested his all in this land. Yet they considered *him* the outsider.

The bird effortlessly rose, a symbol of freedom. It didn't need a Galil or Black Thunder, it didn't even need to see the thermal to fly – it just felt the air, that was all. It directed its wings to catch the invisible columns of warmth, climbing rapidly, circling, all the while searching for food down below – the perfect predator.

But it wasn't alone. There was another hunter in the sky.

Uri caught a glimpse of something flying, silent and lethal, below the buzzard. Unmanned, piloted by an American miles away, perhaps in the US, the drone was the ultimate assassin, small and hard to detect, so unlike the Black Thunders, and he watched with fascination and admiration as the little aircraft continued on into Lebanon. There was a little puff of smoke, then another, as the MQ-9 Reaper fired two missiles at a target out of his sight. The only proof of the shots was the little column of smoke a couple of miles away as the Hellfire missiles destroyed a house and fifteen members of the family within.

Thursday 15th September

09.21 London

Jack Case hated this city now.

When he was younger he had commuted to London each day with building excitement. Passing by the Sarson's Malt Vinegar building down near London Bridge station, he would feel his heart begin to pound. Standing on the commuter trains, there was little to see, only dingy rows of Victorian houses, the shells of the warehouses and wharves of the old docks, all bombed in the war and left derelict for want of money to rebuild them. But, as he looked out from the train each morning, this sight had given him his sense of purpose: this was why he joined the Service, to protect his country from enemies who sought to destroy England.

Then, in the 1980s, there was no doubt who the enemy was. The looming presence of Soviet Russia dominated Europe; the threat of annihilation by their nukes was real. There had been so many times when Europe had almost ceased to exist and, as a young Service agent, he had devoted himself to his job. Keen on fitness, he had learned Karate with an inspirational Shotokan instructor. He had also joined a gun club in London Wall in a basement beneath a 1960s tower block, and learned how to use pistols of all types. He used his own handguns every weekend. A niggardly government offered agents only 25 rounds a month, and that wasn't enough to be safe with a handgun, so he used to shoot five hundred a week, honing his skills at drawing and firing. A North London martial artist who specialised in English fighting skills taught him how to fight with knives and staffs. Jack soon had a reputation as a 'gun nut' and some looked at him askance but, when he travelled to East Berlin as a new agent, he knew he could defend himself.

In 1983 a computer malfunction lead to Russian alarm bells ringing. The Lieutenant Colonel in charge, Stanislav Petrov, had orders to launch an immediate counter-strike if Russia was attacked, but his intuition told him the computer was at fault. Only one missile showed on his systems. More alarms rang: there were two missiles, three… but he knew an attack would be an all-out affair. The Americans knew that a Russian response would be overwhelming, so why try to risk annihilation with a paltry few weapons? Petrov sat

24

anxiously waiting, sweating, hoping his guess was right, and by doing so averted a nuclear holocaust that would have wiped out Europe and America. There were no American missiles: it was a software fault.

Jack had been a case officer in London a year later, and it was due to one of his contacts that the story was pieced together. Rumours of a Lieutenant-Colonel who had been taken away from his post, stories of his questioning, his deteriorating health, and how he was pensioned off all because he should have launched an all-out response. By averting tragedy he failed in his duty to the Soviet Union.

It was that which gave Jack his first step-up on the greasy pole. He and his networks brought back intelligence on Petrov, and that informed British and American negotiations on missile treaties and, eventually, eased the gradual, peaceful breakup of Soviet Russia. Grateful for his efforts, he was promoted, briefly.

That success was also to be the ruin of his career. Without the Russian bear, there was less need for humint - human intelligence, or spies on the ground. The cadres he had painstakingly built were cast aside as budgets were slashed, and he saw the men and women he had recruited thrown on the scrap heap. It was shameful.

*

Vauxhall Cross was state-of-the-art, a curious mixture of yellowish stone and green glass, reminding Jack of a ziggurat, a symbol of a dead, pointless religion. It was the embodiment of all he thought wrong with his Service. It had lost its way. The leadership thought this was the way to achievement: a centralised block, much below ground, with copper mesh throughout the walls to prevent electromagnetic snooping, bulletproof glass and walls to protect the staff. It cost millions, and was filled with the most modern technology, and was prone to the problems that are endemic with cutting-edge equipment. Computers failed, if they weren't lost in a pub. The telephone systems were broken more often than not, the clever satellite communications systems was rendered useless when a building was constructed in the line-of-sight of the main dish, and now the whole place was a scurrying ant heap of panic in the wake of the 7/7 attacks on London. Suddenly the Service had realised that home-grown terrorists were as much of a threat as any foreign ones.

He entered the building, walking through the secure areas in front of the foyer, past the scanners, submitted himself to a close body search when his steel watch bracelet set off the lights, and waited to be taken inside.

Once, he would have been welcome here. No longer. Now, wherever he looked there were suspicious faces.

'Morning, Jack.'

He hadn't seen her approach, and now he turned with a rush.

'Karen… I didn't…'

'No, of course not,' she said.

Karen Skoyles was shorter than him, only five-five or five-six, and had a mass of brown curls that fell to her shoulders. The plump thirty-three year-old had an amiable appearance that had deceived many, with lively brown eyes that sparkled. It was her eyes he had first noticed when he hired her thirteen years ago.

Today they were cold and hard as she studied him with distaste. She had not liked the idea of the Scavengers at first, and she evinced interest only when she saw in them a means of advancing herself. She had taken on the Intelligence Directorate, reporting to the deputy director general himself, and soon succeeded in bringing Scavengers under her own aegis. She had grown to loathe Jack since the split, when he and Claire had separated and then got back together again. Maybe she thought he was weak to go back to his wife, or scorned Claire for being so malleable as to take him back. In any case, Starck had been set in charge of Jack's Scavengers last year. Starck's Scavengers. Maybe he was picked for that reason – the alliteration, like Broughton with his 'Bullies'.

Jack would never know, and he didn't care. Soon he would be out. He had created the unit, he had been the first Scavenger, and now he was the first to be burned.

She gestured towards the lifts.

'Come with me.'

'Where are we going?'

'I have a briefing room on the third.'

He nodded as they crossed the foyer. That was a relief. The truly secret areas were all below ground. He followed her to the bank of steel gates; she used her card at the nearest, and it opened. At the lift she had to use it again to activate the doors. Once inside, she had to press the card on a receiver before she could press the buttons to the third floor, and then the two stood in silence: an older man who was at the end of his service, and the younger woman who had taken over

26

much of his responsibilities. Neither meeting the other's eyes, both travelling in mutual distrust.

'How is Claire?' she asked as the lift's doors opened.

'She's fine. We were starting to get to know each other, until this happened.'

'I'm sorry,' she said without emotion, striding along the corridor.

It was disorientating, here in the building. On this floor light grey carpet silenced their feet, and they passed a series of little cubicles, some with open doors, most with their doors closed and lights on to indicate that meetings were in progress. A neat line of concealed fluorescent strip-lights lit the corridor from shining metal grilles overhead.

'Here,' Karen said, pushing at a handle and standing back to let him in first.

Jack gave her a glance and walked inside.

There was a single table and a quartet of armless chairs set around it. On the table was a manila envelope with stamps marking it as secret, and a half-drunk mug of coffee.

'Morning, Jack,' Paul Starck said. He was standing at the back of the room, staring out at the river like a man who must wait at least another half hour before his next nicotine fix. 'There's your reading, old cock. Be quick – you fly at two this afternoon.'

*

11.39 Croydon

Detective Sergeant David Yates hunched his shoulders, trying to keep the warmth in, but the chill in this bleeding house made it impossible. Damp – the place reeked of it. That and piss where the local scrotes had come in for an evening's strong cider or glue sniffing. He'd been here keeping close surveillance on the house in Alma Street for over a week now, working in shifts with the second team, peering through the camera's 600mm lens, and straining his eyes and his back in the uncomfortable position within the tiny bay window. And so far nothing.

This house had been empty for years. There had been some youngsters squatting, but they'd been evicted a month before this operation began. Someone had told the police that they were farming skunk in the place, and the locals came down on the kids really heavily. Too late they learned that their 'drug cartel' was made up of fanatical Christians who wouldn't touch alcohol, drugs, or even have sex, and the last thing on their minds was growing hash. The fact

27

they'd tidied and decorated the place should have been a clue, but instead the plods broke down the doors and stormed all over it, doing enough damage to undo all the squatters' efforts. The tip-off had come from neighbours hacked off with God-botherers knocking on doors and trying to give them all Christ's message when they were trying to watch X-Factor. Stupid, bloody arses.

It was a crap street, and a shitty duty. The only bright and gleaming aspect about the stakeout was Wendy Grayson.

He'd worked with a number of WPCs over the years – hard not to nowadays, there were more women than men in some teams – but Wendy was one of those girls who just fitted in. She had the sort of face most blokes wouldn't look at in a busy room. But when you did notice her, you just saw how bright she was: clever, sharp, caustic as hell when she wanted, but a bloody good team player. And when you made her laugh, when she grinned, she had the most gorgeous dimples. Long dark hair and eyes so dark they were like black holes sucking you in. A man could do a lot worse. And his wife didn't understand him. Shit. The old, old story. And Wendy had heard it from all the other cops. Yates felt it like a pang. He could watch, dream, but never touch. She'd just think he was a randy old git, at his age. Sod it.

Moving away from the camera, he glared at the house opposite. These hundred-year-old terraced houses were good. Why the fuck they were filled with foreign bastards was more than he could understand. English houses ought to be for the English, but they were just handed over to any bunch of freeloaders. Not that he was racist – he was as scathing about white Romanians, Polacks, and Krauts as he was about Indians and Pakis. No, but this had been a good little street, once. Now he reckoned the people who infested the area should be deported. They were all scum.

The man they were watching was worse than the rest. As Yates stood carefully away from the window to stretch his legs, he kept his eye on the house, searching for any sign of Abu Fazul Abdullah, or whatever his real name was. He was supposed to be a victim of repression in the Sudan, but there was sod-all evidence to support that. It was rumoured that he had prepared bombs for terrorists, and that's why he'd been put under constant watch. It had been said that his real name was different, and that he'd helped the terrorists blow up the US embassy in Nairobi. The Yanks would want him if that was the case. They were bloody welcome to him.

28

Well, Yates would like to see Mr Abdullah try something here. He'd have pleasure in blowing the scumbag's head off.

Up the road, he saw her approaching, iPod phones in her ears, swinging her long-handled bag, just like a teenager coming back from the shops. God she looked good. So young, so taut and fit. His wife was just sort of flabby now. Sagging. The comparison was... but Wendy was young enough to be his daughter.

No harm in reading the menu – you didn't have to buy. Yates leaned over to get a better view. If he could have got away with it, he'd have taken a photo of her – but the fact that the photo would show as being deleted put him off. There was too much care taken with things like that now. A guy who took a photo and removed it would leave that number's gap on the camera's card, and someone would spot it, and then he'd get a bollocking.

He had his camera phone, though. Pulling it out, he held it up, shakily, trying to hold it steady. The picture was grey and poor, but he could see her legs, her figure, and he smiled as he pressed the shutter, only to pull a face as she turned away. Picture ruined.

It would take a moment to snap another, this time with her looking more at him... but why had she turned?

It was a bike, a big, red Honda, burbling along the road. The rider, a slight figure in body-hugging red and white leathers, drove the bike in-between two parked cars directly in front of him. It had two panniers, and another large bag over the petrol tank. The rider slowly climbed off and set it on the side-stand. He locked the handlebars, before wandering off, casually pulling off his gloves and unzipping his coat.

Disinterestedly, Yates watched him for a moment and then turned down to look at Wendy. She was staring at the biker, and Yates wondered why she was so fascinated with him. There must be something...

Yates peered, and suddenly something grated. The man didn't remove his helmet. He just kept on walking, and then glanced down at the phone in his hand. He's sending a text.

And Yates slammed his fist on the window and shouted to warn Wendy but it was too late and the bike just evaporated in a bright white blue then red flash and the whole of the house opposite was engulfed in the wash of fire. Yates felt the glass before him shatter into a million fragments each cutting his face and blinding him. The window was gone and he couldn't hear anything except for a low

29

moaning and it was him as he sat slumped at the back of the room with blood for a face and no eyes, and a four foot splinter of wood from the window frame jutting from his belly.

Friday 16th September

00.07 Anchorage; 09.07 London

It was a clear, dark night when Jack arrived at the airport and stood outside breathing the chill air, eyes screwed against the exhaustion that was threatening to overwhelm him after nineteen hours of travelling.

The cab ride from the airport was just like that in any other American city, but the streets were quieter. Somehow he was reminded of Canada and, as he gazed about him, he saw a lanky creature lumbering about at the side of the road as they swept past.

'Moose,' the driver said unnecessarily.

Jack grunted and closed his eyes. First the flight to Toronto, connected with a flight to Seattle, where he had to wait for Alaska Air, which then took another five hours to deliver him here in Anchorage. He hadn't realised how much farther up the coast Anchorage was from Seattle; the journey left him drained.

Karen had briefed him herself, which he found interesting. Paul Starck stood at the window, sneering at the world and biting his nails, desperate for another nicotine fix. But he wouldn't leave in case Karen let something slip. Jack knew Starck too well, and could appreciate his panic. The bastard was a corporate whore, he'd used anyone and everyone he could to get up the ladder, and he'd be happy to shaft Karen if he could. But she had outmanoeuvred him. She was bright enough to bypass him. All her early efforts had been invested in ensuring that her name was known. The DG liked fresh, young faces, and to him Starck was an anachronism. Smoking and drinking was no longer the way to the top, and while he really wanted the top job, Starck knew it was too late. She would soon be in glorious control of all Scavengers and Broughton's Bullies, as well as Operations.

Starck was there to listen for any snippets he could later use to damage her but he was over-optimistic. There was no chance of her letting anything slip. Not in front of him.

Once Jack would have warned Karen. She had been his second-in-command for so long, but not now. Secrets were too much a part of his life for him to give away something for free. Everything had value, and in his business the commodity of choice was secrets.

31

Besides, she was bright enough to know Starck. The 'Ice Maiden', she'd been called when she first turned up. It was obvious that she was determined and ruthless, but not many realised that she had a clear, analytical intelligence when it came to humans; she appeared to read them. If anyone was safe from Starck, it was her.

*

When Jack lost his Russian group in '98, he had been terrified he'd lose his job. It was then, when the Service was gradually shedding all unnecessary officers, that he had first thought up the concept of the Scavengers. In 2004, after the recruitment of so many youngsters post 9/11, he proposed it again to the deputy DG, but it didn't fly. The Service was full of bright ideas that, as he knew, were routinely squashed by the politicians. Too many of them hated and distrusted the security service.

Instead an army of accountants and consultants materialised, none of them with operational experience, who were called in to pronounce on every new scheme for protecting the realm, who could be guaranteed to argue against the 'Oxbridge' teams at the top of the Service. The poor bloody infantry went out and got themselves shot at, sometimes killed, and the managers shook their heads and carried on planning the next lunch with their trusted consultants to discuss more blue sky thinking.

It was the recruitment that caused the problems.

After 9/11, senior staff enjoyed heady days of money and influence again. They were told to go and hire, and if they didn't get enough heads through the doors, recruitment officers were sent head-hunting for them. Suddenly the whole building, which had been empty at the end of the Cold War, became cramped; it was bulging at the seams as it filled with youngsters.

And the balls-ups began from then, in 2003.

Too many recruits meant that HR could not weed out the mediocre – there wasn't time. Instead, the political demand for humint meant that even when senior officers had concerns, it was hard to get staff assessed. There weren't enough filters. The Service became overloaded with untrained personnel, more than had ever been employed before, and the quality diminished as political considerations were allowed to dictate policy. No more were Oxford and Cambridge the favoured recruiting grounds; instead, any university with an Arabic Studies course was sufficient.

Too late, Human Resources realised the paucity of their skills. And that although employing fluent Arabic and Pashtun speakers was desirable, the fact that they were young, idealistic and Muslim, made some less than perfect. There were too many who were utterly incapable of holding a pistol, and when they went live and had to defend themselves, things often went pear-shaped. More worrying were the ones who clearly knew how to handle firearms. In a country where all pistols were banned, that was enough to make them sources of deep suspicion.

The Service was drowning – management and HR were overloaded with personnel – when the 2005 terrorist attacks blew away any residual complacency. Suddenly someone remembered Jack's idea for Scavengers and the concept was dusted off. They had to avoid a repeat of 7/7 at all costs. To the surprise of many, his idea was accepted at last and Jack had his own small empire.

When youngsters caused problems, Jack's men would take away incriminating evidence. They would dispose of firearms, blood, bodies, and generally leave crime scenes looking less like battlefields and more like the after-effects of a tea party. That was why, after the usual bureaucratic bickering and delays, Jack's Scavengers were finally formed in 2007 – to clean up the mess.

It all ended a year ago when the body was found. Immediately all eyes in the Service fell on Jack. Scavengers had created their own fearsome reputation; it didn't matter that he denied any part in the crime: the mere suspicion of guilt was enough. Scavengers were known to be ruthless. Their reputation for fierce determination only added to the cautious distrust with which he was viewed.

Jack was put on gardening leave, unwanted. The breakdown of his marriage was common knowledge in Vauxhall Cross, and added credibility to the rumours. The murder was put down to an error of judgement brought on by his wife's infidelity. Karen had spread that rumour, he was sure. She wanted the top job.

*

'I used to bring my agents in upstairs,' Jack said to Paul Starck's reflection.

Starck looked back bleakly.

The third floor was a general ops and meeting floor. 'Upstairs' meant the sixth and seventh, where senior staff worked. It made agents feel wanted to be allowed to tread the hallowed carpet of the DG and DDG.

'So did I,' Karen said. 'There's more security now. Some prick on the sixth, I think.'

'It happens,' he shrugged.

'You realise who you're dealing with, don't you, Jacky?' Starck said. 'You are with one of the high priestesses of analysis. The blessed Karen here reports directly to the top. To the DDG himself.'

'You are here by my permission,' Karen said, glancing through notes, not looking at Starck. 'You are here for the briefing, but only as an observer. You are not required to comment. Remember, you will be having your HR review shortly. Don't make me have to be honest with my section.'

'See, Jack? She's superior to me, even. My boss. Direct to DDG, that's where her reporting line goes. Bypasses HR, Legal, Information Systems, the lot. With Scavengers and her own Technical Ops unit, the pick of the data passes through her. She even has her own kings, her Liaison and Info teams with their grubby little fists clutching at everything they can grab from Langley and the NSA. Some say she has a direct line to the DG of the CIA. And the rest of us? We serve the priests and priestesses at their altar. Ours is not to reason why, you see.'

'I think I can still hear you talking,' Karen said shortly, and Starck was silenced.

The briefing was short. Karen read him a summary; he pored through the files about Dan Lewin, studied the photos of the man before and after his tour of duty, and then Karen started on Jack's profile. She sat opposite him, unsmiling, firm, earnest, and began to run him through his story and his objectives. He was to fly to Anchorage, view the body, check the cabin where Lewin had killed himself, find any written diaries or journals, and bring them back. He had cover as Lewin's lawyer, which should serve to protect him from too many questions, but in the meantime, he had a full series of documents to read and learn. One set about Lewin himself and his record he had to learn now, the other about his own supposed business affairs with Lewin he could take with him. It had been arranged as a client file for a solicitor's office.

'Take your phone with you for normal emergencies, but if there's anything you have to tell us, don't use it. The Americans monitor all cell phones routinely. Get to Seattle and speak to our resident spook there.'

'Who is he?'

A man called Stephen Orme. Jack had met him once.

They agreed on codes and systems for contact before moving back to discuss Lewin.

'Did he have friends out there?'

'Not before leaving,' Karen answered. 'He may have had some drinking buddies, but he wasn't in Whittier long.'

Starck interrupted. 'He was hiding. Over here, he moved to Manchester, to get away from the enemy and us. He was very scared by the thought of a cell coming here to kill him.'

'Why?' Jack asked. 'What'd make him think he was in more danger than the thousands who'd been there?'

'He was involved in some harsh interrogations,' Karen said. 'And he questioned some important people.'

'Important, Jack. You hear that? The sort of chaps the Americans wanted to learn a lot from. Not the sort to be lumped together with the Guantanamo proles. These were the tops. They got special treatment: multiple translators, their own cooks, the works. So, Lewin was the kind of man their friends would want to speak to.'

Jack nodded.

'To learn which beans had been spilled.'

'And to reward him for his enthusiastic questioning techniques,' Starck said.

'But you wouldn't help.'

Karen took up the story, 'We couldn't. And then, when the police refused to provide him with twenty-four hour support, he went mad. Tried to buy a gun…'

'I told him all that,' Starck said.

Karen spoke over him.

'Then he ran abroad to the first place he could think of that was deserted and where he could buy himself a pistol: Alaska. Probably saw the pictures of Sarah Palin with a rifle and thought it'd be ideal, the prat.'

'The Americans aren't too supportive of immigrants without a job. How'd he get in?'

'Probably on a holiday ticket. I don't know.'

Starck shrugged.

'He had friends in the US military from his time in Iraq. Perhaps he was able to win someone over and get their help.'

Karen continued, 'Originally he took a room in Anchorage, but then moved to a quieter area, a cabin a mile from the town of

Whittier. That place is weird enough. Only one road in, and that's on a railway line.'

'What?'

'Seriously. There's the one tunnel to the town, and it's shared by trains and cars – one lane wide. I don't think he could have found a more deserted location if he'd tried.'

'Why?'

'Why there?' Karen stood and went to a coffee machine, pouring them both a mug. She didn't offer one to Starck. 'He wanted seclusion, and he wanted protection. Like Paul said, protection he could get from a handgun, and in Alaska they've got pretty relaxed laws on guns. Over there he might feel he could protect himself.'

'Instead he blew himself away.'

She had pulled a face at that, but it was the thought that stayed in Jack's mind as he reached Anchorage. It was incomprehensible to him that a man should travel halfway around the globe for safety and, arriving there, kill himself. If he was going to do that, it would be easier here, in the UK. But Lewin didn't strike him as a man seeking his own death. He was broken as an intelligence officer, true, but that didn't make him suicidal. Rather, the fact he wanted a gun showed him as seeking to preserve his life. If he wanted death alone, he'd have rigged a rope from a rafter, or a hosepipe from the car's exhaust. The pistol, to Jack, proved he wasn't interested in ending his life.

He was seeking to defend himself.

*

The taxi dropped him at the Hilton's entrance. It was on the corner of the building, and he thought, at first, that he was being delivered to a petrol station as the car swept into a broad parking area. Inside, the foyer was a shiny, gleaming facsimile of Hiltons the world over, and he was soon checked in. He took his bags to his room, set his case on the bed, and methodically searched for bugs, but there was nothing apparent. Not that it meant anything. The listening devices used by the US were ever more sophisticated.

Taking up his small rucksack, he returned to the ground floor and walked to the bar. At the top of the short flight of stairs to the bar were two glass cages. In one was a rearing grizzly bear, paws raised to display immense claws; in the other an even larger polar bear. Plaques stated when the bears had been shot, by whom, and with which guns. Jack stood staring at them for a while before walking down a short flight of steps into Bruins' Bar. He took a seat on the left, his back to the wall and ordered a large bourbon from the smiling waitress before opening his folder.

This should be a quick in-and-out job. Still, just in case, he had brought two spare identities. His day-rucksack had a plastic moulding inside, where the grab handle sat. Before leaving Devon, he had converted that into a space for two passports, some credit cards, and other ID. He was, at heart, a scavenger still. Best always to be safe.

Occasionally, he shot a look at the TV screens. There was a baseball match playing, but as he watched there was a commentary about an explosion in a street in London, England. Apparently there had been a gas leak, and a family was killed. It meant nothing to him.

*

18.32 Pakistan; 13.32 London

In Pakistan, in a small house four miles outside Hangu, a bearded Muslim knelt to pray with four of his sons at his side.

Hangu was known for its beautiful countryside with hills and rivers, but there were few visitors now. As a region within the North West Frontier of Pakistan, it was a place tourists would avoid. Suicide bombers and terrorists were common, wandering at will; Talib fighters from over the border in Afghanistan came here to recover from their injuries; and even the locals were worried as the Pakistani military and police attempted to douse the flames of revolt. In the midst of the fighting and lawlessness, foreign Special Forces were rumoured to watch and occasionally assassinate the leaders of the Afghan freedom fighters. It was a time of terror.

This place was safe. It was known to be the home of a most religious man.

The murmur of the men's voices inside the house rose and fell, and the oldest daughter, Sadiqah, could hear them as she played outside with her sisters. The twelve-year-old was proud today. There was a guest in their house, a great man, one of the leaders of a clan from inside Afghanistan, Maulana Fazlullah, a man noted for his passionate defence of his country. A warrior from his childhood, he had first taken up his rifle against the Russians when they invaded, and later won great renown for bringing down a helicopter with a missile. But the effort was almost too much for him. He had lost so many children; he had hardly any family left. Although he hated the Taliban, as any free-born Pashtun must, preferring always to rule his own lands in his own name and alone, he had accepted that they were the strongest force and submitted to their rule. But when the hated

English and Americans invaded, he took up his rifle again. For no man may take an Afghan's lands without suffering the consequences. No Afghan would tolerate a conqueror. Those who sought to overrun their lands and offend their faith must die.

She knew this. It was the way of their tribe.

At the call of her sister, Sadiqah was startled to see a trail of dust rising from beyond the sugarcane fields. Peering at it, she felt quickly anxious. There were very few here in Hangu who possessed a car – only the corrupt and the police could afford such luxury. She ran to the house, grabbed her father's heavy AK-74 from where it stood by the rough table, and hurried outside, hefting it in her hands as the sound of the car grew louder.

There was more than one. Large vehicles, all with dark windows against the intolerable heat. The first began to slow, and she watched with sullen suspicion as the dust billowed around it. And then there was the howl of a racing engine as the throttle was pushed wide.

It was enough to make her frown, bend and jack a round into the breech, for the road here was very poor, and even carts would slow for the potholes.

Sadiqah lifted the rifle, pointing it at the car, and that was when the first of many rounds hit her, and she was thrown back against the wall of the house as the four cars screamed to the house, stopping in clouds of yellowish dust, doors already open. Dark-green-camouflaged soldiers sprang out.

Men ran to the doors, firing as they came, but the soldiers were prepared, and their submachine guns spurted flames. There was a *wopwopwop* from overhead, and a black helicopter sped around from behind the house. She could only gaze in wonder as her blood oozed. One of her brothers ran from the house, firing from the hip, hoping to hit the flying monster, but there was a loud hissing and crackling, and she saw fire from the open door of the machine, and her brother fell at her side, his face cut in half by a burst from the helicopter's cannon. She stared at his pulsing brains.

She was still alive as the men fired their grenades; she heard the double thud of their explosions; then the rapid crackle of submachine gun fire; the solid bark of pistols; and the hectic, haphazard sounds of a firefight, while her breathing grew more laboured and her sight darkened. And then there was a sudden peacefulness, a moment's calm, and the helicopter seemed to float around in front of her. It settled, dangling in mid-air, dust billowing in all directions, and three spirals of white smoke erupted from a pod at the machine's side, and she saw streaks of silver whistling past. Shortly after, the ground rocked and bucked. She heard nothing, but the detonations struck her like a fist, leaving her with mouth agape, desperate for air.

Soon afterwards a soldier dressed in black saw Sadiqah. He walked to her, tested her pulse, and smiled down at her. She could make out his pale face, and thought she could see kindness in his eyes. He said something, gently. She didn't understand his words – she had never learned American – but as he closed his eyes, urging her to do the same, she understood. She closed hers too.

A moment later, the pistol bullet crashed through her temple and she was dead.

*

09.13 Anchorage; 18.13 London

The air was chilly in Anchorage. Jack Case had glanced through the menu of the Hooper's Bay café in the hotel, but preferred to take a walk. His mind still fuzzy from jetlag, he decided to take it easy for the morning – he would have work to do later.

He picked up his rucksack and headed up E Street, until he came to the Paul Egan Centre, and along 5th Avenue. For all his time here in America his rucksack would remain near him. The spare passports and ID nestling under the grab handle were too important.

Opposite a JC Penney there was a small café, and he stopped there for a mug of coffee and a plate of bacon and eggs with toast. While he sipped his coffee, he read through the reports again, and ran through his cover in his mind, checking the details of his life story.

His Blackberry's light flashed, and he pressed the select button. It was only a warning message to say that there was no signal. Strange. He turned the phone off and threw it into his bag before reaching in and pulling out his book. Whenever he travelled he always brought a book. Other agents preferred their iPads and Kindles, but he still held to the fact that a machine with wifi or Internet access was a machine that would allow others to track him. A book with pages was safer. This time he'd brought Quintin Jardine's *A Rush of Blood*, which would keep him entertained on the flight home, hopefully.

For now, with time to kill, he opened it and began to read.

*

It was lunchtime when the taxi dropped Jack at the coroner's building – a low, new block on South Boniface Parkway – and while he waited inside, he was struck by the way that St Boniface was remembered over here, in America. Boniface was a man born in Crediton in Devon, not far from Claire's house, and was known for his work converting German tribes to Christianity. It seemed odd to meet with his name here in Alaska.

A door opened behind him and a man called out, 'Mr Hansen?'

Jack turned to see a chubby, smiling man of about five feet seven, in a dark suit with glasses that reflected the strip lights of the ceiling. He wore a plain grey suit, but his tie was loose and his top button open. He shook hands with a smile.

'Sorry to keep you so long, Mr Hansen. I know you'll be in a hurry to get matters completed. You were Mr Lewin's attorney?'

'Yes.'

'Fine. So, if we can go through the ID, then I can release the body.'

'There is no doubt? Of his suicide?'

Jack felt cheated. He had been so certain that Lewin wouldn't have killed himself, that this confirmation irritated him; he felt like a poker player who had misjudged an opponent's hand.

'No. He had bought himself a six-gun. Ruger GP100. Several people saw him with it. He used it out in the woods, and folks had seen him plinking occasionally.'

'So you are sure he committed suicide?'

'I've no doubt. He was a loner, and very nervous. I think things just got too much for him. Was he depressive?'

'I am afraid so. He'd been in Afghanistan, you see.'

'Oh, he was a soldier? So many of our boys are coming home traumatised. It's a terrible war. You know it's lasted longer than Vietnam already? The thought's appalling,' the coroner said, shaking his head.

He led the way into a large room. It was high-ceilinged, and had two stainless steel autopsy tables and a cloying smell of antiseptic and formaldehyde. It made Jack feel claustrophobic; he could feel sweat prickling under his shirt.

A white-coated aide had already fetched the body on a gurney, and now stood at the side of the white-wrapped body. Jack wondered whether the bodies were stored in sheets like this, or whether they were kept in body-bags, and only displayed more sympathetically when visitors came to identify them.

'I should warn you,' Jewson said more quietly, 'a .357 in the head isn't pretty. Are you sure you are ready?'

Jack nodded, and Jewson nodded to the assistant. The man pulled the sheet away, and Jack stared down. He pursed his lips after a moment, and nodded.

'It's him.'

'I am very sorry you had to see him like this,' the coroner said, motioning. The sheet was pulled over the ravaged mess, and Jack stood a moment, staring down at the sheet.

'Would you like a coffee? Perhaps you need a seat? I know it's a shock to see a man you knew like this. If it helps, there's no doubt he died instantly,' Jewson said, as the gurney was pushed through a double door at the far end of the chamber.

'Yes. Thanks,' Jack said. He wanted to be sick; he felt that he and his Service had betrayed this man.

*

13.46 Virginia; 18.46 London

The car rolled up silently outside the church and two SUVs parked a short way behind. The driver remained in his seat, but the guard in front got out quickly, stood still and surveyed the broad street ahead, while the passenger collected his thoughts. Then the rear door was opened for him, he climbed out, placed a grey fedora on his head, and walked smartly up to the doors.

He stood at the entrance a moment, scanning the room, before marching down the aisle to a chair up at the front. Here he bowed, genuflected, and moved off to a seat, staring at the altar.

It was a simple table, which he found satisfactory. There was a cloth upon it, which ran from side to side without concealing the plain wood beneath. A silver cross stood upon it, and behind there was a magnificent mosaic in gold and yellow, of a Caucasian holding his hands up to a bright sun high overhead while trumpets intruded. He always felt that this church had a belief in loud blasts.

He bent forward and hid his face in his hands as he prayed. There was so much to plead for. For God knew all the threats to the nation in these troubled times. So many countries hated all that America stood for, their populations were convinced that America was evil, and they sought to thwart her in all she did. They didn't realise that American had a divine purpose – she was there to help to save the world. And she would do so. With God's help, they would bring the rest of the world to the recognition that there was only the one God, and that He was supreme.

41

But he also prayed for the men who had been employed. He begged for their souls, asking that God forgive any excess of enthusiasm. Occasionally the innocent would be harmed. He regretted that, but it was a simple fact. God would understand. God would forgive.

He heard the door open, but made no move until he had finished his prayers, and only then, after standing again, making the sign of the cross, and turning from the altar, did he look up at the man in the doorway.

'Sir, a call from Islamabad.'

The deputy director of operations, CIA, took the STU-III telephone from his guard.

'Yes?'

'Mission accomplished.'

'Thank you.'

Peter Amiss passed the receiver back to his guard, and before he left the church, he glanced back at the altar with a small smile.

His prayers had been answered. Now it was time to move to level two.

*

11.51 Anchorage; 20.51 London

It had been a relief to leave the coroner's offices and get back to his hotel. On the way, Jack had the taxi stop at a liquor store, and he went inside and bought a bottle of Jack Daniels from the man at the till. He took it back to his room at the Hilton and had finished a quarter of the bottle before the shaking would leave him.

Lying on the bed afterwards, he had closed his eyes for a moment. But when he did, he could smell that stench again: preservatives and cleaning fluid. A noxious mixture that made him want to vomit.

It was plain enough that Lewin had died quickly. The bullet must have been soft lead. It had entered at the right cheek bone, and bone had slammed into the soft tissues with the bullet, making an exit wound that must have taken half his brain with it. Quick, certainly. The impact of the slug had distorted his entire head, almost forcing his left eyeball from its socket. As Jewson had said, it wasn't pretty.

But it left the question of his journal. Did he keep one, and if he did, where would he have hidden it?

The first thing to do was to get to his house and start to search.

Jack phoned reception and asked where he could rent a car. Then he took out his mobile phone, but there was still no signal. Muttering to himself, he called reception again, and learned that his tri-band phone wouldn't work here in Alaska. The receptionist was sympathetic. She had to tell almost all her guests, she told him. Alaska had its own network operator with their own frequencies and ordinary mobiles wouldn't work.

'Can I connect you?'

Soon he was talking to a helpful woman in the police station, who gave him the details of the cabin where his client had been found dead.

'His name was Lewin. Daniel Lewin,' he said.

*

16.10 Langley, Virginia; 21.10 London

Roy Sandford was only half awake. The last night he'd managed to finally persuade Janice 'Very Nice' O'Hagan to accept his offer of a meal, and the result had been better than he had hoped.

He settled his shoes on his desk and loosened his tie. It was still strange to be back here in the real world. The last few months he'd been out in Pakistan, a volunteer CIA agent teamed with the NSA checking the communications between tribal groups, trying to get decent intel on their activities, but the social life was shit. He was thirty, in Christ's name, and the nearest he'd got to a woman was sitting next to a sergeant in the 142nd Military Intelligence Battalion. The 142nd were everywhere, because the 142nd came from Utah – it was a National Guard unit formed mostly of Mormons who'd been missionaries. Their knowledge of languages was superior to most others in the NSA. But their knowledge of laws regarding sexual relations on military service was just as hot, and their damned morals meant they stuck to them.

Last night, with Very Nice, he'd got rid of a whole lot of frustration. With luck he'd be able to see her again after work tonight. So long as he didn't fall asleep on the job. This morning's early shift on the Echelon liaison desk was painful. Even now his eyes would hardly stay open.

His screen was already turned on, even before his first coffee, and he eyed it blearily as the system logged him in, trying to concentrate on the job.

Echelon was a network of computers designed for espionage. Any conversation in the world: fax, telex, text or computer message could be snatched up for US intelligence to look at.

There was no need for the operators to do more than type in a few criteria or key words, and then sit back and wait. Compared to the misery of Pakistan, where there was the ever-present risk of a bombing or shooting, it was cool. Especially for Roy, who enjoyed hiking and shooting, because the South Fork Valley was in the mountains of West Virginia, on the edge of the George Washington National Forest. Not that he could tell that from inside. There were no windows, and while sitting at the desks, it was impossible to tell what time of day it was, let alone what the weather was like.

He heard a bleep and stared blearily at the screen. A list of names appeared, then the timer telling him to wait. A light flashed on the boxes behind the screen, and then a little window opened. He read it through once, then sat upright, and read it again, frowning.

At the side of his desk was a notepad, and he grabbed it, leafing through the pages until he came to a code name. Staring back at the window on the screen, he checked the letters one by one before snatching up a telephone.

'Echelon Duty Officer, sir. I've had a hit.'

'Yes?'

'Your coding "White Fuchsia", sir.'

'OK. Give it to me.'

'It's a telephone call from the Hilton in Anchorage, Alaska, to the police station at Whittier.'

'I see. You have it recorded?'

'Yes. And it's transcribed, too.'

'Send me the copy.'

'Yes, sir.'

Sandford put the phone down, shook his head and returned to thoughts of Very Nice, but even as he did so, a small part of his mind was wondering what on earth Ed Stilson, the private assistant to the deputy director, would want with a call to some obscure little town in Alaska?

Saturday 17th September

It had taken an hour for Jack to drive along the Seward Highway to the tunnel. An hour of driving on the edge of the Turnagain Arm, a long inlet heading south-west, had first bored, and then entranced him. It was a broad stretch of water, and opposite all he could see were mountains with their peaks of grey rock above the treeline. Here the trees did not survive higher up the slopes because of the extreme winter cold, he assumed. Yellow leaves made golden mists out of the woods, with occasional darker pines breaking up the softness, while the water looked grey and uncompromising, like the sea off Scotland, but for a man who adored the wilderness, this land looked perfect. It was an alpine view mingled with Norwegian fjords: steep, craggy rocks on all sides, grey roadway, grey rocks, and the gorgeous colours of trees in autumn. Every so often, he saw white crests, and then he realised that these were not spray from the water, but the pale grey fins and tails of whales. It almost made him drive off the highway.

The road curled around at the end, and he had to stop, with the engine idling, in a queue of other cars at a tunnel's entrance. A train came through, a huge yellow diesel hauling a line of tanks, and only when it was past could the cars move up to pay the tolls. Gradually the cars disappeared into the triangular housing that hid the entrance.

It was a long tunnel. He measured it, and the car's digital readout told him it was somewhere near two and a half miles long, a channel blown through the middle of a mountain. The roadway itself was flat concrete, and rumbled rhythmically as he drove. There was only one lane – clearly there hadn't been the money to make a second – so while cars waited at one end, the cars flowed through from the other. Trains used it when there were no other vehicles. At first it was a little alarming to think of the weight of rock overhead, but Jack soon forgot that as he saw a pinprick of light in the distance and realised it was the exit. He carried on in the line of cars, and was impressed by the construction. Every so often there were what appeared to be wider spaces, with a door set in each. Safety chambers in case of fire or some other danger.

He only appreciated the length of the tunnel seven minutes later when he came to the far side. Leaving the darkness, the daylight was a blinding, searing whiteness that made him wince and turn his head away. He drove carefully behind the car in front, following it while he blinked and frowned. Pausing a while at the side of the road, he glanced down at the map beside him and checked it against the address he had been given. Shotgun Cove, he read, and searched for it on the map.

Whittier was a strange little town. A Cold War town, built by the military, and here, Christ, the war had lived up to its name.

The place had first been used by fur trappers, and the Portage Glacier was where they had 'portaged' their boats, carrying them over the mountain passes to the water down here. Now it comprised a small looping road, with a trail that led off along the waterside, Portage Bay, and out towards the sea – not that it went very far, only a mile or two, according to the map.

He was directed to this road by a cheerful man in a plaid jacket, and he took the car slowly along the rough tarmac. Mostly it was good surface, but the extreme winter weather had broken the edges down so that they were shredded into the waste at the roadside. The road led him out of town, past low buildings, including what looked like a small hotel, and on past the enormous military building. It loomed up on the right: a grey concrete block constructed in sections, that stood impressive and forbidding, strangely like a derelict Soviet apartment block, as though they had invaded but had been forced away again. All around it was luminous tape, tied to posts in the ground, and warning signs were everywhere. It looked like it was going to collapse soon anyway. There were builders all about, and cranes and JCBs stood idle. A sign he passed said that it was being made stable. Just another dump being demolished, he guessed.

Once past that, he was into the trees. Tall pines rose on the right, the road turned away from the water, and the trees enclosed him. The road climbed, and he had to keep in a lower gear as the surface deteriorated further, the car bucking as the sedan's two-wheel-drive slipped and slid on mud and twigs, the engine revving as he kept the pedal down, trying to keep the car heading up the track.

It was a stiff climb but, after a while, the trees fell back and he found himself in a wide parking area. There was a footpath leading onwards, so he carefully turned the car around and reversed it so that it was pointing straight down the track again. Elementary fieldwork: a car should always be positioned ready to drive away.

He shut off the engine. It was quiet here. There was some birdsong, but nothing like as much as in England in woods. Here, he felt the countryside had already shut down for winter.

Climbing out, the door's slam seemed unnatural in these surroundings. There was a constant background hissing, which he realised was the water in the Portage Bay down below him. If he peered hard through the trees, he could see a greyness that must be the water.

He glanced about him one last time, and then began the walk up the pathway. There were five or six steps, each formed of wooden planks held in place by pegs, that led to a path of gravel, now heavily invaded by weeds, that curved past some large outcrops of rock. Soon, he could see a dark building up ahead.

It was obvious why Lewin had chosen this. Jack stood a moment and took it in.

He had seen cabins like this in old films of the gold rush. Formed from the trunks of a number of great pines, notched and locked together at the corners. The gaps between the timbers had been filled with mud or clay, to form a thick, insulated wall. It had a steep roof to allow the snow to slide away, and a window was next to the door, directly in front of him. There were steps leading to the door by means of a small stoop.

Yes, it was like a cabin from an old film – but it was also a solid, easily defensible fortress for a man who sought safety. It would be difficult to broach the walls, and someone had cleared and maintained a kill-zone all around. Anyone attacking would be seen.

Jack walked to the door. There was blue plastic police tape across the door, which he tugged aside, and then he was in.

It was one large room with a log-burner over to the left and a metal chimney rising up through the roof. A single wooden armchair and a low table stood beside it. On it was a glass. Heavy curtains hung at the windows, and books were spread all over. A larger table was over on the right, and that was where the sink stood, as well as a cupboard. On top were some unmatching plates, while beneath was a larder. The door to it was open, and Jack could see that there was more whisky than food inside. He stood a while in the doorway, staring in, imagining Lewin's life in this little chamber. Solitary, miserable, it

47

would hardly be surprising if his depression had grown more intense out here. It was a breeding-ground for madness.

There were some shreds of material on the floor. One or two had been rugs once, but now they had been washed and wrung out too often. A lone comfortable chair stood near the kitchen table, with more books lying on it. Jack walked over to one, which was still open, upside down. It was *Fear Up Harsh*, by Tony Lagouranis. Jack flicked through some pages and pushed it into his pocket for studying later.

Then he began to walk the room.

It was the old process. First he took a series of photos with his mobile phone. Much like a forensic officer, Jack went through the clear, obvious areas first. He opened the cupboards, looking carefully inside. He reached up behind the doors, behind the cupboards themselves, into every nook and cranny. Looking at the walls, he tapped at any newer-painted areas, set his head along the wall, closing an eye to try to spot any lumps or bumps. He felt under the chair-seats, under cushions, behind the single picture, which showed an amateurish rendition of an old pine, the top blown away by lightning, and around the windows in case a hiding place had been cut out.

He stared at the picture on his phone, and then idly pressed the call button. There, in the recent list, was Claire's number, and he pressed it. He was lonely here without her. The last months had been so tough while they tried to patch their marriage. He just wanted to speak with her but the phone flashed a message. "Call Failed. No Signal".

Frustrated, he stuffed it into his pocket. All the modern technology in the world and he couldn't even call his woman.

That was when he finally opened the bedroom door.

The smell was not as bad as it might have been. Someone had come in here to wash away the worst of the blood, and the sodden sheets had been removed, but there was still the sickly, sweet stench of decaying blood and brain matter.

It was all over the floor. Where the simple bed lay, there was a shaded patch where the mattress had protected the floor, but away from that the floor had been liberally sprayed. It reached over the floor towards the walls, and there was some blood on the door, even. As he glanced about the place, he noticed that there was less staining on top of a chest of drawers near the bed, and the wall behind was clear of splashes, although the wall above had been marked.

48

It made Jack narrow his eyes.

He shook his head to clear it of the suspicion. There was never anything straightforward about a death scene. He had witnessed enough killings in his time to know that. So he began to go through this room too, quickly and carefully so as not to disturb things so much that a new visitor would notice. He took photos to remind himself where everything had been, and then attacked drawers, cupboard and boxes. He knelt to feel under the bed, he lifted the mattress. Nothing. And then, as he pushed the rugs back to see that there was no safe beneath, he saw the hole in the wood.

It was quite large, big enough for his forefinger to slip in, and it was at an extreme angle, about forty-five degrees from horizontal. The splinters at the edge were all stained dark, but that could have been the person who came in and washed the blood away. Any blood would have pooled here. Still...

He stood, the vague suspicion growing more certain as he looked about him.

The coroner, Jewson, had told him that the bullet had been a .357, and from the head of the body, the bullet must have deformed badly. That meant a soft-nosed bullet. It was perfectly consistent for a man to shoot himself in the head, and a .357 would expand and deform as it hit bone, if it was made of soft lead. Thus it would make a hole larger than .357 of an inch if it subsequently penetrated a plank of wood. But the angle seemed entirely wrong. A man shooting himself in the head would naturally angle the gun upwards. For Danny to have shot this bullet, he would have had to have been lying on the ground, or almost lying. It made no sense.

'You didn't top yourself, Danny, did you? Someone else saved you the bother, just as you'd said. You poor bastard.'

*

18.31 London

Sara was exhausted. She had to stop and rub her back as she trudged up the road towards the house, and all the way, the resentment built in her.

She was no shrew, but the sense of utter futility against so implacable a foe was enough to make anyone despair. When she had been a young girl, she had been made aware of the differences between her pale flesh and that of foreigners. Hers was white, her father told her, not like those with 'a touch of the tar brush'. He had railed against the 'Pakis' and 'blacks', and refused to use Mr Singh's

49

shop up at the corner. When she was fifteen, he took her out of her old school, because there were too many of 'that sort' in it.

It was no wonder she had rebelled.

She met him when she was at university. The campus of The City University was multi-cultural, as a London college would have to be, and she found herself suddenly thrown in among Muslims, Jews, Buddhists, and all kinds of faith that fell between them. And in the bar, and in the lectures, she had noticed the tall, lean, ascetic boy with the deep brown eyes and a confident, gentle nature. She had fallen head over heels in love.

The day she brought him home, expecting her parents to welcome him, had been the worst day of her life. Her father, always a doting parent, must surely love Mohammed as much as she did. He had never refused her a thing before. When he saw how much she adored Mo, her father would naturally accept him. She knew it.

But he didn't. He wouldn't let Mohammed into the house, and when she begged him, he turned his back on her.

'If you don't want to break your mother's heart, you'll drop him. Don't ever bring *his* sort back here.'

It was his decision, and it was final. She had felt her heart tear in her breast at his words, and she felt that it was the moment when she grew up. Although she hadn't told her father, she was already pregnant with Mohammed's first son. And when he was born, Sara swore to herself that her parents would never see him until her father had personally apologised to Mohammed.

Mohammed was as good a man as any could be. He was calm and amiable, a slightly lapsed Muslim in that he smoked and drank a little – not much, but he had a passion for good malt whisky and enjoyed Guinness. As a father, he was devoted to the children and to her, and she could not imagine him ever trying to impose his will on their daughters, telling them who they were allowed to see or even marry. It was not in his nature. Urbane, civilised and cosmopolitan, he sought only to see his sons and daughters educated and happy. He had ambitions for them, but he would not impose them on his children. He hoped that his own example would show them the benefits of education.

And his legal practise flourished until the disaster.

Sara could remember the day so clearly. A quiet morning, as the birds began to sing in the trees outside their bedroom near Crystal Palace. They lived in a pleasant street of Victorian terraces, and the

50

morning's chores began early for Sara. She was glad of the peace before the dawn. Always a poor sleeper, she rose and went to the small room next door to read a book, as she often did. The house was restful; the sound of her husband and children snoring was music to her ears. It was peaceful, the home of which she had so often dreamed when she was a child.

She could remember even now that first jerk of utter terror as the house shook. A tremendous slamming concussion went off beneath her, making her chair quake, throwing her to her feet, to stand, staring about her wildly. It had felt as though it was inside her, in her heart. Then she thought it must be an earthquake, but even as the idea sprang into her mind, she heard another crash, then three quick crunches, *bang*, *bang*, *bang*, and there was a hideous clattering in the hallway.

Rushing to the top of the stairs, she saw her front door shattered, and black-clad men with helmets and masks gripping enormous guns, running in, shouting, pointing their rifles at her, and pounding up the stairs. One man shoved the butt of his gun into her belly, taking her arm, twisting it behind her back, and forcing her face to the ground. Her nose bled, her hand crushed as though he had snapped all her bones, and a thin, agonising strap was secured about her wrists. Her arms were tightly gripped, and all she could hear was her daughters screaming with terror, her sons protesting vehemently, and the wet, horrible slapping sounds of men punching her darling Mohammed.

They were soon gone. Sara had been released before long, and she sat rocking herself in the front room, cradling the youngest two children in her lap, while the two older boys stood nearby, watching her with their petrified eyes, none of them knowing what to do to soothe her as the tears ran down her cheeks. That afternoon, Mr Blenkinsop had come around from next door. He said nothing, but stood in the doorway and stared at the hall. Later he returned with his toolbox and quietly refitted her door, mending it as best he could where the sledgehammers and door breaking bars had struck, while his wife cooked for Sara and the children in the kitchen.

That was the beginning.

Mohammed was accused of crimes under the new anti-terrorism laws, Sara was told. The house was invaded by police officers who had removed flooring, dug holes in the walls, opened chimneys that had been blocked for decades, and confiscated their computers. That cost their oldest boy all his project work for school.

The family papers, Mohammed's mobile telephone, their answering machine, all disappeared. So did their bank account details. Suddenly Sara had no money, no means of contacting anyone – she was alone. Utterly alone. Unable to fend for herself, when the media arrived on her doorstep, she was keen to speak with them, and gave out all the information she could, in the hope that someone, somewhere, would correct the injustice. Clearly there was a mistake.

But there was no mistake. Mohammed was the man they wanted. He had been born in Kenya to a Pakistani family, and when he became a lawyer and set up his own practise, he attracted one or two clients who were later found to have disreputable pasts.

Not that Sara knew that. She was not allowed to know what her husband was accused of, nor who accused him, when they accused him, or when he was supposed to have committed the crime – nothing. All the evidence was presented to a judge, and on that basis, poor Mohammed was thrown into Belmarsh Prison. None of the media interviews Sara gave were broadcast. They were all stopped in the interests of 'national security'.

The children were bullied at school, and soon both boys were excluded. They had been fighting with other children who called them names, and said that their father would be deported and then he'd be killed.

Sara's worst terror was that her Mo would be extradited. Everyone knew about 'rendition' by then, the process by which men were captured and flown sometimes thousands of miles, to a land where they could be tortured. It was hard to believe that it could happen today, in the twenty-first century, but it did. Where were the men and women who believed in civil rights, who wanted to uphold the Geneva Conventions? They were all silent. A few Muslims being hurt didn't matter.

When the law changed, because the Law Lords held that imprisoning men and women without fair trial was illegal, Sara had thought that the nightmare would, at last, come to an end. She watched the news, read the papers eagerly, in anticipation of the day when her husband would be free and could come home. The thought of the look on her children's faces was wonderful. Perhaps they could take the boys to a new school and begin again.

It was because of her growing expectation of his freedom that the news of the Control Orders had come as a body-blow.

Her husband was free. But he must wear an electronic tag at all times. He was free, but he was to remain in the house for sixteen hours every day. He was not permitted to leave at night. While he was allowed to share his house with his wife and children, no other members of his family were permitted to visit without explicit Home Office approval. Nor could any friends, outside a small proscribed list, visit them. Neither his friends, nor his children's. The telephone was taken away, as was Sara's mobile and the children's. Now, if their children were late or held up, they could not even call their parents to let them know. But at least he was home, she had thought.

She was wrong. It was the beginning of a new hell.

Mohammed sat in their front room and watched the window with fear in his eyes. He was a non-person. His family were marked with the tag of terrorism, and had lost all contact with their friends.

Sara had tried to maintain a placid exterior, but the experience was draining. They still had no idea what Mohammed was accused of – there had been no trial. And yet he was here, held still, on the order of the Home Secretary. Mohammed could not explain why. He denied having done anything to merit this treatment. He had no business, no money, no hope.

Last week Sara had finally lost it. A policeman arrived and walked in without asking permission. He didn't need to. As Sara had learned early on, the police could enter without warrant or permission whenever they wanted. This one barged past her when she opened the door, and then walked upstairs while a colleague remained down with Mohammed, as though he was likely to leap to his feet to attack someone. Ludicrous! He was so drawn now that it was a wonder he could still sit upright. Haggard, pale, anxious, he was gradually withdrawing into himself like a mussel hiding in its shell.

It was the scream that made Sara run. She hurtled up the stairs, and found her daughter in the bedroom, the policeman standing in the doorway. He turned to her guiltily, but Sara was like a tiger protecting her cub. She grabbed his anti-stab vest and swung him around, shoving him hard. He didn't fall, but she didn't care. She was about to run at him and slap his face, claw at him, in God's name, to protect her girl, when she saw he had already unholstered his extending baton, the steel ball shining wickedly.

'Try that again, bitch, and I'll hit the girl first, then you,' he spat. 'Out of the fucking way.'

Sara was tempted to spring at him, but her daughter's hand on her forearm stopped her. Sara bit her lip, and then drew Aaeesha to her. Aaeesha meant 'life', 'vivaciousness'. Now, the little six-year-old was mute, terrified. There was no safety for her, not even in her own bedroom.

The memory was acid in Sara's mind. That night she had wept as she had never wept before. The tears wouldn't stop, no matter what. Mohammed had come to her, but her anger at him was unlimited: it may not be his fault, but this misery was his responsibility.

'I *hate* you!' she had burst out, pushing him away. 'All this, it's all you! If you weren't here, at least we'd have a life! Look at us! Look at what you're doing to us! I hate you, hate you, *hate* you!'

It had been unreasonable. She knew that – but who else could she have lashed out at? Not the police. Any attack on them would lead to her being arrested too, and then? Then they'd put the children up for adoption, perhaps extradite Mohammed, and imprison Sara herself. There was no good that way. It was all so appalling that she even considered suicide. But she wasn't brave enough to kill herself, nor coward enough to leave her children behind.

She sighed, picked up the shopping again, and walked up the road once more. The house was here, a left turn at the top, past the little Chinese take-out, past the closed windows of the shop which had sold second hand children's clothes before it went bust, and into her own road.

There she stopped and dropped the shopping, hearing a bottle smash. She ran, uncaring, towards the blue flashing lights, the chattering radios, and to where Aaeesha was shrieking with terror.

*

13.39 Langley, Virginia; 18.39 London

It had been another slow day for Roy Sandford. Since the rush yesterday when he'd picked up the call about Lewin and forwarded the package, he had been pretty much left alone, just as he liked it. He was planning a long weekend with Very Nice, and the memories of her long, warm thighs and mane of chestnut hair were occupying more of his thoughts than his line manager would have liked, when his phone rang.

'5219, yeah?'

'Is that Roy Sandford?'

'Yes, sir.'

'This is Ed Stilson, assistant to Peter Amiss. He would like you to come up to his room now.'

The line clicked and went dead.

Roy stared at his screen as though it might provide an explanation. Peter Amiss was a legend. He had been a rookie during Vietnam, but before the Tet Offensive he was one of the few who warned that it could be a serious assault. Many thought that it was impossible after the huge casualties the North Vietnamese had suffered in 1967 – almost 90,000 dead – that they could mount any kind of large operation. That was the view of General Westmoreland. He told President Johnson that the end of the war was in sight.

Then, in January 1968, the North Vietnamese began their offensive. More than 70,000 men and women attacked over a hundred towns and cities and the American forces reeled under their onslaught. It was a military failure. The US troops lost less than a tenth of the casualties of the Vietnamese, but that wasn't the point. The American public had been assured that the fight was almost over, that the will of the enemy was broken. To suddenly have a major escalation of the war like this was a disaster.

For Peter Amiss it was a significant success. The religious Texan from Austin had established himself as a ruthless strategic thinker, and his methods had been proven to bring results. Within ten years he was one of the senior officers in intelligence. Now he was Deputy Director of the Agency.

Sandford knocked at the glass door. Inside the bright room, he could see a hard figure at the desk. Amiss was in his shirt sleeves, his jacket thrown over the back of his chair, and talking on the phone. A pugnacious man, he was short and wiry with stubby fingers and thick arms. While talking, he jabbed a finger across the room as if the guy on the other end of the phone could see him. Greying hair was cut slightly longer than was fashionable in the Agency, but his fitness was not in question. He had no paunch, and the flesh under his square jaw was still taut. The sun bronzed his face during weekends on his yacht, and the only apparent concession to his age lay in the washed-out colour of his once-blue eyes. They were grey now, as if all the pigment had seeped away and left behind only the base coat beneath.

Amiss carefully placed the handset on the cradle, then looked up.

'Sandford?'

'Yes, sir.'

'Come in. Shut the door. Good.' He had an entirely blank expression on his face as he studied Sandford. At last he said, 'I've heard good reports about you. They say you did well in Afghanistan.'

Sandford nodded, feeling a mixture of pride and anxiety.

'Sir?'

Amiss stared up at him. Sandford was standing warily, almost, but not quite at attention, and the grey eyes studied him thoughtfully for a moment or two. 'I have a need for a liaison specialist in Seattle. You go there, set up the systems with the local comms specialist, and wait for incoming traffic. Your task will be to work with the local FBI and help them any way they need. You'll monitor the Echelon net from there for them. Is that clear?'

'Yes, sir. What is the operation about?'

'You don't need to know. You'll receive all the briefing you need while there,' Amiss said.

He looked away from Sandford and down to the papers on his leather desk, which, Sandford knew, was glass-topped so that no one could read what he had written on the soft leather. There could be no impression left on the glass. Sandford had heard about that just like he'd heard that the deputy director prayed each and every morning and was a committed Catholic who would bring out a crucifix and pray over it in times of extreme stress.

'Your operational leader will be Frank Rand of the FBI,' Amiss frowned, still staring at the table top before him. Then he set his hands down on the glass and spread his fingers. 'I am concerned, Mister Sandford. I believe that there is something going on in Alaska that we should be aware of.'

Sandford could think of nothing to say. He nodded.

'There has been a suspicious death. It may be nothing, of course. But we are investigating. You will keep abreast of matters and let me or my assistant know.'

'Yes, sir.'

'You know who that is?'

'Sir, Mister Stilson, sir.'

It made no sense. Sandford was a communications specialist, not a crime scene investigator, but no one argued with the deputy director.

'The Russians are a matter of miles away from Alaska. It used to be theirs. And the Bear is growling again,' Amiss said. He looked up at Sandford with his watery eyes. 'If you see or hear anything that disturbs you, anything at all, I want to hear all about it. You understand me?'

*

19.02 London

Sara was furious when she got to the police station. It had taken all her patience to hold back from shouting and screaming when she saw the white van and Vectra driving off, but there was no point.

The house was trashed again. They had used a battering ram against her front door, shattering the hinges, smashing the lock, buckling the panels of the new door, so recently replaced. It lay upon the hall table, which was itself crushed with the weight of the door, and the family picture of all six of them was broken beneath it.

It was enough to make her weep tears of rage and frustration. She had the feeling that the whole of her world was toppling. She loved her man, but the last months had made her almost want to see him taken away, and now that he had been removed, she felt an intense guilt that she had ever wanted him out. She wanted her husband back. Back here, in her home, back as he was, a powerful, intelligent man with a fierce belief in justice and the rights of his fellow men.

She was sitting on the stairs, swamped with abject misery, when Mr Blenkinsop tapped on the shattered doorframe.

'Mrs Malik, are you all right?' he asked.

He was a short, skinny, truculent man who'd retired before Sara moved here. Once he had been a soldier, she knew, but now his chest sagged, and his shoulders were stooped. He was no fool, though. Bright blue eyes studied her with some anxiety, as though he feared she may break down again at any moment, but his jaw was firm.

'I just want my Mohammed home again. Why have they taken him this time? It is so unfair!'

'Mrs Malik, you need to look after yourself,' he said. 'Can I make you some tea?'

'Mr Blenkinsop, I need something a bloody sight stronger than tea!' she snapped.

He nodded, and disappeared. A few minutes passed, and he was back with a half-full bottle of Teachers. She took it gratefully and poured herself a large one in the tea mug she found on the floor. The handle had been snapped off, but it made no difference to her. She took a large gulp, and felt the raw burning in her throat.

'Why did they take him?' she said again.

'Has he been breaking his terms? If he wandered too far from the house, they could arrest him again. Or if he broke the tag or something.'

She was about to answer when she remembered the policeman who had threatened her and her little girl.

'They just want to hurt us all,' she whispered.

The thought that the policeman might have reported her for obstruction or something hadn't even occurred to her. She had thought that it was a single, foul incident, soon completed. But instead now she was forced to confront the thought that she may have been responsible for her husband's rearrest herself. Because she had stood up to a bully in her own house, her man was taken away.

'It can't be that,' she breathed.

'What?' Mr Blenkinsop said.

She explained the incident and, as she did so, an appreciation of her inadequacy rolled over her, crushing her spirit. It *was* that, surely. It was all her fault that her man was taken away again. If only she had been more sensible, more rational in her response to the policeman, her Mohammed would still be here. A rebellious part of her mind pointed out that he would still be sitting in the chair in the front room, vegetating, but she thrust the thought from her. Better to have him here than back in the prison; better here than on a plane being exiled to some foreign land where they would use whips and electrodes just to satisfy themselves that he was truly broken.

It decided her.

No more would she sit back and accept the position of victim in this great, obscene conspiracy. She would shout from the rooftops and demand that she be noticed. Her husband must be returned to her, and at the least she would force her case into the media.

She looked at her neighbour.

'Mr Blenkinsop – could I use your telephone?'

*

12.12 Whittier; 20.12 London

The light was thin when Jack returned to Whittier. It was tempting to drive on back to Anchorage and report to London that the journey was a waste of time, but something made him decide against. The hotel room would wait, and he may as well stay here a little longer. Tomorrow he could speak with the police who investigated the death and find out whether they had taken any paperwork. Important papers, bank details and insurance policies, would surely have been taken for safe-keeping. And then there was the matter of the bullet in the floor. He was no expert in forensic science, so surely someone from the local police must have noticed the same troubling angle.

He parked outside a small café and bar and asked whether there were rooms available. The woman behind the bar, a slim, short, pugnacious woman in her early thirties, with a tip-tilted nose and shrewd blue eyes nodded and offered him a room.

It was not perfect. A tiny room with a sink in a corner, a shower down a short corridor, and a TV with a perpetual mist over the screen, but it was warm and clean. He took it.

He sat downstairs at a table with a view over the bay, staring out to the south and west as the sun sank and the sky darkened. Here, with the high hills behind the town, and the low sun, it was dark almost as soon as twilight started. A mist moved in from the water, drifting towards his window like a wraith, and he was struck with a feeling of utter serenity.

Out near the bay itself, he saw a girl. She was dressed in pale blue puffa jacket, thick and warm, and had a woollen cap over her head, but her long blonde hair whipped about her back. She had a multi-coloured scarf about her neck, and stood staring out over the water with a stillness that made him think of a film he had once seen, in which a woman stood staring out to sea waiting for her lover to return. She looked painfully sad.

Simple sadness was an emotion he had not experienced while he was a spy. In his life in the Service, he had known panic, fear, and the thrill of action – but generally he had been most aware of the mind-numbing boredom of administration. In the early years, he had been abroad, and that had been fun. Entering East Berlin and having his luggage searched for incriminating items, firearms or bibles, had made him fall in love with the life of an agent. Being a dealer in secrets and lies, snaring opposition agents, forcing them to turn and spy for England, occasionally killing; he had found it exciting. It left him with a sense of power that did not diminish until the Russian collapse.

That had not been foreseen. He certainly hadn't spotted it himself, and the senior officers in the Service hadn't either. There was such a swift change from Russia the enemy, to Russia the friend under Gorbachev, and then the decline into madness, with the attempted coup that was thwarted by Boris Yeltsin. If anybody had told Jack in 1985 that his career would soon be over because of the end of the

Soviet empire, he would have laughed. But it had happened, and he had fallen behind a desk, there to grow bloated and disillusioned.

In Vauxhall Cross, he had become depressed. It felt as though he was incarcerated in a prison, and at the same time Claire was withdrawing from him. His teams were rolled up, all the men and women he had gathered with threats, bribes, or cajoling, disappeared. Some had been found and murdered, some retired themselves, while others became leaders of the new Russia. One had somehow found funding and bought a large share of an oil company, then moved into television, and now was an exile from the St Petersburg mafia living in London.

Scavengers gave him a second chance. He was still an agent with skills, and he could use them to organise new teams. Infiltration, spying, covert observation, the full gamut of Service work was his again, and he began to spend more time exercising, practising Karate, getting fitter 'just in case'. Soon he was able to use his skills. One of Karen's women in the Caucasus was raped and murdered in 2007 and, when it was realised her computer and communications kit was missing, Jack was sent to tidy up.

Arriving under cover as the father of the victim, he viewed the photos of her body for a long time before going to negotiate with the men responsible. There were three. In less than an hour he delivered the stolen gear to the British embassy at Tblisi. No one found the bodies. It was a perfect demonstration of the Scavengers' skills.

And while he found a new purpose, Claire grew more distressed.

Once she had asked him exactly what he did, and he had felt the question like a punch in his breast. The whole of his life from that moment stretched out before him, and he could discern the two tracks: one of honesty, one of deception. Honesty would involve cursing her forever, because she would be a partner in his deceits; lying would at least spare her the shame of complicity. He loved her. The thought of starting a relationship based on lies was hard.

He told her he was a salesman with a petrochemicals firm, just as his cover demanded. Which was fine, until she learned the truth.

*

The sun was gone now. In the gloom outside, there were no lights visible on the other side of the bay, and he thought it was the mist at first. It was only a little while later that he realised that there were no lights, no habitation whatever on the opposite shore. Only the trees rising from the rocks.

Jack sighed. He ate a thick stew, drank some beer, and stared through the window into a blackness so intense he felt it reflected his soul.

*

20.14 London

Mohammed felt the tears on his face, but he was still too petrified to make a sound. He had no idea where he was.

They had not bothered to knock. He had been in his front room, cradling a hot mug of tea, when the front door slammed open. They must have had a battering ram, he thought, and then he was thrown to the floor, the tea scalding his hand and forearm, while black-clothed men with masks forced him onto his belly. They grabbed his arms and yanked them round to his back, and then fitted the plasti-cuffs, pulling them tight.

'Come on, you bastard. We want a word with you!'

He was jerked to his feet, and he moaned with panic as they hustled him to the door.

In the hall a man was taking a small box and fixing it to the phone cable where it entered the house. Mohammed was made to stand still while the man held a scanning device to his leg tag. When the scanner bleeped, he pulled what looked like a SIM card from the back. He nodded at the men, and they hustled him out. Mohammed glanced back and saw the man push the card into the box dangling by the phone wire, and then he was through the door.

He couldn't know that this small box sent an electronic signal which overrode that of Mohammed's leg tag. This box could fool the police into thinking he was at home when he was not.

Outside, Mr Blenkinsop stood glowering, while other neighbours watched, most with arms folded in demonstration of distrust. They all believed he was guilty. He only wished he knew what he was supposed to have done. It made no sense to him.

He stumbled, but hands under his arms kept him upright. A white windowless van was parked in front of his house, the back doors wide open. He took it all in, it and the similarly unmarked white Vectra behind it, as would a man given a last sight of the world before he was blinded. Then he was hurried up the metal steps and into the back of the van, where he was shoved to the ground again. The doors were slammed, the engine roared, and he was rolled to the back of the vehicle as it sped off.

It was strange, he thought, that there was no siren.

13.43 Whittier; 21.43 London

The room was still warm when Jack returned to it and lay on the bed.

He picked up his mobile phone and flicked through the photos he had taken at the cabin. One was of the kitchen, and his eye was drawn to the picture of the solitary pine. Blasted, it could have been dead, he thought. Whatever could have persuaded Lewin to buy that, he didn't know. Presumably the man had wanted the picture there – if it came with the cabin's rental, surely he could have taken it down from the wall. Jack would have.

Setting the phone beside him on the bed, he tried the TV, but the picture was so fuzzy that he couldn't face it. Instead, he found the book he had taken from Lewin's room. It opened at the page where it had been left and, as Jack looked, he realised that the book had annotations in the margins. He frowned as he read, 'Just like me!' against a paragraph, and read it. The section told of how the author had suffered from post-traumatic stress, and had woken to find himself in the kitchen, crying, naked. Clearly it was a scene that Lewin had associated with, because the whole passage was underlined extensively.

Flicking through the pages, Jack began to get a feel for Lewin's experiences. *Fear Up Harsh* was based on the experiences of one interrogator in the American army, and told how he had gradually slipped from basic interrogation into more intensive questioning, allowing the prisoners to believe that they were going to be attacked by dogs, electrocuted, set on fire, or shot – all were used, and the book told of the constant choices that a man must make when ordered to find out what a prisoner knew. If the man denied knowledge of anything, he could be questioned more and more harshly until he broke down – but the intelligence was rarely useful. Most snippets of information were clearly invention, created in the heat of the moment by a man so desperate that he would say anything to stop the questioning, the sleep deprivation, the cold... Men would say anything to stop it.

Lewin had gone through the same experiences. He had volunteered to help the effort against terrorists, and when he arrived he had been an idealist, keen to do all he could to save lives. His job, as he saw it, was to take in those arrested by the troops, and to break them so that their intelligence could be used in the fight against the enemy. Troops would be sent out each night to snatch those against whom there had been allegations. Those brought back were questioned, intimidated, terrified, and forced into stress positions while troops punched, kicked, shouted, and spat at them; the men were given no sleep until they confessed to a crime or gave information themselves. After which it would be assumed they knew more, so they would endure still longer periods of torture until the army interrogators grew bored and sent them away, either to a local prison, to a foreign prison where more overt torture could be used, or to Guantanamo Bay. They were to be broken, because the administration of information did not allow for the innocent to have been captured. The army had declared a man suspicious, and that meant he must know something. If he then gave a snippet of information against another, both were necessarily guilty. Both must be broken so that every shattered memory could be sifted for data.

But when Jack interviewed him, it was Lewin himself who had been broken.

*

22.06 London

The van rocked and bucked along the streets, and Mohammed found himself being thrown across the van as they went around corners. There were a lot of corners.

Mohammed was close to collapse. Years of solitary confinement in gaol had blunted his faculties, and the grim, relentless emptiness of his last months of close confinement in his house had torn away any last vestiges of self-reliance. Life happened to him, he was without power or authority. When he had been a solicitor running his own practice, he had been confident and proud. His family gave him enormous pleasure, his work was a source of gratification, and he felt as though his efforts gave him standing in the community.

All had been ripped from him by the grotesque nature of his arrest and incarceration. The prison in which he had first been held, Belmarsh, had been rigorous and brutal. All the warders plainly viewed him as an ally of Satan himself, and he was regularly spat on and tripped or kicked. After a few months of that, he had retreated into himself. Complaints were pointless. Asserting his innocence was merely a source of amusement for those who took malicious pleasure in causing him pain.

The thought of his family was like a knife in his belly, slowly twisting. He hated to think what his poor Sara would think of this

63

latest disaster. She would probably be better off if he was being taken away. At least the children would be free again. There would be no more threats of them being frisked as they entered the house to prove that they weren't bringing in contraband – a mobile phone, or perhaps a laptop that their father could use. All communications with Mohammed must be monitored permanently. Without him, the house could perhaps return to normal.

With a sudden jerking rock, the van drew to a halt. Mohammed slid over the floor, his breast catching a loose rivet in the floor, which tore his shirt and ripped a long scratch in his chest. The pain made him hiss.

The door in the side of the van was drawn back with a low, rumbling rasp. Two men climbed in, and went to his legs. One man knelt on his calves, which was excruciatingly painful. The second had a stainless steel tool that looked like a pair of scissors, or pliers. Mohammed threw a look over his shoulder at them, and when he saw the tool he began to moan and wail. He thought some form of torture was about to be inflicted upon him, but instead the men removed his watch and then cut through the reinforced strap holding the tag to his ankle. They took them to the door and hurled them out.

'No good now. No one knows where you are, fella,' said one of the men, and both laughed as they clambered out again. The back door rumbled shut, echoing in the empty metal container, the doors to the cabin slammed, and the van began to move off once more, rocking and bucking on the uneven surfaces.

Mohammed was terrified. Not only by the fear of why he had been taken, but also because of the man's voice. He hadn't expected to hear that accent. Not here in England.

The man was American.

Sunday 18th September

02.20 London

Sara al Malik lay weeping in her bed. The crushing desolation of losing her Mohammed was more than she could bear. There was a dreadful emptiness in her soul. What could she do, what would her children do, without him? All they had was the result of all his efforts.

She looked at the clock glowing green in the darkness. Two twenty in the morning. There was a sobbing from the bedroom next door – Aaeesha didn't understand why her daddy was gone, and already both the boys were talking in undertones. She had heard one mutter something about the 'fucking fuzz', but she couldn't tell them off. She couldn't say to them that they must try to ignore what had happened – how could she? They had seen first hand how the police behaved with people of their faith. They had seen the results: the smashed doorway, the broken photos and table, and the stain on the carpet. All for what? They had done nothing, but their lives had been stolen away in the last few years. Their father was gone. And...

And what had she done? She had cried. Like a pathetic little girl, she wept in the face of the injustice. She was *pathetic*.

She had phoned her lawyer, Mr Lomax, and he had listened patiently to her as she explained what had happened; he seemed to grow more and more silent and quietly enraged as she spoke. Lomax had known Mohammed from his time at Braboeuf Manor in Surrey, where they had both trained for the law, and knew him better than any in the profession. The idea that the police should have broken in again like this was enough to make his libertarian soul rebel.

He called back later to say that they had a meeting arranged with the local Superintendent of police in the morning to learn why Mohammed was arrested again. There was no time to fix a meeting sooner, Lomax said. They should learn all they needed in the morning.

Sara had put the phone down without another word.

Now, lying in her bed, sobbing silently, she prayed again that her husband might be returned to her.

Without Mohammed, she was lost.

03.32 Glasgow

Mohammed al Malik slept very little that night. He couldn't work out what was happening to him. He had been convinced that his captors were the police at first, but now, having been packed up and locked in here for so long, he started to doubt that. The police would have taken him to Scotland Yard, or their special terrorist prisoner cells at Paddington. He knew that. They took him there last time.

This was different. They had travelled solidly for ages. He had no watch, and for all that time he had been left alone in the back of the van, shivering with the cold, thrown from side to side at first, but then the vehicle settled down and the engine took on a steady roar. He guessed he was on a motorway but he had no idea where they could be taking him. It was so far, and even though the slow rocking and the continuous rumble were soporific, he could not rest. His mind kept running over the brief assault when they captured him. Whoever 'they' were.

And now, at last, the van was slowing again. There was more of a rocking motion as it slowed and then started going round corners. A lurch and bang told him they'd run into a pothole, and then they were on again, and there was a loud roar from outside that made him frown. It sounded like an aircraft, but surely, if they were going to take him to Heathrow, they would have got there in minutes, not in hours. It made no sense.

It stopped. The van rocked and two doors slammed, and then the rear doors were thrown wide, and he had to cover his face against the appalling brightness. Two halogen lamps were nearby, and their terrible illumination seared his eyes. He had to hold a hand over them as the two men grabbed him and pulled him from the van and out onto tarmac.

'Come on, Mister Malik,' one said, not unkindly.

'Where are you taking me? Please? What is happening?'

'You don't have to worry about that, Mr Malik,' the other man said.

'Where are we now?' he demanded.

It was the first of the men, the one who had cut off his tag, who said, 'Prestwick airport, in Glasgow. You're taking a plane ride.'

He wanted to struggle to free himself, but he knew it would not work. The last weeks of self-disgust and despair had left him a weakened shell, incapable of fighting. He only prayed that Sara might

66

be safe. He hated to think what could happen to her. She would be distraught.

They were propelling him towards a small aeroplane and, as the light began to grow more tolerable, he saw it was an executive jet. They took him up the stairs and he was thrust into the cabin. As soon as he entered, a large man with gingerish hair stood up and snapped a handcuff onto his wrist. The other went on his own.

'Where are you taking me, please?' Mohammed asked.

But there was no answer. He was led to the back of the plane, and there he was forced to stand, while men and women in black cut his clothes from him and peered into his ears, up his nose – *everywhere* – until satisfied. And then they unlocked his arms and made him dress himself in a jumpsuit, and then bound his hands and feet, before pulling a hood over his head.

'Please,' he said, shivering now with the fear.

But the only answer was the prick of the hypodermic needle in his arm.

*

08.42 France; 07.42 London

It was a small, sleepy little village, a few miles from Poitiers, in the flat plains that were filled with enormous fields of sunflowers every summer.

André Bouvier had lived here for almost four years now, and he was glad to have been able to set down some roots. Here, in his own little garden, he felt as content as he ever had. It was as his father had always told him: a man needed land. Without land, a man was nothing. It was land that defined a man; that gave him strength. Once he was aware of his land, he was aware of himself, his father always said.

It is not always so easy to know yourself, André knew. He had been born in French Senegal in the early 1960s, and he had been happy there. It was different to this place, he thought as he smiled to himself. In Senegal his father was a house servant to a Lebanese family, and it was from them that the young André had learned what little schooling he had. They had been decent, kind people, devoted to their children, and fond of André. He adored them in return, and their son Charles who was two years older than him. André loved him, too.

Then Lebanon had been the playground of the rich, and André had been proud to be asked to join them on their trip to their homeland in 1974, and when he arrived, he had walked about with his jaw hanging

67

open, astonished at the sight of enormous sparkling tower blocks rising up into the sky, the glorious Mediterranean Sea glistening like silver, the cars, and the markets full of colour and scents that were so alien and beguiling. He loved every moment of his time there, and when he was told that they would be returning to Senegal, he wept. But he went back with them, and if that had been all, perhaps his life would have been content enough.

But it wasn't. The next year, civil war struck Beirut. The city was cut in two, with Christians battling against Muslims, and the young André was distraught at the thought of all those generous, kindly folk. He wanted to do something to help them, but of course there was nothing he could do. But when Charles told him that he was going to go and join the war, little André knew he must too. And so the two took a ship and sailed to Lebanon, a fourteen year old Muslim boy who could barely read or write, but who was desperate to join with the people who had shown him kindness, and a sixteen year old boy who was learned, but had never handled a gun.

Charles did not last a week. He was shot by a machine-gunner on their third day. André was lucky to be missed. He was only three feet in front of his friend when the staccato burst came from the top of the street on their right, and when he looked back, he saw Charles lying in a welter of blood, trying to scream, but making no sound. He looked at André, and André saw the life fading from his eyes as his blood soaked the rubble in the street. The horror was so profound that André could never speak of his friend's death from that day on.

André remained. His luck held all through the vicious fighting. Even when his fortune might have failed him, when the Syrians arrived and removed all obstacles, his fortune held. But he was left with an undying hatred of Jews. He had heard how the destruction of Beirut was caused by the hundreds of thousands of displaced peoples – Palestinians evicted from their own lands by Israeli invaders, and he blamed the Jews without hesitation and without limit. He detested the ground they polluted with their martial feet. They had trampled the innocent, women and children alike, in their greed for ever more land, and he would do all he could to avenge their victims. All of them. Especially poor Charles.

It had been good in the 70s and 80s – hard, but good. He was involved with the PLO for many years, moving gradually from the Arafat arm into a splinter group that sought to harm not only Israel, but her friends too. 'My enemy's enemy is my friend', he might have said, and he was quite convinced of the corollary: 'My enemy's friend is my enemy'. Thus it was that he became involved with the attacks on America in the gulf, helping with the assault on the American embassy in Nairobi, even trying to design bombs for cars and trucks to detonate under the two World Trade Centre towers to bring down those monstrous symbols of American dominance. Sadly that attempt failed, and from the moment of that failure, he had been forced to go on the run. Never remaining in a house more than one night at a time, constantly moving from town to town, city to city, nation to nation. It was a wonderful thing, to learn how the people would help a warrior.

But every year it grew harder to maintain his determination. It was less and less attractive to see young boys and girls who were prepared to dedicate themselves to Allah and go to kill others. He had no compunction about killing Americans, Jews, or other unbelievers, but he was less convinced by the wholesale slaughter of other Muslims. They may have followed a different leader, and their religious conviction become perverted, but still, he saw only young boys and girls being sent to their own deaths, and they reminded him too clearly of his Charles.

And then, for some reason he did not understand, there came an offer to come here – to live in France. The DST , the counter espionage arm of the French government, managed to pass a message through an intermediary, and within two months, he was here. New name, new life, all signs of his past wiped away as if it had never been. It had all been a terrible dream and nothing more. In return he told of some missions he had participated in. It was worth it.

He ran the hose over the gardens in the early morning light and watched the early morning sun play with the fine drops, creating a mist of glowing chips of colour. Reds, golds, and blues all danced in the air before him, and he watched with fascination. It reminded him of seeing fountains in Beirut in the good days before the war. He had come from the dry, poverty-stricken Senegalese landscape to that land of water richness, and that shock had never left him. To see fountains of water, that was to see true beauty.

There was a car, and he turned and watched the lane cautiously. Here he was free, but there was always that wariness. It could never leave him entirely. He was wanted by Americans, by English, by so many enemies. So long as the intelligence arms of Israel or Saudi Arabia did not discover him, he was happy. Those were the two that gave him most reason to fear, he knew. They were ruthless and without compassion.

It was an old Citroën. Battered and dented, the red car rattled and thumped over the badly pocked road surface. While he was fairly sure that the Americans would have a better, sparklingly clean vehicle, he was on alert. The Jews wouldn't hesitate to make use of the most dilapidated and antiquated equipment if they thought it might give them an edge.

The car rolled up to the first house and stopped. There was a momentary pause, and then a heavy, Gallic-looking man grunted loudly, shoved the door wide and pulled himself out. He was a fat man, with a drooping moustache, in a sweat-stained linen suit, crumpled like an ancient bag, wearing a straw Panama. He did not look at André, but stared up at the house itself, shoving a Gauloise into his mouth and breathing heavily as he lit it.

Then André heard a step behind him, and he was about to move when the tranquiliser gun fired the dart into his back, and although he managed to take seven steps, each grew harder and harder against the resistance of the air itself, and he found himself collapsing. He felt the stony ground against his cheek as men moved purposefully around him; then he felt himself being lifted as engines raced towards him. Finally, he was dropped into a trunk, and his last memory was of the fat man blowing smoke in his face, before slamming the lid shut.

*

09.24 London

The police station was at least quiet as Sara stormed in. Behind her, trying to keep up, was Mohammed's lawyer, Ian Lomax, who struggled to maintain an outward appearance of calmness as his anger overwhelmed him. His face was ruddy, making him look like a farmer dressed in an unfamiliar grey pinstripe suit.

'I want to see the superintendent,' he said to the desk sergeant. 'Now.'

Soon they were buzzed through the security doors and taken into a long room. At the far end was the superintendent of the station, a young man, slim and serious-faced with dark hair and pale green eyes. There was a sergeant with him, an older man with grey hair.

'I wish to speak with my client.'

'I don't understand. Please, sit down. Mrs Malik, isn't it? What has happened?'

70

Sara could not contain her rage and shouted, 'That is what I want to hear: what has happened to my husband? Where is he?'

'Mrs Malik, I have no idea...'

'Even under the anti-terrorism laws you have to tell us where he is,' Lomax said. 'It is a disgrace that you should send armed officers to arrest him and...'

'Wait!' the superintendent said, and held up his hands. 'You are not listening to me. I have no idea – no idea whatever – what you are talking about. No one from this station has been to speak with your husband, Mrs Malik. That's right isn't it, Bruce?'

The sergeant at his side nodded. He had a square, kindly face.

'Mrs Malik, when was this supposed to have happened?'

Sara glanced at Lomax.

'Yesterday.'

'How many men were there?'

'I saw four – they were in a car and a van.'

'Did you see what sort of van? Was it marked?'

'No! They were plain white, that's all.'

'With lights? Blue lights?'

'I don't... no... I don't think so – but what of it? They were police, I know they were! I saw them, and they took my man and threw him into the back of the van and drove away before I could get to them.'

The superintendent was watching her carefully. Now he looked up at Lomax as Sara collapsed into a chair.

'I assure you that I have no knowledge whatever of this. None of my own officers have been involved so far as I know. If it's true that officers from another force have encroached on my patch without telling me, I will be demanding explanations, I assure you.'

'Where is he, then?'

'I will try to find out. Has he removed his tag? Or perhaps he has been using a mobile telephone or communicating with someone else?'

'No!' Sara cried. 'How could he? This is all about that officer, isn't it? The one who hurt my daughter. He has invented all this.'

'Mrs Malik, I don't know what you are talking about. All I do know is, there has been no operation from here to arrest your husband. I will investigate, and will inform you when I have heard anything.'

71

'You had better be quick,' she said. 'I will be writing to the Home Office and my member of Parliament, as well as all the papers and... and...'

'Mrs Malik will see that no stone is left unturned in her pursuit of justice. That may well include bringing a charge of wrongful arrest against all the individuals involved,' Lomax said.

'I am sure you will,' the superintendent said, barely concealing his dislike. 'In the meantime, you could also write to the Commissioner of Police to ask him. He is more likely to help.'

Sara walked out of the station with Lomax behind her and, as she came into the roadway, she suddenly felt squashed with the pressure of the disaster. There was a weight of grim misery that fell upon her shoulders. She stumbled and almost fell down the steps to the pavement. She was going to be sick.

Lomax caught her and helped her to a wall, where she leaned, panting and waiting for the nausea to pass. She felt disorientated, confused in the midst of all the traffic, and stared about her wildly. It was an alien state, this. She had grown up in a free England, but in recent years all her certainties had been first challenged, and then shattered.

In the country in which she had been born, the police had no more powers than a citizen. It was a fundamental principle that all were equal, that no man or woman could be held without a warrant, that no one may be gaoled without a fair court hearing in front of a jury, that all were innocent until proved guilty. All these underpinned her belief in her country – and all were gone. It felt as though she had been lifted and transplanted into a foreign culture, dumped into Soviet Russia or North Korea. She did not understand her own land.

'Mrs Malik, I am sorry. I need to get to my office to find out what I can. I won't let this rest, I promise you.'

'Where is he, Mr Lomax? Who has taken him? They can't just do this, can they?'

'No. They have no right to kidnap. Whoever did this will pay for it,' Lomax said definitely.

Sara tried to smile, but found that her eyes were brimming again.

*

Unknown

Mohammed woke to a rumbling drone, and he felt an incredible urge to vomit. He was lying on his back, but he couldn't remember what had happened, where he was, why he was here.

72

The ground beneath him was quivering, but it was at least comfortable. It felt warm to the touch, and he stretched, nausea held at bay while he tried to assess his surroundings. As soon as he felt the tightening at his wrists and ankles, he stopped, his heart thundering a warning.

Slowly, he opened his eyes. It made no difference. All was entirely black. He could have been in a pit miles beneath the earth, but for that noise, that vibration. And he knew where he was in an instant: an aeroplane. The sickness returned with force, and he had to struggle to swallow the bile, because now he realised he was hooded. He could drown in his own puke like a drunkard. He would not.

It was disorientating. Under the sky a man could tell where the earth was, where the sun stood. Here, he was able to reassure himself that the pressure of the mattress or couch on which he lay was surely down. The Newtonian proof was there on his back, his buttocks, and his scalp. And yet, in this never-ending blackness he felt the weird sensation that he associated with alcohol: like a drunken teenager shutting his eyes, it felt as though the room was spinning about him. He could have been in a plane that was about to crash. The fuselage could have been whirling through the air for all he knew, and the picture of the craft twisting and falling, to crash in a blossoming cloud of flame and destruction, was all too gripping. He shivered with anticipation and his heart pounded with the terror, until at last he was persuaded that surely no disastrous fall could take so long. And if the craft were to tumble to its doom, it would not rumble so smoothly. It would whip about, and there would be screams from others on board as they panicked.

Here there was no panic. He listened attentively and although he could make out some quiet conversation, there was nothing else. Where was he? What was this? Where were they taking him? The aeroplane was well furnished, surely. Now he was sure he could discern leather in the upholstery through the hood. He sniffed, the only sense other than hearing and touch that he could use to the full.

His hands and legs were bound with painful, thin restraints. Not metal, more likely plastic. He pulled at them experimentally, and in response he heard a muttered grunt. Soon there was a step, and he felt a hand on his throat. It was so unexpected that it made him recoil and jam his head back into the chair.

'Keep still, fucken asshole,' a voice muttered, and he was suddenly still. It was a woman's voice. He remained there, listening with every nerve tingling, and felt her hands at his neck again. Now, he realised, she was untying a lace or some other fixing under his chin; he waited patiently until he found that he could begin to see again. The fabric was opened down towards his chest, and he could vaguely discern a woven pattern. And then the hood was dragged from him, and he snapped his eyes shut in pain at the brightness of the light.

'There you go, honey,' the woman said. She was short and solid, with a mousy bob, and had a hard, shrewd, oval face. She surveyed him without compassion through dark brown eyes. 'Don't want you to die before we get there, eh?'

'American?' he said. He was startled by how rough his voice sounded, as though he had not used it in years. 'Where are you taking me?'

'Aw, honey, that would take away the surprise, now, wouldn't it?' she said with a throaty chuckle.

*

07.42 Whittier; 16.42 London

Tony Burns, Whittier's Police Chief, was tired that morning. He had already been up for some hours. A bear had gotten close to hikers and their screams of terror could be heard for miles around.

'Morning, Chief. How's it going?'

'Gimme a coffee, Suze,' he said, slipping his backside onto one of the stools at the bar counter.

He was shortish man, wiry, with an amiable face, brown eyes behind thick glasses, thick brown hair and perpetual shadow on his jaw; he pulled off his thick plastic spectacles and eyed the menu with a sneer.

Suzie Parker passed the mug to him.

'You want to complain about it?'

'Shit, no. It looks great,' he said.

'But you want your special?'

'Nope, not today. Today, Suze, I'll have two eggs over easy and a little toast.'

She set her head to one side.

'No bacon? No pancake? No syrup?'

'OK. You sold me. Some bacon too.'

'You've had a bad night.'

'Worse'n you'd believe.'

'Didn't hear of trouble.'

'Two hikers up near the glacier. Damn fools left their garbage out.'

74

She winced.

'Bears?'

'They thought they'd be OK. They had a handgun – forty-four. Reckoned they were Dirty Harry or something.'

Suzie rolled her eyes.

'Don't they listen when they're warned?'

'I guess they just thought a forty-four was big enough to pull down even a grizzly.'

'You know what Earl used to say? He saw a guy with a gun like that once, and he said "What's that?" The fool said to him, "It's a forty-four magnum, the most powerful handgun in the world." Earl said, "What you got it for?" "It's in case of bears." Earl just looked at it, and said, "You'd best file down that foresight, then." "Why, to give me a faster draw?" the guy asks. "Nope. Because it'll be less painful when the bear shoves it up your ass."'

Tony chuckled, 'Yeah. I miss old Earl. Used to like yanking the chains of the tourists.'

'Yeah. But he'd been here long enough, he felt entitled,' Suzie said.

'One of the good guys,' Tony agreed.

Earl Wallace had arrived with the construction crews in the '60s, which helped to rebuild the town after the earthquake all but destroyed the place, and had chosen to stay.

'So what happened to the hikers?' Suzie asked.

Tony Burns pulled a face.

'Assholes must've got a cub, I guess. Some reason the little brute didn't attack. All I can say is, they're damn lucky.'

'Neither of them hurt?'

'Nope. I think they let off their guns and the noise scared the bear off. Didn't hit the bear. Just good fortune that there wasn't some other guy up there who got shot, I guess. Could have been spraying slugs all over Portage Glacier from where they were. What the hell city boys were doing up there at this time of year, I don't know.'

'Well, I'll thank God no one was hurt,' Suzie said. 'I don't want news like that getting out and scaring off all the tourists.'

'Yeah. Fair enough.'

'Excuse me, are you the chief of Police here?'

Tony glanced over his shoulder and nodded, 'That's me.'

'Could I have a word with you?' Jack said. 'My name is Hansen – I am a lawyer from England. My client was Dan Lewin, who lived in a cabin near here, but died last week?'

'From England, eh? You've travelled a long way.'

'He was a good client.'

'Really?' Chief Burns nodded pensively. It would be a surprise if the man out there had been a good anything. Millionaires tended to come here for the fishing in the summer, but they were all gone with their boats before the first frosts. And men who rented little cabins and then committed suicide were rarely wealthy. 'I wouldn't expect him to be much good to you. Didn't look the kind of guy to have too many dollars. Not for long, anyhow.'

'May we talk?'

'While I'm eating my eggs, you can have any spare attention I can afford,' Chief Burns said. 'But if it's official, let me finish eating first, eh?'

There was a screech of tyres out in the road, and Tony turned quickly to gaze out.

'Who's that?'

Suzie returned from the cooker, peering through the thick glass and answered, 'Bob, I think. Who's lit a fire under his ass?'

The door was thrust wide and heavy-set man with a heavy, padded, red fleece jacket leaned in.

'Chief, you gotta come quick.'

'What is it?'

'My cabin out on Shotgun Cove? Some mother's burned it down, God dammit!'

Chief Burns turned a face of tragedy to his eggs. 'Bullshit,' he muttered, and shovelled eggs onto toast, ramming it into his mouth. Grabbing rashers of bacon, he stuck them into a napkin, took another bite of egg and toast, slurped his coffee, and glanced at Jack. 'Mr Hansen? This is the place your client used to live. You want a ride?'

*

08.11 Whittier; 17.11 London

Tony Burns started the engine as soon as he sat in the seat and methodically pulled the seat belt around and snapped it into the lock. He shot a look over at the lawyer.

'Mr Henson, I'd like you to do up your safety belt too, sir. I wouldn't have a man's death on my conscience, not with my driving.'

'Oh, yes. Sorry. And it's Hansen.'

As soon as the other seat belt had clicked, Chief Burns reversed out of the parking bay, and pulled the shift down. 'Strange this. You arrive here yesterday, and today the place goes up in smoke. Quite a coincidence.'

'Perhaps so. But the place didn't look as though the fire department had much of a say in the building of the place.'

'Yeah?'

'I only mean that the place was potentially a fire risk. It wasn't a modern apartment, was it?'

'Strange for it to go up just after you visited, though.'

Jack nodded and added, 'By the way, did you investigate his death yourself?'

Chief Burns glanced across at him.

'Why?'

'It looks strange to me.'

'You have experience of murder investigations?'

'No. I am a lawyer – my realm is more probate.'

'Oh. But you reckon you can question me about investigating a murder scene?'

Jack sat back in his seat. This guy was a redneck cop from a town of maybe two hundred people. He was hardly going to appreciate questions about his methods from someone who came from another country and had no experience. He should have kept his mouth shut.

'What struck you as odd?' Chief Burns asked.

'It's probably nothing.'

'What is?'

Jack did not look at him. 'The guy shot himself, but the bullet ended in the floor.'

'Yeah. We reckoned he was lying on his bed and the bullet went down into the planks.'

'That makes no sense – the bed was too far from the gunshot mark.'

Chief Burns looked across at him, and then swung the wheel to go up the track to the cabin. 'The bed was moved when the room was cleaned.'

'Oh.'

Jack winced and looked away. He had not thought of that. Suddenly his desire to pursue this as an enquiry fell away. Perhaps he hadn't killed himself. Maybe the fire was a mere accident. It didn't matter, anyway – no one in England would know or care. He could wind this up and get back to Anchorage. There was no book, no journal, and the idea of waiting around here was ridiculous. Soon he would be back home with Claire. If she was still waiting. He prayed she would be.

'There was one thing strange, though,' Chief Burns mused, breaking into Jack's thoughts. Burns expertly took the track at speed, and then lifted off the gas as he hit some scree. Stones and gravel shot off to the right as he gunned the engine again, traction restored.

'What?'

'He used a hollow-point to kill himself. But I couldn't find the ammo in his cabin. All he had there was round-nose, full metal jacket.'

That made Jack frown. Full metal jacket bullets were military style, with a copper casing that covered the whole bullet so that when it hit flesh or bones it punched a neat wound, rather than expanding and tearing a ragged hole in the victim. Expanding ammunition, especially hollow point, was designed to balloon as soon as it hit flesh, so that it would rip a man's body apart.

'Seems odd.'

'Yeah,' Chief Burns said. He swung the wheel and the car came to rest at the parking bay. 'I thought that, too. Then I reckoned, if I was desperate and wanted to get out, I'd probably want to have one bullet I could rely on. I've seen a guy took the top of his head off with a solid slug. Missed almost everything, but it tore his head and face around. Just the pressure of a handgun bullet can do real damage.'

Jack nodded and said, 'Could he buy a single round like that?'

Chief Burns opened the door.

'Hey, he could've borrowed one from a guy at a range, could have stolen one from a club – one bullet, who's going to care?'

The two walked up the path, and before long both could smell the charred building.

'Ah, shit!' Chief Burns muttered. 'We used to get a few artists and the like up here. All brought good money. Looks like we're going to have to get a new cabin built for next season.'

Jack walked to the door and peered about him. The roof was burned away, and the interior was ruined. Most of the walls had gone, but the mess was still smoking, and he could see a red glow in among the blackened logs when the wind gusted gently about them.

'Can you smell anything?'

The police chief gazed at him, puzzled, and joined Jack at the door.

'What, Mr Hansen?' he began, but then he frowned. 'That smells like an accelerant.'

78

Jack peered at him. It was a technical term for a redneck local cop, he thought so he added, 'Smells like petrol.'

'I reckon you got a suspicious mind,' Chief Burns grunted as he walked in, stepping gingerly among the mess. 'If I had to guess, I'd reckon that this was an electrical fault, or maybe the water heater had a failure. It happens on occasion. And many homes will have a gallon of gas somewhere. For running a leaf blower or chainsaw. Don't think this'll be any different.'

Jack entered, but kept away from the chief. With the heat from the fire, he wasn't sure how badly the floor would have been scorched. He saw that the picture of the tree was ruined, and stood staring at the burned mess. The picture had been painted on a board of wood, and it had burned fiercely where the oil paints and varnish had lain.

'Shame about the picture,' he muttered.

'Eh?'

'Nothing. He had a picture here of an old tree. It had been hit by lightning or something,' Jack said, stepping towards the table in the kitchen which, by a miracle, had survived the collapse of the main beam overhead, although all the books on the surface were now burned and black.

'Must have been the Shotgun Pine,' Chief Burns said absently. He pulled up a beam of wood and peered under it. Stepping through the opening where the bedroom door had been, he continued. 'I know he used to go that way to paint.'

'He painted?' Jack said.

'Yeah. Saw him myself a couple of times, sketching and scribbling. He had an old book. Leather cover to it, but never let anyone see inside it.'

'How big?'

'You seem all fired up again, mister. Something you want to tell me?'

Jack smiled and took his passport from his pocket.

'This shows I am who I say I am. If you want, I have my driving licence, photos of the children, everything here in my wallet, too.'

'There's no need for all that,' Chief Burns said, taking both and looking at them carefully. 'But thanks. Yeah, they look good, Mister Hansen.'

'Where is the tree?'

'Shotgun Pine? Out near the point. You just take the Shotgun Cove road and keep going. It's rough, though. All a Jeep track. You'd best keep your Ford off it. The rental firm wouldn't like to see it all scratched and dented.'

'You knew I had a Ford?'

'This isn't a big town to take care of, and the most dangerous folks tend to be visitors,' Chief Burns said.

'I'll take a walk out to see this pine,' Jack said.

'Okay. You do that. And then, when you're back, do you want to view his effects? All the stuff that looked valuable I took back to the station and kept in the safe.'

'What was there?'

'Cash, his watch, just personal effects.'

'His sketchbook?'

Chief Burns looked at him. 'I wouldn't take up my safe's space with that. It's not like it was valuable, eh? Or was he a famous painter?'

'Nope,' Jack smiled. 'Only a soldier who'd gone to ground.'

'Yeah, we knew that. He came into town a couple times. Drank in Suzie's bar. Seemed alright, but a live wire. Know what I mean? He was always wired, like he was ready to go off the deep end any time soon. Guess it was true, too. Poor bastard.'

Jack walked through into the bedroom. It was wrecked. The mattress had gone up quickly, and the smell of burned foam rubber was an assault on his sinuses. Jack scuffed the rugs from the floor, but the fire had burned well here, and the floor had only a dimple to show where the bullet had finished in the planks.

Chief Burns watched him with narrowed eyes.

'For an attorney with an interest in wills, you spend a lot of time looking at bullet holes, Mr Hansen.'

'It strikes me as strange that the man came all the way here to commit suicide. Why didn't he do it at home?'

'Good question. Why was he here, Mister Hansen? It's a long way from home.'

Jack considered. There seemed little need to conceal much. It was likely that Lewin had spoken of his time in the army, and if he didn't, people would guess from his carriage.

'He was with the British Army in Iraq and Afghanistan. I think he had a bad war, and wanted to hide from the world.'

'Uhuh. And he reckoned this'd be a good place, I guess. Yeah, that's what I reckoned when I spoke to him. Reckoned he wanted peace and quiet, with his painting and drawing, but then the black dog came down on him. Know what I mean?'

'Churchill used to call his depression his black dog.'

'That's right,' Chief Burns chuckled. 'I used to think of him as my greatest hero. Other kids thought Superman was the one: me, I preferred the hoary old fighter.' He grew serious again. 'Think that's what got to your client. He was alright when he first got here, two months back. About three weeks or so, he looked good. But then something happened about four weeks ago. He was real jumpy all of a sudden. Wanted to keep an eye on the doors all the while, like he expected a felon to walk into the bar when he was there. Then he stopped coming into town. Just turned up once in a while to get supplies, and then he was kind of watchful, you know? Like he didn't trust anyone any more. Not even Suzie, and everyone likes Suzie.'

'Did anyone keep an eye on him?'

The police chief looked at him.

'I said I saw him sketching a fair amount, eh? I was up here often as I could be, and when I wasn't, I tried to get one of my guys to drop in. We did what we could. We're a small community here, we don't get too many problems and, as police officers, we take our pastoral care seriously. But I wouldn't have him arrested and checked by a shrink just because he seems kind of depressed. That's for him to decide.'

'So he died.'

'Yeah.'

Jack shrugged.

'I doubt anyone could have stopped him. He was pretty determined. The bullet shows that.'

'Well, I'm surely sorry he took his life up here. If he'd come down to the town, maybe someone could have helped him bit more. Ach! What do I know? Look, you want a ride down to the Jeep trail?'

'Yes, I'd appreciate that.'

'Don't mention it,' Chief Burns said. 'I still ain't figured you out, Mister Lawyer. I reckon there's more in your head than just a little dead client here. Still, none of my business.'

Jack smiled and nodded, but his mind was already on the pine tree. Shotgun Pine seemed a long shot for a journal, but the fact that Lewin had been up there so often, the fact that he had painted it in his home, both showed that he had some feeling for the tree and the view from it. Jack should at least check it out.

10.18 Whittier; 19.18 London

The tree was easy to find. As soon as Chief Burns let Jack out of the car and pointed, he could see the splintered, broken top of the tree through the smaller pines all about it.

'It was the last of the old ones round here,' Burns said, as he sniffed and scratched at his ear. 'The army came up here and drove the road through, but they didn't cut the old Shotgun Pine down. Don't know why. It was left as a landmark, I guess. Reckon it was after the earthquake. Maybe it's the last of the trees from before the quake of '64.'

'Quake?'

'We're close to the fault line here. In '64 the place was trashed. Quay, fuel stores, the lot. The military buildings survived, but that's about all.'

'Right.'

'The land here shifted by feet. Hell of a tsunami, too. We're kind of used to the elements fighting back around here. Look, I have some of Mr Lewin's belongings back at the station house. You want to come take a look? Fine. I'll be busy rest of today, but you can find me there any time tomorrow. We're in Kenai Street. Ask Suzie to show you the way.'

Thanking him, Jack closed the door and trudged up the roadway. It was very poor here, little more than a bed of loose chippings, and the ground rose, leaving the water far below. Jack stopped when he crested a hillock and stared about him. The sea was grey and inhospitable. Opposite him, on the other side of the bay, the mountains rose from the water, lush and green at the base, thinning as he found his eyes drawn upwards, and grey and bleak at the top. It was all the same around here: pines and rock, and little else.

He liked it. Turning back to the track, he continued up until he came to a wide space.

The tree stood at the edge of the track, which curved about it, and looked entirely out of place. It was as though an army engineer, guilt-ridden at the destruction of so many other trees, had finally selected this one remaining bough to live on. And then, ironically, because it was so much taller here and solitary on its little hill, it had been the easiest target of lightning when it struck.

He approached the tree cautiously. If this was a blind drop, there would be nothing for the casual observer to see. But for Lewin, it must have been easy to find originally, when he first began to look for a secret hideaway. He wasn't a trained agent, but an interpreter and interrogator. Finding suitable caches was not part of his job.

But he had made that painting. Looking about him now, Jack could appreciate why. The place was higher, secluded, and yet gave good visibility of much of the track leading here, and over the water. A man up here could be sure of seeing when someone approached.

Pulling out his phone, he looked through the photos he had taken in the room: two showed the painting, although neither was well focussed, and the picture on his mobile was not as clear as it could have been. He wished he had taken a photo of the picture itself, but it hadn't seemed important enough to justify it.

He stood with the phone at eye level, comparing it with the tree. Moving around the tree to match it with the photo, he soon found the exact position where Lewin must have sat to paint. It was a tree stump, ancient and rotten, and standing beside it, Jack wondered whether the painting had held a clue. Perhaps there was something that distinguished the location of the journal? But if that was so, the clue had been lost. The phone's screen was poor, and the resolution of the picture terrible.

Putting the phone away, he walked to the tree. From this side, there were only cracks in the wood. One looked hopeful: a broad fissure that rose to some height, but the bottom was covered by a brittle layer of bark, and when he touched it, the bark fell away. If anything had been installed there, the bark would not have survived. Still, he reached inside and quested with his fingers. Nothing.

For an hour he prodded and tapped, checking roots, testing the bark and wood, fingering the thin soil all about it, and found nothing. The whole area was a mess of chipped stone and loose soil. Even grasses found it hard to survive here with the freezing winters, but there was no obvious hiding place, no matter how hard he searched, and he wandered to his starting point where the stump stood, and sat upon it. It rocked as it took his weight, but he remained there, staring at the Shotgun Pine, glancing at his phone every so often.

And then he closed his eyes.

'You prick!'

He stood and studied the old stump. It was a little proud of the ground and, as he pushed it, it shifted. Some old plants had grown about it, and there was a loose flap of lichen and moss at one convergence of the roots. He pulled it aside, and peered in. There, among the roots, he could see a carrier bag. He tugged it free and opened it to find a clear plastic box. And inside was a leather-bound journal.

*

12.03 Whittier; 21.03 London

Jack didn't look inside. That could wait until he was back in his room. For now, he had the boxed journal stuffed into his coat, the zip done all the way up to his chin. Even with the thick down inside the coat, he was aware of the chill, and he stuffed his bare hands into the side pockets to try to warm them.

The town appeared before him sooner than he would have expected. Here the roads were so poor that driving along the track meant a speed little better than a trot, he guessed.

It was a curious place, this. Whittier suddenly appeared from the east through the trees. First the quay and a huge passenger ship at the dock came into sight, and then the rest of the town began to sprawl away on his left. It was like a huge scoop had been lifted from the side of the hill here, and a 'U'-shaped road network inserted. Surely this was where the glacier had once lain because the pines were all a darker mass nearer him, while in the bowl of the rocks there were low bushes or scrub. That must have been the glacier's position. Amazing that it had moved out of view.

Next to come into view was the hideous old block. It loomed up on the extreme left, a foul cancer of concrete, with black, glassless windows. It was vast, and stared out over the rest of the town with a malevolence Jack could almost feel.

At its foot he saw the girl he had seen the night before – the blonde, slim girl with the fear in her eyes. She looked over as he approached, and he smiled.

'Hello,' he said.

She didn't reciprocate his smile.

'You're new here.'

He nodded.

'Just visiting. A man I knew died. Did you know Dan Lewin? I am his lawyer.'

'He killed himself.'

There was no emotion in her voice. Only a dull conviction.

Jack motioned towards the building.

'Horrible old place.'

She turned away from it.

84

'I nearly died there. Johnny did. A walkway fell on him. So loud!'

'I'm sorry.'

'He thought the Buckner Building would be safe. He'd made himself a place in there, but it crushed him. Do you think it's haunted?'

Jack glanced at her. She was plainly sad, but there was no harsh edge to her misery, no cracks from which the tears could spring, and he guessed that she must be medicated to seem so stoic.

'Why should it be?'

'I don't know. I seem to hear things.'

He pointed to the building.

'Buckner? Why's it called that?'

With a sing-song lilt ,as though repeating a mnemonic from many years before, she replied, 'He was the army General who did so much to make this town.'

'What of that one?' Jack said, pointing to the only other apartment block in Whittier.

'That's the Begich. It was named after a politician who died in a plane crash. Lots of men died here,' she said, and suddenly began to sniffle, as though the immensity of her grief had returned to take her. 'So many die.'

'Really?'

'You know, if you come here late at night, you can hear them. The screams and sadness. All the ghosts of the Bucky.'

Jack had been going to ask her where Chief Burns had his office, but the girl's fey manner affected him. He felt as though he would be trampling her feelings into the mud by bringing her back to such mundane affairs. It was a relief when a woman gave a cry and ran towards them. She took the girl's hand, throwing a suspicious look at Jack, and hugged her.

'I was worried about you, honey.'

'I went to look at it again.'

'You have to keep away from that place. You know it's dangerous, Kase. Keep away from the Bucky.'

'I will.'

Jack felt he should add his own comment.

'She didn't go inside, I don't think. She was watching from out by the road when I came by.'

The woman nodded, but said nothing more. Instead she turned and took the girl with her, walking over towards the tall block. Jack went to his room at the bar. He tossed the journal in its wrapping on his bed. There was nowhere to hide it in his small chamber, he realised, looking about him. He dare not leave the journal here. The thing was too important for him to risk losing it. He wanted to keep it on him at all times. So thinking, he took it from the box and shoved it into the lining of his coat, before pulling it on again and going down to the bar.

He asked for a coffee, and sat at the same table as the previous night. This time, when he looked out through the window, the blonde girl, Kase, wasn't there, and it seemed as though the view was incomplete without her. He would have liked to have been able to help her. She had a strange, fragile manner about her that called to a man to try to comfort her.

Suzie was soon there with a mug and a pot of cream.

'There was a girl I saw in town today,' he said. 'Kase?'

'Oh, yeah?'

'She was talking about ghosts and things.'

Suzie chewed her lip.

'Well, Kase is a nice girl. Don't think anything else. But she went up the old building over there with her boy, Johnny Durham, and there was an accident. A walkway fell on them. Killed Johnny outright, and it sort of loosened her mind, you know?'

Jack turned back to his coffee a few moments later with a sense of real sympathy for the girl. To have her boy crushed to death in front of her… And Suzie's reticence to talk about it spoke much about the horror of the girl's experience.

It was that horror which made him think of Claire. She had none of that fragility and vulnerability about her before, but she did now. Perhaps it started when she first realised his real job had nothing to with petrochemicals. It had taken her a long time to accommodate the truth, and then they had started to drift apart, with her growing increasingly withdrawn. But it was only when they separated that she had displayed her anxiety openly.

She had become more alarmed, like a trapped animal, when he first joined the Scavengers after 7/7. The more she understood about his job, the more the implications seemed to knock her down, both mentally and physically. She even walked stooped. It had been utterly different when he was in charge of his network in Russia because she had no idea about his work. He was at home most evenings after his day's work, and she never guessed that he wasn't working in the oil industry. When he established the Scavengers that all changed. He was confronting real danger, having to face situations he had never anticipated before, and, worst of all, he found he enjoyed it. It drew him away from Claire, and she could sense the gulf opening up between them.

The house in Devon had been in her family for a couple of generations, and although she had agreed to convert it to a semi, and sold off the second half, she was adamant that she would never sell the rest. Even when they came so close to the final break up, and he demanded that she move back to London with him – God that had been a row to end all rows. He could still remember her tear-ravaged face as she shrieked at him that she would rather die than go back to live that empty, wasted life with him in London. He had only ever seen her like that once again. That time when he saw her...

That wasn't a scene he was going to dwell on. Instead he took a glug of coffee, pulled out the journal and opened it.

And saw why this journal was so dangerous.

Monday 19th September

'I went there thinking I was going to help in a war,' Jack read, and stopped to take another gulp. It was hard to read this. He felt he knew what he was going to learn.

'I was appalled when I heard of the tragic attacks on the two towers. New York had always seemed a place of excitement to me. I loved it after visiting twice, and to see it brought so low showed me that there was genuine evil in the world. As a Christian, I saw it as my duty to help eradicate the murderers who could do such things. They had to be stopped.

'I was an enthusiast for the war. It could not come soon enough.'

The whole journal was plain paper, A5, unlined, and there was a thin leather covering that was bound with a thong. It was written in a hand that varied wildly, with pencil mostly, that slashed at the paper with vicious strokes, or a dark blue fountain pen that seemed to match a happier mood. When the pen was used, the characters were more rounded and appeared calmer. Sketches filled certain parts, some being pictures of walls, of bars, or scenes from the countryside which looked as though they might have come from around here: pines and bushes, fireweed and stark, bare trees. Pictures of the cabin, from several sides, and a series of the Shotgun Pine from varying angles.

But it was the faces that were the most common. Stark, gaunt faces, with eyes that haunted. The cheeks were deeply sunken, the skin lined and haggard: faces from Belsen or Auschwitz. They leapt from the pages, and Jack had to hold the journal away. He couldn't bear to have them too close to him, as if their horror could slip into his own soul – his soul that was already so scarred. It was hard for him not to pick up the phone, but a glance at his mobile told him that there was no signal still. He couldn't call Claire. It made him feel empty.

He turned back to the beginning. It took a little time to decipher some of the pencil writings, but once he was used to the harsh, angular scrawl, he found he could read it much faster.

In the main, the book told of Lewin's arrival at Iraq, and how he spent a lot of time travelling about the country with his regiment. He had been seconded to them in order to help interrogate the prisoners who were caught as the troops passed through certain areas of

Baghdad, and in the main, although all were nervous, the population gratefully received them. 'They are an ancient race, and they show it. Urbane, gracious, generous, nothing we wanted was too much trouble. We were invited into their homes...'

He was sent into Fallujah to help the American troops just before the big push to destroy the rebels within, and there he was impressed with the professionalism of the soldiers. In this, his first six month tour of duty, he appeared to enjoy the work, and his enthusiasm for the country grew.

And yet it also meant that his tolerance of the men whom he considered terrorists, those who were prepared to bomb or shoot the ordinary Iraqis, was growing ever more fragile. He hated those who could harm others for no reason, and he could see no good reason for the continuing raids and attacks.

'My first descent into hell.'

The title of that page drew Jack up short, and he sat for a long time reading the passage.

It told of a time when he had a boy in his custody. The lad was not yet eighteen years old, younger than the British soldiers who brought him in, and yet Lewin was convinced that he was a terrorist. Lewin had been told as much by the major in charge. This prisoner was guilty of storing weapons. He had been found with a handgun in his room. Usually a pistol was no indicator of criminality, but there was a strong belief that intelligence proved this boy had been aiding a group of disaffected Iraqis who had tried to bomb a police station. He knew their names. He must give them up.

Lewin questioned him. There was no response. He tried to shout and swear to induce fear, so that the boy would begin to talk, but the lad watched him from those large, bovine eyes, and said nothing of any use. He denied knowing the bombers, denied helping anyone. He was a supporter of the Americans, he said. The pistol was only there so he could defend his mother and himself. He didn't want to see his mother harmed or raped. Everyone needed a weapon for defence.

There appeared to be no way to break him. There was no proof that the army could give Lewin, there was only more force. Over time, since arriving in Iraq, Lewin had been happy to use increasingly harsh techniques. He had brought in trained dogs to intimidate prisoners and he had set electrodes on his desk and left prisoners staring at them while he went out of the room. This time, though, with this prisoner, he lost it.

Too many nights of demanding answers that were not forthcoming, too many days in the middle of the desert, fearing the next explosion from an IED, too much time listening to the stories of soldiers who had wept as they told of their comrades blown to pieces or shot dead. This time, Lewin ran out of patience. He punched the boy on the nose. He felt the bone snap under his fist, saw the smudge of blood, the way the boy's head jerked back, and rather than feel shame or guilt, he felt power, power mingled with pleasure. The boy made some comment, snorting and his nostrils bubbling with blood, and Lewin felt only rage. He slapped the boy with the back of his hand, then again with the front, knocking his head from side to side, lost for that moment in his own rage at the futility of his questioning, and at his impotence. The boy closed his eyes, and Lewin bunched his fist to punch him again, when he saw that the boy was crying. Not sobbing like a man, but simply crying, like the boy that he was.

That was Lewin's descent into hell. It was a rapid fall, and climbing out of that pit of despair was a long, painful, weary climb.

From that moment, there were more pictures of the men he had already questioned. The interrogations of men who had been deprived of sleep, who had been forced to stand in stress positions, who had been beaten, and who had been threatened with death, now began to be reviewed by Lewin, and he did not like the conclusions he was reaching. Where in the past he had routinely assumed that his comrades were naturally telling the truth, now he questioned that. In almost all cases, they did believe that they were doing the best job they could in order to stop the terrorism, but now Lewin felt certain that the men they were bringing in were the wrong ones. As he analysed the data on his own victims, he began to see patterns. All those who were brought in tended to have been named by others who had already been interrogated, usually harshly. The expansion of intimidation in interrogations had brought about the natural result: those who were scared for their lives gave whatever information they thought would help save them, no matter whether it was true or not.

The whole system was based on a military view of administration. There were men there who had committed crimes: troops found someone nearby, therefore he was involved. Mere proximity implied guilt. The 'criminal' was questioned to learn what he knew, whom he knew, and those named were also captured and questioned. If a man denied having anything to do with the incident, it could only mean that the questioning was not harsh enough. In a results-driven organisation, that meant increasing the pressure on the victims fast. The *data* itself was not validated – it was the quantity that mattered.

It was a nervous breakdown, of course. That was what Jack had seen when he met Lewin all those weeks later, not that it helped: Lewin was desperate and needed both mental therapy and physical support. But then, although he was given some counselling, the Service set him loose.

He flicked through the pages and saw that Lewin's mind was starting to grow ever more irrational. He suffered from mood-swings, and the pages were alternating from pencil to biro, to fountain pen many times in each day. Pictures of the men he had questioned – except he now explicitly used the word 'torture' – appeared more and more often. On one page, he had drawn eight faces in squares, each more gaunt than the next, and the last was more like Munch's *The Scream* than a real human. Jack almost turned the page before he realised that this was Lewin himself, the torturer displaying his anguish at what he had done.

The journal told of his journey into self-loathing. He lost his position, and he wrote about moving to Manchester where he hoped to lose himself in the thousands who thronged the city streets. But there he was confronted by others who, he thought, looked at him as though they knew what he had done. Paranoia became an ever stronger element of his make up and, as Jack read on, he winced to learn of Lewin's increasing terror. The man should have been sectioned and helped, not arrested for trying to buy a gun to protect himself.

He read on, and saw a reference to Alaska. It made him pause, and he reread it carefully. There was a mention of a place with space, away from other people, somewhere he could feel safe. Someone had told him of this place, a man Lewin referred to as Brain, whom he knew from his time in the army, and he had come here, to Whittier. Jack wondered who this friend could be. It was an odd name for a soldier, but then soldiers would often give each other nicknames. They were rarely challenging: the short called 'Lofty', the chubby 'Slim'. Brain was probably a soldier known for foolishness. Although it was possible he was just good at crosswords.

But why here, to Whittier? There was little explanation of that, but Jack reckoned he could understand his motives. Leaving England would have felt like leaving prison in his state. Coming to Alaska would mean arriving in a wild, free land, different from all that he was used to, and perhaps, Jack thought, closing the book, because it was cold. It could not be more different from the country in which Lewin had been questioning prisoners.

There was mention of his talks with Jack himself, and Jack skipped that. There was a mention of a meeting with Karen Skoyles, too, discussing interrogations, but as Jack turned the pages he found a piece that really made him pause.

It was a new section: 'I think I can take part again. Brain says now it'll be with genuine suspects. No more hurting the innocent in the hope that I catch the right one: this time, the murderers will be brought to me for full interrogation. As long as it takes, he says.'

Jack stopped. He read back a few pages, and saw that there was a subtle change in the writing on the three previous pages. They started with his arrest in Manchester for trying to acquire a gun to protect himself, and soon after, taking a flight to Anchorage, and finding his way here, to Whittier. And here, he suddenly appeared to be more enthusiastic and motivated. Something had changed.

'To learn that it can all be arranged right at last. Thank God Roger suggested I should come.'

There were several more pages filled with similar hopeful, happy comments.

'The unit can improve. There can be justifiable interrogations. We can get intel, good intel, from people like this. I'd be glad to help them.'

In the last pages, there were some more hopeful comments, but then the tone changed again. Instead a note of tension intruded, a fresh despair.

'*No.* I told them, but they didn't listen. Now they say that it's all wrong again. That I'm wrong. But I remember him! It *can't* have been him.'

There were some lines Jack could hardly read, and then a scrawl in pencil.

'This is worse than Abu Ghraib.'

*

21.32 Whittier; 06.32 London

Those words stayed with Jack as he sat in the restaurant that evening, reading and rereading the journal.

To say that things were worse than at Abu Ghraib was weird. The Abu Ghraib prison had been notorious for the abuse of prisoners: for water-boarding, humiliation, beatings, and mental torture. It read so

92

oddly, to see the way that the blue pen had gradually taken over, as though Lewin had seen some new hope through the prism of his misery. Something had breathed new life into him. And then Jack found the name: Roger Sumner.

The name was one that rang a bell loudly. Jack set the book aside and cleared his mind as he tried to isolate that name from the hundreds in his mind. Sumner. It sounded like someone he'd known. In the Service? No. But military, he was sure. An officer, too. A Captain.

That was it! Captain Roger Sumner, from Military Intelligence, who'd been in Ireland at the back end of the Troubles. Jack had met him a few times at inter-agency briefings, usually regarding Irish terrorists trying to buy guns from Eastern European dealers. Jack had a tab on two arms suppliers, and had passed on information. Sumner had been a bright, calm, quiet man, who listened carefully and spoke little. He was keener on keeping secrets than sharing, and when he was forced to give information, it was plain how difficult he found it.

Jack went through the journal a few more times, but could deduce nothing more. The only thing that did interest him still, and which he could make little sense of, was a list of names at the back of the book.

There were thirty or more, and each had a cross alongside. One name rang a chord in his memory, a man called Abu Fazul Abdullah. It was there, somewhere, close to the front of his mind, but he couldn't quite bring up the relevance. Abu Fazul Abdullah... The name was familiar.

He looked further down the list. There were another fifteen or so, none of which meant anything to him – names like Faisal, al Malik, Abdul-Gaffar, Rasmi, Labeeb... There was no leader of the Taliban or al-Qaeda that he knew of. The letters made no sense to him. If only they were Russian, he told himself with a weary grin. Then at least he may have understood them, perhaps remembered one or two.

He would check on the internet to see if he could make any sense of all the names when he returned to Anchorage.

And then, he would go back home. There was nothing for him here.

*

13.12 London
Sara al Malik snatched up the telephone as soon as it rang.
'Yes?'
It was Lomax.

93

'Sara, I'm getting nowhere with the Met. They deny all knowledge. I've been all the way to the Commissioner's office, and no one is giving me anything more than a polite brush off. They even suggested he ran. They've found his tag, apparently, somewhere off the M25 near the A3 junction. I've already asked how his tag could have got there without them noticing, but they don't know. Said something about a fault with the signal: they say that they were still getting the message that he was at home. The main thing is, they deny absolutely any knowledge of his arrest. No one can tell me anything at all!'

Sara's stomach seemed to fall from her body. She was empty, a mere shell with nothing inside her. There was a chair beside the telephone, and she took it now, clutching hold of the arm as though it was an anchor to life as she asked desperately, 'Do you believe them?'

Lomax had been a student agitator at university, and more recently fought cases on behalf of asylum seekers, squatters and union activists. He never trusted what the police told him. 'No. I think they either have him themselves, or they've helped another country take him. Rendition by other means.'

Sara grabbed for a chair's back. Her legs suddenly weak, she fell into it. 'What can we do?'

'What we threatened, Sara. We need publicity to get Mo back. If you feel strong enough, I propose to get all the media coverage I can. I have a friend in advertising, and he's already promised that he will give me all the relevant contacts. We will have the BBC, independents, Sky and God knows who else jumping onto this. There is no excuse for daylight kidnap, no matter what they felt the justification.'

'I see,' she said. 'We tried that before. It did nothing, did it?'

Even to her, her voice sounded small and far-away. The idea that she should have cameras, journalists, and the whole paraphernalia of a modern media storm outside her house again– men and women thrusting microphones at her, demanding answers – was deeply alarming But if this was the only way to find out what had happened to Mo, it was worth it. Surely it was worth it.

'Sara? Are you there?'

'Yes.'

'This is a big step, Sara. But Sara, I can't leave Mo to rot in some cell. He's a friend. Are you strong enough for this?'

'I want him back. Yes, I can do it. But… it scares me.'

'I'll be there with you, Sara. I'll be there with you,' he promised, and then the line died.

And just afterwards, she heard a small, faint click. At first it meant nothing, but then, she suddenly frowned and stared at her receiver with horror.

She had been bugged.

*

09.24 Whittier; 18.24 London

Next morning was crisp, but not too cold. Jack pulled on a thick leather jacket, and shoved the journal inside a larger inner pocket for safety, before setting off to find Chief Burns.

The police station was south of the tower in Kenai Street: a low, flat-roofed building, with a glass front and two steps leading up to the main room. There were two Ford Expedition four-wheel drives outside with lights and marked 'Police', with scenes of mountains behind the lettering. It made it look like a ski-school's vehicle more than a cop's, Jack thought as he went up the steps.

'Glad you could make it,' Chief Burns said, as he walked in through the door. 'Take a seat. Coffee?'

'Thanks,' Jack said, and took the warm mug gratefully.

'Cream? Sugar?' Chief Burns asked, and appeared disappointed when Jack rejected them. 'Any luck?'

'What with?'

'Whatever it was you were looking for at the pine.'

'It was a good view. I can see why Mr Lewin would have wanted to go there,' Jack said.

'Oh. Sure.'

Chief Burns led Jack from the main room into a small office. There was a plate glass window from here looking into the main room. The other side looked out towards the Begich Building. Chief Burns sat at his plain, steel framed desk with a light wood top, and motioned to Jack to take a seat in front.

'We only have two guys working through the winter months,' he said, seeing Jack's eyes watching the large space. 'Whittier only has about two hundred people here during winter. But in the summer, when the sports fishermen come, and the walkers and the folks wanting to see the glaciers, then I have more guys hired. We need the space then.'

He had a small box, the size of a shoebox, on the desk, and now he leaned forward and pushed it towards Jack.

'There you go. All his valuables. All I could see, anyways.'

Jack took the box with a certain reluctance. There was a feeling of trespassing on a man's misery in opening this. Lewin had done his best for the country, and was then ditched. When he was anxious, he began to learn how insular the Service could be. When he started to lose his faith and became a disbeliever, he was thrown aside. Much as Jack himself had been.

'You want some peace?' Chief Burns asked. 'Look, take it with you, eh? There's nothing you have to leave with me. You have power of attorney, right?'

'Yes.'

'Right, I'll need a receipt, then, and you can take it away.'

'It's all right,' Jack said and took the paper Chief Burns passed to him, glancing down the sheet.

Opening the lid to confirm the contents, the first item he found was a box. Inside he found the pistol.

'Is that the one?' he asked.

'Yes. It's empty, don't worry. I put it back there myself.'

'Don't think the police at Heathrow will let me bring that back,' he said, picking it up.

It was a heavy gun, a Ruger GP100, weighing at least three and a half pounds in his hand. All stainless satin steel, it was not as violently shiny as a nickel-plated gun, and had a more utilitarian appearance with its short, stubby barrel. He pushed the cylinder latch with his thumb and looked at the six chambers. All empty. There was no blood on the metalwork or the soft, black rubber grips with wood inserts.

'I had it cleaned soon as the case was closed. Didn't want some member of the family coming here and finding it covered in his brains.' The chief eyed Jack for a moment. 'There are fifty or sixty rounds with it.'

'Can I see them?'

'You can take them,' the chief said, as he opened a drawer and pulled out two boxes. They were green, with a golden cross. 'Here you are. Full metal jackets – unlike the bullet he used on himself.'

'Yeah,' Jack said, taking the boxes.

One was heavy, full, but the other was almost empty. He opened it and pulled out a round, glancing at it. The brass casing was shiny and new, the copper bullet gleamed.

'He came a long way to buy that gun,' the chief observed. 'Then blew himself away. You won't do anything like that, eh?'

'No. I have no desire to kill myself,' Jack said.

'Good. Wouldn't want anything like that to happen to you,' the police chief said, leaning back in his chair and eyeing Jack over the rim of his mug. 'So, you have all you need?'

'I'm afraid so,' Jack said. 'The case is sad, but I can wind up Mr Lewin's affairs now I can confirm his death. It'll make the probate process more straightforward.'

'Good. So long as that's all. You sure there's nothing more you would like to tell me?'

Jack looked into Chief Burns' shrewd eyes. 'I don't know anything you'd want to know.'

'I see. Right, well there's one last thing. Look in the bottom of the gun box.'

Jack lifted the box. It was a simple cardboard box with the Sturm & Ruger sign on the outside. Peering in, he saw that there was a roll inside. It looked like a roll of banknotes in a plastic bag. He tipped the box and the wrap fell into his hand.

'So, Mr Hansen, what do you reckon to that lot?'

Jack unwrapped the plastic bag and pulled out the roll. It was a series of newspaper cuttings all held together by a rubber band. He took the band off and began to flick through the cuttings. They were all stories from different newspapers: some print outs from a paper's website, the BBC, New York Times, CNN, and Fox News. Some were deaths of terrorists, others were stories of men and women killed in attacks against presumed terrorist bases. There were photos of the dead men, of buildings blown to pieces, and over all were notes in the ragged, angry pencil that Jack had seen in the journal. 'The WRONG one!', 'He was in Abu Ghraib', 'He was supposed to be released', and 'INNOCENT' were scrawled over them. Jack looked at them, and shrugged.

'I have no idea. Perhaps he was conducting some research.' As he spoke, he felt a sharp, electric excitement pass through his belly. The names he read were the same as those in the back of the journal. There was Rasmi, al Malik, Abdul-Gaffar, Abu Fazul Abdullah ...

'You think so?' Chief Burns leaned forward. 'Mr Hansen, I honestly don't know too much about this and, to be honest, I don't think I want to. But I do think something smells real bad about this. First him dying, then these cuttings and his cabin. I don't like this sort of shit. I think I'll be glad when you're gone. You understand me?'

'Of course,' Jack said, rolling the cuttings back together. He dropped them back into the Ruger box.

'Right. That's it, then. Good to meet you, Mr Hansen.'

He stood, and Jack rose at the same time to shake hands. And that was when the world seemed to boil about him.

There was a flash. The floor rose and rippled in front of him; the ceiling lifted, and he felt his body being flung forwards towards the chief. His knee hit the table, even as he curled his body into a ball, covering his head with his hands, and then he was past the desk and rolling over the floor the other side with Chief Burns in front of him. There was a rattle and clatter of concrete and metal and shards of glass all about him, and then Jack knew nothing more.

*

10.57 Seattle; 18.57 London

'Sir!' Roy Sandford cradled the phone in his shoulder as he spoke, the keys rattling quickly on his computer as he frantically read the screen. 'Yeah, there's another report. Sorry, sir!'

'Well?'

'Sending the package now, sir.'

'Very good.'

Roy put the phone back on the cradle and peered at the screen. There was something really screwy about all this. Something was happening and he had no idea what the fuck it was. Jeez, he wished he was back with Very Nice. He'd been here in the FBI field office in Seattle all day, and the cramped offices reeked of old tobacco, sweat, and cheap disinfectant. He didn't want to think what might have gone on here before the FBI took it over.

He rose to fetch himself a coffee, but the machine reeked of sourness as soon as he went into the kitchen. Instead he took a paper cup and filled it from the water fountain, standing at the door to his office and sipping it.

There was some kind of mission going on, he knew that much. So much SIGINT was flying around the systems, he was sure it was a big one. Like Amiss had said, some guy was dead. But not a US agent. This guy was foreign, that much he had gathered.

Well, Roy was going to keep his ear to the ground. In a world where intelligence was all, where secrecy was prized over all else, there was never a man or woman who was so fascinated by gossip. And Roy liked to know what was actually going on.

And then, naturally, he would have to pass on the information to Amiss. It was strange, though. Why was the deputy director of operations so interested in this one death in Alaska?

*

09.58 Whittier; 18.58 London

And then Jack was aware of a whiteness, a ghostly vision. He was a mass of pain, and couldn't speak or cry out. He saw two men in drab grey who wandered into the room, and stepped carefully and swiftly over the ruins of the office, pushing spars and timbers aside as they came, and quickly patted Jack down, before pulling the journal out of his coat. Jack was unable to keep his eyes open, and his head lolled from side to side, all control gone. He had to close his eyes, just to stop them falling out of his head, and the chief's body was beside him, but he wasn't moving, and Jack let his head slip to the side, and closed his eyes...

... And there was a shout, and coughing, and three more men were with him, and they pulled Jack aside, from under a beam which would have cut him in half, if it hadn't fallen on the chief's metal desk, and he began to feel he was alive, and then he felt the roaring of exhaustion rushing up through his spine, his head fell back, and he was out again.

*

14.34 Whittier; 23.34 London

'You're doing pretty well, for a guy should be dead,' a voice said, and Jack's eyes snapped wide.

He looked around the room, and saw only clear white walls, a blue rail, and a smiling woman's face.

'Where am I?'

'Not the most original first words,' she chuckled, moving around him and moving pillows to make him more comfortable. 'You're in the Begich Tower, in the medical centre, Mr Hansen. That was a bad knock you got on the head.'

He closed his eyes, and in an instant he was back there, in the chief's office once more, the room flying about him.

'Shit, Chief Burns, is he...?'

99

'He'll be OK,' the woman said. 'His head's hard as fossilised ironwood. But that's nothing for you to worry about. You just have to get yourself better.'

'What happened?'

'I'm not sure, but I think the gas tanks behind the building blew. A freak, they're all saying. I don't know, but I do know it was real bad luck. You sit back and rest, now.'

Jack allowed his head to fall back on the pillows, and tried to piece together the last moments. He knew that he had been in the chief's office, and had been handling the gun, a Ruger GP100, then a roll of papers, when there had been a flash and he had been thrown through the air.

'Where are my things?'

'Your clothes and all are in the wardrobe there,' the nurse said, pointing. 'Don't you get up until you're feeling better, now. You've been out for a while.'

'How long?' he snapped.

'A few hours,' she said, checking his pulse and registering the result on a clipboard. 'Now, you just rest there.'

He felt his head for damage – there was a series of bumps at the back of his skull, but apart from that he felt only a horrible tiredness.

'Any fractures?'

She watched him with a patient expression on her face and said, 'You aren't going to listen to a word I say, are you?'

He grinned weakly.

'How would you feel if a building had fallen on you?'

'Pretty sore, I guess. Still, you take care you don't make things worse, you hear? You don't want to have any more injuries.'

'No.'

He waited until she had left the room, and then hobbled painfully to the cupboard she had indicated. His thick leather coat was there, but now it was shredded. His trousers had a tear in the rear of the right thigh. But then he started feeling his coat, and swore. The journal was gone. That part of his hazy memory of men in the smoke was no dream. There was nothing inside his coat.

'Shit!'

*

14.06 Whittier; 23.06 London

Jack went to his room, waving to Suzie as he went past the bar.

100

'I heard,' she said, giving him a quick look. 'You need new clothes, you know that?'

'I could tell from the breeze up my backside,' Jack said ruefully.

'You hear how Chief Burns is doing?'

'They said he'll be OK,' Jack said. 'Should be out before long, I hope.'

In his room, he pulled on new trousers and a clean shirt, balling the old clothes into a bundle and throwing them into the bin. Packing quickly, he glanced around the room to make sure that he had left nothing behind and, as he did, he saw that the chest of drawers had been moved. There were dents in the carpet to show where the legs had stood, and they were a half inch or more out of true.

Someone had been in here. Either to bug the place or to hunt for something – perhaps for the journal.

He could remember those ghostly figures with ease. Two men, both moving quickly. They had the journal, and perhaps Lewin's other possessions, too. He would have to go and check. And then, get out. It was clear that they were after something, and while they hadn't killed him, he couldn't know if he was safe or not. He spent more time staring about him, making sure he'd left nothing behind, before wandering downstairs.

Settling the bill, he had a coffee, watching with apparent disinterest as people wandered about the streets. In reality he was scanning for anyone keeping Suzie's place under surveillance. He was convinced that the same men he had seen had tried to blow him up and they could be watching for him. At last, seeing no one, he went to his car and threw his belongings in the back. Then he climbed inside and drove to the police station, watching all the while for any men trailing him.

The building had been devastated. Where the entrance had been, now there was a mass of rubble and twisted metal. It reminded him of the 9/11 photos he'd seen, with bars and handrails, windows and pieces of furniture all broken and bent out of recognition. The roof mostly remained, a timber frame held it up, but much of the insulation had fallen through and lay in a thick carpet over the floor and wrecked furniture. It was enough to make Jack's belly curl in on itself. He felt nausea and dizziness begin to overwhelm him as he realised how lucky he was to have survived the blast. This was a bomb intended to kill everyone in the building – he had no doubt of that.

101

There was a young police officer standing where the door had been, a thick coat against the freezing air. 'Can I help you, sir?'

'I was here with Chief Burns,' Jack said, staring at the wreckage. 'I just wanted to see what fell on me.'

'Pretty much all the building, I guess,' the man said. He was younger, perhaps thirty, with a narrow face and thin black moustache. 'Hey, I'm glad you're OK. How's the chief?'

'I heard he'll be out soon.'

'That's good. You were both lucky.'

'Any idea what caused it?'

'The fire chief reckons the gas cylinders round back blew up. Christ knows why – maybe the metal was just old, eh?'

'Yes. Look, there were loads of my things in there. Is it all right to go in and look for them? They all fell out of my pockets, and I don't want to leave them.'

'If you don't mind me coming too,' the police officer said. 'There's nothing much more can fall on you now, anyhow.'

It was hard going in his weakened condition, with every footstep a danger to the ankles, broken glass lying all about, and the smell of singed fur and burned plastic everywhere. Jack found himself having to concentrate harder than usual just to stop himself from toppling. It was a very curious feeling, especially since he had a strange sweatiness, as though there was a fever building in him to join with the awareness of the vertigo, but he swallowed the dizziness and continued.

'Where were you: in the chief's office?' the policeman asked from a few feet further on.

Jack nodded, made a guess and said, 'Over there?'

'Yeah, that'd be about it,' the younger man said.

Soon they were sifting through the rubbish together. All around was thick insulation material, wisps of fibres floating off on the air. Jack felt the chill wind on his leg as he bent and tried to make sense of the mess about him. Roofing, cedar beams, metal supports, all lay about over the area where Jack had been sitting with the chief. Two spars rested on top the desk where Burns had sat, and Jack felt a sickness in his belly to think that it was this metal desk that had saved his life and the chief's. The solid metal legs took the weight of the roof.

It was twenty minutes before he saw a glint in among the rubble, and pulled out the Ruger. It was unharmed, so far as he could tell.

The ammunition was here, too, and he picked up both boxes. There was a sheet of paper nearby, and he saw it was the receipt for the items, which he showed to the police officer. He seemed uninterested. There was no shoebox, and, when he hunted all about, there was no sign of the journal.

But then he had some luck. He saw the red label of the Ruger's box, and when he pulled it free, the roll of cuttings was still inside.

He stuffed it into his pocket quickly before making his way from the room.

Tuesday 20th September

01.12 London

Karen Skoyles was asleep in bed when the news came through.

She always woke quickly. The phone had only rung once before her eyes opened. As it rang a second time, her hand was already on the handset.

'Skoyles,' she said softly.

Glancing at her watch, she noted the time with a wince. She'd never get back to sleep again after this.

'Hargreaves, Miss. There's a report coming in from Alaska, and you asked to be warned...'

'I know. What is it?'

'Our man has been taken to hospital, apparently. There has already been a telephoned claim for medical insurance, which is how we heard. Apparently our man Hansen was involved in an explosion at a local police station in Whittier, and he and the police chief were both injured, Hansen less seriously. He is out now.'

Karen lay still as she mused the problem.

'Very good. Thank you for letting me know,' she said.

She pressed the button on the handset, replaced it in the cradle by her bed again, and then lay back, staring at the ceiling, before rising, pulling on a dressing gown, and walking through the apartment to the kitchen. There she went through the routine of filling the kettle and boiling water. She spooned coffee into her cafetière and waited for the water to boil. Soon, a mug of black, sweet coffee cupped in both hands, inhaling, she could consider the news.

The loss of Lewin was bad enough. He had the potential of creating enormous embarrassment with his journal. But if Jack was clumping all over the place with the subtlety of a rhinoceros on steroids, things could get much worse. For a moment she felt a flare of sympathy for him. There was little chance of garlands for him with this job. At best he could return to obscurity and take his redundancy cheque, but at worst he could become a greater embarrassment to the Service than even Lewin. The last thing the Service needed was to see an agent causing problems with the Americans. The Brothers could be very tetchy about British agents on their territory, and the Service had to maintain good relations with them.

She considered that. In her mind she had a picture of Jack as he had been that last time she saw him: cold, stony-faced, like a prisoner before his parole board. With good reason, she knew. This was his last chance, and she had told him so.

Poor bastard.

*

16.38 Whittier; 01.38 London

Jack was in two minds as he walked away from the ruined police station. He stopped at the roadside, and looked about him at the wreckage, feeling utterly disorientated at the sight. He knew that this mild confusion was the after-effect of the blast, the result of the blow on his head and the explosion that had thrown him forward. It was a miracle he was still alive.

That was the thought that was uppermost in his head: how lucky he had been. That and a certain guilt at surviving mostly unscathed while Chief Burns was in a hospital bed still. He shook that off with a shudder. Better that the cop was there than Jack. He had work to do. Since the journal was gone, Jack had to collect his thoughts and figure out what to do to recover the situation. Karen would not be happy, nor the DG.

'Shit!' he muttered viciously. Starck's words came back to him. The threat of failure: he could lose everything he had saved up for. Two mistakes he had made in his life. One had cost him his career, and now this one was likely to cost him his future and his wife if Starck was vindictive, and Jack knew he was. He swore again. There was no safe bolt-hole, not for him. Someone had taken the journal.

The building had not been detonated accidentally. Someone must have planned to blow it up. Then they had come in for the book – either because they thought Chief Burns had it, or because they thought Jack had, in which case they could come back to kill him, or the chief.

In his pocket the Ruger was a comforting weight, dragging his coat down, the ammo boxes balancing it on the other side, but he would have to find a better way to store it if he was going to keep it for defence. The sights would catch if he had to draw it fast, and just now he was sure that he would have to use it. Those two shadowy figures in the murk after the explosion would come back for him.

Why? Who were they?

He should get back to the car. Get out of here. Whittier was too dangerous for him.

105

But first he had to know whether Chief Burns had anything else on Danny. Perhaps there was something else he could tell Jack, something that could help Jack understand who he was up against.

He turned and made his way to the hospital section of the Begich Building again, pushing through the broad doors and into the reception.

This place was only small, but when he walked out earlier it had seemed busy. Now, for some reason, the place was deserted. The reception desk was empty. Jack assumed the woman had gone to the washrooms, and he glanced along the corridor quickly before peering down at her desk, to find the room where Chief Burns was recuperating. The hospital ward only had a few rooms. He found Burns' name and walked along the clean passageway.

His own room was on the left, one of the nearest to the nurses' room, and he glanced inside as he passed by. His bed was still unmade, but with so few staff here, he wasn't surprised. They'd be busy for a while. Further up he passed two empty patient rooms, and then, on the right, he found a room with the blind down at the door's window. He knocked gently and walked in.

Chief Burns was lying in his bed with a large plaster over his brow on the right, covering his temple. His face was raw-looking where the heat from the blast had caught him, and there were innumerable tiny scratches and puncture marks from the fine shards of glass that had lanced into his face. His eyes had been protected by his thick plastic glasses fortunately, but Jack saw a mess of pin-pricks covering the rest of his features.

'You're not looking too bad,' the chief said ruefully.

'My back's sore,' Jack said. 'How are you, apart from the cuts?'

'Not too bad. A beam hit my head, they tell me, but it rested on the desk. Otherwise it'd have cut me in half.' Burns looked him over. 'Your hands OK?'

'Yeah. Nothing much,' Jack said, flexing them. 'My leather jacket's wrecked, though.'

'So 're my glasses,' Burns said ruefully. 'I'll have to get to Anchorage to buy some more.'

Jack nodded him. Then added, 'They're saying the tanks behind the station exploded.'

Burns looked at him, eyes narrowed as he struggled to focus without his spectacles. Even without them there was a shrewd assessment in his eyes as he said, 'You know, I've been a cop for a while now. I've seen cars in crashes; I've seen pools of gas with morons dropping matches into them to see how long it'd take before they blew – all that kind of shit. Never seen them go up like that before.'

'Sort of what I thought, too,' Jack said. 'You take care of yourself, Chief.'

'Oh, I think I'll be all right,' Burns said. 'Once you're gone, anyway.'

'Hope so,' Jack said.

'You look after yourself, Mister Hansen.'

Jack was about to shake hands, but just then there was a knock on the door, and he turned to see Suzie with a small bunch of flowers. She walked in, smiling at Burns, but giving Jack a frosty look, as though she felt this was all his fault, which it probably was, he thought.

'Hi, Chief. Wanted to see how you were doing.'

Jack looked from her to Burns.

'Well, I'll be off now, then.'

Suzie nodded coldly. She would obviously be happier without his presence. It made Jack feel a pang of jealousy. Chief Burns had his admirer, and Jack was having to fight just to maintain contact with his wife.

Out in the corridor he pulled the door quietly behind him and set off for the lifts beyond reception. There were footsteps approaching, but he paid little attention. He was thinking of the smile and how it lightened Suzie's expression as she saw Chief Burns. It was a curiously depressing sight, he thought, and his head was down as he walked.

There were two guys leaving the elevator. They walked on past him, and Jack continued to the elevator in a hurry to reach it before it could depart. The doors slid shut as he got there, but opened when he pressed the call button. As he slipped inside he was struck with a conviction that something was wrong. Before the doors closed, he glanced back along the corridor, and he saw the two men outside a room. One stood back, looking towards him, while the second reached for the door handle, and he was sure that both had hands under their coats.

The lift doors slid shut, and it was as they thumped together that he realised the two were at his own hospital room.

All his training screamed at him to run. The men at Vauxhall Cross would not want him to stay here. Karen Skoyles would order him to leave immediately. Even Starck, for all his faults, would not want an agent to knowingly put himself in danger. Jack was convinced that the two men were there for him. They might have wished to catch him, but he was certain they were determined to kill him. Why? Because of the journal. It must be that.

And they may well try to kill Burns. Which would mean they'd kill Suzie too.

Jack quickly pressed the button for the next floor. As soon as the doors opened, he was out and running along the corridor. There was a fire escape staircase at the far end, he knew, and he ran for it full tilt, slamming into the door and shoving it wide to thunder into the wall behind. Then he was on the stairs, running up two at a time, pulling himself up with the handrail and, when he reached the top, he remembered the Ruger. He stood at the fire door fumbling with the box of cartridges, fumbling bullets from it into the chamber. They were so long and slender that they were hard to slide in, and one refused utterly. He pulled it out and shoved it in his pocket, before selecting another and thumbing it home. Then, pistol in his hand but behind his back, he stepped into the corridor. Suzie was still in the room with the chief, but Jack's room was a little further beyond, and he walked along quietly and carefully, the tension in his back and scalp sending electrical tingles along his entire spine.

There were doors on both sides, but Burns's room was halfway to the lifts, and Jack could see his own doorway three or four beyond that. He sidled along anxiously, the pistol's rubber grip with the reddish wood inlay feeling slick in his hand.

A man came out from Jack's room, quickly, and set off towards the lifts. He was large, bulky, wearing a heavy plaid jacket, his gingerish hair cropped to a stiff-looking bristle over the whole of his skull. The second came out, a shorter, stockier man, with a similar haircut but darker hair. He looked almost Hispanic, with narrow features and dark eyes set close together. And he saw Jack.

Everything slowed. Jack saw the pistol in his hand, the stubby silencer attached, and heard the shots striking the walls behind him before he was aware of the puffs of smoke from the barrel. Something hit the ceiling, and a cloud of dust erupted from the tiles overhead, and then Jack was throwing himself through the nearest door, landing on his bad shoulder on the floor.

'*Shit*!' he shouted.

A severe nurse with black hair tied back exposing the nape of her neck turned from her patient to glare at him, and he stared back at her, frozen for a moment. Then he bellowed as he clambered to his feet,

'There's a gunman out there!' and saw her eyes go to the Ruger in his own hand, but then he saw the connecting door leading from this room to a second, and ran to it, throwing that door open and passing through as the nurse and her patient stared after him.

He was in a dispensary, and the door to the passage was half-glazed. Hurrying to it, he peered out, ready to snatch his head away at the first sign of a shot. There was no one visible. He opened the door and cautiously looked out. No one. He stood still, his mouth open as he moved into the corridor, breathing with exquisite care, listening for any strange noises: a footstep, perhaps the noise of a man racking a pistol, reloading it, but there was nothing. Quickly now, he went to Burns's room and glanced in. Suzie and Burns had not heard the silenced gun, and were talking, Suzie sitting on a chair, her back to the door. There was a wide space between them, Jack thought. They were friends, not lovers. Burns looked up, but before he could say a word, Jack was gone.

The reception area was clear. He went to the lifts, and there was still no sign of the two men. Walking round the elevators, Jack carried on through to the next section of corridor, and section by section made his way to the end of the building, taking the staircase to the ground floor, where he stood staring out, looking for those two men. They weren't there either.

He thrust the Ruger into the waistband of his trousers, in the small of his back where it was hidden and safe, opened the door, and stepped out, moving quickly.

*

16.46 Whittier; 01.46 London

Jack was worried. The gunmen had not tried to kill Burns, and that meant they were probably after him. Glancing up at the sky, he hastened his steps. Soon he was in the car and driving towards the tunnel, the Ruger on the chair beside him, the full box of ammo beside it. He cast a glance down at them, and realised that even in an open society like this, the police could frown on such a scene. He had his jacket on, and pulled over to pull it off and throw it over the gun. Then he sat for a moment, taking deep breaths and slowly letting it out. There was a coldness in his breast, a tightening in his lower throat, the feeling of shakiness in his hands, and he shivered suddenly, resting his brow on the steering wheel.

He was not exactly scared, It was more an awareness of danger approaching. He had been in real danger before now, in Russia, and even earlier in East Berlin when he was a rookie plodding his way around the old Iron Curtain, but this felt less focussed. He had no idea who the enemy was. All he was convinced of was that it involved Danny Lewin's journal, and because he had seen it, someone had decided he should be killed. The men leaving his room may not have realised who he was when he walked down the corridor. They must have thought he was still bed-ridden after surviving that explosion. If they had realised he was up, they would have looked more carefully for him, and killed him before he could get to the lift.

'*Fuck* them!' he muttered. 'Why?'

There must be something about the journal that was to be kept secret. Something Danny Lewin had written in it. He only wished he knew what it could be.

For now, all he wanted was to get away from this town. He'd be happier, feel safer, in a city. He pulled out into the road again.

Ahead of him he saw a large truck pull out, and slowed. It was not quite time for the passage to Bear Pass yet, and the line of cars, trucks and a coach, stood waiting with engines idling until the way was opened.

The lights changed, and the traffic began to move off. Jack put the Ford into gear and trailed off after the truck, following along the road and under the great inverted 'V' of the snow that led into the tunnel itself.

Even with the lights, it was oppressive. It made him think of the darkness in the wrecked police station as he began to come to, and the mere thought was enough to make him shiver suddenly. The strip lights flashed past, one after another, in a mesmerising sequence, and Jack began to feel the effects of his injuries in the last few hours. He puffed out his cheeks, opened the window, and let the cool air wash over his face to keep himself awake, but before he had reached the halfway mark, he felt his eyelids starting to close. The car wobbled, and he jerked back to full wakefulness, but with an appreciation that his concentration was blown. After-effects of action, he told himself. Gripping the wheel with both hands, he shifted in the seat, focussing on the truck, and suddenly realised that it had slowed. He had

110

narrowed the gap between it and his car, and he pressed on the brakes, wondering what was happening.

There was a jarring lurch, and his head snapped back onto the rest. 'What the...?'

Again, the car jerked, and he looked in the rear view. There, the car behind was so close that he could not see the headlamps. It slammed into the back of his car again, a third time, and now it was shoving him forwards, into the truck. He tried to stand on the brakes, but the car behind him was much heavier, and the engine more powerful. He could do nothing as the Ford started to slide, the tyres screeching on the concrete. He stared in the rear-view, and then he saw Ginger and the Hispanic in the car.

He took his foot off the brake and swerved, trying to lose the car, but even as he did so, there was a *phut-crack*, and a hole appeared in the windscreen near his head. A starred hole, with lines radiating. He didn't need to wonder what that was. His scalp began to creep with the thought of how close the bullet had come to his head. There was another crash behind him, and a whipping sound, and particles of fine glass showered around his head as a second star appeared in the windscreen, then a third, and a loud crash as a bullet slid along the lining of the roof over his head and smashed its way through the top of the windscreen in front of the passenger seat.

There was no chance of survival. He had to escape the trap.

With a savage wrench, he pulled the wheel round, to see whether he could get past the truck, but there was not enough space. The truck filled the whole tunnel. But then he saw a wider section. It was one of the safety chambers. A heavy steel door in the wall, behind it a secure chamber for drivers to escape from fires or other dangers. As the car behind jolted into him again, trying to shove him into the truck, and the truck itself slowed, Jack slipped down a gear and raced the engine. Slipping the clutch, he angled his car's bonnet under the bed of the truck and then off to the right, into the broader space. He saw a door, grabbed the Ruger and box of ammo from the passenger seat, threw open the car door and ran out, the pistol in his right hand, pointing at the car behind.

Two men in the car saw him, but saw the gun too, and ducked quickly. A shot went off, slapping into the roof of the tunnel, a whining ricochet flying past his head, and then he was diving over the bonnet of his rental and rolling over the far side as a series of shots rattled about him, each almost indistinguishable from the one before.

111

Then there was a hideous ripping sound: a submachine gun. The car's windows were punctured and then exploded in clouds of glass as he rolled over to cover his head from the shards. There were thuds as the slugs pounded through the metal of the car. Large holes opened and peeled back, and Jack felt one tug at his jacket as he rolled over the floor. The big safety door was in front of him. He couldn't reach it without being shot to pieces.

Bellowing defiance, he cocked the hammer on his Ruger, then span and rose, firing straight at the car. As he stood, he saw Ginger standing, in the act of reloading an Uzi, surrounded by a mist of gun smoke. Seeing Jack, he ducked his head, but slammed the magazine home and, as he lifted the gun, Jack began squeezing the trigger.

There is little any man can do when a pistol is firing at him from close range. He will always hurl himself out of the way if he can. Ginger was no different. As Jack fired all five remaining shots, Ginger leaped away, rolling over the bonnet of his car, and dropping at the far side.

Jack yanked open the big security door and threw himself inside the chamber beyond, pulling it shut behind him.

Gasping, he opened the gun's cylinder and fumbled with the box of ammo. The cardboard flap opened, and a plastic tray fell out, scattering cartridges in every direction. He scooped up a handful, and tried to load them. His fingers were shaking, and the heads of the first two rattled and missed their chambers, but then, suddenly, ice flooded his body. A pure wash of rage calmed his heart and his head, and the last four slid into their positions with ease. He took up another few and dropped them loose into his left pocket, even as a slamming ring struck the door. Then two more. Each hideously loud in the confined space.

Looking about him, he saw that he was in a long chamber cut out of the rock. It was walled and ceilinged, and there was a pair of bench seats back-to-back in the middle of the floor, but they were bolted to the ground, and he couldn't use them to bar the door. There was no time to be imaginative.

He knew how they would come, if they were trained. One either side of the door, and then the door would open, and they'd rush in, one to each side, and cover the room. They'd begin shooting as soon as they could.

In a hurry, he pelted to the wall, and lay on the floor. The GP100 was in his hands, and he cocked the hammer. It moved smoothly, and he tried to remember what he had learned about pistol shooting: grip tightly in the right hand, cup the right with his left, maintain a clear picture of the target area, and squeeze the trigger, don't jerk it…

The door slammed wide, and a shape moved. He fired, twice, as quickly as he could move his trigger, and saw the body of the Hispanic hurled back. The man crashed against the door, then fell outside.

Jack could hear nothing. The magnum cartridges had thundered in the confined space, and he could hear only a muted echo of sounds as he waited with his finger on the trigger, the hammer cocked. He thought he felt rather than heard an engine revving. He rolled away from the wall, and darted to the other side of the room. There he heard a crunch, a rattle and thump, and when he rose to his feet, the Ruger was still in his hands. Warily he edged towards the door.

Outside, he saw that the truck was gone. The car that had crashed into him was already moving off, and the rear door was slamming shut as it went. There on the ground he could see blood from the man he'd shot. He only hoped the bastard was badly injured.

He lifted the gun to fire at the car, but the weight was too much. He leaned against the wall, and sank to the ground as the next cars in the line stopped, and men climbed out, watching him with caution and some trepidation.

*

17.59 Whittier; 02.59 London

The view over the lake was impressive. On another day, Jack might have stared at it with wonder, but not today. He sat at a table by a massive window looking out over the Portage Lake, hugging a mug of coffee and staring down with a frown on his face.

Around here even the police seemed impossibly polite. There was an aversion to rudeness that was almost pathological.

'Mr Henson?'

'Hansen,' Jack responded automatically. He could get genuinely cross if he was to remain with this cover for much longer, he thought. 'It's an "a" then "e", not an "e" then "o".'

'Ah, right.' The trooper who had brought him here to the Begich, Bloggs Visitor Centre stood back, and Jack found himself looking up at a tall, slim African American. His hair was short, and he had laughing, cheerful eyes that took in Jack's appearance with a calm, professional interest. His features were regular and attractive, with sharp bone structure leading to a pointed chin. His white shirt and dark blue suit were impeccable, but Jack saw that his black shoes looked out of place. They were scuffed and messed.

'This here,' the trooper said, 'is Mister Frank Rand.'

Jack nodded.

'Please take a seat. You with the police?'

'Not exactly, Mr Hansen,' Rand replied.

He smiled and Jack noticed that he rarely blinked, as though Jack was so fascinating he could not tear his eyes from him.

'Another agency, then?'

'I am with the Federal Bureau, sir. When there is a crime that runs across state borders, it's for the FBI to get involved.'

'Feebies? This was well inside Alaska, surely? Someone tried to shoot me in a tunnel. That's hardly across a border.'

'But you're a Brit. That makes it kind of interesting to us. And the fact that your friend was here and has died, his house has been torched, and you and the local police chief were almost killed in a freak explosion – those all kind of add up to a slightly bigger issue than just a shooting.'

'I see.'

'Then there's the other thing: he was from the army, I've heard. No secret around town.'

'Chief Burns said the same. He knew that.'

'But he didn't have a report I have from the National Security Agency that says he was commended for his help in questioning suspects in Iraq, I guess. Did you know Mr Lewin was commended for his help in intelligence gathering?'

Jack shook his head.

'So, what do you want from me?'

'I want a full explanation as to what has been going on here.'

Jack shrugged and glanced through the window.

'I'd like that too.'

Rand followed his look. 'Your friend, this Mr Lewin. Any idea why he could have killed himself? Why someone would want to burn his cabin after? Could this have been terrorists?'

'He wasn't a friend, just a client. I came more because I've never been to Alaska than because of him. I just thought I could mix business with pleasure.'

'You're a lawyer, right?'

'Yes.'

Jack felt Rand's eyes range over him.

114

'You'll excuse me if I say you keep pretty fit for a lawyer.'

'Even lawyers can go running.'

'Uh-huh. Tell me, I hear in Britain pistol shooting's illegal. That right? No one can protect their house or anything with a gun?'

'Pretty much.'

'You handled that pistol of your client's pretty well, I guess.'

'I used to do some pistol shooting before it was banned,' Jack said. 'I don't like revolvers, though.'

'Yeah. Don't like wheel guns myself. Much happier with my auto.' Rand appeared to make a decision. He leaned forward. 'Right, Mr Hansen. So, here's my problem: Someone burned the cabin just after you got here. Makes it look like they're trying to conceal something. Unless it was you set fire to it, of course. But that wouldn't explain the attack in the tunnel, now, would it? Or the police station. I haven't seen it yet, but the place is trashed, I'm told. And now I hear that there was some kind of shooting at the Begich in Whittier too. While you were there.'

'Really?'

'I am not going to arrest you for that. From all I've heard, and I've spoken to the cars behind you in the tunnel, it's clear enough that you were attacked, not the attacker. But I do want to find the guys tried this. Who was it, Mr Hansen?'

'I don't know. They just came out of nowhere. Two men in the car behind me,' Jack said helplessly. 'I'm a lawyer – I'm not used to this sort of thing.'

'Not many folks are,' Rand said drily. 'You know why this place was built?'

The change in topic made Jack blink.

'What, this building?'

'Yes. It's twenty-five years old now. They put it up to give people a view of the glacier. Back in the day, this was the main portage way for the trappers and all to get to the sea. They'd make their way up here then carry all their gear over the glacier, down to the sea beyond. So they built this place to celebrate the old ways. But it's gone. The glacier's retreated all the way round there,' he said, pointing, 'because of the new way of life. Global warming melted the ice.'

'And?'

'Just thinking. They were too late with the visitor centre here, just as I seem to be too late to help you.'

'Well I'm leaving the state,' Jack said reasonably.

'Oh, I think I could still help you a little,' Rand said. His eyes were fixed on Jack again. 'Tell you what. Your car is in no state to be driven now. The rear end's all dented and hanging off. How about I give you lift back to Anchorage?'

'That's kind, but…'

'Good,' Rand said.

*

18.37 Anchorage; 03.37 London

Jack was glad to leave Rand in the lobby, and went up to his room. It looked the same as before, but he didn't trust to appearances. The phone could be tapped from Langley, and he wouldn't know. Modern telephones could electronically be set to work as microphones, feeding a recording system even when the receiver was on the rest. Lasers could be set to a hotel window to sense the microscopic trembles in the glass and decipher a conversation. Bugs were old technology, but now were so tiny that Jack would never be able to find one if he searched this room for a week.

He needed to send a message back to the Firm, but for now that could wait. His body was complaining everywhere. His back hurt from the explosion, and his head was still sore. Now he could add the bruise to his hand where he'd rolled over the car to the concrete in the tunnel, and the headache from the gunshots in the enclosed chamber in the rock. He was tired, aching, and aware of a rising anger.

Someone had made two determined efforts to kill him, presumably after murdering Danny Lewin and burning his cabin, and the only reason Jack could see for the attacks was Lewin's book: his life story. And Jack had no idea why.

Jack walked into the bathroom and ran the taps for a hot bath. The sink had a mirror over it, and he leaned on the sink and stared at himself. His eyes were raw, his face still marked by the tiny fragments of flying glass, and he closed his eyes for a moment, bone-weary.

When he opened them again, he studied his face bleakly.

It was a face that had experience. He had known joy, he'd known disaster and catastrophe, but his was not a face to love. No one could love him. His nature was against love. He was outside the usual realms of life: where others fell headlong in their passion, he would watch, analyse, reflect, and say the right things, but without the same fervent conviction. When others said that if they were left on a desert island, they would fade for the lack of a lover, a friend, a companion,

116

he knew he would survive. He needed no one. There was no one person who ranked highly enough in his estimation to cause him misery at their loss. The only one who came close was Claire.

Claire. He was fooling himself. He did need her. She was his rock, his anchor to the world and real life.

He took his shirt off, then the rest of his clothes, and studied his body in the mirror. There was a bruise on his left, and a tingling all over his back and scalp. Both his hands were scratched and his right knee was swollen from when he had been flung aside by the explosion. Standing here, it was as though he was surveying the injuries on another man. This was not really him. It must be shock, he guessed, but it didn't feel like shock. More, it was like a kind of rage that seethed deep within him.

Claire was still the only woman he had felt close to. She was his single point of attachment. Without her, he thought he would have to give up on life. When she left him, he had understood. There was an irony: most cops' wives despaired, constantly fearful, wondering, as they kissed their men goodbye in the morning, whether he would come home or be killed; for Claire it was the fear not that Jack wouldn't come back, but that someone else would not and that he would return with another man's blood on his hands.

Yes, he understood her reasons for leaving him. He didn't forgive her, but he did at least possess an empathy for her feelings. She was miserable when she learned that his entire life, so far as she understood it, had been a series of elaborate lies. Yes, he had appreciated how fierce her wretchedness was. So she left him and went back to Devon without him. And there she embarked, he learned, on an affair with Jimmy McNeill, another guy from Vauxhall Cross, the bastard.

Jack could not function without her. When she went, he grew to realise how much he depended upon her. Not her as a person, not her as a lover, but her as a rock that gave the scenery of his life a colour and vividness. Without her, he became less than a two-dimensional character. He became nothing.

That was the real cause of his rage at being sent over here. He must get back. She wouldn't have an affair again, but that wasn't the point. He had to return to her so that he could become whole again, because out here he was beginning to feel that the fragile ropes that held his sanity firmly to his soul were fraying.

Sliding down to sit in the bath, he tried to rest, but the hot water stung the cuts and scrapes all over his shoulders and neck. While his leather jacket had saved him from much of the slashing of the glass particles, there were plenty of needle-points of pain, he felt like a man who had slept on a bed of nails. Less anguish than a series of pin-points that gave the impression of a sore rash. He waited until the warm water eased the worst and shut his eyes.

He had to get back to the UK before his cover was blown. If it became known that he was working for the Firm, he'd find himself in even more trouble. As it was, he wanted to escape back to the real America – back down to Seattle. There was a British office in the city, and he could meet Orme, the resident spook, to make use of his communications gear. The Ice Maiden would be keen to hear from him, and he could not call her from an unsecure line. That would be to make a gift of the truth to the Americans. Their technology for listening to all calls was unbeaten, and he had no desire to be arrested. He only hoped that the roll of cuttings would be some compensation for his losing the journal.

Yes. He'd get out to Seattle and contact the Firm from there, and hopefully be on a plane home within a day. He closed his eyes and settled down in the warm water, and then, for some reason, his mind brought up a memory of Lewin. Danny looking so haunted and petrified in the interview room, and then the picture he'd drawn of himself, the Munch-like screaming face.

But then in his mind's eye he saw the girl again, Kasey from Whittier, the vacant-eyed, scared and sad teenager who spoke of ghosts in the empty building, and he shivered.

*

20.14 Anchorage; 05.14 London

It was the phone's ring that woke him.

The water was cooler now, and he was aware of the change in temperature as he rose, dripping, and winced. Since settling, several muscles in his back had decided to remind him they had been torn in the bomb blast, and there was one at the right of his neck that felt like it had been slashed by a blunt carving knife. Any movement of his head was accompanied by a sharp stabbing just over his back, between his shoulder blades.

He pulled the bathrobe on and limped to the phone by the bed. On the way he checked the door to make sure that the locks were secured, and then chose to stand by the bed. 'Yes?'

'Frank Rand, Mr Hansen. I wondered if you'd eaten yet?'

'No.'

'Well, I'm going down to eat in ten. There are a few points I'd like to discuss with you.'

'Give me thirty minutes. I'll see you in the bar.'

Jack put the phone down and dressed in sober dark olive moleskin trousers and a plain cream linen shirt. He felt better for the wash, but there was still the list of names he'd found in the journal that needed looking into. He would try to check them now. He still had the roll of cuttings which told of each man.

The hotel relied on visitors who wanted to use their own computers, but Jack only had his mobile phone, and he wasn't going to use that to surf the web. Its screen would give him a headache. And then he remembered it didn't work over here anyway.

There was an internet lounge, and he was soon sitting at the computer, his backpack beside him. The first was the man called Abu Fazul Abdullah, he recalled, and he typed in the name. And sat back as if punched as the name came up.

'Shit!'

Now he remembered vaguely hearing of the gas explosion in Croydon. It was the day he left the UK, wasn't it? Yes, and two cops had been killed, too. The man had been a suspected terrorist, and no one was going to mourn him too much.

What of the others? Jack began to type the names in, and gradually his frown deepened. Each of them had died: Faisal, al Malik, Abdul-Gaffar, Rasmi, and Labeeb were all men who had been accused of terrorism. Two had been at Guantanamo Bay, but neither had been considered too much of a threat. Well, that was no surprise to Jack. He had heard that the serious, dangerous suspects were all kept elsewhere. Guantanamo was deliberately kept in the public eye, like a magician who keeps one hand in plain view, while he performs his tricks with the other. The serious suspects were held in Diego Garcia, or in unknown prisons in Afghanistan, Uzbekistan or Pakistan. Lewin's main job, he recalled, was to interrogate and then propose who should be sent where.

A thought struck him. He took up the roll of cuttings again, glancing about him as he unrolled them, studied the names, and began to whistle. All had been listed as terrorists; all had been arrested and held by the Americans, and all had died.

119

Some of them had been blown apart by Hellfire missiles, one was killed in a suspected attack from a suicide bomber from a sect opposing his own, one had been shot by tribal enemies, a third was run down in the street by a hit and run, three were killed in a car crash, and two in a fire. As he pored over the cuttings and checked with the computer, he saw that all the names, both those in the cuttings and those he recalled himself, had been killed. All suspects, and all dead.

Jack was about to shut down the computer, when he frowned again. He typed in the name of Sumner, the officer he had known in Belfast. Too many hits for comfort. He typed in 'British Army Captain Sumner' and the screen refreshed. There were still 30,000 hits, from Napoleonic War heroes to the Korean War, but it was only when he had scrolled through five pages that he saw a piece from the British newspaper, the Daily Telegraph, dated June 21, 2008:

Captain Roger Sumner said, "The Aid to Afghan Veterans Trust is enormously grateful to the people who've lent us their money for this trip. For all of us it'll be an adventure as well as a way to help with the strain of the last months." He created his charity to help those, like himself, who lost limbs in the Afghan War or Iraq, and he hopes that this journey to Machu Picchu will be only the first of many adventures. For a man who has done so much, it is a testament to his spirit and enthusiasm.

Jack ignored the rest and scrolled down the search engine. It told how Sumner had decided to form a fundraising charity to make money for the rehabilitation unit at Headley Court, which had done so much for him. Then as part of the charity, he developed a separate wing that would help those coming out of Headley to acclimatise to life outside, and a third arm that would provide exciting opportunities for those who had come back severely mentally or physically injured. But then there was an item that spoke of a man dying on a journey across Central America, and how it had impacted the charity. Funds dried, and creditors were left impoverished. The charity was shut down in 2009.

It left Jack feeling doubtful about the man's business skills. Sure enough, there was another piece from the autumn of 2009 bemoaning the collapse of his charity. 'Captain Sumner was not available for comment.' A piece responding to critics in 2010 said that the police had not found evidence of fraud, and underneath that, a short piece from the Guardian in 2011 stated that the charity had suffered from maladministration and had lost a lot of money, but also noted that the Captain had left England and was now living in Las Vegas. It was as though the reporter was trying hard not to say that the Captain was an inveterate gambler who had squandered the charities funds on fast living, but there was more than a vague hint of censure in his writing.

'Prick,' Jack said to himself.

Journalists could afford to be judgemental. They never put themselves into danger.

Sumner was worth noting, Jack reckoned. He glanced at his watch and stood, quickly erasing all history from the computer before turning it off and walking out to the bar.

*

20.45 Anchorage; 05.45 London

The bar was entered by a set of stairs leading down to the circular tables with a bar at the far end. On the left as Jack descended was a plasma screen set into a large wooden surround like a fireplace standing up from the floor. Ahead, behind the bar, were three more TVs, all showing sports and news channels. There were two tables occupied, one had a heavy-set man in his thirties: square jaw, strong shoulders, buzz-cut hair, and encroaching stubble. He sat staring at the plasma over left, his jaws moving rhythmically, a beer before him. He wore a plaid shirt, sleeves rolled up, and old jeans. His back was to Jack. The others were more suspicious. A young, attractive strawberry blonde woman in her twenties, and man looked like he was nearer Jack's age. They were close, leaning together over the table, but not quite touching. Both glanced at him, then away at each other again. A suspicion of guilt was in their eyes and movements, and he fleetingly wondered if they were there to watch him. If they were, they were too obvious out there in the open. More likely they were trying to enjoy an illicit affair, he guessed, but neither dared make the first move.

He strode to the left, and sat on a bench at the wall, watching, putting his backpack beside him. He was to the side of the plasma, and commanded the whole of the bar area as well as the stairs leading to it, which gave him a feeling of security. It put him in view of the couple and he could tell if the chewing buzz-cut's attention moved to him.

The brunette bar girl came and he asked for a beer. As she left, he saw Frank Rand at the top of the stairs. For an instant, he wished he'd still got the Ruger. He'd already had to give it to Rand. After the shooting in the tunnel, the FBI wanted the gun to check the ammunition and the rifling in the barrel in case they could match it with a bullet. They still hoped they would find a man with a bullet in his shoulder. Anyway, without a holster it was an unwieldy weapon – too heavy to carry tucked into the waistband of his trousers, or in a pocket. And Jack had the feeling airport security would look askance at him if he tried to board a plane with it on him.

Frank Rand glanced at him oddly as he walked to the table. He was wearing a pale suede jacket, an open-necked oxford shirt with a small silver crucifix glinting brightly against his dark skin, and jeans. He stood looking at the screens, and then pulled a chair out and instead of sitting opposite Jack, he drew it across to the side. Sitting, he looked over at the other people in the room. When the barmaid appeared with her tray, he ordered himself a club soda.

'You still on duty?'

'In the Bureau it's best not to get a reputation as a drinker,' Frank Rand said easily as he sat back, his eyes flitting quickly over the other people in the bar. 'And I don't like to think of alcohol mixing with a handgun.'

'Very true.'

'Good. Generally lawyers have it easy, from what I've seen. Rarely have to play with guns in England. I used to watch *Rumpole of the Bailey* on pay TV. I liked that guy.'

'The hero for every downtrodden victim,' Jack said.

'How long you been a lawyer?'

'I qualified in eighty four.'

'Where?'

'Why do I get the feeling I'm being interrogated?'

Frank Rand smiled disarmingly, but said nothing.

Jack sighed.

'I studied at uni, and then went to qualify at Braboeuff Manor, in Surrey, near Guildford. It's called *the College of Law* because lawyers go there to learn the job. OK? Since then I've been in private practise.'

'Uh-uh. How'd you meet with this guy Lewin?'

'He came to us in Manchester. That's where my firm is based. Beyond that, Mister Rand, I don't think I need go.'

'You knew about his background, eh?'

Jack shrugged.

'He was in the army, I know.'

'Better than that. I told you I had a report on him. I ran his name through a couple of our other systems. He was liked by the CIA – helped with training a few of our guys, apparently, as well as interrogating prisoners. He was intelligence, you see.'

'Really?'

'You didn't know?'

'There are many things I am careful not to remember. Especially things that involve the security services,' Jack said.

'That's very sensible,' Frank chuckled. He sipped some of his soda, glancing at the plasma. 'Crappy game, that. You happy to eat something here?'

Jack nodded, and Frank beckoned. Soon the girl was back with them, and Frank ordered himself a King Crab salad and Jack opted for a fresh Halibut sandwich.

'So, what's your plan?' Frank asked as they waited.

'I just want to get out of here.'

'Understandable, but we may well have some questions for you.'

'You can always contact me through my firm,' Jack said. 'You have my business card.'

'Yeah.' Frank Rand eyed him for a moment, before nodding. 'And now?'

'I'm planning on getting to Seattle and visiting the Consulate there. I reckon I ought to tell them what has happened.'

'I see. You haven't called them already, then?'

'I didn't think to do that, no,' Jack said.

Their food arrived, and the two men were silent. As soon as the waitress left them with a cheery, 'Hope you enjoy your meal,' Frank leaned closer.

'You see, I'd have expected someone to call them in a hurry after being shot at and all.'

Jack held his gaze and said nothing, but Frank Rand was clearly comfortable with the silence. He eyed Jack for a long moment.

'Looks like you were perhaps a guy had been in danger before, maybe?'

'Why d'you say that?'

'Mister Hansen, you seem a man who's on edge just a little all the time. I know it's a shock to be in an explosion, and worse to learn that someone's trying to kill you in a tunnel. That's not good. But you seem to have taken it pretty much in your stride, that's all.'

'Perhaps I am a little more resilient than the sort of people you usually meet.'

'Perhaps. Or perhaps there's a little more to you. You see, I would seriously doubt that if one of the CIA's best was suddenly found dead in a foreign country, the Agency wouldn't send one or two of their own to see if all was well. Perhaps, if the guy had been involved in interrogation of possible terrorists, the Agency would want to know that the death was an accident, or at least natural. And if there was any chance incriminating papers or computer data was lying around, they'd prefer to get to it first. You see the way my mind's working?'

'I suppose I can understand.'

'Well, let's say there's this hypothetical guy. He died abroad, but some in the Agency reckon he might have been killed. The Agency would have at least one guy out there in a hurry, searching for anything, wouldn't they? And if there was something underhand, then he could be in danger. The bad guys may even try to blow him up, or failing that, shoot him.'

'I wouldn't know,' Jack said.

'Of course not, you being a lawyer and all. But if you ever reckon to talk to someone who could help, let me know, that's all I'm saying.'

'Yes, of course.'

'You have to bear in mind, sir, that if this guy was interrogating Muslim terrorists, it's just possible that some of them got to find out where he was living and took out their idea of revenge on him.'

'Perhaps.' A flare of bitterness made him add, 'That's what he feared. It was why he came here, I think. In England he wasn't allowed to protect himself. No pistols, no Tasers, no mace or pepper spray. He was just left to hang around. He was a sitting duck.'

'Right. We understand each other. So, I may have a couple of terrorists trying to kill off military guys involved in intelligence. Your Lewin may just be the first.'

It was a thought, Jack admitted. A possibility. 'If I learn anything more, I shall let you know.'

'Good.' Frank finished his meal, setting his fork on the plate and wiping his mouth with the napkin. 'You leaving on the morning flight?'

'Yes.'

'Well, have a good flight. I may see you there. I'm taking a company jet early in the morning.'

'That would be good,' Jack said.

Frank smiled, then reached into his pocket and pulled out a business card. 'Call me if you need anything, Mister Hansen. I may just see you in Seattle.'

'Thanks.'

Frank Rand rose and nodded to him. He was about to turn away, when he appeared struck by a thought.

'One last thing, before I forget. The man you shot in the tunnel? There's been no reports of a man with a gunshot wound turning up at a hospital anywhere round here.'

'You think he's dead?'

Rand sniffed, considering. 'I think if he isn't, he probably soon will be. He was hit well, from the look of the blood in the tunnel. If he doesn't get plasma in him soon, I don't reckon he'll live very long.'

'Good.'

Jack watched Frank Rand walk away, and he looked down at the card in his hand. The number was easy to remember, but Jack had no intention of calling it. When he left Anchorage, he was going to get to the Consulate, and then disappear back home. In a couple of days he had been shot at and almost blown up. Someone was serious about killing him, and he wasn't going to wait and give them a chance a third time.

*

20.54 Seattle; 05.54 London

Roy was sitting back in the chair at the FBI office in Seattle. It wasn't a bad one, this. Leather-faced, with a tilt mechanism, and the back could go wa-ay back, too. Meant he could get a doze every so often when he needed to, and tonight he was screwed. He'd been up early, and his eyes were raw from staring at the screens all the long day. There were times, like this, when he was alone in the office, when he was bored, when nothing was happening, when he really regretted joining the service at all.

His thoughts wandered. Very Nice was there again. Her long, curling hair ran down her back as she turned to look at him over her shoulder with that sort of wanton look in her face. Jesus, she was gorgeous. He was lucky she'd picked him. Last time he'd been back home, she'd been all over him, giving him something to remember her by, so she'd said. She'd been like – well, a nympho, and it made him feel great, knowing she wanted him so much too. God, she was good...

125

Why was he here in fuckin' Seattle? He ought to be back there with her, rolling all over her before some other bastard got to her. She'd said that last time, that she hoped he'd soon be back because she couldn't face things without him.

She was there waiting for him, and he was here, with a boner like a lead pipe, and no way to get rid of it. He couldn't keep on thinking about her. He had to try to concentrate.

There were three files he'd opened just before eating some late supper, and he sat up now, and reopened the first and began to read the code, analysing the function as he went. Yeah, that looked good.

It was when he was halfway through his editing that the red flash caught his attention. A flash, then the window opening, and the Echelon logo.

'Shit!' he muttered, all thoughts of Very Nice and his code evaporated as he grabbed for the phone and dialled.

'Sir? It's Roy Sandford, sir. Echelon has another hit. This time it's your code "Maki-e".'

'Thank you, Sandford.'

*

06.23 London

Karen Skoyles stood in her office, pacing in front of the window as she considered the implications of Case's attacks. There was a churning anxiety in her belly that would not go away, and she was irritable from lack of sleep.

In the beginning the whole game had been such fun. There were few risks to her. As an analyst in Vauxhall Cross, she had not been troubled by the risks of work in the field and getting shot or garrotted. They were the dangers presented to others, not her. And she could work on her career strategy.

Some reckoned the most important work they could do was the stuff they did in the field. That was balls, and she knew it. The way to get up the chain of command was to show your face, do good work, and make sure it was presented well to the bosses. The more they saw of your competence, the more likely they were to promote you. It was certainly the case with her boss, Richard Gorman, Deputy Director General. It was he who had seen her ability and who had promoted her over Starck and even Case. They had originally set up the first Scavenger unit, now called Squadron One, the first of the three Scavenger teams, and Karen had taken it from them, later adding two more and her own Research and Resources division. Later she had brought in the liaison unit as well, with one of her staff seconded to America based in the CIA offices at Langley. Her latest empire-building exercise should see her absorbing Broughton's Bullies, after the cock-ups they'd had in recent months.

Broughton was like Starck and Case: they were all dinosaurs. They'd had their day. It was time they were cleared out, time that younger folks took over. She was going to be head one day: Director General. Then she'd take early retirement and have a series of jobs with private companies who would each pay for her expertise. It was a golden future.

And it was all at threat now, because of Case.

Why hadn't he just gone in and come back quietly? There wouldn't have been any trouble, then. But she had to get that journal. She had to know what was inside it. Otherwise her career could be quickly finished.

*

21.36 Anchorage; 06.36 England

Jack returned to his room a while after Frank Rand left him. He wanted to rest, and being here, in a public area, felt safer somehow than going back to a small room. He could not forget the faces of the two men in the tunnel: Ginger was still uninjured so far as he knew, even if the Hispanic had been wounded.

But the games on TV bored him, and the couple were growing more affectionate by the minute. It was enough to make him feel slight disquiet – perhaps it was frustration at being so far from his woman. He had never known such a feeling before, but he hadn't been shot at before. In Russia he made sure that he was safe. It was ironic that he had been in danger here, in America, in the country of allies.

He opened the door, and slipped the metal loop over the ball at the doorframe to secure it, manually locking the handle as well. If someone wanted to break in, they could pick the lock, but breaking the security loop would make a lot of noise.

About to walk to the bathroom, he paused and stared around the room. There was something that was not quite right. Not as he had left it. He sectioned the room, peering at specific items of furniture as he worked out what was wrong. His bag looked all right. The door to the bathroom was open, as he had left it. At the bed the covers looked fine... And then he noticed that the bedclothes had been moved slightly. As though someone had been feeling around under them, looking for something. He strode to the bed and lifted the sheets, but there was nothing to make him think that a weapon had been installed while he was down with Frank Rand.

Someone had been in here. Either a colleague of Rand's, or perhaps the man with the ginger hair. He had no way of telling, but Jack suddenly had a tingling sensation in his arms and back.

He felt like a hunted animal.

*

08.13 London

Karen was already convinced before she sat at her desk, preferring to pace her room. She delayed making a decision until she could review the whole matter, but in the back of her mind she knew that she would have to go into damage limitation as quickly as possible. Case was just too dangerous.

The computer was the natural tool for her work. There were many, like Starck, who still preferred to keep everything to paper, but Karen had worked her way up from analysis clerk to manager by keeping her eyes open on the various resources available. Now she began to search for information on Alaska and the news channels on the web, looking for anything about the town of Whittier and the explosion in the police station. It didn't take long. And then she saw another piece about a shooting in a railway tunnel.

It was enough. That was the report that made her pick up the telephone.

'Jessica, I would like see the DDG, please.'

'Is that an urgent request, Karen? I've only just got to my desk.'

'Yes,' she said. 'It is urgent.'

The line clicked, then, 'Five minutes, Karen.'

She took the stairs, her files in her hand. It was rare that she would take the extreme measure of going to the DDG, but that meant that she had instant access when she needed it.

The room on the second from top floor was immense. It took up the whole western corner overlooking the river, with a view over all the river traffic. Karen looked about her with the growing certainty that one day this could all be hers.

But only if she controlled this problem quickly.

'Sir, I am sorry to trouble you,' she said, and quickly summarised events in Alaska over the last days.

'You sent Case out there?' Deputy Director Richard Gorman peered at her files expressionlessly.

He was a details man, she knew. Never an active agent, he had, like her, worked as a research analyst for years and progressed through the levels of management on the basis of his ability to quickly assess an issue and dissect it into elements that could be individually countered. He had few skills with people, and always delegated responsibility for management, which was why Karen's rise had been so swift. He trusted the brunette with the willing smile, incisive intellect, and reliably compliant analysis of problems. In contrast he tended to distrust those who had been agents on the ground. Their reports often were not detailed enough, their analysis too coloured by their feelings for their agents.

'Well?' he said, sitting back.

Short, rotund, dark-haired and genial in appearance, he reminded her of a bank manager from the 1960s: bumptious, affable, but suburban and unimaginative.

'Sir, I had to send an agent who was competent to look for the journal. Someone who had some knowledge of Lewin, and the only man available was Case. I can see now it was an error.'

'Too damn right it was an error,' Gorman said. He picked up the report of the shooting in the tunnel. 'And this indicates that he is now in danger.'

'He may have found the journal. If so, so much the better.'

'Why do I sense that there could be a "but"?'

'He has not reported in. There's been no call yet. I'd have hoped he would have put in a call, if only to say he's OK.'

'So?'

'It is possible he cannot call. It may be that the lines are too open and he feels it wouldn't be secure enough. Perhaps he is waiting to get to Seattle. That is where he was supposed to deliver the journal if he found it.'

'Right.'

'But just in case – I don't want any risks to the Service – I'd like to have approval to ditch him.'

Gorman looked at her. 'Case has been in the service a good few years.'

'Until he went rogue.'

'He was on your staff at the time. I would probably have supported him if I were his line manager.'

It was the first criticism she had heard from the DDG. He stared at her coolly without moving, waiting.

129

'It was Jimmy McNeill he killed,' she said firmly. 'He killed one of our own.'

'Was that proved?'

'No, but …'

'McNeill was found drowned after falling from his horse, wasn't he?'

'Case was, is, a Scavenger. He's an expert at killing without leaving evidence. We taught him. He learned McNeil was sleeping with his wife, and the conclusion was too obvious to ignore.'

'Did you ever find any proof? I assume you would have removed him from post if there was real evidence found?'

Karen took a series of sheets of paper from her manila file and passed them to him. 'I didn't want to show you these,' she said. 'It seemed better to let him go as natural wastage.'

'While we're recruiting,' Gorman said. 'So, these are phone records. And show he regularly travelled about the country. Dated last year.'

'The ones dated second July are the relevant ones,' she said. 'You can see there that he went to Devon, to the cells that are located in northern Dartmoor around the eastern fringes of Okehampton. From analysis of the signal strength at the time, it's clear he was around the Fatherford area.'

'And?'

'That is where Jimmy died, sir. On the second. And Case always said he was in London that day. All day.'

Gorman put the papers to one side and steepled his fingers.

'You have authority to remove him if he proves an embarrassment. We cannot afford to upset the Brothers. If the CIA gets to learn that he was ours, it would be very embarrassing. So create a cover ready to burn him if necessary.'

'If the CIA realise he's there on our business, I'll have a cover story ready,' Karen promised.

'Good. And well done for spotting this, Karen,' the DDG said, peering at her thoughtfully.

She left his office filled with the warm certainty that what might have been a disaster for her career had been turned into an opportunity.

*

08.18 London

Sara al Malik was to see how effective the media could be that morning. From the first call before seven thirty, she was on the go. Calls to her house phone, journalists demanding to speak with her, radio interviews, men and women appearing out in the road, all was loud, brash, confusing. She was used to a peaceful life, and this intrusion was appalling to her. The children were petrified, cowering upstairs at first. It was only when they heard that there was a film cameraman outside that they began to display a more confident enthusiasm for their situation.

'Yes, I came here with my shopping, and saw them taking my husband away...'

'What do you mean, did he surrender? Did they give him a chance to surrender? Look at my door. Look at how they destroyed my door. Look at this stain on the carpet! That is where they knocked him to the ground...

'He was sitting here drinking a cup of tea, and they beat it from his mouth, smashed my cup...

'Why did they take him? I don't know! No one has told us anything, nothing! I don't know why they took him, where they took him, nothing!

'He didn't break the rules. He maintained his curfew – he didn't call anyone or anything! But we don't know why they caught him in the first place, what he was accused of...

'Do you know what it is like? To have been accused and declared guilty, to lose your bank account, your job, your phone, to lose internet access, to have your children's friends vetted before they would be allowed to visit you? This is medieval, this is. It is torture!'

She kept the facade as long as possible but, when the next knock came to her door, she was already so exhausted it was hard to force herself to her feet to answer the summons.

It was Lomax. He smiled thinly as she stood aside to let him in, staring wide-eyed at the people milling outside her house.

'I have a statement for you to read and check,' he said.

She took the paper from him and glanced at it, but shook her head. 'I can't... Explain it, please?'

'It's a statement for the media that states our position: that Mo was kidnapped from here by the police or security services, you don't know who took him, why he was taken, or where he was taken to and as far as you know, he has never been involved in criminal or terrorist activities, and has not broken the terms of his incarceration here at home. It says,' he continued, 'that Mo is an innocent, kind husband and father, and that you are desperate to have him back. It says you and he are being punished for something but you have no idea...'

'Yes, yes,' she said impatiently. 'I understand that. What now?'

'You sign this, and then I begin to twist the legal knife in their guts. I start to demand details about who was responsible and—'

'They will deny it, won't they?' she said weakly. 'What then?'

'Not all the police are corrupt,' Lomax said grimly. 'Someone there will see your distress. Soon as they see how you're affected, they'll regret their actions. They must come to appreciate how you're suffering.'

'What if they don't?'

'We'll cross that bridge when we come to it,' he said soothingly. 'This is my job, to rattle the cages and demand. Yours is to sit and try to hold things together, Sara. You have to be strong. For Mo.'

While they spoke, Sara saw, from the corner of her eye, a man in grey coveralls with a tool kit in his hand at the open front door. He stood smiling.

'Yes?' she asked sharply.

'Sorry if it's not a good time. You've got an old NTE5?'

She held her hands open despairingly.

'What?'

'Sorry, love – British Telecom. It's the box coming into the house,' he said, glancing at the wires on the skirting board. 'There it is. Mind if I swap it out?'

'But it's all been fine!'

'Even your computer speed? This new one's faster with broadband.'

'We aren't allowed computers,' she said bitterly.

'Well, when you get one, it'll be faster,' he said reassuringly. He knelt as he spoke and unscrewed the box cover, removing the front plate and fixing a new one.

'There you go,' he said, rising.

Neither Sara nor Lomax noticed that the little box beside it that had duplicated the tag on Mohammed's leg to make it appear that he was still in the house, was now gone.

*

08.21 London
Karen called Starck.
'Yes?'

'I'd like to see you, please. Now,' she said.

'It'll be a joy and delight,' he said with that sneering manner of his.

She replaced the receiver, refusing to be intimidated or irritated by him. He was a dinosaur who saw everything in black and white, like so many older members of the Service. There were allies and enemies, and the two should never mix, in his opinion. And he resented being passed over in favour of a woman, of course, especially one who was younger than him. That was a double insult to him. Tough.

She stood and walked to the window. Not yet high enough in the hierarchy to have a view over the Thames, at least she did have her own room. Glass walls gave her a view of the analysis centre for the Middle East, and she watched the men and women at their desks for a while as she waited, considering her moves with care as her fingers played with the cross at her neck.

He knocked, and she pressed the little button to release the door. One of the innovations she had implemented on this floor. Since so much data was held in offices like hers, it made sense to make sure that it was as secure as possible. She had a key, and the security desk downstairs had a master key in the safe, guarded day and night by two armed guards on secondment from the SAS. They were known by the agents as the Gorillas: burly, over-muscled fighters with a contempt for all Intelligence staff.

'What is it, Karen?' Starck asked mildly.

He walked in and sat on a chair, crossing his legs.

She slid the printouts over the desk to him.

'Have you seen these?'

He picked them up and nodded slowly, whistling through his teeth. 'Is he all right?'

'There are no more reports about him. The tunnel report came from the internet, not our agents. I've already asked Orme in Seattle to see if he can make any contact, but there's no news as yet.'

'Ruddy hell,' Starck muttered, reading the report of the tunnel shootings again. 'What are they up to?'

'I don't know. But clearly Jack has rattled a few cages. We do not know what he has found, if anything. Someone clearly thinks he has.'

'Who?'

'God knows. Was there anything Lewin was involved with that could have led to this? All Jack was supposed to do was find the bloody journal, for Goodness' sake!'

133

Starck nodded, but he was reading down the page again.

'I don't get it. This has all the appearance of an assassination. Who'd want to kill off our Jacky?'

'He has some enemies,' Karen murmured. 'But for now, he is growing to be an embarrassment, and I won't have him coming back to give us problems.'

'So you want them to kill him, you mean?' Starck smiled, yellow teeth showing. 'Good corporate attitude, Karen. You should be in HR.'

'If possible I want him back without any problems,' she said defensively. 'But if this gets nasty, we don't want it to hurt us here.'

'We?' Starck smiled. 'Sounds like you're more concerned with the perpendicular pronoun.'

'What?'

'Never mind, dear. You're worried in case the Brothers in America realise he's with us, I suppose? You don't want them to know we have one of ours over there without permission, do you?'

'We have scrabbled our way back to the top table with America. It's taken us years to get here,' Karen said. 'When you were a junior agent, we had Philby, Burgess and MacLean, then Blunt, and constant whisperings about another spy. Remember? It's taken us all this time to win the Americans over again, and prove to them that we were worth dealing with. If they learn we're working over there, in their jurisdiction, they'll be furious. And I don't want that.'

'So, having sent him out there, now you want what, exactly?'

'I want you to start concocting our exit strategy. I'd hoped he'd be back here in a day or so without any trail, but he's failed. Get me a means to deny him.'

'How?'

She threw a copy of the cell phone report across the desk to him. 'Speak to his wife. If it goes tits up, I want to be able to prove he's a loose cannon, entirely on his own, nothing to do with us.'

Starck lifted an eyebrow.

'I don't understand what you mean.'

'Don't be a moron, Paul.' Karen took a deep breath. 'Ask her about McNeill. Make sure she knows our suspicions.'

'There was nothing proved.'

'I didn't say there was.'

'What good will it do?' Paul asked.

'If she thinks he did it, she could try to contact him. Ask him. And that would tell the Yanks about him and McNeill.'

'You want me to speak to her so she lets them know Jacky's a murderer, you mean,' Starck said, and his lips curled up into a cynical smile. 'What a clear-thinking mind you have.'

Karen thought it looked as though he was snarling.

*

09.32 Anchorage; 18.32 London

Jack was at the airport in plenty of time for his 11.55 flight. A cab took him down L Street, into Minnesota Drive, then along W International Airport Road to the Ted Stevens airport, and Jack marvelled at the lack of traffic. Anchorage was the biggest city in Alaska, but it felt like a small town – friendly and safe.

He made time to speak at some length to the car hire firm, and learned that Frank Rand had already called them to talk about the car. Jack had a number of documents to sign, but apparently Frank had told the hire company that the car itself would have to remain at Whittier until the CSI team had been through it. They could arrange for its return afterwards. There was little for Jack to do, which he was glad of.

It was a pleasant airport. The decorations of Native American Inuit peoples were everywhere, and even after the horrors of the last days Jack was aware of some regret to be leaving. He would have liked to have visited this land for longer. As it was, he was looking forward to seeing the consulate and passing over all the information he had: the description of Danny Lewin's journal, the roll of cuttings, and the men he had written about: especially Roger Sumner. That was surely a man who was worth hunting down and speaking with. Trouble was, Jack knew he'd be in trouble. He'd lost the journal itself.

Idly, he wandered about the airport. There was a display of the Iditarod, with photos of mushers calling to their dogs, the sleds rushing over virgin snow, and Jack stood staring for a moment. To pit yourself against the land like that, you had to be a particular kind of man. He would have loved to have done it himself, when he was younger. To live on the trail with a pack, travelling over a thousand miles in a race, pitting himself and the dogs against mountains, frozen lakes, and the brutal winds – that was life. He could almost taste the cold air in his mouth at the thought.

He had booked in, and now he submitted to the searches for weapons, and once airside, fetched a coffee and loafed about with his book, and all too soon it was time for his flight to Seattle. It took little time to line up and filter onto the small Boeing, and he took his seat in the window, glancing out at the terminal building as the airplane's engines whirred quietly.

And then Jack froze as he saw in the window of the departure area the square face and short hair of the man in the hospital. The man in the car in the tunnel: Ginger.

*

19.49 London

It was past supper time when Claire returned with the dogs.

Her daily routine was rigid, now that Jack was gone again. She would rise at half six, go out to check on her chickens and the pony, and then have breakfast by eight. Soon after, she would take the dogs out along the road, over the main road, and down to Fatherford. It was her duty, she felt.

The walk followed the river all the way from the Okehampton College towards Belstone, and she would wander up it, past the great shelves and cliffs of granite, the waterfalls and gentle pools, up to the high moors, where she could stop and rest a moment. Remembering.

Her daily act of remembrance was a penance, she felt, for those few weeks when she had been unfaithful to her husband. A time of joy and sudden freedom that she had not expected. To be free, truly free of London and the round of socialising with men and women from the Service, because no one outside was fully trusted, ever, was a wonder. She had felt like a teenager again. And then it all went horribly sour.

Claire had a job with a local kennels, which was easy enough. It paid appalling money, but she was happy just to leave the cottage for a while, and while cleaning up after a kennel-load of dogs was hardly stimulating, the company of the dogs was relaxing. Playing with them, grooming them, feeding them. All menial enough tasks, but she didn't have to worry about other people talking about her behind her back or hushed conversations quickly stilled as she entered a room. Instead she was granted the unjudgemental companionship of up to thirty dogs. It was enough for her.

Today, still feeling tense in Jack's absence, she had eaten an early supper and taken the dogs out again. The Spaniels bounded about the roadway, all along to the main road and over to the copse at the bottom, where they scurried about searching unsuccessfully for rabbits or cats. For an hour she walked about the copse until she felt

136

ready to return home, and then she called to the dogs and made her way back.

The dogs in their bed, she walked through to the kitchen and set the kettle on the Aga, before turning on the radio.

It was then that the phone rang. Without thinking, she picked it up and gave her number.

'Claire, my darling, is that you? It's Paul. Paul Starck.'

She felt her face freeze.

'Paul. What do you want?'

'Only a chat, Claire. Only a chat. Are you in all day?'

'No. I'm busy.'

'Then tomorrow.'

'No, I will be…'

'I do need to speak with you, Claire. And it won't make any difference if you try to put me off,' Starck said gently, but there was iron in his tone.

'Tomorrow,' she said, and put the phone down, slowly.

And then, as the foul memories returned to her, she sobbed, quite quietly, into her hands as the kettle whistled and rattled beside her.

*

16.21 Langley; 21.21 London

'He is on the flight.'

'Good. To Seattle?'

'Yes.'

Amiss put the receiver down and sat back.

'He is on his way.'

His assistant, Bruce Stilson, was sitting in the upright chair opposite his desk and nodded, 'You want me to get over there and deal with things?'

'I hope there's no need. There's nothing he's got that could connect to us. Not now he's lost Lewin's book, and while there is the list at the back, I doubt whether this guy will have made connections from that to us. I think we're in the clear.'

'But he knows the book's gone. He knows somcone's been chasing him, and from the look of all we've heard, he saw the guys at the hospital and in the tunnel. He knows we're after him.'

'It's a serious business to kill an ally's agent. He's supposed to be a friend to America.'

'But he knows someone's tried to kill him. What if he starts to piece things together?'

'It's possible.' Amiss frowned to himself. 'We can leave the local Feebies to keep an eye on him. They're already in place. Hopefully in a day or less, he'll be on a plane out of here.'

'He's lucky to make it.'

'Yes. Our efficiency has been sorely strained in the last few days. We need to tighten the training. He should not have made it from Whittier. Still, if he leaves us, it will be better than him dying here. And at least we have the journal.'

'What if there was a message in the journal that he read and understood?'

'A coded message for another English spy?' Amiss grunted as he considered. He remembered times in Vietnam and in the Gulf, when risks were assessed, possible options evaluated. It was always better to be prepared for the worst. 'Perhaps you're right. Go and join our team. Activate them and monitor. Keep a close eye on this Brit. Just in case we need to remove him. We can't afford to have any more balls-ups, though. Remember that, Stilson. If I give you the order, I expect results this time.'

*

22.43 London

Karen Skoyles drove to her apartment in the Barbican and parked her VW Beetle convertible in the bay in the underground garage. She left it, pressing the fob until the lights flashed, before making her way to the lift.

In her flat, she set her case down and walked to her sitting room. From here she had a clear view all over London. The landmarks, from St Paul's cathedral down there, over to the river, and beyond. A panorama of perfection, she thought. And she wanted to weep at the thought she might soon lose it all.

Her career had progressed nice and steadily until now. Hopefully by abandoning Jack Case she could retrieve things. But it was only as she sat and went through things today that she realised the emotional impact her decisions must take. It was one thing to evict a man like Case from his position in the Firm, to leapfrog Starck and make his life miserable in the hope he would take redundancy, and another to order that a man should be deserted, perhaps even killed.

And it would probably come to that, she knew. Case was too much of a threat to her, even if he didn't realise it.

Karen had begun to work with the CIA some years before, when she had herself been seconded to a liaison role. At the time only

GCHQ staff had been give the US liaison jobs, but she had argued that it would be good to have an analyst on the team, and Richard Gorman had agreed.

When Amiss had spoken to her about a new operation, she had been pleased. It proved that the Americans were keen to involve her with their plans. And all they asked was a few clues about suspects. They were allies, so the information they wanted was justifiable, she felt. Why not help Britain's allies? Especially since they intended using the data to help in the war against terrorism.

Yes. At the time it had seemed so logical. And Amiss had in return ensured that her influence was remarked upon. The Americans praised her, and that helped her at the Service.

But if news of her passing on information so that Americans could capture people for torture came to the ears of the DG or DDG, her career would be ended.

She trembled at the thought. And then she picked up a telephone and put a call through to the number Amiss had given her.

If she gave out Case's name and details, the Americans would soon find him. And then her problems would disappear. If Case was dead, her secret could remain just that: secret. It was the only way she could ensure her own safety.

And she knew how to make the Americans keen to kill him.

Wednesday 21st September

16.32 Seattle; 00.32 London

Frank Rand cut the call and returned to his desk.

The local FBI offices off 3rd Avenue, Seattle, were all new and modern, with Steelcase desks and partitions and trunking that hid the cable runs from the main computer servers. Roy Sandford was shut away in his own private little chamber over on the left, with separate feeds in from the main comms boxes up on the next floor, and this area before Frank was where the main team congregated. Not just now, though. Most of the men were out in the field, at the airport, at the ferry terminals, at the coach station, all of them searching for the man they knew as Hansen.

He looked about him with frustration. He wasn't used to losing a subject like this. They'd set up the surveillance well, too. The taxi should have been ideal but Hansen, if that was his real name, had lost them easily. The cab that was driven by Frank's driver edged forward, and was in position to pick him up, but almost at the moment he slid to a halt beside Hansen, the bastard had smilingly given up his place to an elderly couple three behind him. The next cab was a fall-back, but Hansen was engaged in talking then to the despatcher, and he waved on the next man in the line. It was only the third cab he took, to Qwest Field Stadium, Frank learned later, where Hansen took a quick walk over the road and got a bus towards the university campus. But from there the trail died. There was no spoor to follow.

Across the table from him, Debbie Stone crossed her short legs, tapping a pen against her legal pad.

'Why'd he go and hide? He's a victim, he ought to be trying to get away from here, and he could use our help to make sure he was safe, couldn't he? Running makes him look like a felon himself.'

'He's a Brit. Perhaps he was scared,' Frank Rand guessed. But then he remembered the look of cool calculation he had seen in Jack's eyes at the bar in Anchorage. 'No. He wasn't scared. More, he was angry.'

'Then what's he up to?' Debbie demanded. She narrowed her shrewd grey eyes. Debbie was shorter than common for the FBI, and had short legs and a round face that looked like a sulky teen's. Her complexion was very pale, matching her blonde hair, but her dark grey eyes were striking. Frank was happy to keep her in his team for her eyes alone. They held his attention for some reason. But in addition, she was one of the top marksmen in his team with her issued Glock 23 and her privately owned Glock 27, both in .40 cal. She was definitely not the sort of girl who would suffer a fool gladly. For two years she'd worked in the Behavioural Science Unit, and she was always interested in the motivations of the felons they hunted.

'Who knows?' Frank said, as he sucked at his teeth and leaned back in his chair, staring at the ceiling.

'Did he strike you as dangerous?'

'Nope. He seemed perfectly normal. Just not a lawyer, from what I saw. And I'd guess he could be worried that the same Muslim terrorists who killed Lewin could be after him now. Lewin came here because he wanted to get a handgun.'

Frank swivelled his seat away from her and stared out through the glass-panelled wall at the team in the main room. A series of desks were in there, giving seating for eight men and women at computers, while behind was a Steelcase-built unit with similar space, but this time with high partitions creating pod spaces for agents to work in private.

It was a long time since Frank had worked in an environment like that. He missed the camaraderie of the team never more than now. As soon as he had taken the first step on the rungs of management, he had become aware of his separation from the others, and he missed them.

'And?' Debbie said.

Her matter-of-fact tone brought him back to the present. She was never one to become sentimental or maudlin. She stared at him seriously now, and he said nothing for a few seconds, feeling his purpose return under her steadfast gaze.

'And now he's gone to ground somehow. That means he must have cash. Any credit card transactions would have shown up. He's not using his own phone, and it can't be turned on, or we'd find it and him. It'd be easy to find a foreign number on the local cells. He's not registered to a hotel with the passport and name he gave me in Anchorage, so that means he's deliberately hiding.'

'Which sounds less like he's got a phobia about cops and Feebies, more like he's got his own reasons for hiding. Perhaps he's got something else he's hiding, boss?' Debbie said.

'Like what?' Frank said.

'If he was a felon, and he was involved in firebombing the shack where this guy Lewin lived, he'd have reason to hide, wouldn't he?'

'I don't think there's anything to say he's a felon.'

'Uhuh. But he's got some reason to want to hide.'

'You don't buy the idea he's just scared of being shot at again?' Frank grinned.

She didn't.

'Do you? If he was that scared, like I said, he'd have asked for protection. Did he? Did he call his consulate? The embassy?'

'Ah, shit!' he muttered and picked up the phone again. 'Look, we don't know if he's here or not, but I guess we have to assume he'll do what he said he would, and visit the British Consulate. Get all available teams over there. I want all entrances and exits monitored.'

And meanwhile this British son of a bitch could wander the city at liberty.

'*Shit!*'

*

17.29 Seattle; 01.29 London

Jack took a cab from the airport as Hansen, but when he arrived at downtown Seattle he was already a new man.

The sight of his attacker at the airport had shocked him more than he would have expected. It was one thing for someone to warn him away from the place of Lewin's death, although he had no idea why, but it was a different matter to be followed all the way to Anchorage and from there to the airport. The man was in the departures area, too, which meant he was taking an airplane himself. But he wasn't on Jack's flight, which was some relief.

However, he could have been taking a later flight to Seattle. Jack wasn't going to have that. He didn't want to find the man in Seattle, maybe waiting for him in his hotel room. No, he was going to have to disappear. With a new identity, he would be able to register in a hotel and find some peace for a little while.

He found a Best Western hotel off Pioneer Square. Sitting on a bench at the square, he picked up his backpack and reached round under the grab handle. The thin plate of plastic under the handle was perfect for concealing his spare passport and ID. He had two credit cards there as well, and now he had space to pull out his spare documents, and shoved Hansen's ID away into the recess, before walking to the hotel and checking in using his alternative identity:

Rod Avon. He had never been to Seattle before, and all he knew was that the city was renowned for coffee, seafood, and an internet retailer that had taken over the world. He needed a place to buy a phone, and the best place he could think of was a market or mall. As soon as he had washed, he picked up his rucksack and his book and walked out of the hotel and on to Yesler Way.

With a city map from reception in his hands, he strode fast. There was a mall up to the north, a scant mile from his hotel. Walking up 1st Avenue, he kept a wary eye open for surveillance.

All about the market Jack routinely noted faces. It was a principle he had learned when he had spent a little time with the Watchers in London, the Service undercover surveillance units: that a man's clothing was irrelevant. The Watchers all had reversible coats, changes of trousers, hats, gloves and everything they needed to give different combinations of clothing to confuse any alert watcher. But a man or woman would not be able to so easily conceal their eyes and the outline of their faces.

On the way there, he had changed his pace, he had stopped, doubled back, hesitated to read notices, taken a road east to Second Avenue, and wandered up there, and while outside a large building called Benaroya Hall, under the pretext of reading a stone tablet in the Garden of Remembrance, kept a wary eye open for anybody who could have been loitering. It made a fifteen minute walk take three quarters of an hour, but it was worth it. He had no doubt that Frank would have put a surveillance team on to him if he had the opportunity. There was a water feature a little farther back along the road, and he walked to it, his eyes keen for any sign of recognition or alarm, but saw nothing. He studied the water rippling over a series of stone steps of some black rock, and every sense was alert.

It was a little after that that he heard the jarring screech and horns of emergency vehicles. A massive red fire truck came along first, honking and bellowing as it thundered up the streets, then a smaller truck with a box cabin behind the cab, and "Medic One" printed on the red bonnet. The two hurtled past him, and he kept his head low, but his eyes scanned the people all about. If there was a team trailing him here, they were good. So good, he could spend a year looking for them and still fail.

No. There was no point. He turned and made his way north again, and soon he was in the market.

All the while a cool breeze blew from the sea to the west. Snuffing the air, he remembered that scent. It reminded him of days with Claire at Dartmouth. That port, now little more than a tourist's playground, had been one of the Royal Navy's greatest centres in its day. He remembered sitting on the benches near the ferry over the river, eating fish and chips or pasties, while the sun played over the rippling waters. Once they had climbed down to the little fort at the mouth of the river, and they had made love on the hillside behind it, careless of the boats passing by en route for the sea. That was when they were first courting, and their passions had seemed all-devouring.

It was hard to believe that they had been so happy then.

*

17.35 Seattle; 01.35 London

The team had calmed down for a short while, but now there were more men and women in the rented offices off 3rd Avenue and Roy Sandford was forced to keep his head down as he worked on the transmissions.

In the past, there was always a single wireless comms officer on missions like this, but in recent years the development of new forms of electronic communications had rendered many of the officers obsolete. There was a firm belief that men like Roy weren't needed any more. With automated systems like Echelon, the view went, you just typed in the keywords you needed checking, and Echelon would do the rest. The supercomputers could sift through billions of emails, faxes, text messages, and even phone calls. In many countries now, it was a policy with all businesses never to discuss patents over the phone in case Echelon heard the discussions, because then a series of patent applications would quickly appear in American Patent offices. It had become the single biggest tool for industrial espionage ever created, and because the British, Canadians, Australians and New Zealanders paid for their own hubs: the NSA had computer rights to impose their own keyword searches over them, it was a cheap form of espionage, too.

But the success of Echelon had created its own problems. Just as in the Gulf before the second Iraq war there had been too much information for the intel officers to pick what was relevant and what was not, with Echelon and the other listening devices, there was ever more information to be sifted. More and more telephones meant that there were ever more officers needed to listen and evaluate data, and Homeland Security, the FBI, NSA, CIA, DEA and others didn't have the manpower. So when there was a specific mission, there was even more need now to have a specialist on communications with a field team.

Roy Sandford yawned, smothering it with the back of his hand, his fingers returning to the keyboard while his mouth remained wide, and carried on. There were seven main feeds coming in to him now: a main switchboard from the British Consulate, a second that was supposed to be a secure line from the Consulate to the British Embassy in Washington, two which were telephones used in British safe houses, and the rest were feeds from mobile networks used by British staffers. Roy had no qualms about listening in to the British. This was merely one mission amongst many. He glanced up at the screen behind his monitors. There where three ranged about him on the table top, and a rack with three more above them, while on the wall above was a plasma with feed from various other sites.

'Sandford?'

'Hi. What do you need?'

Roy responded automatically. It was Frank Rand, he realised.

'Any traffic from Hansen?'

'Nothing yet. He's not turned up at the consulate yet, sir.'

'Any telephone intel?'

'Nothing from any known numbers,' Roy said. 'I checked with the UK phone companies and found three guys with his name. One of them was in the area of Manchester, and his address agreed with the one Hansen gave you, but that number's still not responding. I have checked the cell network, but there's nothing showing for that number. I'm guessing if he's got a phone, it's a throwaway.'

'So we're stuck with the numbers for the Brit agents over here.'

That was their problem, of course. There were potentially many more British agents here than they knew of, and while the FBI and other agencies were theoretically forced to cooperate with each other under the Homeland Security regulations, in reality each was still a separate, competitive organisation determined to see to their own interests and maintain their own budget. It was likely that the other agencies had information on agents that wasn't being shared. For this mission, Amiss had gained additional clearance for Roy, and he had a separate feed from his systems into the Homeland Security's system that linked to the other main agencies, which was a help, but he was looking for someone using a phone number he didn't know.

145

'So as far as you know, he hasn't made contact with the Consulate,' Frank said.

'No. I've no way of telling. But I don't like the idea he has a throwaway. That makes him seem more suspicious.'

'Yeah. I'm sure he's an agent. He had tradecraft written all over him. Which could mean he's set himself up with another alias for a hotel room.'

Frank grunted.

'So, we have no idea where he could be?'

'He's in Seattle, I'd guess. None of the feeds from the car rental firms have showed him getting a drive. He could have taken a train or bus and paid cash, I guess. And if he does have another passport or ID, we're fucked.'

Frank Rand said nothing for a moment, then, 'OK. Keep looking for him, and if he uses a phone to call in, you get a trace on it.'

'Sure,' Roy said. And how, he added to himself, how the fuck am I gonna find him without knowing what number he's got, or the number he's calling? There ain't nothing here for me. It's just fuckin' guesswork.

He'd have to call Amiss and let him know what was going on. This whole mission was screwed so far as he could see. The line went dead, and he waited a moment before pressing the speed dial for Amiss.

The calm voice on the other end of the line was soothing. 'There is nothing to worry about. If he's a British spy, he'll turn up again soon.'

'Down here the local Feebies are getting kind of pissed at him.'

'It isn't surprising. They will have had some concerns since he has been present at an explosion and a shooting.'

'I just hope we can find him soon.'

'Yes. We don't want any more violence on our streets. Hopefully you will find him, and we can put him under protection. Then we can send him on his way. The Brits can deal with him when he gets back home. The sooner he's off our backs, the better,' Amiss said, and the line was cut.

*

18.13 Seattle; 02.13 London

At the Pike Place Market, Jack savoured the smells and colours of the fruit and vegetables. There was an atmosphere here that soothed him. A little of the nervous panic that he had felt since seeing Ginger

146

at Anchorage dissipated as he eyed the chillies hanging in brilliant bunches and the tomatoes and squashes in baskets beneath. There was a stall with handmade glassware, another with sculptures, and all around was noise, bustle, and happiness.

There were a pair of guitarists at the entrance to Pike Place Market, and he used the opportunity to pause again and monitor the people browsing the wares. The odour of fish was all about, and he felt the temptation to stop and buy some food, but quashed it. First he had work to do.

In Pike Place there were no phone vendors that he could find, and after a frustrating half hour, he gave up. Looking at his map again, he saw another mall a few hundred yards away, and he made his way to it. Here he was more lucky. A bored boy in faded denims that sagged almost below his groin said 'Yuh,' when he asked about a pay-as-you-go phone, and soon he was in the street with his new Nokia.

There was a coffee bar he remembered from his walk up here, and he retraced his steps to it. A pleasant little café it was called the Online Coffee Bar, and he walked in and ordered himself a large Americano, taking his seat at a comfortable leather chair. Next to him was a plug, and he set his phone to charge. By the time he had finished his coffee, he was happy that the phone was good to go, and he put the cardboard cup into the trash bin as he left.

In the street he dialled the number he'd memorised in London.

A man's voice responded.

'Hello?'

'This is the tourist. Is there a message for me?'

'Strange – I was just talking about you. Sounds like you've had some fun. We should meet up.'

*

21.17 Langley; 02.17 London

Amiss had been at his desk since lunchtime, and while it was growing late, he remained there, waiting with a faint frown on his face. In the darkened room, shadows from his desk lamp made his face a hideous mask.

He did not, as a rule, believe in arriving too early nor in staying too late. Easier by far to do urgent work at home in the morning, and read background material at night in front of his fire. The guards and safes he possessed were adequate for the papers he took home. While he could subsist on four hours of sleep in a night, he often found that the best ideas and reasoning came to him during the hours of sleep. Often he would wake, refreshed, with a problem resolved, and then he would have his secretary come in for dictation while he was still in his bed. It freed his mind, he felt. Sometimes, like today, he would vary his routines. It was good on occasion to have his chauffeur drive him to the office and to walk up to his floor alone, without the bustle and hectic noise of all the other staff. To come up here and sit at his desk and cogitate, considering the different possibilities and risks. Threat and opportunity, those were the two headings he used most often on paper when he was reviewing options.

Today he had been in very early, before six, just so that he could sit in silence and compose himself. Because today was the crucial one, as he had said to Stilson earlier. And now he must wait for the information that could set in motion plans to kill again. He was at one of those crossroads when the wrong decision could ruin his network. Which was why he had Tullman in the room with him now. The Council demanded that all decisions required a minimum of two senior members, and Amiss would not act against the Council. That was as unthinkable as selling state secrets to a foreign enemy.

The phone's light flashed to show he had a call and he had it to his ear before it had finished its first ring.

'Amiss.'

'Sir, it's Stilson. There's no sign of the target, sir. Frank Rand and the others are looking for him, but it's like he's just disappeared since he landed.'

Amiss turned his swivel seat around and he nodded.

'Thanks for the heads-up, Mr Stilson.'

'What do you want me to do?'

'Hold on a moment.'

He set the phone down on the desk, and then leaned forward, his head bowed, as he faced the crucifix on its little shelf, and clasped his hands before his nose as he prayed and asked for direction.

It was the same whenever he asked the Good Lord to aid him. A wave of conviction seemed to rise about him and buoy him up, bringing him that confidence that could otherwise be so lacking. His string bracelet slipped along his wrist, and he smiled, his eyes still closed, as he felt that reminder. It was almost as though God was placing His hand on his, in gentle reminder.

Enough. He knew what he must do.

'Mr Tullman, he has disappeared. Somehow he managed to give the waiting agents the slip.'

148

Tullman turned his pale eyes on to Amiss. He spoke in a soft, Boston accent, 'It is the trouble with these, ah, Feds. They don't know how to, ah, keep their eyes on their targets. Had it before.'

'Are we agreed?'

'We have no choice,' Tullman said, nodding his head with that quick, jerky manner of his.

Amiss picked up the handset.

'We must find him, Mr Stilson, and kill him. And then, to be safe, I think you should take a flight to Nevada. The desert can be lovely at this time of year.'

*

18.58 Seattle; 02.58 London

The walk back to the hotel took Jack a circuitous hour. There was no hurry. The resident spook at the Consulate had sent him a text message in a series of three coded number sequences. Not as secure as some systems, this was adequate for an agent in a hurry: the page was today's date multiplied by nine; the next two numbers gave the line; the last three the position of the letter. Jack looked at his copy of the agreed book: *A Rush Of Blood*. It was a new book by the best-seller Quintin Jardine, not one that could raise eyebrows. Besides, Jardine was one of Jack's favourite writers, which was why he had chosen it.

The numbers were stored on his phone. He needed somewhere to sit quietly and transcribe the message. Not here in the open, but back in the privacy of his hotel room.

He felt the urgency of the situation, but while he felt sure that he was not being followed, he took no risks. Even when he reached Pioneer Square, he didn't go inside at first. There was a wariness about him – almost a superstitious sense that he was in danger here, although he had no idea why. There was a large Victorian cast-iron covering, which was a Victorian covered market of some sort, apparently, and he stood in the shade of a tree behind it, his eyes on the hotel half a block away. Beyond it he could see a freeway on tall legs, the cars racing past metres over the roadway, and behind that there was the occasional glint of the sea. Gulls wheeled overhead, their cries piercing in the clear air. Their calls were clear even over the rumble of the traffic.

Their calls took him back to Exeter and a day, years ago, when he had been at the cathedral, lying on his back, his head in Claire's lap. He had been so full of love for her then. Their early married life had been one long joyous adventure, and even when he was sent away on his occasional rounds of meetings with his Joes, he had always felt that warmth at knowing he would be going back to Claire.

The sourness had only set in after she had realised about his job.

Others he knew had experienced the slow, debilitating destruction that was so common among his peers. Men who were incapable of forming close relationships with their wives because of the cynical conviction that no matter who the woman might be, she must in the end betray him. Doubt and deceit came so easily to those in the Service. And for many of the wives, the sudden discovery of an affair was enough after years of isolation. It was the natural way for an agent to treat his wife, as though she was not to be trusted, and must instead be kept secluded, like a victim of interrogation – like those whom Danny Lewin interrogated. But the women resented it when they realised that their husbands were off with other women. For the first time Jack wondered how the husbands of the female agents felt. Even the Ice Maiden had been married once, he knew, but now she was single, and all the more determined in her job. Only her religious faith kept her sane, Starck had said once, and Jack could easily imagine that religion would become a prop to a lonely woman.

Not all marriages broke up because of infidelity. There were many which broke apart because of the cops' curse: the fear that lurked in the breasts of so many of the wives of police officers – that one day they would wave off their man and never see him alive again. There were all too many women who found that dread to be more than they could cope with. For a year, for ten, perhaps, they could cope. But as the children grew older and the number of colleagues who were themselves victims of violence began to increase, the women started to withdraw into themselves, until something snapped and inevitably there was the ultimatum: you can have me or the job, not both. And with only a few exceptions the women found that their blackmail rebounded.

At first, he had thought Claire had fallen out of love with him when she had discovered he had lied. It was almost eight years after they had married, and Jack had thought nothing could spoil their self-contained contentment. God, was he wrong. She had learned who his employer really was, and there was one thought uppermost in her mind: that for all those years, her life with him had been a lie. Still, she got over it. She was content to know he was involved in research

150

and analysis. For a time, she even seemed proud of him. And then it all went sour.

He didn't understand. She hadn't known exactly what he did, but that was irrelevant – they'd been happy, for Christ's sake. Not many women could say that. He had done all he could to keep her happy.

He had thought she had been happy – until she left him in 2011 and shacked up with Jimmy McNeill.

There was a movement farther along the street, and he peered around the tree-trunk towards it, but it was only a workman at the back of some truck. They were digging up a section of road.

He should have returned to his room, but he had an overwhelming reluctance to go back and sit there alone. Reflections of his life with Claire had brought on an emptiness in his chest. He could see her again on the day they had separated, the shrieked hatred she had flung at him, the accusations, and the horror in her eyes.

Turning, he headed back towards downtown along 1st Avenue, and started to look for a bar. He could transcribe the message there.

*

19.03 Seattle; 03.03 London

When the call came through, Frank Rand winced at the number on his screen.

'Rand.'

'Good. Can you come and see me, Frank?'

His operational chief here was Bill Houlican, a short, heavy-set man in his late forties. His grey hair was trimmed neatly, his blue eyes were steady, and in Frank's opinion he was the epitome of the old-fashioned, lantern-jawed agent. Back from the good old days when there was a strict colour bar. There was never anything said, but Frank always felt that there was a noticeable frost when he was around, and it wasn't the same when others were with Houlican.

'Sir?'

'Sit down.'

Houlican was in his shirt-sleeves, the cuffs rolled to the elbow. It was said that he liked to have his arms on display because they were so intimidating. He believed in intimidation. Once, it was said, a trainee agent had been called to his office for a bawling out, and Houlican had gone with the anxious recruit to the window, and gazed out with him at the people in the street seven stories below and said 'D'you believe in reincarnation?' to which the boy replied

'I... I don't know, Sir. Why?'

151

'Because maybe, if I threw you out of the window, perhaps you could *come back as a fuckin' agent*!' Houlican bellowed suddenly, shoving the hapless man towards the window. His scream, apparently, could be heard half a block away.

Another time, when his temper got the better of him, Houlican responded to the release of a known felon by a clever attorney by hurling his desk's chair across his room and through the plate glass window overlooking the agents' room.

Those days were past, luckily. Management by physical aggression was frowned upon, as was promotion because of skin colour and nepotism, but old habits died hard. Houlican just now appeared to be unsure how to continue. He had a sheaf of papers on his desk, and he tapped them square against his Steelcase desk before eyeing Rand.

'We've lost him, I hear.'

'Yeah. He gave us the slip in the taxi, and so far we've had no luck tracking him down.'

'Not good.' Houlican murmured the words softly, and Frank ignored them.

'We're monitoring the British Consulate in the hope he'll turn up there, and as hotel registrations come through, we keep tracking them, but apart from that, it could be a long, hard job.'

'Then we need a little luck to bring him back,' Houlican said. He stood, and stared through the window behind his desk. For a moment Frank wondered whether he would get a repeat of the reincarnation speech, but then Houlican turned back to him, shaking his head. 'What do you think he was doing here, if he was a spy?'

'I guess it's what we thought: he was checking out the death of an intelligence officer, making sure the guy Lewin did kill himself, and wasn't murdered. There could have been evidence on him.'

'You seen the report from the police chief in Whittier?'

'Yes.'

'He mentioned that this Hansen, whoever he is, was off up to some place Lewin used to visit to draw and paint.'

'Yeah.'

'Strikes me as curious.'

'Yes, sir.'

'Do you think Lewin was a suicide?'

'No. If it was, why would Hansen be in the firing line? I think he knows something about the whole thing, and the fact he's gone to ground just reinforces that view.'

152

'If Hansen is his real name.'

'Yes, sir.'

Houlican nodded to himself. Then the phone rang; he picked up the receiver and barked his name, but then listened, his face becoming strangely blank, and then he looked at Frank as he nodded, said, 'Got that. Yeah,' and began to scribble in a notepad. He thanked the caller and set the handset down again. 'Looks like we have more to worry about. There's news from England, according to the CIA. Our liaison guy in London has brought us some data on your friend. Apparently he's wanted for murder. That's nice, eh?'

Frank Rand felt that like a punch in the stomach.

'Anything else?'

'We have his name and we have his English telephone number. Go get the asshole, Rand.'

*

19.23 Seattle; 03.23 London

The bar had been quiet enough when he walked in, a pleasant, long, narrow room with dark wood. Tables were set out on one side of the room, with tall bench seats covered in soft leather, and Jack walked to the middle of the room, taking his place at a two-seat table. He had a good look through the windows, satisfied that a surveillance team would not be able to peer in through the darkened windows while the street was in daylight. There were too many reflections.

A young waitress appeared, chewing gum, and he suddenly felt ravenous. He ordered a sandwich with fries, washed down with an ale. The beer arrived first, and he sank half the glass in the first gulp. It was a long time since he'd felt so thirsty. It was a long time since he'd felt so alone.

He had his book opened already, and since this was the 12th, he multiplied it by nine and went to page 108. Eight lines down, twelfth letter was "m". First line, third letter "e", and so on. Soon he had the message: "Meet Buenos Aires grill 220 Virginia Street tomorrow 1300".

Jack memorised the location and time, and set his book to one side as his food arrived.

'Thanks.'

*

19.26 Seattle; 03.26 London

Frank Rand sat back at his desk with a feeling of sick tension in his belly as he threw the papers back onto his desk.

153

So 'Hansen' was actually Jack Case, a British spy for many years. How Houlican had got the information, he didn't know, and didn't need to know, but it was clear enough that someone in Britain had spilled it. Just as it was plain that Jack Case had not been honest with Frank.

Rand had been fairly certain that he had been a spy, but it was a shock to have it confirmed so baldly. And that he was a rogue was very worrying. Why, if he was suspected of murder, had they allowed him to fly to the US? Because they wanted him off their own territory, so he could come here and commit death by cop in a shootout? From the time Frank Rand had spent with Hansen, or Case, he hadn't got the impression he was unstable. Merely very self-contained. And that went for plenty of special ops guys he had known in his own time. Even his friends in HRT, the Hostage Rescue Teams within the FBI, men who were trained to kill in a moment in their anti-terrorism roles, were not madmen. They were like Case: cautious, thoughtful, considered men. It was just that when they pursed their lips to peer at a bar, you knew they weren't thinking of the effort of pushing through the line to reach the drinks, but were wondering how much plastic explosive it would take to bring the place down.

But Case was a killer, and his own had called to warn Frank and his team. The ultimate betrayal. Whatever he was guilty of back home in England, it must have been bad for them to tell the Americans. And the Brits would know that this would hurt them. To send a spy undercover to a friendly country was bad. Not unforgivable, since they'd lost a guy, but bad. But for him to turn out to be a killer, that was much worse.

Frank picked up his phone and called through to Roy Sandford. 'I have something for you to send out to all the operatives on this case. Ready?'

*

19.41 Seattle; 03.41 London

There was little else to do, but Roy believed in keeping busy. He was already monitoring all the cells he could, trying to find any sign of the man he knew as Hansen, but the systems were eluding him. They had the Brit's UK phone number for a Blackberry. If his phone was turned on, Roy would easily be able to track it down with a fair degree of precision, but while it was turned off, there was no chance. And Rand and others thought he had bought a throw-away phone, too

154

– a pay-as-you-go that would be untraceable. Still, there was a chance he would be using his Blackberry occasionally. If only he could learn when it was going to be turned on...

He brought up a list of phone numbers that had called the various Consulate lines, hoping that Case had called one, and began to check them off. None was the same as the listed phone owned by Hansen, but that was no surprise. If the guy was intending to fall off the radar, he would just leave his phone turned off. Easy.

Roy shook his head. He was an Echelon analyst. He ought to be back in his computer suite with Very Nice, not cooling his butt here in Seattle. He glanced at his phone, thinking he ought to call her, but he didn't dare. She could be in a meeting, or with friends, and he daren't phone in case he was overheard here.

Overheard. There was something he vaguely remembered: a case from a couple years ago. It was there, in the back of his mind, but he couldn't quite remember... something about cell phones... He chewed at his lips. Jeez, this was maddening! Must be something...

He rose, walked to the coffee machine, took a Styrofoam cup and held it ready, grabbing the jug, but didn't pour. The memory was so close. Something to do with cell phones, and – it was a mobster, he remembered: the Ardito/Peluso case. The FBI officers involved in bringing the mobsters to book had bugged their properties, the restaurants where they did business, everything, but the Mafiosi had routinely swept for bugs. They found two, so the FBI had to go in and quietly remove all the others in case they were found too. But they'd thought up a new scam. Instead of fixed, detectable bugs, they checked on the cell phones the two used. A hacker managed to design a programme that turned on the mics in the phones, and the FBI had the software sent to the phones by the cell network. Bingo! All discussions held by the mobsters were recorded and sent in real time back to the FBI.

There was a guy involved in that. Roy picked up his phone and called Amiss. He'd be able to get the software patch if anyone could. And perhaps with that set up, they'd be able to turn on the microphone in Hansen's phone.

And then he paused, thinking. If they could turn on the microphone, why not turn on the phone itself, and when they had, they could triangulate to get a fix on the guy's location.

'I'm going to get me a pay rise for this,' he murmured to himself as the phone speed-dialled Amiss.

155

15.14 London

Claire had already walked the spaniels, and when she was back she was tempted to pretend she'd forgotten Starck was coming. She could go to work, behave like normal, like an ordinary woman. But if she did, he would likely turn up and question her there. And it was likely he'd make trouble for her. She knew he could. He was a complete bastard when he wanted to be. So, instead, she had called in and said that she was feeling sick and couldn't work. The kennel owner was solicitous and concerned, and that itself made her want to burst into tears.

She was sitting at her table when Starck turned up. He tapped gently at her back door like a friend, but Claire stood watching him without moving for a long time through the panes of the door, frozen like a rabbit in a car's headlights.

It was painful to see him here. Let alone invite him inside. It hurt more than she could have anticipated.

'Good afternoon, Claire, my love,' he said, baring his yellowing teeth. 'What are the chances of a cuppa?'

She moved automatically towards the kettle.

'What do you want, Paul? I didn't ask you to come here. I don't want you here.'

'That's hardly friendly, Claire.'

'Because we aren't friends.'

'I've always been fond of you.'

'Really?'

He had walked into the room and now leaned on the back of a chair across the table from her.

'Claire, what happened to Jack wasn't my fault. I tried to protect him.'

'You destroyed my life, you know that?' she spat. She had a cup in her hand, and it was in her mind to hurl it at his head, but her rebellion died as she looked at his face. 'What do you want of me? I've nothing to say to you.'

'You know Jack has been asked to work again?'

'You came here. He told me. I said he should refuse, but you knew too well how he'd bite, didn't you? You knew he'd agree.'

'There were limited options for him,' Starck said. 'If he hadn't gone, his pension could have been in trouble, as well as redundancy and so on. He had no choice.'

156

'So you blackmailed him.'

'He's the best I had.'

'So it was you?'

'Mostly, yes,' he agreed. He left the chair and crossed to her side. 'Sit down, Claire,' he said, and took the cup from her. He busied himself with the kettle and teapot as he spoke. 'You see, he does have some unique talents. But you know that already, don't you?'

'Yes,' she said dully. 'He's a killer.'

Starck smiled with his yellow fangs.

'Oh, darling, he's much worse than that.'

*

08.04 Seattle; 16.04 London

Roy Sandford blearily stared at the screen when the little electronic *zzip* sound came. For an instant he was confused as he gazed at the screen in front of him. He had snatched a nap from one through seven, and the six hours made him feel a bit better, but his head was still woolly, and his thinking was more than a little confused. Then he blinked and studied the other screens. It was when he saw the email pane that he stirred himself and then a grin spread over his face.

The mail package contained the programme written for him by the technicians at the NSA, and he opened it and smiled broadly at the contents. There were some instructions for him as to how to upload it to the cell phone he wanted, and he read them carefully before he copied the file to his disk.

'Right, Brit spy, let's see if we can figure out where you are,' he said, and his fingers began to race over the keys.

*

16.24 Devon

It was the reason Claire had left him in the first place. So often it was the women who grew bitter, resentful of husbands who preferred their work to their families who broke the fetters and fled. Some were so scared that they were only a temporary lodging for their men, and had to leave because of their fears that they would otherwise see their men off one morning never to see them again.

That was never Claire's fear. Her genuine, personal terror was that he would return every night. And she would know every so often that he had once more killed. He was a thoroughly professional assassin.

When she first realised what he did, she had been too stunned to cope. Her brain had shut off, as though to protect herself from considering the truth. When he put his hands about her, she felt them

157

tensing as though preparing to throttle her; when he reached for her, she flinched in case there was still a man's blood on his fingers; if she smelled something on him, it was not another woman's scent she feared, but the chemical tang of gun oil.

It was not shocking – it was overwhelming. The whole of her life before that moment had been based on lies and half-truths. She realised that now.

'I am truly sorry, Claire,' Starck said.

'Just shut up! Why don't you go, and leave us both in peace? What do you want from us?'

'Claire, you don't have to like me or what we do in the Service, but I do need your help. You see, there are some problems which are causing us a little concern.'

'What are you on about?'

Starck had filled the pot, and now he set it before her, two mugs at one side, and the jug of milk nearby. He drew out a chair and sat, watching her with a stern compassion.

'Claire, I have to take you back to that day last year, in March 2011, when you realised what he was.'

'I don't want to!'

'I know. But I must demand it. Where were you when you learned?'

'At the apartment in London,' she whispered. 'I hate you.'

'I remember that apartment. Very pleasant.'

'It was hideous.'

'Lucky Jack sold it, then. Do you remember who was there?'

'Poor Jimmy was there,' Claire said, and her eyes tingled with the promise of tears at the memory. Jimmy McNeill had been so sweet, so kind to her. 'And Jack had asked you, too. And Karen. It was when it was announced that he was going to work for you. Eighteen months ago, roughly.'

'Yes. And how did you actually realise? That Jack had killed people?'

'We were having a party, to celebrate. And I didn't realise still. I knew he was in the Service, but it didn't matter to me then. Not before that night. When we married I'd thought he was a commodities salesman or something, but after we'd been married eight years I realised that wasn't true, and I confronted him.'

'What did he say?'

158

'That he was with the Foreign Office. Gradually I learned his job wasn't diplomatic at all, but I still thought he was a spy. A researcher. I could have borne that. I could,' she said with spirit, looking over at him.

'I'm sure you could,' he agreed.

'But then, that night… we were all in the sitting room, weren't we? And Jimmy was over by the big window that looked out over the river, and Karen and you were toasting Jack, and it was all so good, and fun, and you said that he was being promoted – I didn't even know what his money was, or what the grades were. But he was pleased, and so was everyone else, and they started singing *For He's a Jolly Good Fellow*, but Jimmy wouldn't sing. And I went to him to see how he was, and what the matter was, and he wouldn't look at me, and kept his eyes on Jack all the time, and then he said it.'

'What? What did he say, Claire?'

'You were *there*. He said, "So, Jack, how many souls did this promotion cost?"'

'Yes. And the evening went downhill rather rapidly after that.'

She wiped her eyes with her hands.

'And I left him a few months afterwards. I couldn't bear to think of his hands on me. His hands, after he'd killed…'

'What did he say to you about it?'

Claire shrugged and pulled a grimace. 'He said he only did it rarely, when it was necessary, when he had to. The usual pathetic excuses: that he was in a war, and he was a foot soldier. That he had to do what he was ordered. And I spat it back at him, saying that was the Nazi prison-warders' excuse – "Not my fault, I was only following orders". It wouldn't hold water.'

'He didn't lie to you,' Starck said softly.

'I don't care! I don't want to be married to a killer, Paul! To a murderer! It made my flesh creep to think of it.'

'So you left him.'

'I came here. I came home.'

'But he joined you?'

'He swore to me that he wouldn't kill again. He was leaving the Service and we'd forget all about the job, Jimmy, and *you*! And he'd still be here if you hadn't lured him away! We were making a go of things. He had stopped his work; you stopped him. And then you came and took him away again! I hope you can live with yourself!'

'Sometimes,' Starck said softly. 'Sometimes.'

159

16.29 London

When the phone rang, Sara al Malik swore under her breath. There had been so many calls yesterday, and while today the calls had sloped off since lunchtime, she had a conviction that this must be another newspaper calling for a fresh angle on her misery.

'Yes?' she said curtly.

'Sara, it's me.'

The voice of her lawyer was enough to ease her spirit a little.

'How are you?'

'Fine, fine, Sara. Look, I've some bad news.'

'What could be so bad compared to what's already happened to me?' she sighed.

'It's pretty bad. There's been a D-Notice issued over all the news stories about Mo.'

'What?'

'It means none of the papers can report what's happened. All the TV companies, all the radio, all the media, have a blanket ban on all reporting of anything to do with you or Mo.'

'Can they do that?'

'Yes. If it is deemed to impact national security, they can stop anything they want. Look, Sara, I have to ask you: are you quite sure in your own mind that Mo had nothing to do with any terrorist plots? You are absolutely sure?'

'How can you ask that about my Mo?' she demanded. 'You know him as well as I do myself! He would no more hurt a human than kill himself!'

'All right, Sara. All right. I had to ask. I just don't understand what is happening.'

Soon after, he made some apologies and hung up. Sara held onto her phone, thinking, and it was while she sat there that she heard the soft little click again. She drew the phone from her ear and stared at it before carefully setting it down on the receiver.

She had never felt so lonely.

*

08.34 Seattle; 16.34 England

Roy Sandford smiled as he set the file to the main testing system he was using. Best always to test new software and ensure that there were no glitches in it. Once he had set this up, he would push it onto the live machine.

160

His phone rang. It was Amiss.

'Sir?'

'I believe you have received the package you asked for?'

'Yes, sir.'

'Can you just tell me again what it'll do? I'm not the most technical guy in the Agency.'

'Yes, sir. It's a piece of software that will fire up his telephone, hopefully. When that happens I can tell you exactly where he is. We can triangulate using the cell network to figure where he is within a few metres.'

There was a pause.

'Could you tell me first? Before you let Rand know.'

Roy blinked.

'Well, uh, yeah. I guess.'

'That is good. Roy, this will seem a strange question, but I have noticed looking through your files that you are a Catholic. Is that so?'

Roy was about to chuckle and admit that he was severely lapsed, but then something in the question sank into his consciousness. This was an important question to Amiss, and when Roy thought about all those rumours about a crucifix hidden behind Old Glory in his office, and the stories about the number of times his driver had to take him to a church, he thought better. This could be a career defining moment, he thought.

'Yes, sir,' he said.

'That is good. Roy, I would like you to be very sure you understand me here. I can help your progress through the Agency, but I do have to know that I can trust you. You understand me? I may make peculiar requests. You have to respond immediately and without question. Is that understood?'

'Sir.'

'Good. Now, get on with that software.'

'Yes, sir.'

*

17.03 Devon

'Has he ever shown signs of irrationality with you, Claire?' Starck asked.

'Why don't you just go away?'

'You know I can't. Has he?'

'Then *fuck off*! He's the man you and your lot made him!' Claire burst. She turned and faced the window. From there she could look out over the fields to the new trading estate. 'You took him and moulded him to your will, didn't you? You took an ordinary, decent man and made him a monster.'

'Possibly, Claire. But possibly we took a monster and gave him a direction that made him safe.'

'Safe so long as you kept feeding him, you mean? You Romans had your lion, and all you needed to do was keep on finding a Christian to throw to him.'

'Perhaps. But these were dirty Christians,' Starck said blandly. 'If it's any consolation, I didn't want him to do it.'

'Why, in case he got a taste for it and came after you?'

Starck placed his cup down, and when he spoke, his voice was cold with growing resentment, almost anger. 'Why do you keep on at me, Claire? You know Jack was never a saint. He is the man he is. I did nothing to him except give him a purpose and point him in a useful direction. He's a spy, Claire, and sometimes it can be a shitty job. But better that someone does it, rather than we all suffer.'

'He was never irrational except when he had seen you last week,' Claire said, thin-lipped.

'Did he ever mention Jimmy McNeill?'

'That is none of your business,' she flared.

'You left Jack for Jimmy soon after the party. You ran away with him.'

'I couldn't stand the hypocrisy – I couldn't stand people like you, Paul. It was you, who made me run away, not only Jack. He tried not to lie to me, he tried to keep us stable and together, but when I learned he was a killer, that was enough. Jimmy wasn't a killer. I loved him. But you, you were happy to keep on lying to me. You lied from the very first moment you met me to the last. And I expect you'll be lying to me again today, won't you?'

'You came back here to your home. And Jimmy came too.'

'I had nowhere else to go. I hated London. The surface-skaters, that's what Jack called you and the others. Did you know that? He had more contempt for you than even you for him. He hated you. You were always so shallow and dishonest.'

'He knew you were back here?'

'Where else could I go? He knew that.'

'Jimmy told you he had nowhere you could go with him?'

'What?'

'He didn't have his own place, did he? Only a little flat in Hounslow.'

'That's right,' she said, and then faced him. 'What do you mean? What's this about?'

'So Jack knew to come here to find you? You wouldn't be anywhere else, would you?'

'I didn't hide from him. I wasn't that much of a coward.'

'So Jack came to find you. And you had a row.'

'He never came here after our split, no. Not until after Jimmy's accident last year.'

Starck eyed her closely.

'No? You didn't see him here?'

'I don't understand what you're on about, Paul.'

'You didn't see him here?'

'Of course not!'

Starck nodded to himself.

'What is this about?'

'He was here, according to the records in Vauxhall. Apparently he didn't turn off his phone. We could trace him. We hoped he was here to have an argument with you. That's what the records show.'

'When? What do you mean?'

Starck pulled a face.

'Does it matter now?'

'When, Paul?'

'The day Jimmy died. The records show Jack was here that day.'

*

10.45 Seattle; 18.45 London

The restaurant was ideal for him. Jack arrived an hour and a half before the due time, and lounged at a street corner with a hot coffee, watching the place and keeping his eyes on the passers-by. When he was convinced that there was no surveillance, he left and walked around the block a couple of times, never too far away, always monitoring the other people in the area. It was as his watch told him it was one fifteen that he returned, stood eyeing the place, and finally entered.

'Glad you could make it.'

Stephen Orme was tall, fair, and almost too good-looking. In a profession that depended upon hiding in a crowd, he was a rarity: a perfectly featured man with the blue eyes of a god. He had the narrow waist of a natural athlete, and the long, slender fingers of a pianist, and women invariably fell at his feet when he murmured softly in their ears. It was a shame, as Jack knew, that he was gay – or perhaps bisexual. He had certainly been successfully utilised in several honey traps. One had involved a Russian spy who had been living in America for some years and in whom the British Service had developed an interest. After four months of his assiduous attentions, the poor girl had left her husband, deserted her Service and country, and was now living a quieter, embittered life in British Columbia.

'You would appear to have been rattling a few cages, old fellow,' Stephen said once they had ordered beers.

'Unintentionally. Lewin appears to have been killed – I don't believe it was suicide. I had found the journal that he left, but the damn thing's gone. It was taken from me.'

He briefly set out the events at Whittier and in the tunnel on the way home. Stephen was recording his words on a small digital recorder and, as he came to the end of his story, Stephen began to ask questions, running through all the details that Jack had given him again, not in order to test him, but purely to confirm the story.

'What did you do with the pistol?' Stephen asked.

'The police kept it after the shooting,' Jack said. 'I couldn't have kept it. I don't know what the rules are, but I guess the cops would be unimpressed were I to turn up with a handgun at Anchorage Airport.'

'Very true,' Stephen said. 'Is that all?'

'Yes. I've told you everything,' Jack said. But he hadn't. He had held back on the roll of newspaper cuttings. From a desire always to keep secrets, but also because he was wary. Someone had followed him to the airport, and that made Jack... nervy. He felt happier keeping some details to himself. In any case, there was no need to talk about Sumner. The poor bastard had been injured fighting for his country, and then his charitable efforts collapsed. There was no need to hound him further. He couldn't have had anything to do with Lewin. He wasn't even in Alaska. He realised Stephen was talking again.

'Eh?'

'I suppose there's no possibility that we could recover the journal? Could you recognise the fellows who took it from you?'

Before Jack could answer, the waiter came and took their orders: Orme's steak, Jack's salad Niçoise, and both were silent as the waiter scribbled.

'I've thought about the bastards wandering through the police station often enough,' Jack said viciously when the man was gone. 'But I can't visualise them, no. I was swimming in and out of consciousness all the while, and I'm just lucky to be alive. If the beam had landed on me, I wouldn't have stood a chance. But the ones who tried to get me at the hospital wing – those two I'd recognise anywhere. One, I think, I hope, is dead. He was a Hispanic. The other was a bigger guy, a ginger-haired man. It was cropped short, like a Marine, you know?'

'What of this Frank Rand?'

'He's a bright FBI agent. I don't think I should cross swords with him again. He suspected me, I know that much.'

'Then we'd best get you home,' Stephen said. He smiled and passed an envelope over the table. Jack took it thankfully and slipped it into his inside pocket. He knew that it would be a passport and tickets under a new name. Soon, with luck, he would be on a plane and on his way homewards by tomorrow night.

'Are you listening?'

'Sorry, Jack said. 'I'm still jet-lagged.'

'I said,' Stephen repeated, 'that you had best be careful. Keep your head down, so these fellows don't shoot it off for you. They do not sound pleasant.'

'No,' Jack said, remembering the two in the hospital, the Hispanic he had shot in the tunnel. 'At least one of them is down.'

'You're sure you injured him badly?' Stephen asked.

'There was blood all around, and the FBI reckoned he would be badly injured, but last I heard, there was no reports of a man like him turning up in a hospital. So yes, with luck the shit's dead.'

*

13.12 Seattle; 21.12 London

Roy Sandford whistled as he put down the phone.

'So, Mister Case, you're a bad dude,' he muttered, and grinned to himself.

He was not a field agent. He had no appreciation of the dangers of such a post, and all he knew was that the man he was hunting was listed as dangerous, even by his own peers in Britain. 'Right, man, let's get you sorted, eh?'

*

21.43 Devon

165

Claire dialled while holding the glass of gin in her hand so that the ice rattled with every button pressed. He had said she could call him by using his mobile, but what was the code to dial to America? There was some stupid set of... she took a long pull at the gin, wincing. It was much stronger than her usual drink at the weekends, but, although this was only Wednesday, she had needed it when Starck finally went. The house still reeked of his stale tobacco smoke smell. It made her feel sick, almost as sick as his comments had.

'I need you talk to you,' she said, sniffling. She gazed at the telephone book, reading off the sequence of code numbers for American international calls, but the figures made little sense to her. She tried pressing the buttons again, and sobbed to herself. Taking a deep breath, she set the glass down on the table and dialled with careful deliberation. It was ever so quiet. Like there was nothing there, just a void sucking her call into it. An electronic black hole. Obscurely she wanted to giggle at the thought, and then, as she picked up her glass again, she heard the soft click.

'Jack?'

'Hello. Leave a message after the tone and I'll get back to you soon as I can.'

'Jack,' she said, and the weeping began again. 'Starck was here – he was horrible, Jack. He said you might have been here on the day Jimmy died. Jack, I need you... to talk to you. Please, Jack, call me back. I don't care what the time is. Just call me!'

*

15.20 Seattle; 23,20 London

Jack was back at the Pioneer Square hotel by mid-afternoon, and while there he ripped open the envelope. Inside was a passport, new wallet with credit cards made out to new identity, as well as a mixture of dollar notes that totalled two hundred and thirty-four bucks, all of them used.

He was happy, when he saw the plane tickets, as he would be leaving the next day. Only one more evening here, and then he'd be on a flight up to Vancouver to catch a connection. Then home, to England.

There was a sharp tone, and he frowned for a moment. It was familiar, but unexpected. Then he remembered it: it was the tone that his phone made when it received an answerphone message. He turned back to his passport, before the shock hit him. *The phone should have been turned off*!

15.21 Seattle; 23.21 London

'*Yes*!' Roy Sandford punched the air as the screen registered the phone. He grabbed his phone and punched the numbers for Amiss. 'Sir? We've got him. Pioneer Square, the Best Western Hotel there on Yesler Avenue.'

'Excellent, agent Sandford. I can see you will be soon required for other jobs I have. Thanks.'

Roy closed the line, and then phoned Rand, giving him the same details.

'Good. Keep an eye on him.'

'If he has a throwaway phone, he may use it shortly. I'll keep monitoring the cells,' Roy said gleefully. There were two other technicians in the office, and he called them next, instructing them in what they must do, before turning back to his own screen and cracking his knuckles. 'OK, buddy! Let's see how good you really are!'

*

15.22 Seattle; 23.22 London

Jack grabbed the phone and stared at it. The Blackberry's small light winked at him to show that it was on a network and, for a moment, he was too surprised to react. He saw the little symbol showing a recorded voice message, and without thinking he pressed the button to view the message. He saw Claire's name, but then he quickly turned off the phone, pressing and holding the power button until it came up with a shut down message. Even then he wasn't sure he was safe. He wanted to remain off the radar, so he took off the back and pulled out the battery.

He was sure he had turned it off. But now it was on again. Perhaps he had missed the button. When he'd spent so much time drumming into his lads the fact that they had to be careful about technology – he felt as stupid as the British escapee from Stalag Luft 13 who responded 'Thanks' when the Gestapo wished him good luck, after he'd taught his comrades to be on their guard for exactly that trick.

Then his mind turned to his wife. What could Claire have phoned about? She knew never to try his number when he was abroad. They had a rule that he would call her when he could. This was weird. He would have to call her back. It may be important. But not now.

Sitting on the bed, he wondered whether the phone could have betrayed him. It *shouldn't* have done. The thing was registered to his real name in England, and unless the Americans had been hugely fortunate, they would not have found that. Instead they would have had the name of 'Hansen', and *he* didn't have a phone. Yes, he must be in the clear, he thought.

But there was no point taking risks. He packed his bag quickly, took up his rucksack, and made his way downstairs, leaving his suitcase in his room. In the foyer he stood in the entrance, looking up and down the road, searching for any signs of surveillance. There was nothing obvious. He checked out, and asked if he could leave his case to be collected later before pulling his rucksack onto his back and leaving the hotel.

He felt very alone. In Berlin and other postings the language had meant that he was always aware of his difference, but here it was worse, somehow. The very normality of the city, the logic of using English, all tended to make him feel still more endangered. Chattering passers-by made him feel he was under surveillance at every moment. The sight of a man with an ear bud in his ear made his heart stop for an instant before he recalled that this was America, not East Germany or Russia, and that half the population walked about with iPods or Bluetooth earphones inserted. There was no point worrying. He had seen nothing to merit concern.

There was a car's tyres screeching some distance away, and he snapped his head about, but there was no sign of a vehicle hurrying to him. No, just an ordinary noise from an ordinary street, he told himself as he continued along the roadway. He needed to find somewhere to sit and kill some time.

He found himself looking down into the Seattle Mystery Bookstore and, without a second thought, he plunged down the stairs into the shop. It was dedicated to crime writing, and he browsed among the shelves considering the irony that he was here while he suspected someone was searching for him. Someone who might well have murdered Danny Lewin – Danny, the sad boy with the horror in his eyes.

Jack saw nothing as his mind whirled. Every time he heard a car engine gunning up the hill outside, his attention was dragged to it, expecting at any moment to see a convoy of dark cars with agents spilling from them, but all appeared well.

'Can I help you? You looking for a specific author?' the shop keeper asked, a jovial looking man some years younger than Jack with a thin black beard.

'No,' Jack said with a smile. 'I'm just wondering about a gift for a friend.'

'Do you know what they read?'

Jack shook his head.

'I'll know it when I see it,' he said.

There was a sudden harsh screech of brakes, and he saw a black sedan rocking outside as three men leaped from it and ran down the road towards Pioneer Square.

'Wow! Someone's in a hurry!' the shopkeeper said, but he was already talking to himself.

Jack was at the window, staring out. Now, as the three disappeared down the road, he hefted his backpack, He selected a softcover by Zoe Sharp, and walked to the till.

'She'd like this, I think.'

'Ah, a good choice. I like her work. Really strong storylines and from a girl who knows how to write.'

'Thanks,' Jack said, shoving it into his bag as he waited for the change from his twenty, and then walked out of the store and turned up the hill away from Pioneer Square.

*

15.27 Seattle; 23.27 England

In his pocket was his new phone. He pulled it out as he strode up the hill, stopping before a plate-glass window and studying all the people nearby in case he was being watched.

He wouldn't have called Stephen Orme again unless he had felt threatened, but those three guys looked too much like agents, and it was too much of a coincidence for them to appear just now, after his phone had turned on. Stephen might be able to give him a room, access to data comms, or even concealment in the Consulate, just for a day, until he could get out of the city. Reluctantly, Jack came to a decision. He studied the keyboard and dialled the Consulate.

Stephen's calm voice answered. 'Hello?'

'It's the tourist again. I think I need help.'

'Where are you?'

'Not far from my hotel.'

'Give me your precise position. I'll come and get you.'

There was something in his tone that grated.

'Good.'

He had the street map out already, and Jack looked at it as he spoke. 'I'll be at Pier 50, waiting to get a ferry to Vashon or one of the islands. Can you meet me there?'

'Sure. Look, how long till you're there?'

'I'll be there in about forty-five,' Jack said. He looked west from the road, and beyond the flyover he could see the straight line of lights lining the walkway and road to the ferry.

'Good. You wait there at the entrance, yeah?'

'There's a kind of water fountain there. I'll be beside that,' Jack said, and closed the call. Then he called a cab.

*

15.28 Seattle; 23.28 England

As a means of tapping an individual's phone calls or emails, Echelon was useless, but that wasn't what the network was created for.

Echelon operated by searching all communications and listening out for specific keywords that it had stored in a suite of programmes called 'Dictionary'. These watchwords were selected by the alliance of the UK/USA services, the 'Yookoosa', which comprised the larger Anglo-Saxon Commonwealth countries and the USA: so there were hubs in Leitrim in Canada, Waihopai in New Zealand, Kojarena in Western Australia, and Menwith Hill in England. Trawling through millions of messages constantly, Echelon sifted them for those messages that were of specific importance to certain teams.

Roy Sandford knew all this, just as he knew that millions of messages each half hour were being checked and discarded, and he knew that the Dictionary was all. It was the basis of the whole system. Without it, Echelon was so much expensive metalwork. But the Dictionary meant that all the agencies that had access to Echelon could seek information on specific areas of interest. So, for example, the Australians would be interested in Triad gangs and smugglers from Asia, while the English would be more keen to know about possible arms sales to Irish terrorists. Echelon had been designed to allow each nation to have their own Dictionaries, so that they could take responsibility for their own areas of influence.

Except although the design that was demonstrated to the UK/USA teams by the NSA provided the separation of interests, the NSA ensured that such separation did not exist for themselves. All the Dictionaries used by the junior members of the consortium, the Brits, Australians and others, were transparent to the US team; while the others could insert their own keywords and have searches conducted over their own spheres of influence, the US agents could see these too, and the results were copied to the NSA. While the other consortium members had access to only their own reports, American agents saw all of them. But there was another trap door, which the NSA had designed and implemented. All the US searches were transparently conducted over the entire international network, without the junior members seeing them.

And Roy had access to the entire network under the Order given by Amiss.

He had already inserted the relevant details known about the agent. The name he had used in Alaska: Hansen; his friend's name: Danny Lewin aka Daniel Lewin aka Dan Lewin aka D Lewin; the town where Lewin died: Whittier… everything Roy had been told about the man they were hunting. Having done all that, there was nothing for him to do with Echelon, so he was working on the telephone systems, and it was while he was working on them that the screen on the right bleeped. He looked up and saw the red box flashing. And then he saw the Echelon signal.

In his hurry, he missed his phone and slid it across his desk, almost to fall on the floor.

'This is Roy, yeah, I think we got something here!'

'What?'

'An English guy, one we've not had under surveillance, who's supposed to be a tourist operator, has just called a UK number and mentioned our friend Case. Says he's going to be at Pier 50 waiting for a ferry in about three quarters of an hour.'

'Great: tell the team to meet me there,' Frank said, glancing at his watch.

*

23.31 Devon

Claire was sitting on the floor. The spaniels were beside her, one with his chin resting on her thigh as she sniffed and wept. The bottle of Plymouth gin that had been half full when she poured the first drink was empty now.

She had no idea what was happening. Her head was fuzzy and light from sobbing and alcohol, and all she could see in her mind's eye was Starck sitting there at her table, his yellowing features, his yellow-stained hair, the yellow stains on his fingers and hands, all equally repulsive to her.

171

When the noise assaulted her ears, she could scarcely recognise it at first. It sounded alien to her. But then she realised that her handset was ringing, and reluctantly picked it up. 'Yes?'

'Claire, it's me. I was worried, love. I saw your...'

'You did it, didn't you, Jack? I can see it now. Starck told me you were here when Jimmy died. What did you do? Hit him with a stick? Throw a rock at him?'

'Claire, no! Don't start imagining things that didn't happen. I couldn't have hurt him – I was in London.'

'He showed me your telephone log. You know that? If you have a mobile phone, they can tell where you are at all hours of the day. And yours showed you were down here.'

'That's bloody impossible!'

'You killed Jimmy. He was the only chance I had to get away from you... to escape. But you murdered him, didn't you?' She said, before choking with the sobs that took her over. 'I loved him, Jack. I was prepared to try again with you when you begged me to, but I didn't realise you'd killed him! You murdered my lover! What worse thing could you do to me?'

'Claire, not only did I not do it, my phone was in London all that day. I was nowhere near Devon the day he died. Starck made it up!'

'Why would he make it up?' She sniffed and spat, 'He's not the one trying to lie to me to climb into my body, is he? It was you. It always was you. I don't want anything more to do with you, Jack. Never! Nothing!'

*

23.57 London

Sara al Malik was in the kitchen sitting at the small pine table. Not drinking tea or coffee, not hunched over a plate, but sitting upright, staring at the far wall.

She had lost. There was nothing else. The blank-faced officials had won. They had taken poor Mo, and now she couldn't even raise her voice to demand his return. The papers, the TV companies, all of them would ignore her. She could talk to friends, but nothing more. None of the media wanted to know.

And then she had a sudden thought. The BT engineer had mentioned the computer. Although Mo's computer was taken by the police, and he wasn't allowed one under the terms of his parole, Sara could get one for herself. Or use one.

On the internet, there were ways to make friends with many people, very quickly.

Thursday 22nd September

Jack climbed out of the cab near the water, and walked along the roadway until he was close to the railings by the sea. The breeze was chill on his neck as he stared up north and east towards the skyline. From here he could see all the buildings clearly. The strange tower piercing the sky, the tall tower blocks housing offices, the array of harbour front shops and restaurants.

And the ferry terminal.

Jack stared out over it with his thoughts in turmoil. He should never have called Claire, but the message had demanded it. He couldn't leave her wondering what was happening. But the response he had gained was plain enough. She was deeply hurt. Starck had presented her with proof that Jack had been there, indisputable proof in the form of his telephone.

Except he knew that his phone *had not* left London. It had been there all the time. So how had Starck found proof that was untrue? It was easy enough to falsify a report on a computer, of course. Just type up something into a genuine-looking form, and print it. It would not have to be terribly detailed or clever to convince Claire, after all.

Jack shook his head. This was crazy! He had no idea what was happening, but he did know that someone was setting him up for the murder of Jimmy McNeill. But just now, he didn't have time to worry about the implications of that. He must first see whether there was a risk from Orme.

Behind him was a park, and he saw a tourist binocular up at the top. Dismissing Claire from his mind, he climbed to it. A sign told him this was Hamilton Viewpoint Park, and mentioned something about a newspaper owner who'd given his name to it. Jack wasn't interested. He was more taken by the metal binoculars on their plinth in front of parked cars. Crossing to it, he put in his money and studied the distant pier. There was a large building to the south of the ferry terminal, but he could still see the entranceway distinctly in the clear air. No sign of anything as yet, he thought. And then, as he watched, he noticed that on the Alaska Highway, the flyover freeway that was only a short distance from the terminal, a car had stopped, and two men were peering over the concrete wall to the ferries. From this far, even with the magnification of the binoculars, he couldn't see what they were doing, but it was plain that they were not fixing a puncture. One climbed back into his car and drove away, but the second remained where he was. As Jack watched, another pair of figures moved along the roof of the large building to the right of his view.

'You're early, lads,' Jack muttered as he let the binocular lenses face skywards. He stood a moment, his forearm resting on the binoculars as he stared out towards the ferry, before shouldering his bag again and setting off to the road back to Seattle.

Orme had given him away, somehow. His last contact in the US had betrayed him. He pulled out his pay-as-you-go phone and was about to drop it into a little bin, when he reconsidered. He turned it off, and put it into his pocket again.

With his job gone in London, with Claire deserting him, and now knowing he was being hunted by American agencies, he was left with a sense of utter loneliness, and a perverse calmness.

Because now he had nothing to lose.

*

16.12 Seattle; 00.12 England

Frank Rand waited in his car with the tension mounting. At his hip, his Glock 27 dug into the soft flesh and made him shift in his seat occasionally. It didn't matter how much you spent on a holster, the damn things were always literally a pain in the ass when you sat in a car.

He looked over at Debbie who was parked in the road over the other side of Yesler Way, in a car park of an Italian restaurant. Her eyes were not on him, but flitted about the roads, occasionally glancing up at the overpass.

There were twelve of them around here. Four on the ground at the ferry, in case they had to head the guy away from the passengers waiting in line, two more up north of the terminal, two south, both with drivers waiting in their cars so that no matter where Hansen or Case, or whatever his real name was, tried to go, there would be bodies on the ground to stop him.

But he wasn't here yet. Frank felt the first pricklings of adrenaline-fuelled sweat. He had a hollowness in his belly at the thought that this might all go wrong. To divert himself, he called Roy Sandford.

'Roy. It's Frank. The call you were talking about, you're sure that the guy mentioned he was going to be here?'

'That's what he said, yes.'

'There's no sign of them. No one at the fountain, nothing.'

'Oh. Well, just in case, I am running a check on all the phone calls made to the guy who phoned Britain. The one called Orme. There was only one call to him or from him in the moments before he made that call.'

'The number we were given for his UK phone?'

'No. This is different. It's unlisted, but it's not on contract, and registered in the US.'

'Where is that cell phone now?'

'Moving away from you, heading south.'

'How close can you put me to him?'

'I've only got triangulation from a couple towers, but within a few yards, for sure.'

Frank stared ahead at the fountain. He should not leave this site, but he also couldn't afford to run the risk of losing the phone. 'OK, you lead me to him. Put a call through to Daniels and Markham, and get them to join me and Debbie. You keep an eye on that phone, and we'll chase him down.'

'I think I can help,' Roy suddenly said with excitement. 'It's heading to the airport!'

'Shit! Forget Daniels and Markham – I'll go with Debbie,' Frank said, turning the key in his ignition. He blasted his horn three times rather than calling, waving to her as he gunned the engine until he was alongside her. 'Get in!'

*

17.12 Seattle; 01.12 England

Stephen Orme worked in a small office near the Union Lake, in a shop front on Eastlake East. The place suited him well, because not only was it an ideal site for him to maintain his cover as a tourist officer, his apartment above the shop looked out over Fairview to the water, and he could walk down the stairs to his little boat at the jetty beyond. From there, on his days off, he could carry on his clandestine surveillance of the ships entering and leaving Puget Sound while he maintained the fiction of going fishing. It was a job he adored.

He had spent much of his young adulthood as a naval officer, and if he had been told that in a few years he would be here, living in one of America's most beautiful, friendly and attractive cities, so that he could indulge his fascination for submarines, he would have laughed out loud. But after some years in the navy, he had suffered a bad fall when his helicopter was blown by a gust as he was transhipping, and he was thrown from the open door to the deck. He still had a slight limp from the damage done to his pelvis. Shortly after he had been warned that his active service in Her Majesty's Navy was at an end, a grey little man with a grey smoker's complexion visited him, and soon recruited him to the Service.

His work was done here in his office for the day. Stephen locked the doors, shut down his computer, turned off the plug sockets, and picked up his phone as he walked out to the back. There was a private staircase from here that led upstairs to his apartment on the second floor, and he walked inside with that feeling of freedom. Out behind his apartment there was a deck, and from there he could see out over the water to the Gas Works Park. A nineteen acre site dedicated to the firm that had once taken in coal to make gas for Seattle's lights. Odd to think that people wanted to celebrate the industry of the past, Stephen thought, staring at the dark bronze tanks and pipes. Yet it was always quite full of cars and sightseers.

He walked through to his bedroom and pulled off his suit, carefully hanging his jacket on a hanger, dangling his trousers by the legs until the creases lined up, and inserted them into his press, before pulling on a pair of old blue jeans and a thick pullover. It was an old one his parents had given him when he first became a submariner, and he was as proud of the jumper as he had been to pass the rigorous entrance tests. The only test he had failed was the infamous escape. Each submariner was forced to enter a column of water, and swim up to the top. It was supposed to simulate an escape from a damaged sub, but in Stephen's case it only simulated a bar fight. He had always had a weak vein in his nose, and it burst as he rose through the water. A common enough fault, though, and all he needed was a minor operation before he was eligible for the additional money a submariner could earn.

Tugging on his boots, he crossed to the French window leading to his deck, and unlocked it. As soon he had slid the doors open, he hurtled down the steps to Fairview, crossed the road, and was on the jetty. He loosened the ropes, and dropped into the boat, pulling open the door to the tiny galley and entering. He set the switches on, returned to the outside to turn on the small diesel engine under the deck, and stopped.

'Fancy seeing you here, Stephen,' Jack said.

*

17.34 Seattle; 01.34 England

'He's leaving the airport now – he's turned around and leaving!'

'Shit!' Frank said. 'What the fuck is going on?'

They had followed the signal for the phone all the way to the airport, and now Frank and Debbie were at the main entrance but, as they threw open the car's doors and leaped from the vehicle, Roy's urgent tone came across clearly. They sprang back into the car and Frank jerked the shift into drive again, spinning the wheel and shoving down on the throttle, pressing the bud into his ear. 'The asshole's running us on purpose.'

Debbie said nothing, but she opened her phone and made a call. 'Hi, it's Debbie. Any sign of him?'

She closed the phone a few moments later.

'He's not there. No show.'

'You thought he could have sent us on a chase?'

'Still do. He threw his phone into a car, left it in a cab, put it on a truck. Who knows?'

Frank pursed his lips, and then gave a short nod.

'Call Sandford, tell him to patch the signal through to the locals and have them pick up the driver, see when he could have got the phone. Bloody Case must be back in the city itself. Why'd he send us down here?'

'He isn't a fool. He realised he was being set up,' she said.

'Who by, though?'

'The guy who called through to the UK, I guess. Can we find him?'

'Get on to Sandford. If anyone has a reason to chase him down, it's Sandford after this,' Frank grated and pulled onto the slip road to head back downtown.

'Why him?'

'Because if he doesn't, I'll have his balls for golf.'

*

17.41 Seattle; 01.41 England

Jack watched him as Orme busied himself about the boat. It was a small craft, with a galley and cabin that could have fitted inside a wardrobe, and one diesel engine that chugged like an asthmatic bulldog.

'What was the idea?' Jack asked as they moved away from the jetty.

'You're *persona non grata*, Jack.'

'What's going on?'

'You need to ask the Firm,' Stephen shrugged. 'I'm only a local. They don't tell me anything.'

178

Jack knew that was true. The agents in place would never be told the reasons behind a mission or the planning that went on in the background. Stephen would almost certainly not have any idea about the reasons why he would be thrown to the wolves.

'It makes no bloody sense,' he muttered.

'You've got some enemies, that's all I can say,' Stephen said.

'You were told to betray me, then?'

'I was told to leave you in the cold. I was not to go to meet you at the ferry, and not to meet you again afterwards.'

'On whose orders?'

'Jack, you know better.'

He probably didn't know. And if he did, he wouldn't admit to it. Jack looked round at the water opening up before them. The little engine was puttering smoothly now, and they were moving at about ten knots, he gauged. The wind in his face was cold, and the fine spray that occasionally splashed on him made it feel all the more freezing as he surveyed the grey waters.

'I just don't understand it,' he said.

'Perhaps you've made too many enemies in London?'

'That's no reason to discard me.'

'Really?'

Jack looked up at him. Stephen was staring ahead at the boats, keeping an eye on a yacht that was tacking slowly across the lane.

'What's that supposed to mean?'

'Nothing.'

'What did they say to you?'

Stephen looked down at him and his face was carefully blank. 'I heard about your wife and Jimmy McNeill.'

'What about him?' Stephen said.

'He died, didn't he? Do you think everyone is stupid in the Service, Jack?'

Jack said nothing. He turned and stared ahead as Stephen continued.

'You were one of the very best, I'm told. The networks you had in the old days were supposed to be used for training purposes, they were so efficient. You recruited only the best, and you maintained them well. But when you joined the Scavengers, your wife didn't like it. That's what I heard. She didn't like it when she heard what your job was.'

'She didn't understand. She thought I was just a paid killer.'

'You weren't?'

'No! We were sent in to tidy up when others screwed up, that's all. And sometimes we had to get a bit heavy, but not all the time.'

'But how heavy did you get with the man who took your wife, eh? When your missus leaves, it makes it easier to kill, I suppose.'

'That's bollocks. He was riding his horse and fell into the river. That's all.'

'Not what others think, I'm afraid.'

'I know that. I'm being set up. Starck went to my wife to show her the cell phone traffic on that day. It showed me being near her. Near him, when he died.'

'You should have thought of that. Cell phones don't lie, Jack.'

He gave a dry laugh.

'Really? How about the little fact that my phone never left London?'

Orme looked at him. It was clear that he was struck by the honesty in Jack's face as he asked, 'You sure?'

'Of course I'm bleeding sure. You think I'm a moron who doesn't know phones are guaranteed location finders? Who'd be prick enough to take a phone with him to commit murder in this day and age?'

'Karen told me you'd done it.'

Jack swore. 'So you think they're hanging me out to dry because of that? They'll see me arrested over here to remove me?'

'Yes.'

'Except I'd hardly be less embarrassing if I was in prison over here, would I?' Jack said. 'They'd want me professionally silenced. Is that what they thought, that I may get shot if they send in the FBI to catch me at Seattle?'

'You were supposed to have been armed.'

'What, and they told the cops that I was?' Jack said, shooting a look at Stephen.

'They said you might have had the gun Lewin shot himself with.'

'I had to hand that in, though! Why'd they say that?' Jack wondered. Frank Rand knew he had no gun, but Stephen's words implied that the Firm wanted the police to think he was dangerous.

'Starck told me on the phone.'

'But that's secure, isn't it?'

'Not that line, no,' Stephen said, leaning slightly as the wash from a faster craft pushed his boat until it rocked.

'What were you doing on an unsecure line?' Jack demanded.

'*They* called *me*, Jack,' Stephen said.

'Shit! So they wanted the Yanks to know I was a crook, a killer, and armed, just before they discussed where I was going to meet you?'

'And then told me later on a secure line not to go. I was told you were in the cold. You'd blotted your copy-book, and I wouldn't have to worry about you any more.'

'Shit!'

'Sorry, Jack,' Stephen said, glancing down at him.

'But they wouldn't want me in prison shooting my mouth off,' Jack shook his head. 'So I was supposed to get shot by the cops over here: instant removal of all embarrassment.'

'That's about it, I guess.'

Jack stared unseeing at the waves ahead. There were plenty of small pleasure craft strung along the water heading out to the Sound, and he felt a weird unreality as he gazed at them. Here they were, a series of happy sailors in their boats, sailing along in a line towards the sea to go fishing, to enjoy the sea, or just to enjoy the feel of a rolling deck beneath their feet, and here he was, a marked man. The finger was pointing at him, and he had no escape because all the supports, all the companions and friends he would normally depend upon had decided he was disposable. A slimy piece of old garbage, unnecessary, unwanted. He'd been thrown into a bag ready for disposal, and now he was to be left on the street.

The fucking pricks!

'Starck, then,' he muttered.

He'd get that bastard somehow. One thing he was sure of was, he wasn't going to wait to be caught by the FBI.

'What're you going to do, Jack?' Orme said.

*

17.51 Seattle; 01.51 England

Amiss was in the apartment near the Potomac when his telephone shivered in his pocket. He took it out and studied the picture of Stilson before pressing the receive button.

'Yes?'

'We have them. We followed Orme to his boat and there he met Case. The problem should be resolved soon.'

'Good. Make sure that there is no trace left behind to tie us in. Understand?'

'Yes, sir.'

17.56 Seattle; 01.56 England

Stephen Orme was still eyeing Jack between watching the way ahead.

'Well?'

'How the fuck should I know what I ought to do?' Jack grated. 'I need time to think.'

'If London thinks you're guilty, and they must do if they're going to lay you out to dry like this, you'd be best to disappear, mate,' Stephen said. 'I'd often thought I'd bugger off to Mexico or somewhere, but that's less appealing now because of the drugs gangs. I wouldn't want to end up in the bottom of a Tijuana ditch. Perhaps I'd go further south. Colombia is dangerous for some, but I think you'd find places out in the country that would be safe enough. The rebels have been pretty much wrecked in the last few years. Then there's Argentina. Supposed to be good there. Cheap beef, and good beers.'

'Shut the fuck up, Stephen, will you?' Jack said.

The whole thing made little sense. He was doing his job fine. Sure, Starck said originally that they'd cut him off if he didn't go on the mission, but now he was on his way back, where was the sense in getting rid of him?

'You gave in my report, didn't you?'

'Yes. And the Ice Maiden seemed really interested. The details about the ledger grabbed her, or I'm Pinocchio.'

'So why cut me off now?'

Jack was sure that there was some kind of connection. There had to be: something would make sense of his being left adrift in America having done what he was told. He reviewed his actions in the last week: he had obeyed his orders and gone to Whittier, viewed the shack where Lewin died, assessed his death as murder, and found the ledger. Sure, it had been stolen from him, but that wasn't his fault. The attacks on him were hardly his fault, and he had done nothing untoward since reaching Seattle. Events had forced him to react, that was all. And the responsibility for that lay with the Firm, not him.

'Are you going to shoot me?' Stephen asked.

Jack gave a short laugh.

'Here? In the middle of the lake, with how many hundreds of witnesses all around? Do you think I'm as mad as London seems to reckon?'

'I don't know, Jack. I mean, you're here, on my boat. And since we both know our Service has tried to have you killed, that itself I find a little curious.'

'I have no intention of killing you or anyone else,' Jack said. 'Apart from the guys who tried to shoot me.'

'Ah.'

'Look, can you drop me over there?'

Stephen looked where Jack was pointing. 'Sure. What are you going to do?'

'I wish I bloody knew,' Jack said. 'But I'm bleeding sure Mexico doesn't appeal to me. I've nothing saved or put by.'

'Things are cheap out there,' Stephen said.

'Including my life, if they track me down,' Jack said.

Stephen looked down at him. There was a little grin at the side of his face, and then he cleared his throat with a surprised look on his face. The front of his white Aran jumper grew a huge blotch of red and, as the boat rolled, he toppled forward to his knees.

'What the...?' Jack shouted, and then he heard the crack of the gunshot.

Stephen was smiling still, but now he coughed and a gob of blood came up and trickled from the side of his mouth as he collapsed to lie in the floor of the boat.

'Stephen, shit, man! Don't bloody die, mate!' Jack said desperately, staring about him wildly as he looked for the source of the shot. There was a crunching sound, and he ducked as a splinter of wood two inches long was torn from the steering wheel. Another crackle, and he saw the window on the port side of the cabin suddenly grow a hole. That was when his mind suddenly cleared.

Stephen Orme shivered, and his eyes turned to Jack with the terror of death. He died as Jack tried to think of something soothing to say to him.

But nothing came.

*

17.59 Seattle; 01 59 England

Frank Rand was not in a good mood when he returned to the office. 'Well?' he snapped as he walked into Roy's little chamber.

Roy Sandford looked over at him and felt the strain of the last hours as he shook his head. 'The locals found it. A yellow cab, with a happy Nigerian driver. A legal, but he's unaware of the guy who left the phone in the back. He's had nine or ten payers this afternoon. The one sounds most like your guy was a man he picked up near Hamilton Park over West Seattle.'

'Hamilton?' Frank said, moving to a map on the wall in the main office and staring at it. 'This place?'

'Yes. I've checked. It's got a perfect line-of-sight to the ferry terminal. A way off, but still, with clear air and binoculars…'

'Yeah. Makes sense. The prick!' Frank glared at the map a while longer as though it could give him some inspiration. He was still there when Debbie entered, sipping a coffee. 'You get one for me?'

'Try any sexist bullshit on me, Frank, and you'll be limping for a week,' Debbie said mildly as she went to a free desk. She typed in her password. 'Where'd the cab drop him, Roy?'

'How did you hear that?' Frank demanded.

'I asked around. The guys at the coffee machine were gossiping. They said he was seen taking a metro bus downtown, and then an inspector saw a strange guy with a rucksack take a cab. Well?'

'He was dropped off outside the Benaroya Hall. The Garden of Remembrance there. You know it?'

'Yes,' she said. 'I wonder why?'

Frank shook his head and added, 'There's a reason for everything this asshole's doing, I reckon. And it's not just to make us look stupid.'

'Is he rational?' Debbie asked. 'He isn't behaving rational.'

'What isn't rational? He sure seemed it in Anchorage and Whittier. The only thing I noticed was a dislocation. You know, like a guy who's not all there. But I thought it was just the reaction. He'd just been shot at, after all.'

'Or was he just dissociated from people. I've known some who are sociopaths. So 've you, Frank.'

'He didn't strike me like that. He was used to action, and I guess if he was a Brit agent, that ain't surprising, but I didn't see him as a crazy.'

He considered his own words for a moment. 'I'm going to go look at the place he was dropped, just see if there was something there. You reckon it was outside the Benaroya Hall, Roy?'

184

'Yeah,' Roy said. He was about to say more, when his phone rang. 'Agent Sandford? Yeah. Oh – OK, sir, yes.'

He cut the line and glanced at Frank with a worried look in his eyes.

'I've been recalled.'

Frank nodded, but not without a tensing of his jaw muscles.

'Who by? We are in the middle of something here.'

'It was Peter Amiss, sir.'

'Shit!' Frank said. 'Debbie, get hold of HR and see if you can get someone else with Sandford's skills, will ya? I'll be back in an hour or so.'

He strode out of the office and over to the lift, where he thumbed the button.

It was infuriating the way that personnel could be pulled out halfway through a mission like this. Usually agents would be left in place until a situation was declared complete, an investigation finished. But since the cutbacks and the reorganisations post-Waco and 9/11, specialists were considered too important to be left in field offices. He was still smarting as he entered the lift and took the ride to the underground car park. It was tempting to go beyond, to the huge underground target range, but he didn't have time and the release of firing twenty or thirty rounds could wait.

He climbed into his car and started the engine, the tyres screeching on the surface, and took the ramp up. At the top, he looked both ways before booting the engine and pulling away, still in a fury.

The black Ford sedan that pulled away from the kerb as he passed didn't grab his attention, nor the two men inside.

*

18.03 Seattle; 02.03 England

Jack darted to the wheel and took hold, spinning it about and taking the boat over across the middle of the lanes, earning himself an angry blast on a horn from a fast-moving motor boat that had to swerve to avoid him. Jack paid it no attention; he was still searching for the men who had fired at him. There was a fast boat over towards the northern shore, but he saw no one on it. If he could guess, the bullets were from a handgun. There was no significant noise, which made him think there was probably a silencer on the gun. He knew that the target of a silenced gun could sometimes hear the shot, because a silencer could act like a laser, focusing sound waves in the one direction, behind the bullet, while the silencer's baffles dissipated all

185

the other sound energy. While a revolver wasn't efficient because of noise blowing out between chamber and barrel, and automatics threw out noise with the discarded shell case, either would be quiet enough here on the water.

Whoever it was, he was a good shot, Jack guessed, but thrown off by the bobbing of Stephen's boat or the motion of his own. He must make more of the moments he had. He pulled the wheel around again, crouched behind the cabin, and searched all about him for the source of the shots, but there was nothing he could see.

And then he caught sight of a flash and whiff of smoke, and knew he had them.

It was a low, fast motorboat with two Yamaha engines at back that had been two or three boats behind him, further into the middle of the lake. There were two men aboard, both in dark trousers and with leisure jackets on that looked out of place, as though their trousers were from suits. One wore a pale brown hoody, the other had on a university-style jacket with pale body and darker sleeves, and both were staring at him. The university man had the look of the partner of the Hispanic in the hospital, and Jack nodded to himself. He was being chased, then.

The other guy with the hoodie crouched, and Jack saw him stretch out his hands. A puff again, and Jack threw himself sideways as though hit. He peered back over the gunwale, but he saw that his feint had not persuaded the two. The boat edged closer to the middle of the lane, and now it was past him, it began to make a long turn to follow him. Once behind him, the two would have a clear field of fire, Jack knew.

He pulled the map from his pocket and peered at it, steering with his left hand, and then yanked on the throttle and pulled it wide. This little boat was never going to beat two Yamahas, but he didn't have to make it easy for them.

To the north, he saw the bronze towers and pipes of the old gas works and, on instinct, he steered for it. There was a marina to the left of it, and he thought he could see another to the right, but he aimed the boat straight for the towers, hoping he could survive the distance.

There was another whack and a starburst appeared in the fibreglass of the cabin. He looked down, and saw Stephen Orme was not going to get up again, and then concentrated on the beach dead ahead. He would have to pass through all the queue of boats which were heading out to sea, and he knew that he would make some enemies when he did that, but better some enraged boatmen than a bullet in the head. Another strike, but at least the engine was still working, and when he glanced back behind him at the fast boat, he saw that the men were arguing. One probably wanted to hurry and finish the job, he guessed, but he was also convinced that the other was reluctant to commit murder in full view of all the pleasure boats in the lake. They were running risks enough just firing at him. Fortunately they were only shooting when they thought that they wouldn't be seen, and that knowledge gave him an idea. As he and his boat concealed the two men from other boats, he yanked the rudder around, and the boat rolled wildly. It made the next bullets miss the boat completely.

And now he was in among the boats, earning himself bellowed insults, and he gave them the finger, hoping that at least one would remember him and his face, before he was through and nearer the shore. Now, when he looked back, the two in the boat were concealing their weapons below the gunwales as they passed through the line of boats, but soon they would be through, and then they could push the throttle wide, he knew, and even as he had the thought, he saw the prow of their speedboat lift suddenly. They were coming straight at him, the vessel bouncing more on the tops of the waves, jerking and splashing as it thundered on. He had a few moments, no more. As he held his course, he reached down to Stephen and felt his pockets. There was a wallet in his rear pocket, a set of keys in another. No sodding gun, though. Jack took them and stuffed them both into his pocket. They may come in useful if he escaped.

He set his boat at the marina on the right of the steel columns, and edged nearer and nearer to the shore, casting a look over his shoulder as he heard the slap, slap, slap of the water on the speedboat's hull, and then, as he thought they must be about to slow to shoot him from close range, he flung his boat about. It turned sluggishly, but the pursuers hadn't expected even such a simple manoeuvre, and they couldn't stop in time. He carried on while the two Yamahas roared, and the speedboat took a wide turn to follow him again, but now he was within yards of the shore, and he turned in, deliberately running the craft up the mud and shingle beach. He snatched up his rucksack and ran forward to the prow, leaping down into the edge of the water and hurrying on up the grassy bank. The speedboat was thundering on towards him, and then it slowed, and he broke off to the left as he heard that, because it must mean that the men were preparing to shoot again. He heard a bullet strike soggily into the grass near him, then

187

saw another pockmark appear in front of him and to his right, and then he was behind a tree, and he could open his stride as the ground levelled. He passed by the great gas storage tanks, pelting on as fast as he could, the breath thundering in his lungs, until he reached the farther edge of the towers.

Chain-link fencing surrounded him; he followed around it until he saw a path ahead that led through some bushes to a car park beyond. If he could make it to that, it would be difficult for pursuit with weapons.

Glancing over his shoulder, he saw that the two had leaped from their launch and were following him with determination. That itself was a shock. He had half expected them to give up the chase when he reached the land, but now they were running straight at him.

He concentrated on the way ahead. There were people all over the grass here, walking about and enjoying the sun with children in pushchairs or strolling hand in hand. Jack felt the pain starting in his lungs as he ran, and it grew to be too much, and he could have fallen, sobbing. But to stop meant death. He ran on, the agony flaring like a starburst in his chest, panting with the effort. There was only a matter of yards, then feet, then he was on a flat pathway, and he threw himself forwards through trees to the car park beyond, and at last he could stop. He threw himself behind a truck, hurling his back against the rear tyre, and took a long, gasp of air, before grabbing for Stephen's keys in his pocket. Gripping them in his fist, two keys protruding between three fingers, he felt ready.

*

16.11 Seattle; 02.11 England

The first came pelting round the truck like he was never going to stop. A large, bull-necked bastard with cropped hair. Jack rose in one fluid movement: his left hand grabbed the man's university jacket by his lapel and pulled him round, over his out-thrust leg. The man couldn't stop himself falling: Jack used his momentum against him, blocking his legs, and the spin hurled the man headfirst into the rear panel of the truck. His head struck the vehicle on the corner where the rear of the cab bent around to form the rear bed, and there was a sickening crunch as bone broke under the force of the impact. Jack didn't hesitate. He punched, a Karate blow, the keys puncturing the thin bone of the man's temple. He was taking no risks.

Jack dropped to his knees and grabbed the guy's waistband. There was a gun there, in a holster at his hip. Jack had it in his hand, a

188

Glock, he knew, and he racked it quickly to make sure it was loaded. A cartridge ejected, and Jack knew it was loaded and ready. He felt the comfort of the safety bar under his forefinger, his left hand supporting, and crouched, peering under the truck to see where the other man was, looking for feet, and it was that which saved him. A slug passed over his shoulder, creasing his coat, and slapping into the metal of the truck's bed. It dented, but the bullet fragmented, and Jack swore as he ran, bent double, round to the other side of the truck. The bullets must be frangible rounds, designed to expand on hitting soft tissue. He paused a moment at the other side of the truck, gripped the Glock like a priest holding a crucifix against a demon, and then he was away again, darting quickly past the truck, then a Chrysler, then a Ford Fiesta, until he was concealed behind a Ford Taurus.

He grasped the wing mirror and pulled. It bent back and he swore, and then he reached inside the housing and jerked hard. The glass came away, trailing some wires, and he used this as a periscope, quickly searching until he saw a low figure with a hoodie slip around the Chrysler. Jack could see where he was heading, and quickly moved to the front of the Taurus, keeping low, the mirror held under the car. He saw legs, and dropped to his belly. There were two feet visible below the Fiesta, and he fired without thinking. Two shots quickly, aiming just below the ankles, then three more; he fired until he heard the scream and saw the body fall.

There were shrieks at the sound of the shots, a wild, panicked scream from a woman and, as Jack rose, he saw people scurrying away in every direction. He approached the fallen man cautiously. He was in his early thirties and heavily built. His Glock, fitted with a long silencer, lay a few feet from his hands. With his ankles lacerated, he must have been in agony, but still he flailed for his gun as Jack approached. While Jack watched, he pulled a small crucifix from under his shirt and kissed it.

'Don't try it,' Jack said. 'Come on, give up.'

'Fuck you!' the man blurted, and threw himself bodily towards the gun.

Jack fired until the gun was empty.

*

18.23 Seattle; 02.23 England

The Garden of Remembrance was a pretty little scene, Frank Rand thought. He stood, staring down at the plaque in front of him. 'And so it's goodnight, my darling,' he read. 'I send you all my love.' All the comments were from the dead to their parents, to their women, to their loved ones. It was the sort of honest, admiring display that his countrymen did so well, Frank thought. It made him proud for their sacrifice.

There was little here that he could imagine was relevant to the investigation, though. He sat at a bench and listened to the sound of running water from a water feature and tried to put himself in the mind of the man he hunted. The guy was a Brit, so he probably had little idea about this city. If he was still here, and hadn't taken a rental or caught a train ride, he would be feeling pretty lonely. He must know that someone had betrayed him and, although he knew the Americans had the technology to catch him, he would be feeling pretty desperate.

That thought brought on another. Was it right that Roy had managed to track him down? After all, with all the technology at his disposal, it had been the error made by the Brits that had led them to him. And it was unlike the Brits to make such an elementary error as calling on open lines. Especially since they knew all about Echelon from their own involvement. And someone had passed information to Houlican about the man, too.

It was enough to set him thinking about the whole course of the hunt for Jack Case, and the conclusions did not strike him as satisfying. He was still sitting there on the bench when his phone trilled.

'Rand.'

'Frank, we have multiple shootings at the old gas works up at the park, you know the place?'

'Yeah – why, what's been... you think it's him? Have they found him?'

'No, but sounds like he found some people.'

Frank ran to his car. He didn't see the black vehicle half a block away that pulled out behind him.

*

18.31 Seattle; 02.31 England

Jack didn't have any blood on him, which was a relief. He needed to escape this place, and that meant getting away without people staring.

The gun was empty, and he hadn't time to search the bodies for more ammo. He walked away from the place, pulling out a fold of his shirt and wiping the pistol as he went until he was sure it was clean,

190

and then he dropped it into a bin at the edge of the car park, walking quickly but without urgency. He was a man on the way to a meeting, not a felon leaving the scene of a crime. He took out his map of the city and held it in his hand like a tourist. Sirens were approaching, but he kept on going. Hopefully there would be no one with a description of him yet. Chances were, no one would be able to. Witnesses of shootings tended to notice the gun, not the gunman. Their eyes were drawn to the muzzle, and their testimony was at best doubtful.

Crossing a road, he found himself in a residential neighbourhood, and he kept his eyes on the cars parked at either side. It was some while before he found an old and battered vehicle that suited him. It was a VW Rabbit, and with the windows wide, he could see the tatty interior. It was parked along a narrow alley, and he slipped inside it, pulling at the wires while his other hand moved the steering wheel to make sure that there was no lock. There wasn't. It took a couple of attempts to start, but then he was away, driving north, and checking his route on the map. He found his way to North Pacific Street, then to the Eastlake Avenue, heading back down to the apartment where Stephen had lived.

He parked the car four blocks away in a dark little alley, and left it, striding purposefully to Stephen's place, approaching from the lakeside.

It was a pleasant flat: neat and tidy, with prints of the sea on the walls. Jack moved through it in a hurry, his eyes searching for the safe that he was sure must be here. He went into the bedroom and looked at the door. It was immensely heavy, and had solid hinges and a Banham lock. This was the secure room for Stephen. The houses of spies and other diplomatic staff would usually have safe areas in their homes so that if they were endangered for any reason, there was always a place to which they could run and lock themselves inside. And inside there would be the safe, too.

Jack had not been on the more recent safe-breaking courses, but he didn't think that a safe here in Seattle would have been changed recently for a newer, high-tech model. The city was not high on the list of dangerous locations, unlike those in Arab countries and European capitals. There the lack of trust from the Foreign Office tended to ensure that diplomatic staff had the most up-to-date safes and security.

He was right. The safe was partly concealed in the floor of the bedroom under a rug, and when he looked at it, he was relieved to see that it had a simple key, which was on the key ring he had taken from Stephen. He opened it and reached inside.

There were no codes. Only an ancient Browning Hi Power, two magazines of 9mm ammunition, and five thousand dollars in cash. Jack took out the money and riffled through it. Luckily it was all in different denominations. He put two hundred dollars in his wallet and stuffed the rest into his rucksack along with the magazines, but he hesitated over the Browning before putting that in there as well. Brownings were invented before the Second World War, and this one had the look of a collector's piece. The slide was browned, the original steel blueing worn away. Jack pulled the slide open, and peered in. It was clear, but the slide rattled slightly – very old, very worn. He sniffed at it, and could detect the chemical odour of gun oil, but there was not much. Still, it was better than no gun at all. Men who were determined to kill him had chased him halfway around America, and he had no idea why, except for Lewin's story and the ledger. It had to be something about that. And all he could do was try to return to Alaska to find out what they wanted with him.

No – there had to be another way to learn what he wanted. But first he had to leave this place. The cops would soon be here.

He shut the safe, locked it, and walked to the back, locking the door as he went. Then, crossing the road, he shouldered his rucksack and marched back towards the town. And as he walked, he threw the Orme's keys into the water.

*

18.46 Seattle; 02.46 England

Debbie watched as Frank jumped from his car and joined her.

'Well, Debbie?'

'A man was on a small boat, rammed it into the beach, jumped and ran up here. All the way, two guys in another boat were shooting at him, and they chased him up to here. He slugged one over there, beside the truck, and then came up and shot this one.'

'Slugged him?'

'He may come round, but if he does, he'll have a headache for a year. Whole of the top of his skull is cracked, according to the medics, and he's some trauma to the temple. They didn't hold much hope he'd live. Took him to the Harborview Medical Centre.'

'Make sure there's a guard on him there,' Frank said, and shook his head in disbelief as he gazed about him. 'How'd he do all this?'

'He appears to have been unarmed. Witnesses say these two were packing and shot at him, but he didn't return. Not until he'd got one down. That one had a Glock 23.'

'Right.'

The Glock model 23 was the big brother to the 27. Both the 27 and the 23 fired .40 calibre bullets, larger and more deadly than 9mm, which was why the FBI itself issued them. The smaller, lighter 27 had a shorter barrel and cut-back grip to make it more easily concealable, but in every other way it was the same gun. The FBI allowed its agents to take that instead of the 23 for concealed carry, if the agents preferred.

'So, if that one had a Glock, what'd the other one carry?'

'I'm assuming Case took his gun. No sign of it around here.'

'Shit. Any idea who these two are?'

'They're not known.'

'ID?'

'Nothing. Not even credit cards.'

'They must have something on them. Driving licences?'

'Nope. Nothing.'

That made Frank frown.

'Anything on their boat?'

'No. Not on theirs.'

'What does that mean?'

'There was another body in the little boat. Before you ask, no, there's no ID on him either. But I checked with the Department for Licensing, and they reckon this was owned by a Brit called Stephen Orme.'

'Who's he?'

'Don't know. But on a hunch I called the number Roy Sandford found. You know, the one talking to the Brits about your friend Jack Case? Made a phone ring in the boat, and when I checked in his call logs, one number was the one from the cab.'

'Show me the body.'

'Over here, boss.' She led him across the grass to the beach where the two boats lay beached. 'You think Case could'a killed him?'

'Could have, I guess,' Frank said. 'I just didn't have him down as a killer. Anyway, he didn't have a gun until he took the guy's Glock in the car park, did he?'

'Christ,' she said, and winced as he set his lips. She knew he was deeply religious and could be offended by blasphemy. She must remember to moderate her language in front of him. 'Sorry.'

'No problem.'

There was a ladder beside the craft already, and Frank ascended, peering down into the craft at the wide-eyed blond man. 'When he was shot, they did it well.'

'He'd have died quick,' she commented.

'In answer, no.'

'Eh?'

'I don't know, but why'd Case shoot this one guy, then get chased by two others? Makes no sense.'

'That's what I reckoned. Case had no gun on him, or didn't return fire anyhow, according to the folks all about here.'

'Anyone actually confirm it was him?'

She nodded.

'Three women pretty certain it was him soon as I showed them his mugshot. You can't be certain of ID in a moment of stress, but two of 'em looked pretty convincing. Reckon it was him in the boat, and the two gunmen took some potshots at him. Sort of looked like one bullet killed this guy, and Case managed to get away.'

'Poor bastard. He'll be running now.'

'If he has a brain, he'll be hiding really carefully. They've been chasing him all the way from Alaska.'

*

18.53 Seattle; 02.53 England

He had no plan. Jack walked as though walking was the sole reason for his existence, his entire body was devoted to it. At first he headed east, and found himself in a quiet suburban area with large houses, grey or brown, with pleasant shaded roads from the tall trees. Then he turned southwards towards the downtown area. He saw a street sign and read 14th Avenue East, and nodded, checking that against the map he had memorised. The attraction of the American cities was this grid pattern. It made navigation much easier, but without a firm destination, he was no better off than in a British city.

Who were those guys? He had to figure out who was trying to kill him. They looked like agents from the FBI or CIA, but that made no sense. Why would they want to kill him? If it was somehow because of the journal and Lewin's death, there was no justification for members of the US counter espionage teams to want to hurt him.

Or was there?

He would find out. He had created the Scavengers to do this. The Scavengers existed to clear up mess and this was worse than any other operation he had known. In the past Jack had worked deep undercover, especially in Russia. There he had sometimes been a rogue agent seeking other rogues, but no matter where he had served, he had been aware of the rules. British agents were not supposed to carry weapons, they were not supposed to kill or maim the citizens of other nations. When he was running his men and women in Russia and East Germany, he was not permitted to take too many risks, to participate in black ops: he was not allowed to move without approval being given first. And when the decision was taken to disband his Joes, he had no say in the matter. He was just told to go and pay them off. And many had died. Well, fuck that! He wasn't going to die here.

Filled with a new resolve, Jack stopped and took stock. Looking about him, he took careful note of the area. This street was pleasant, with its shading trees and comfortable houses, but there ahead of him he could see the first tall towers of downtown Seattle. Right, that gave him an objective: suddenly his mind was operating on a different level.

He had been betrayed by someone – the calls on unsecured lines to Orme proved that. Those guys in Whittier could have been from anywhere, but for others to reach him here in Seattle, for him to be chased and for Orme to have been followed, leading them to Jack, that meant an intelligence organisation. It meant someone was deliberately searching for him, and was getting help, either from the US agencies, or from the UK. He didn't know which, but whichever it was, he was screwed unless he could take the initiative.

The rules had been the rock on which his life had always been fixed. Once, just once, he had stepped outside the rules. Well, now someone else had taken the rule book and tossed it through the window.

Fuck them. He was going to find out who was responsible. Somebody had set him up, and he was going to make them pay.

*

05.12 England

Paul Starck had still been thinking things through as he drove home. All the way since leaving Claire at her house, he had been replaying their conversation in his mind. It had seemed clear to him that Claire had not thought Jack could have been responsible for Jimmy's death, and Paul's words had hit her hard. Too hard, perhaps. It was that which grabbed his attention as he drew up last night.

He had been told to contact the Ice Maiden as soon as he got back, but screw her. She could wait. He lit a cigarette and peered through his windscreen while he smoked, the window down to let the smoke gust out of the car.

The fucking fags would kill him off. There was no doubt in his mind. The medical officer at Vauxhall kept on telling him that at the rate he was smoking, he'd not last another ten years, and even if he did, he'd soon start to suffer from failing circulation, and have one leg or both amputated. Well, that was fine. He didn't particularly mind the idea of death. He had no family, he had no dependents, but he did enjoy the weed, and he'd be fucked if he'd allow some quack from HR to dictate his pleasures. It was bad enough that the do-gooders had managed to prevent all smoking in the offices, so that now he was forced to sit outside on a terrace to get his regular fixes. That would be how Karen would fire him in the end: the amount of time he spent outside. Bitch.

He wound up the window, left the car and slammed the door. Jangling his keys, he climbed the steps to his house.

When he bought this place, Notting Hill Gate wasn't too expensive. It was only in recent years that the prices had rocketed, especially after the film had been made here. Very satisfactory.

It was a Regency house built on four floors, with a basement beneath. He had been advised to acquire this house because the cellar had a reinforced concrete ceiling, installed at some time during the Second World War, and when a fresh, young agent, he had been advised that this could help him. Perhaps after the nuclear holocaust it was felt that there would be a need for spies to ensure the continuation of government. He didn't care what the reason was; it made an excellent storage area.

He walked to the first floor, where he had a large kitchen and dining room, and there he grabbed a large cut-glass tumbler and decanter of brandy, taking them downstairs with him. The door to the basement was under his staircase, and he unlocked the two Banham locks and entered, turning on the light. Pulling the door closed behind him, he walked cautiously down the steps.

It was uncarpeted here, and he walked to the little metal desk which he had liberated from the Ministry of Defence, and sat on the old office chair leaking ancient foam rubber, setting the glass before him and half-filling it. There was a carton of two hundred cigarettes on a low shelf, courtesy of the resident spook in Paris. Beside it was a hollowed out piston from a Spitfire engine, which he used as an ashtray. He took a pack, lighting a cigarette from an ancient Ronson desk lighter and reached down to the safe bolted to the floor and two walls. It took a while to work the fiddly dial and pull out the files.

One was a copy of Jack Case's personnel file, and he read it again. The days in Moscow, in Berlin, and the brief stint in Prague were all well documented, with few obvious holes. That there were holes, Starck did not doubt. Every good officer would keep something back, but Jack's secrets were well concealed.

Starck took a long pull at his brandy. He was tired of all this – the subterfuge, the deceits. He had given up his life for the Service, and had precious little to show for it. With the latest penchant for saving money, he knew full well that his own position was precarious. He was one of the old lags, the kind who was less and less necessary now. Politicians only saw the need for young computer whizz-kids, and there was a positive lusting for some semi-psychopathic bullies to join in with Broughton's lads, to maintain the fiction that the British Secret Service had a purpose and mission in life, but the actual intelligence analysts, like Starck, were not valued at all. Not any more.

Which was why he had become so disgusted with the Service.

There were some who, at his time of life, would have said that they had wasted their whole lives. That was not the sort of whining complaint he would tolerate. Better to try to always keep on going. He had once heard a man say that the most important fights an agent would participate in were not outside the Service with enemies; they were all internal – within. And it was true. An agent could be damned good out there in the field, but if he didn't have cheerleaders back at Vauxhall Cross, all his efforts would be in vain. A man had to have supporters or all his work would be forgotten, or, worse, passed off as another's.

Starck lit another Rothman's from the stub of the last, and inhaled deeply. It may well be toxic, but what a glorious poison it was! He opened the second file and looked through it.

He was irked by the way that good agents were destroyed for no reason. Jack Case was one such. In the past Starck would have moved heaven and earth to protect his Joes, but Karen had forced him to betray Jack. There was a crawling worm of guilt in his belly at the thought of what he had done.

The Ice Maiden was too quick to see her own opportunities. She had shafted Jack as keenly as she was shafting Starck himself now. She was a spider, trapping all power and position in her webs. She didn't even give the poor bastards a shag first; there was no need for her to try to sleep her way to the top, not when so many poor saps were prepared to help her.

That was how she had risen to her own prominent position – reporting directly to the DDG, in charge of Starck and his Scavengers, in charge of Broughton's Bullies, in charge of liaison with the Brothers in America. She had a grasp of all of the power and influence within the Service.

He hated the bitch.

Starck returned the files to the safe. And then he leaned back in his chair and gazed at the ceiling speculatively before draining his glass and refilling it. He lit another Rothman's, and wiped his eyes. Then he picked up the telephone, dialling Karen's home number.

'Hello? Ah, Karen. Yes, it's me. Paul.'

'I was expecting you to call a long time ago.'

He leaned back in his chair.

'I've spent most of the day with Claire. Busy, busy, busy.'

'And?'

'She appeared to have no idea that her beloved could have had anything to do with Jimmy's death.'

'And now?'

'I think it's fair to say that now she has a different opinion.'

'Good.'

'Are the Brothers aware of our man over there?'

'There have been no comments so far,' Karen said. 'I find that strange. I'd have expected them to recognise him against the video of him killing those men. They'd surely have realised he was with us by now?'

'I don't know,' Starck said. He rubbed a hand over his face, suddenly tired. He had been up too long. 'She will do what you want, I think.'

'What do you mean?'

'You want her to try to call him, don't you. So that she will help flush him from his telephone silence. That way, the Americans will be able to find him. Soon as he turns on his phone, he'll receive her call and he'll be nailed. Well, I've done your dirty deed for you, Karen, my dear.'

'Don't patronize me, Paul.'

'I don't think it's me doing the patronizing, Karen.'

He put the phone down and stubbed out the last cigarette before swinging the safe door shut and spinning the dial. Standing, he carried his glass and bottle upstairs, where he opened the two Banhams and climbed up to the next level, and sat at his table with the brandy before him. Grunting to himself deep in his throat, he shrugged and lit a last cigarette before bed.

There was one thing she had said that surprised him. She was right – it was curious that the Americans hadn't kept a closer eye on Jack since the attack in the tunnel. Not only was it surprising that they hadn't kept track of him, it was still more odd that she had allowed Jack to go, knowing the possible risk of discovery.

It was almost as though she wanted him discovered from the outset.

*

05.45 Langley; 10.45 London

Roy Sandford was very glad to be home again. Very Nice was at home, and when he arrived, the first thing he did was ask her if she wanted to go find a bar. His call from the deputy had implied he wasn't needed until the next morning, and after a few days in Seattle he deserved a little rest and relaxation, he reckoned.

Now, when the alarm went off, he woke with a lurch, half expecting to see Frank Rand standing over him accusingly. It was a moment or two before his brain became alive to the fact that he was in his own apartment again. Very Nice wasn't with him. After making love last night, with her long hair cool and silken against his breast and her little silver necklace cold on his chest as she lifted and sank against his groin, she had refused to remain. 'I have to get up early too, Roy.'

'All the more reason to stay.'

'Do these look like my work clothes?' she said, as she pulled on the vest-top and skirt.

He had to admit they didn't, but then he didn't worry too much about that. 'You look good enough to eat whatever you wear,' he said.

'Thanks,' she said, 'but I want to keep my job.'

She threw him a quick smile, and the sight of it warmed him in a way he hadn't known for a long time, and then she was gone, and he had soon fallen into a contented doze.

Today, though, he had a new job, and he wondered what it might be. He was up and dressed by six, and drinking coffee, and it was as he put the coffee mug down by the sink that his mobile rang.

'Yeah?'

'Roy, it's Peter Amiss. I should like to see you this morning when you get in.'

'Sure, sir. I'll be in in a half hour.'

'Come straight up.'

Peter put the phone down and smiled to himself. He had a feeling that he was growing more indispensable to the deputy director, and that was all to the good, he reckoned. Maybe soon he'd get a promotion, something with a raise, and be able to afford a house. That'd be good. He was on his way up.

*

04.21 Seattle; 12.21 London

The rumble of traffic here was loud, and Jack woke with a feeling of deep muscle soreness throughout his back and legs. He was getting too old for this crap. He rolled over, trying to find sleep, but it proved too elusive, and within half an hour he rose and boiled water to make some foul instant coffee from the room's kettle as he mused over the events of the previous day.

It had not taken him long to find his way back to the downtown area of Seattle, and in the middle of the huge Northgate mall he found a telephone kiosk where he could buy another sim card and telephone to replace the one he had left in the cab. He wouldn't chuck out his Blackberry. That he could use again back in England, if he ever returned, but he dare not now. He could be traced too easily. Someone in England had decided to throw him to the wolves, and that meant his number must have been given to the FBI, surely, along with any other details that could help them find him.

Who, though? Why would someone want to ditch him in this way?

Nearby there was a JC Penny store, and he wandered inside. He couldn't return to the hotel for his old clothes now. The hotel would be watched.

Soon he had clean T shirts, spare trousers, underwear, a beanie hat, a warm jacket filled with down, a light jacket, and a small suitcase with roller wheels and an extending handle, into which he threw everything. Nearby, he found a drug store, in which he bought hair dye and a pack of razors. In a toilet, he transferred the Browning and bullets to the new bag. Then he took a cab and rode over to the south and east, watching for anyone following. He had the cabbie drop him off a few blocks away and spent half an hour in a café considering his next move, watching for anyone who could have tailed him.

First, a room to sleep the night, then he would have to leave this city. Those were his priorities.

He paid and left the café, and as he wandered along the sidewalk, he saw what looked like Frank Rand in a black sedan. Without thinking, he slipped in through a large entrance, and found himself in the coach station.

Cops: there were two he could see, and he decided he had little choice other than to continue inside the station to allay suspicions.

The first was loitering near the ticket booth, chatting to the ticket seller; the second was out by the stairs that led down to the coach park below. On the wall there was a small map that showed where everything was in the building, and Jack saw that the stairs leading to the coach park itself travelled along a tunnel. There was a second entrance to the tunnel. The officer by the ticket booth paused and turned to frown at him.

It was enough for Jack. He pulled off his down jacket and shoved it into his new bag. His decision had been made. He needed to win some time to plan his next move. Wearing the same clothes now as in the boat, he reasoned that he must have already been marked. He left the bag at the door and, with his rucksack at his side, strode out quickly with his head down.

He walked out to the steps, ignoring the ticket sellers. He almost made it when there was a sudden shout from the ticketing office and, as the cry came, the agent at the stairs turned and saw Jack.

Jack had little time to cover the distance. Already the agent at the stairs was grabbing for his pistol. Jack leaped forward, hurled his backpack, and dived, legs foremost, scissoring. The cop saw the bag hurtling toward him, and tried to draw his sidearm while avoiding it, but couldn't avoid Jack as well. He got his gun clear of the leather just as Jack's legs caught his knees, and his feet slid on the smooth concrete floor. He went down, his gun hand hitting the concrete to break his fall, but Jack was already there, counting on the fact that the other agent wouldn't fire in case he hit his companion. Jack grabbed the officer's gun, but the agent was strong, and he reached up to

Jack's throat. Jack twisted, both hands on the gun, rolling, but couldn't wrestle it from the man, so he stopped trying. He gripped the pistol as tightly as he could, and slammed it against the floor. The man grunted, but his hand was on Jack's neck now and, as both sucked in the air from between their clenched jaws, Jack knew he wouldn't last long if his windpipe was gripped.

He heard the bellow to '*Freeze*! Hands in the air, Asshole!' but neither man was listening. Jack head-butted twice, hard, felt the crunch as the man's nose was smashed, and rolled the two of them away, aiming for the stairs. He felt himself falling. He and the agent fell down two or three steps. Then Jack could shift – he bunched up his legs, waited, and then shoved hard. The agent was flung away, and Jack was straight after him, grabbing the pistol with his left hand, and chopping down at his throat with his right. The man gave an agonised, hissing gurgle and clutched at his throat, desperately trying to breathe. Jack wrenched his pistol away, and snatched the radio from the man's pocket, before running along the corridor. He glanced around as he went, raised the pistol to the ceiling, and fired two shots quickly in a double-tap, then a third to deter the man chasing him.

*

The second cop had reached his comrade when the three shots rang out; he ran to the wall, slamming against it, his gun ready. He tensed himself, keyed up with adrenaline, and snapped a quick look round the corner. Out and back. At the far side there was a series of stairs rising to the main hall again, which led down to the coach park below.

He risked another look. No sign of the Brit. He took a breath, and was out in the corridor, his gun up and ready. With a one step at a time shuffle, he began to make his way along the wall, sidling with his eye committed to the sight picture over his handgun. No one there. No one there. The first staircase approached. On the left, no one visible. On the right, a gaping maw where the stairs led down. He hesitated, turned and span… No one there. Back, to rest against the wall, and…There was a barrel at his ear. Jack's hand snaked around and took the pistol from his unresisting hand.

'The stairs at the far end go back up top again, you know,' Jack said conversationally. 'Now, I don't know who you are, and I'm really sorry, but I don't have time for this shit.'

He clubbed the man once behind his ear, and he fell like a pole-axed steer.

Jack took his radio, and strode fast to the entrance steps. He hurried up the stairs, took his case and exited quickly. The ticket officer had disappeared. He dropped one handgun into the trash bin by the entrance, dropped a radio on the ground and stamped on it hard, before picking up the second and pressing the send button on the radio. 'Two officers down, gunman in shooting at the—' he looked up at the signs 'King County Metro Bus station. All units respond.' He lifted the pistol and fired twice into the air near the radio, then tossed both away and strode outside.

A taxi was passing down Yesler. He hailed it and climbed in as the sound of police sirens came to his ears. By the time the cops arrived at the bus station, black-clad officers with riot guns and rifles at the ready, he was already driving past the Qwest stadium. He took the cab up to the docks, and left it there.

*

That was last night. Mission accomplished. Now his clothes, his features, his hair, would all be sought. He had changed his clothes behind some old hoardings. He discarded the old ones under a manhole cover in a car park, and he pulled on a beanie hat to conceal his hair before walking five blocks to catch a fresh taxi in his new clothes.

He found a hotel near Eastgate, and used the spare passport and ID that he already had, not the ones Orme had given him that day in the restaurant. This morning he had carefully shaved his hair into a high widow's peak and dyed it a pale blonde. He felt a different man. With his new hairstyle he reckoned he could probably pass by the two police from last night without them recognising him. The photo in this new passport matched his changed appearance.

The rumble continued, a never-ending thundering, and when he stared out through the grimy window, he could see the 405 interstate with trucks and cars shooting past all the time. It was mesmerising, or maybe it was just attractive for him to see such a proof of normalcy. Either way, he stood there, bare-chested, staring at all the vehicles, his mind blank except for the dream of running from here, catching a plane, and hurrying back home. There had to be a way to escape all this, he thought.

He could call in to Vauxhall. That's what he ought to do, he knew. Get back there. Phone them to demand help.

With that thought he had a picture in his mind of Starck, baring those yellow fangs of his as he screwed his face into the semblance of regret as he denied knowing Jack's name, denied knowing anything about him.

Jack knew that he was disposable. And Starck would surely take pleasure in dropping him. Jack was damaged goods. He could see Karen's sad, slightly ashamed smile as she agreed with Starck that Jack should be ditched. He was expendable.

Sod them. Jack knew enough to make more embarrassment than those two could possibly imagine.

But he was lonely. He stared at his old Blackberry, then at the new throw-away.

No. He must wait before using a phone. It was too dangerous still right now.

*

07.24 Langley; 12.24 London

The office was as dark and quiet as before, but this time there was another man with the deputy director.

'Sandford,' he said, nodding to him as Roy walked into the room.

He was a small man in his early sixties, clad in a dark blue suit, short and scrawny, with the look of a professor about him. Pale brown eyes blinked quickly behind his rimless spectacles and he put Roy in mind of a vulture, with his large nose and thin frame, the way his head was held low on his shoulders. He had thinning white hair, and there were age freckles on his hands as he held them clasped before him, his chin touching them.

Roy Sandford knew him. It was the deputy director's opposite number, Frank Tullman, from the NSA. Tullman was in charge of all the skeletons, Roy had heard. Even at his pay grade, the names of men like Tullman stood out. It was said that he had originally cut his teeth as a junior communications operator with the Watergate recordings. He was lucky that time not to have been caught, and his boss had covered Frank's traces to protect his protégé. Now rumour had it that Tullman was the man with all the skeletons. He was the man with access to all the dirty secrets that senators and congressmen wanted kept hidden. When a president needed to be reassured about a man, he would ask Tullman. And when Tullman said a party official should be avoided, the official's career was over.

'Sir,' he said, and now there was a feeling of sick nervousness in his belly.

'This is Mister Tullman. You know him,' Amiss said. There was no question in his voice, only that quiet conviction that Roy remembered from his last meeting. 'You can speak in front of him with absolute freedom. You have just returned from the operation in Seattle. Correct?'

'Sir. Yes, sir.'

'How's the operation progressing?' Tullman said.

'Sir, I think that the team is performing well. It's difficult there. The target is very… um… hard to track.'

'We know that. It's why the FBI put some of their best agents in there,' Amiss said. 'And we put you with them.'

'Well, the FBI guys are good. I'm sure that they'll…'

Tullman interrupted, 'Frank Rand is effective?'

'Yes, sir. From what I saw.'

'The man they are tracking has killed two more men,' Tullman said. 'He is a danger to us and our country. We need you to help bring him down.'

'Sir?'

'From here, Sandford,' Amiss interrupted. 'You can monitor all the information which the team amasses, I assume?'

'Well, yes, I guess so.'

'Good. That is enough. I will have you allocated the room at the end of this hall. You may go.'

Tullman watched as Sandford left the room and the door closed behind him, before asking, 'You think he is safe enough?'

'He is,' Amiss said. 'I have a close watch kept on him. He's a loner, as are so many of these computer whizz-kids. No family, and only one lover, who happens to be one of us as well. He's safe enough.'

'What about his affiliations? Is he with us?'

'I think he may be. I will approach him.' Amiss nodded to himself. 'He would be invaluable.'

'So long as you're sure.'

'If he becomes dangerous, we can deal with him.'

*

06.18 Seattle; 14.18 London

Jack was at the window for a long time. In his mind's eye he saw the walk along the river down at Fatherford with the two dogs, he saw the house, Claire, and even as he was trying to hold a picture of Claire in his mind, he saw again Lewin's face – the white, fearful face as he cupped a cigarette in his hands and stared up at Jack, a young man who had seen and done so much more than his mind

205

could accept. Jack saw him, and then Jack's agents replaced Lewin's face: all those whom his Service had betrayed when they decided the Russian informers weren't needed any more. The agents he had betrayed by not helping them.

He left the window with the scene of endless vehicles and showered, then packed away the evidence of his hair dressing, stuffing the empty dye into a plastic bag long with his shaved hair. Last, he shoved it with his rucksack into the larger, wheeled case with all his clothes. With a clean shirt and pants, he felt refreshed.

Walking down to the street, he hefted his bag and set off westwards. When he found a small café, he sat down and ate a plate of eggs and toast with coffee.

He had a lot to do today.

*

06.23 Seattle; 14.23 London

Frank Rand was up early that morning, his eyes scratchy from sleeplessness, and his temper was not good as he sat at his desk and read through the reports. 'Debbie?' he shouted, and a moment or two later she appeared in the doorway, her hair tied up loosely. It made her look like she'd just fallen out of bed, and Frank saw that her eyes too were red-rimmed from lack of sleep.

'If ya want a coffee, I ain't gettin' it,' she said succinctly.

'Come in and sit down a while, Debbie.'

'Yeah, what?'

'Is there anything more on the two guys out at the old gas works yesterday?'

'They had no ID and seem to have no records anywhere. I don't get it. It's like they had their whole life stories erased.'

'If they were American, we'd have their details somewhere.'

'If they weren't American, we'd have fingerprints, iris scans, Christ knows what,' Debbie said. 'Unless they were illegals and came in over from Canada or Mexico. It's possible, I guess.'

'But?'

'But this is too clean. It looks more like a wipe-job. Like all their data's been erased.'

'Could someone do that?'

'If they had clearance, I guess. I heard once about a British operation in the Second World War. They wanted to make the Germans think there was an attack going to land somewhere, instead of where the invasion was going to happen, and they pretended a man had been killed in an accident, and on his hand was a case full of pretend plans. But thing was, they were pretending this officer was a real character in their planning team. So they had to go back and lose all the real guy's records and invent new ones for the imaginary agent they were inventing.'

'So you reckon…'

'It could be done. Everything's computerised now, so someone with the contacts could get records wiped. But that would mean these goons weren't just hoods. They were agents like you and me.'

'Not like you and me,' Frank said. 'We're legal. If these guys have to have their records removed, even their fingerprints, that means they're not like you or me at all.'

'But they almost certainly were government agents,' she said. 'No one else would be able to get all their details rubbed out like they did.'

'So these two were after this guy Jack Case, and he killed them both.'

'Which is what scares me about him,' she agreed.

'And then he knocked over two cops at the bus station too,' Frank said. 'But he didn't kill them. It was minimum force.'

'They were no threat.'

'No,' Frank agreed. 'He didn't look the kind of guy who'd kill for no reason.'

'But he killed those two guys.'

'So?' Frank said.

'Shows he has skills. He's good on his own, taking down two gunmen.'

'Who'd also killed his companion on the boat,' Frank reminded her.

'That was self-defence, yeah,' she said.

'The cop with the bruised windpipe might have something to say about how much minimum force usually involves,' Frank said caustically.

Debbie nodded, but her mind was already moving on, 'Why'd the Brits hand him to us? He's obviously no threat. He doesn't kill for no reason.'

'You think so?'

'So far, every case looks like self-defence to me. Maybe they think he's gone wild. Think he's a psycho, Frank?'

'Thought you were supposed to be trained out of that kind of thinking at Behavioural.'

'I have been. But I still believe in crazies.'

*

08.09 Seattle; 16.09 London

Jack had definite plans, and he didn't want to be held up with the police. He walked to the rail station and searched for a bank of telephones. With the receiver under his chin, he booked a ticket to Los Angeles from Seattle at three, and took out his credit card in the name of Hansen. It was $198.

He hung up, and went to the next free telephone and booked a flight from Seattle to Vegas on a flight two hours earlier, using the name Rod Avon and with Avon's cards. That was $276. He walked from the phones and into the toilets. There he pulled out the Browning and dropped it into the cistern. There were ways to take a gun onto an aircraft, but he didn't have time to organise it. He flushed the toilet and walked out.

A block or two from the station there was another little coffee bar. He wandered inside and sat at a stool by the window, watching the people passing in the street while he sipped a large Americano.

His back still hurt. It was worse after his impromptu fight at the bus station, but at least he came out all right and his description would hopefully add to the confusion of the police. Now he had firm plans: he had to make it to Vegas to see Sumner, and learn what he could from the man. After that, he would have to see how he could best get back to the UK. That was his one aim now: to get something that would ease his return to Claire. He had to get back to her.

His phone was in his bag, but the battery was still out so he couldn't be traced. Now he looked at it with a sense of regret. He ought to call Claire, to make sure she was all right. She was eight hours ahead of Seattle. It'd be easy to call her. But if he did, he knew that there was too high a risk that Echelon or a similar system could pick up his call. The risk of being discovered by triangulation from cell transmitters was too high to risk. And even if he used his new throwaway phone, he was sure as hell that they'd monitor all calls in and out of Claire's line. He daren't.

Instead, he finished his coffee, picked up his bag, stepped outside, and hailed a cab to take him to the airport.

*

08.32 Seattle; 16.32 London

208

Frank Rand got the call almost as soon as the systems had validated the ticket booking, and shouted at Debbie to join him. The rest of the team was already en route when he reached his car and jumped in.

'So, Frank, think this time he's screwed himself?'

Frank glanced at her as he pulled out of the car park.

'He's not so used to modern computers, is all.'

'Oh.'

He looked over at her. She remained steadfastly staring at the road as he powered down the hill.

'And?'

'Nothing.'

'That "nothing" of yours is deafening,' he said. 'What?'

'Just that he's done pretty well in Seattle for a guy who's no idea about modern computers. I mean, he hasn't shown up on ours, has he? And he managed to buy a ticket to LA without problem. Why LA?'

'To catch a connection? He has an aunt lives down there? Shit, how'd I know?'

'Yeah. Like you say. How'd we know,' she agreed.

He glanced at her again sure she was holding something back, 'What?' he demanded.

'I don't think we'll find him there today.'

'Where is he, then?'

Debbie looked away, over the streets to her right and then said, 'I think he's setting us up so he can get out of here. I'd bet he's got a flight after the one he's mentioned. He'll get us running ragged so he can watch us, and then he'll be on the first fuckin' plane out after we've killed ourselves chasing our tails.'

'Or he is on a plane earlier. Or he's back at the rail station since we're here,' Frank guessed. 'Ah, shit! Nothing's straightforward.'

'Nope. But I don't see how we can figure anything better.'

Frank nodded, but he was thinking fast. He pulled up outside the airport and picked up his phone, dialling Sandford as he went.

'Roy? I got a problem for you. I don't have your replacement yet and I really need some help.'

He outlined the information he had. 'You think you can find out anything from that? Like, where'd he make the call from, or whether he'd made any other calls?'

'What's the timeframe? Do you have a good idea when the call was made to book his flight?'

'Yeah, that'd be at the airport booking, I'd guess,' Frank said.

'You get me the time he called to book the flight, and I may be able to tell you where he called from, I guess, perhaps.'

'Good,' Frank said.

He closed the call and within an hour he and Debbie were with a flustered administration clerk at the airline's offices.

'This really has got to be important,' the little man kept saying as though trying to convince himself as he looked up at the two FBI agents. 'I'm not supposed to give away data like this without a warrant.'

'You have the Homeland Security laws to thank for our authority,' Frank said, deadpan.

'Here it is, anyway,' the man said, ripping off the printout.

'Roy?' Frank said, calling again. 'I have the time of the call for you.'

'Thanks,' Roy said. 'Be back to you.'

Frank and Debbie thanked the clerk and were off, through the door into the airport's main concourse, where they joined their companions at the departure area. They mingled with the crowds, Frank peering over the heads of the men and women in the halls, his hand itching to grab his gun, because the adrenaline rushing through his body was so electrifying. It was a rush stronger than the thrill he used to get from drugs, back in the bad old days before he kicked the habit. He daren't move his hand towards his firearm because he knew that the urge to draw it would be too great. Instead he deliberately pulled his jacket round and buttoned it. He forced himself to walk more slowly and deliberately. He forced himself to push his hand into his pocket. And when the phone in his pocket trembled, the shock was so great that he almost shot through the ceiling

'Rand.'

'It's Roy, Frank. I reckon I've got the guy for you. There was a call made from a payphone in the rail station at the right time. No recording, but the period was right.'

'Did he make another call?'

'Not from that phone. I'll check the ones beside his. He may have moved and called separately.'

'Call me when you know,' Frank said.

*

12.04 Las Vegas; 20.04 London

It was warm as he entered the long walkway to the arrivals hall, but Jack did not take off his light jacket. He felt the warmth as a pillow that cushioned him from the reality of the people about him. He passed the drinks machines, the one-arm bandits, the kiosks with coffee and doughnuts, the burgers. The scent of spicy noodles reached his nose, reminding him he was hungry, but he avoided all the food stalls. Walking purposefully, he smiled at the security guards, his bag rolling at his side, and outside he hailed a cab to take him downtown.

He was relieved to be in the vehicle. It was a new cab, and the seats were still soft and unscuffed. The plastic partition between him and the driver was clear and unscratched, and the air conditioning worked fine. It was a relief to be able to sit back with the sense that so far all was well. But he could not relax. He had evaded the men who wanted to catch him at the airport in Seattle, but there were cops here in Vegas, and there were telephones to call through from Seattle.

The driver dropped him at the entrance to the Bellagio. It was a sheltered entrance. As Jack climbed out and looked about him, he was reassured by the size of the place. This was an enormous, opulent hotel. And one used to protecting the anonymity of its guests, he hoped. Once before he had spoken with a friend who was a committed gambler, and he had always considered the Vegas casinos as being among the most determined to ensure that anyone, be he arms dealer, prince or garage mechanic, should have an equal right to lose money at the casino's tables.

It took little time to check in. He was offered, and refused, a view of the fountains for an additional fifty, and instead took a small room on the fourth floor at the rear. It was adequate. He was surprised to see that the room had no coffee machine or kettle, but a call to reception gave him directions to a series of coffee bars within the hotel complex. He threw his bag on the bed, and took his book with him to the lifts.

The lifts deposited him in the main slot machine hall. He soon realised that the casino was designed deliberately to ensure that a guest must always pass by these machines, no matter what they wished. A coffee? They'd pass the machines. A newspaper? Yes. A meal? Yes again. There was nothing in the casino or hotel that could be reached without passing the militarily precise formations of slot machines.

He ignored them, walking to the nearest coffee bar and buying a cup. It was not so strong, nor as good as his morning's Americano in Seattle, and he pulled a face at his first sip, but it was safer than a stronger drink. Instead he took to watching the punters. Many had bought sprung plastic cords, in various colours, to which they had affixed their credit cards. With the other end clipped to a belt or buttonhole, the contented gamblers could sit at their stools, smoking, drinking complimentary drinks, while their cards gradually emptied their bank accounts. All they need do was press the button or pull the lever, to continue their onward march to bankruptcy, one coin at a time. It left him feeling empty to see so many men and women sitting at their stools, silent, drinking themselves to oblivion, and concentrating their entire beings on the machines before them.

It was depressing.

He had to find Sumner. Jack walked from the hotel and stood outside a moment feeling the sun on his face. It was strange to come here. From the balmy English weather, to the chilly climate of Anchorage, and now to the dry heat of Nevada, his body was finding the adjustment difficult.

Crossing the road, past the glorious fountains that jetted skywards and danced in time to the music from massive loudspeakers, Jack walked along the sidewalk until he came to a store. It was the kind of stuff he would have derided as 'Tourist Tat' in England, but here he didn't mind the clear plastic dice, the spring cords for credit cards, the playing cards in their cellophane wrappers, and all the paraphernalia of the gambling industry. He saw a street atlas, and bought it. At the back there was a listing of different services and stores in the neighbourhood, and he ran his finger down until he found an internet café on Spring Mountain Drive. It was only a short walk away.

*

12.17 Seattle; 20.17 London

Frank's phone rang again and he grabbed at it.

'It's Roy Sandford, Frank. I have it! I think he booked a flight from a second phone just along the way.'

Frank shook his head, staring at two agents hurrying towards him and said, 'He did. Yeah, he called from another phone,'

'How do you know that?'

Frank didn't answer, but shut up the phone as his agents reached him.

'Well?'

'We showed the guy's mugshot to some of the staff over at the other desks. The Virgin desk lady thought she recognised him. Said he caught a plane to Vegas.'

'Vegas?' Frank said. 'What the fuck does he want in Vegas?'

*

15.23 Langley; 20.23 London

Amiss looked up as he heard the knock on his door, and he surveyed Roy Sandford without blinking before pressing the button under his desk. The electronic log clicked and Roy walked in nervously.

'What is it?'

'Sir, the team has found the man called Case. He's managed to escape them again and has made it to Vegas.'

'Where in Vegas is he?'

'I don't know yet, but it won't take long to find him,' Roy said.

'Good. What of the team in Seattle?'

'Agent Rand has arranged for an FBI jet to fly him and some of the team out to Nevada, sir.'

'Good. Keep me informed.'

'Sir.'

Roy withdrew and the door silently closed once more.

Amiss leaned back in his chair and turned it round on its swivel until he was staring at the crucifix again. Then he clasped his hands once more as he prayed for help to overcome this latest problem.

When he felt that he had calmed his spirit enough, he bowed his head to the little figure on the cross, and turned back to his table. He picked up his telephone receiver, glancing up at the windows as he did so. There was the usual click and then sequence of tunes, but then, when the call was answered, he said, 'This is Peter. Could you go secure, please?' and pressed the button for encryption. There was the fifteen second delay, and then he heard Stilson's voice.

'Yes?'

'I have heard that our belief we could remove these problems yesterday was a little over-optimistic.'

'He took out two of my guys.'

'What are you doing to resolve the issue?'

'I have two men on the team leader with the Feebies, but he doesn't seem to have much idea where this man is.'

'I can tell you that. He is in Vegas.'

'What?'

213

'Do you have anyone on Sumner yet?'

'There is one guy who was tracking him down, but had no luck so far. I was on my way there today to help find him.'

'Where are you now?'

'In Seattle.'

'You must hurry. The FBI are on their way by private jet. I do not want them to question Sumner about his involvement. Nor Case. Understand?'

*

12.34 Las Vegas; 20.34 London

The internet café was maybe a little over a mile from the Bellagio, and Jack walked with a firm determination. He had the impression that he was ahead of whoever it was who wanted to kill him, and that itself was reassuring, but he knew that they could still find him if he was careless. He could not afford that.

He entered the café and was soon seated at a computer studying the White Pages. He tried the name Sumner, and there were several men with his name. Against some there were pictures of an envelope, and Jack clicked on one. It brought up a new screen, and on this there were ages, addresses, and other details. Nothing seemed to correspond to the description of the man he had read about in Anchorage, or like the man he had met years before.

There were other resources to look at, and he spent a fruitless two hours searching, before he could sit back and consider. Sumner was clearly not registered here yet. He had no telephone in his own name; he had no accommodation. Jack tried to put himself into the mindset of the man, trying to imagine where he would live.

He had been a soldier. That meant he would try to avoid the worst doss-houses, and he'd try to keep himself tidy, surely. But he would also be on a pensions list, if he had been invalided out of the Forces.

On a hunch, Jack pulled out his mobile phone. The call he'd made to Orme probably meant that phone he had bought in Seattle was as compromised as his Blackberry. He checked on the computer for the British Legion website. There he found a number for the rehabilitation unit in Surrey, Headley Court, which he recalled reading about in the paper. The café had a payphone, and he used a credit card in his new name to buy a call. It was quickly answered.

'Hello, I was trying to locate Captain Roger Sumner,' he said.

'Yes? There's no one here with that name.'

The woman's voice was reserved, and Jack could almost feel the mistrust over the phone line.

'Oh, damn. I wanted Roger's forwarding address.'

'I'm afraid you'll have to call up in the morning, then, sir.'

'What time is it there?'

'It is past eight thirty,' the voice told him rather primly.

'Oh, God, I'm sorry,' he said, smiling. He had heard that smiling while talking on the phone could be heard in a man's voice. 'I'm a fool. I'm here in Nevada, you see, and was hoping to see Roger while I was here. We served in Afghanistan together, you see. He was a great guy. Such a shame about his injuries – he lost his arm. Anyway, I wanted to see him again, but I cannot find his name anywhere. I suppose he's staying in a hotel.'

'Are you with the press, then?'

'Christ, no! I'm a salesman now. I got out when I could. You know, after seeing all my mates injured I couldn't cope with it any more. And it was partly Roger who helped. He put me in touch with my company, so, well, I owe him a lot.'

He could sense the thaw.

'I'm very sorry, Mr…?'

'My name is Rod Avon. I was a lieutenant back then, though!'

'Well, Lieutenant, I am very sorry, but I cannot see what I can do.'

'It was just a try. I wanted to see him again, like I said, but if I can't track him down, that's it. Thanks for your help, anyway.'

'It was terrible how they ruined him,' she said.

'He tried to help so many,' Jack agreed, waiting. She was making a decision.

Then: 'Look, if you don't tell anyone…'

'I won't,' he promised.

'He did write to us when he left the hospital, and it's on the notice board. Can you wait a mo?'

Jack waited with the excitement thrilling in his blood. He heard footsteps disappearing, and in his mind's eye he could see slim legs marching purposefully along a linoleum-covered floor, and then he heard them returning.

'Mr Avon? I have an address. Do you have a pen?'

Friday 23rd September

17.42 Las Vegas; 01.42 London

Ed Stilson flew into McCarran late in the afternoon, and he was in a bad mood, not that it was obvious to the casual observer. His blue eyes were as calm as ever – there was a coolness about them – but it was more an appearance of aloofness, rather than an indication of coldness in his soul. The steel grey hair gave him the look of a manager, but one who had succeeded and was an achiever. It was smartly cut and unfashionably long, for many, but it suited him and his square, rugged features.

He strode purposefully along the terminal's walkways, his eyes noting with humour the three pensioners who sat at their slot machines pulling the handles, before walking through to the baggage claim. Soon he was out at the entrance hall, and hailing a cab.

Ed Stilson had been in the CIA for as long as Amiss himself. He was a firm patriot, and there was nothing that made him so angry as the thought of any man trying to harm his nation. He believed in the superiority of American culture with every fibre in his being, and he had dedicated his life to the protection of it.

It was good to be back in Vegas. He tried to get here once a year for a weekend, and each time he would bring a thousand bucks to lose. He never expected to win at the tables, but over a weekend he could live like a king. He enjoyed that.

It was a shame that this time he didn't have money to burn.

He took the cab to the car rental, and hired a Chrysler with his company card. Soon he was on the highway heading towards Paradise Valley. He had an urgent meeting to conduct before he could go to Sumner, and he dialled the number as he drove.

The phone rang four times, and he clenched his jaw. Bing was a lazy, useless prick at the best of times, but he wouldn't dare to cross Ed Stilson.

'Yeah?'

'It's me. I need something from you.'

'You know where I am.'

The line went dead.

Ed smiled to himself without humour. This should take little time. He gunned the motor and the car shot forward.

Paradise Valley was a good neighbourhood, or this part was. Ed drove up to the driveway, a series of concrete slabs in front of the three car garage, shut off the engine and climbed out, pulling his jacket on as he went. Ed's was a modern, bright, house in Spanish style, with the thick corrugations of the tiles on the roof. Palms dotted the road, and Ed looked about him as he walked up to the door. This place was good – far too good for a cheap punk who made his way to this street via drugs and gun running. But then, most of the men who built Las Vegas made their money from drugs and prostitution so Bing was in good company.

'Hey, come in, Ed. Good to see ya.'

'Hi, Bing,' Stilson said, as he crossed the threshold. The hall was wide, with tiled floors and plants in large vases giving the impression of coolness. From the Mediterranean decoration Stilson would have expected to see a Grecian woman appear clad in a linen tunic, but instead there was a brunette who appeared in a doorway, wrecked. She had large brown eyes, but they were bruised from drugs and lack of sleep, and any beauty she might once have claimed was long gone.

'Get back inside, Ruth,' Bing snapped and, as she turned away, he jerked his head to the patio. 'Come and tell me what you need.'

Bing was so called because his surname was Crosbie. That was as far as any similarity went with the singer. He was short, with a head of dreadlocked hair that was constantly moving about his face as though it was alive. His complexion was sallow and unhealthy looking, and his eyes bloodshot. Ed was convinced that he took drugs too often to be entirely free of them. Now he had a slight twitch about him, as though he was desperate to dispose of Ed and return to ingesting whatever it was that he and Ruth had been trying. His fingers flicked and twiddled as though he was rolling an imaginary joint, and he leaned forward with enthusiasm as he sat, as if on tenterhooks to satisfy whatever Ed needed.

'I need a throwdown piece.'

'Right, right. Throwdown piece.'

'Something can't be traced back to me,' Ed continued.

'Yeah, right. Like, you want to have a gangbanger's toy? Big piece or little?'

Ed had been thinking about this.

'A Saturday night special would be fine. Something like a Mauser HSc or Walther PPK, or small calibre Beretta.'

'Man, got nothin' like that,' Bing said, his head shaking slowly. 'No, but, like, you need it to be a real old one?'

'Just something that is impossible to trace.'

'Got the thing, man. Just the thing. You wait there, while I get it, yeah?'

He was up and away so fast, Ed knew full well he was off to test some more drugs as well as fetch the gun. Ed settled in his seat. He could wait.

It was almost five minutes when he returned, an old shoebox in his hands.

'Oh, this is sweet! Sweet!' he crowed as he passed the box to Ed.

Taking it, Ed was pleased with the weight – clearly not a heavy gun. He opened the box and pulled out a revolver. It was much like the police .38s of the last century. Shit, some of the old arses still used them now in New York. But this wasn't a Smith & Wesson or Colt.

'What is it?'

'It's had all markings taken off, hasn't it?' Bing grinned. 'It was taken from a Mex bringing in some friends to work over here. I reckon it's a Brazilian, you know, a Taurus. Kinda looks like it, eh? Fires .357 or .38. No serial, no registration over here, no traces. Use it and lose it!'

'Good. Do you have any others? A spare would always be useful,' he said.

'Sure. Same deal?'

'No. This I want as a reliable piece. What autos do you have?'

It took only another thirty minutes to find what he needed. A post-war Springfield manufactured Colt in .45.

'Ammo?' he asked, eyeing both guns on the table.

'How much?'

Ed considered. He didn't want Bing to have any information that could implicate him. 'Make it fifty each; a hundred,' he said.

A hundred rounds would be plenty, he thought.

*

17.46 Las Vegas; 01.46 London

Roger Sumner's home was not pleasant.

Jack had rented a car, and now he climbed from it and stared about him. Ahead there was a trailer park, filled with statics that must have been there forty, fifty years. It looked like the builders of Las Vegas could have used them when the city was first being planned. With the

218

dry atmosphere, the most that could be said of them was that they had not rusted too much, but that was the best that could be said – by a long way.

The address was scribbled on a shred of paper he'd ripped from a note pad, and now he studied the place before him. There was a low bungalow nearby, and he walked to it, tapping on the screen door.

'Yeah?'

It was an old man who spoke. He stood at the side of the house, bare-chested, but with cut off blue jeans. On his head was a baseball cap, and the peak shielded his grey eyes from the sun as he peered at Jack.

'You from IRS? You don't look like you're from the IRS.'

'No. I'm from England. I'm looking for Roger Sumner.'

'He ain't here.'

'I can see that. Could you tell me where he is?'

The old man glanced up at the sky.

'Reckon he'll be out near the Strip, probably round the Sahara. Getting some food in before he plays.'

'When will he be back?'

'This is Vegas. He'll be back when he's broke or it's daytime.'

Jack nodded. He glanced about.

'You know which casinos he prefers?'

'Get to the Sahara and ask the guys. He likes it there.'

Jack thanked him and began to walk back to his car. There was a small group of teenagers near it, and he felt the hairs on the back of his neck prickling at the sight of them. They were taking elaborate care not to watch him, he saw, and that diverted his attention from them to his car. There was no obvious damage. The wheels were still on it, but even as he approached it, his thumb on the lock release, he knew something was about to happen.

He moved away from the driver's door and peered at the car. There were sniggers from the group, and he knew someone was behind him, walking slowly and quietly. He span around, and found himself confronted by three youths. All had baseball caps on at an angle, the peaks turned away, and they had grins on their faces that said they knew he had no chance against three.

Without hesitating, Jack stepped in close. The first youth was surprised, and reacted too slowly. Jack thrust his arm forward, fingers locked, and the youth grabbed for his throat, gasping painfully as he hurtled backwards. The second was pulling something from behind his back, and Jack grabbed his elbow, snapping it forwards with all the force he could muster. There was a dry snapping as the shoulder was dislocated, and a scream came from him as Jack continued pulling the ruined arm, taking the little pistol from his holster, and pointing it at the third youth.

His eyes took in the handgun with eyes that widened as Jack dropped the second sobbing youth and walked forward until the barrel was resting on the lad's forehead.

'Drop your gun.'

'I don't have one,' the boy faltered.

'Turn.'

He did, and Jack made sure he was telling the truth. All he had was a switchblade, and Jack threw it hard to land some thirty yards away in the scrubby soil. Then he walked back to his car, paying no attention to the group of teens. He pressed the key to unlock it, climbed in, and drove off, tossing the pistol from his open window when he was some yards away.

*

17.47 Las Vegas: 01.47 London

Frank Rand went to the local FBI office as soon as he had landed with Debbie and two other agents from his team.

'What are you going to do?' she asked him as they pushed through the glass doors into a cool atrium.

'First we'll request all the assistance we can get, then we'll check all the casinos, all the bars, everywhere until we find this British prick!'

'He's kinda got under your skin, hasn't he?' she chuckled throatily.

'I don't like guys who run around causing trouble.'

'But looks like he's the one being run around.'

'Yeah. And that itself makes me wonder what the hell's going on here,' Frank said. They were at the lifts now, and he pressed the button, glancing down at her. 'Look, if all these guys want to whack him, why is that, do you reckon? If he's innocent, what'd they need to do it for? He's just a poor bum with a face that looks like one of their enemies or something? I don't buy it. No, he's got something on them, whoever "them" are, and if he was legit, he'd have told us, wouldn't he? So he's dirty too. That's how I see it. And since the Brits say he's a murderer over there, well, I guess I'll take their word for it.'

'Right, right, Frank. Sorry I asked.'

He grinned at her.

'What do you think, Debbie?'

'Me? Since you ask, I think he's defending himself. But he's, like, a loose cannon. We should shoot the fuckwit as soon as we see him. He's attracting risks all the way and soon some innocents will get killed. He killed two guys back in Seattle when they were both carrying. The only gun he had, you'd taken from him in Anchorage. So I reckon he's pretty dangerous.'

'Yeah,' Frank said. He remembered the face sitting opposite him in the bar at the Hilton. But the eyes he saw there were not the cold, calculating eyes of a murderer. He could have sworn that Jack Case was not a murderer.

But anyone could kill given the right set of circumstances. They all knew that.

The lift opened and they went up, Debbie staring at the dial as the numbers changed.

'So?' she said.

'What?'

'You don't think he's a threat, do you? You reckon he may be a good guy stuck in trouble, but he's not a threat.'

He frowned, eyes narrowing.

'You repeat that sort of bull and I'll have you…'

'In your dreams, Frank. In your dreams.'

*

18.42 Las Vegas; 02.42 London

Stilson drove to the address he had for Sumner. There was a whole load of traffic today, and he was forced to sit with his teeth clenched, his fingers angrily tapping at the wheel as he kept a close eye on the car behind. Should be OK, but he couldn't take any risks. The sun was a problem, too. He hadn't thought of that, but now, sitting in a line of cars, there was a risk of the heat making more trouble for him.

There was nothing he could do. He was committed now. Bing had tried to threaten him with exposure, and he had to make it clear blackmail wasn't going to work.

The ammunition was good. Bing had brought him jacketed hollow-point Hornady FTX in .357 Magnum and .45 ACP. The shells had nickel-bright cartridge cases, with copper-coloured bullet heads. Each had a small red polymer insert in the hollow of the slug itself. Bing swore that they'd expand well and penetrate even through denim or leather, and the little polymer plug made the lead swell more reliably

221

each time. Sure looked like they worked. He was tempted to buy some back home and test them on the range at fifty and seventy five yards, just to see what they were like over distance.

In front the vehicles were moving again, and he gave a grunt of satisfaction. On the passenger seat he had his satnav, and the voice gave him the turnoff warning. In ten more minutes he'd passed onto the slip road and was trundling along at a good speed again. There was a set of lights at the bottom, and he looked around carefully before stepping on the accelerator and heading off to Sumner's.

It was a shabby dump. He had always hated trailer parks. The rednecks and bitches living here ought to be shot at birth. Half were druggies, and the ones who weren't spent their lives drinking beer instead of working. This wasn't the American dream; this was a human garbage tip. He'd be happier when he was out of it. Pulling on his sunglasses, he stepped from the car, slipping into his lightweight suit jacket and tugging it over his holstered Springfield. The revolver was in his pants pocket.

Stopping in front of the entrance way, he decided the bungalow was the best place to start, and walked to the door and banged.

'Anyone home?'

There were some kids out in front, and he smiled at them. Two looked sullen and dangerous, while a third kicked the rear tyre on his sedan. Two girls were nearby. Screw them.

The door opened.

'Yeah?'

'I'm looking for Mr Sumner. You know where he is?'

'How many more a you assholes goin' to come here botherin' me about that prick?'

'Look, I'm just trying to find him, is all. How many others have been here already?' Stilson said, putting his hand to his inner pocket.

The old fool whipped out a .38 revolver. Stilson saw it, and his training kicked in. He wouldn't let an old fuck like this shoot him. He pushed his left hand out, grabbed the gun hand as it came up, and shoved it to the side, past his body, while his right hand drew his Springfield smoothly and rested the barrel on the old fart's temple.

'You wanna die?'

Stilson took the .38 from the old fool and reholstered his gun. This was going to be easier than he'd thought. He forced the man backwards into his sitting room. It was worse than he would have expected, a fetid square room with plastic-covered sofa and chairs facing an old TV. A rug with black burn marks where cigarettes had been stubbed. At the side of the TV was a series of VHS tapes with porn films, from the look of the covers, spilling over the rug. All reeked of old tobacco and sweat.

The old man stumbled, and fell into a chair.

'Who're you, and what d' you want?' he spat.

Stilson wandered past him, hitting him in the mouth with the revolver as he went, and stood at the rear of the room, while the old man snuffled and moaned, holding both hands to his ruined mouth.

Pulling back the sliding latch on the revolver, Stilson glanced at the chamber. There was the reassuring gleam of brass inside. Six rounds, all unfired. He slammed the chamber shut, and swung around into the first room. The kitchen was so tiny that it would have fitted in a small boat. No one there. He carried on over the hall, kicking the first door. It swung back to crash into the wall revealing a bedroom, with the stench of an old man who cared little for his hygiene. Stilson entered, checked wardrobes, and looked under the bed. All was filled with junk. Every spare space had its own collection of magazines or bags of garbage. Flies buzzed about him. On to the next room – a bathroom – no one there. The last room was a minute bedroom with just enough space for a mattress on the floor. This was where Sumner lived, he guessed. There was a clean shirt on the back of the door, some pants and underwear in neat piles under the window. The window was open. He walked outside, but there was nowhere for Sumner to have run to from here.

No, he hadn't been here. He strode back into the house, through to the sitting room, where the old man still rocked in his chair, hands at his mouth. Blood was leaking from between his fingers.

'Old man, I want to know where Roger Sumner is, and I want to know now,' he said.

In his pocket were some disposable ear plugs, and he squeezed one until it was thin, and pressed it into his ear. He did the same with his other ear.

The man looked up at him and took his hands away.

'Go fuck…'

'You ain't bright, are you?' Stilson said, and shot his thigh.

The crash of the .38 in that room was so loud, Stilson was sure he heard a window shatter. The old man's face blanched instantly, and his body jackknifed, his hands not quite touching his shattered leg, his brow near it. For a moment, whether he had spoken or not, Stilson couldn't have heard him with his earplugs still in place. He pulled one out and gazed at the man without sympathy – he had none. This old moron had dissed him, and he wasn't going to get away with that.

'Well?' he said.

*

18.46 Las Vegas; 02.46 London

The Sahara was at the far end of the Strip, away from the Bellagio, and when Jack drove into the car park at the front, he sat looking at it for some while.

It was not dilapidated, but the whole atmosphere was that of a 1950s building that had been maintained for a price, not for safety and definitely not for looks, like a blowsy whore who spent too much time drunk now her looks were gone. Jack turned off the engine and climbed out. The heat hit him after his journey, and he took a long breath. Some years ago he had spent some months in Nairobi in Kenya, and the heat there was much the same as this: dry and physical. It almost felt like a force of its own.

He crossed the car park, his eyes about him as he went. Had he known it, Frank Rand was even then standing in a building only four blocks away, arms folded, staring down along the Strip directly at Jack. But Frank couldn't see his face, and didn't recognise the clothes.

Jack entered the neon-lit entrance and stood staring down at the aisles of slot machines. There was a smell of stale sweat and booze, with an overlay of tobacco smoke. He had been told that Sumner would be near the poker tables, so he glanced around, and made his way through the maze of machines, to where the green baize spoke of cards.

Sumner was not immediately recognisable from the papers. His face was thinner, more haggard, and his complexion was sallow. He had the left sleeve of his sports jacket pinned up, and the scar on his cheek was livid. He had mousy hair which was cut poorly, and it added to the impression of seediness given by the old jacket with leather patches on the elbows, and the slacks. Jack knew without his standing that the backside of those trousers would be polished to a shine from sitting on too many leather barstools and poker chairs.

'Afternoon,' Jack said, as he approached.

Sumner looked up and gave Jack a quick study. It was plain that he hoped this was a new player to complement his party. There was no

224

flicker of recognition. There were only the two players at the table, and the dealer nodded to him as he dealt.

'You want in?' the dealer asked.

'Not yet. I'm here to watch.'

'OK.'

The game continued, but every so often Sumner glanced at Jack as though wondering what another Brit was doing in this casino. After two games, which Sumner lost, he leaned back.

'Excuse me, but do you want something from me?'

'No, Captain. Not directly.'

'Have we met?' he frowned.

'In Ireland. Ninety five or six.'

Sumner peered closer, and there was a spark in his eyes as he realised who Jack was.

'You want to talk?' he said at last.

'I wanted to ask you a few things about Danny Lewin.'

'Danny? How is he?'

'Not very well,' Jack said.

Sumner was nodding to a waitress, who negotiated the chairs and punters with professional calm, the smile never faltering. She bent to give Sumner a good view of her cleavage.

'Sir?'

'Could you please bring me a large bourbon with ice, please?'

'A bourbon on the rocks, sure, sir. Anything else?'

Sumner glanced at Jack and said, 'My round. While you play, they bring you more.'

'Danny's dead. Shot.'

Sumner's face fell.

'Oh, *fuck*.'

*

18.47 Las Vegas; 02.47 London

Frank was pleased at least that the locals didn't resent his arrival. When he described the situation and how the two in the Gas Park had been killed, the team were already moving. He had provided them with the mugshot of Jack Case, and now it was being photocopied for the local police.

'We got good relations with the casinos,' Bert Rankin was saying. He was a large, bluff Chicagoan who had come out to Vegas twenty years ago to avoid the rain and snow, and somehow never made it back. 'Sure, there're a couple there we'd like to have inside and

225

question in depth, but gen'rally they're good. They want to make sure that thieves and cheats get caught more'n we do.'

'Can we ask them for their help in this?'

'We can email the photo and they'll all get on to it. Believe me, out of all those who're likely to respond, the casinos are fastest.'

It was a relief to Frank as he sat and briefed another small team of detectives that the operation here in Vegas seemed so efficient. He ran through his presentation for the fourth time, and it was as he was bringing up the slides of the two men in the car park that a man suddenly sat up and peered.

'When was this taken?'

'Yesterday, at the car park at Gas Works. Why?'

The man was staring intently.

'That guy there, he reminds me of a trooper I met three, four years ago out in Iraq. I was a Marine then. Only quit four years ago, and took this on instead, but I don't forget a face, and that guy was out there. Real sonuva bitch, he was.'

Frank was able to smile regretfully.

'Sorry, don't think so. We took the man's prints and details, and nothing came back. No hits.'

'Uhuh. You say. I'll tell you now, though, he was called Ian McDonnell.'

Frank glanced at Debbie, who was already writing the name on her legal pad. She shrugged when she saw his face.

'McDonnell, huh?' Frank said.

'Yeah. He was out there some time, but when all the stories about Abu Ghraib and other prison abuses came up, he was pulled. Heard he was implicated in some of those torture stories they had in the papers. Easy to believe. He was a Christian fanatic, you know? I mean, I go to church and all that, but this guy's one of them thinks all Arabs could be shot and the world wouldn't miss 'em. Had a job with the prisons – guard or something. Another guy told me he was a real bastard. Just believed all Iraqis were US-hating terrorists. Even kids. There were some shitheads out there, but he was one of the worst.'

'But he got pulled, you say?'

'Yeah. I heard he was going to be charged with some of the abuses.'

'Well, like I say, this guy has no ID or anything.'

'Check up McDonnell. That's him. I'd recognise his face anywhere.'

226

Frank asked which unit the man served with, but the officer didn't know.

'Just check with the staff serving at Abu Ghraib four or five years back. They'll be able to tell you. There must be records of them.'

'Right,' Frank said, glancing at Debbie to make sure she had noted the page and details. 'Any other comments?'

There was a knock at the door, and a woman officer shoved her head through the door.

'Shooting out at Paradise Valley. Did you say your guy was a Brit?'

'Yes,' Frank said.

'This is at a place where another Brit lives. Don't know, but seemed a coincidence to me.'

*

18.52 Las Vegas; 02.52 London

'How did Danny die?' Sumner asked, already halfway down his bourbon, watching the cards as the dealer shuffled and dealt.

'I think someone put a bullet in his head,' Jack said. 'He didn't have too much of a chance.'

'How did you find me?'

Jack shrugged.

'Danny had your name in a book. I found it.'

'Well,' Sumner said, blowing out a long breath. 'Poor Danny.'

'What was he like when you knew him?'

'A good lad. But lousy once he realised what was going on. He cared too much.'

'How do you mean?'

'He was an interrogation officer. And good, too. He managed to get us good intel. But it all got too much for him. His nerves were shot by the time he got back to Blighty. Didn't like to see that it was all bollocks, basically.'

'What, the war?'

'No, the system. See, the army would send people out to round up the nasties. Off they would go, the poor bloody squaddies, round up all the men from an apartment or house, and bring them back, and we'd sort out the wheat from the chaff. Thanks.' He picked up his cards and studied them briefly. 'So he and I would sit in our offices or containers, and question, and question, and question. And since the fellows were brought to us, and the squaddies told us that a known rebel had fingered them, we knew we had to get what they knew from

227

them. And if they sat there looking dumb, we'd do all we could to scare the shit from the bastards. Promise them houris and sherbet if they opened up to us. And if we scared them well and good, they did open up, and they told us their suspicions about neighbours or people a block away, so we'd send the squaddies off to that address, and some other intel officer would have them to question.'

He studied his cards, winced, said, 'Fold,' and turned to face Jack. 'But we never bloody knew. That was the trouble. We never bloody knew whether they were just throwing us a line to get us off their backs. And usually that's what it was. We all went through it. After a while, Danny snapped. He had a young lad in, probably only fifteen or so, and he broke the little sod. Poor bastard.'

'What happened?'

'He had had enough. The work was relentless, and he had this little sod who just kept denying all knowledge, and Danny broke. He punched this kid, three or four times, and then he realised what he was doing and stopped. And he couldn't carry on after that. You see, Danny was a good fellow, really. All he wanted to do was open things up and save lives. Instead he was there with the rest of us in that dirty little war. I got back and kept my mouth shut, so my brag rags grew, but Danny wouldn't play the game.'

'I know. I debriefed him.'

'Well, you know what he was like, then. He was always going to die young.'

'There are always some like that,' Jack observed.

'Yes,' Sumner said with a dry smile as he toasted Jack and drained his drink.

'What about you?'

'Me? Oh, I'm having a high old time of it, I am. I'll carry on enjoying the high life here until I run out of steam.'

'Couldn't you go home, start up the charity again, or some other business?'

Sumner looked at him with a patronizing smile.

'Do you think they'd let me try?'

And then he shocked Jack by weeping.

*

19.04 Las Vegas; 03.04 London

Frank and Debbie followed two detectives from the Las Vegas Metropolitan Police department. They hurtled along the Strip, then off, and soon Frank was confused. The car in front was rocketing from one block to another, and the suspension was bucketing as they hit potholes, and the cheap blacktop was rumbling through the shocks until Frank felt like the fillings in his teeth were coming loose. He was relieved when the cops in front pulled up in a trailer park out near the fringes of the city, and he could switch off the engine and climb out.

There was a crime scene officer with a notepad and pen, who took Frank and Debbie's names and badge numbers before letting them anywhere near the bodies.

As they ducked under the tape, already wearing the latex gloves they'd been given, Debbie complained, 'It's never like this on TV. There the guys just walk straight on in.'

'That's because it's TV,' Frank said. 'I heard a British pathologist once, said he'd been asked to look at a script and gave up when the actor suddenly said he was going to X-ray some blood.'

'Why'd he say that?'

'Because,' Frank said laconically, 'he was an actor. They have to say something. It's why the TV is full of such bullshit.'

They reached the inner perimeter. Beyond this most officers couldn't go, for fear of polluting any evidence, but the FBI agents had authority today. Their DNA and prints would be on file to be cross-referenced against anything found on or near the bodies.

There was a small bungalow, with a car parked out front. Frank could see that the trunk had been popped, and inside were two bodies, a man and a woman. He walked to them and stared down.

It was a long time since he'd been upset at the sight of a dead man, but there was a residual pang each time he saw one – always worse with the women, too. This one was young, a brunette, with a slim figure. Once she had been attractive, but the bullet through her right eye had spoiled her looks.

The man was if anything worse. The bullet had entered through the back of his head, and the shockwave of the bullet passing through the water of his brain had made his features swell alarmingly. They were already blackened, but in this heat that was no surprise.

'Whose car is it?' Frank asked.

'Best guess is, it's that guy in the trunk,' a homicide detective told him. 'It's registered to a Mister Crosbie. Looks like someone took a dislike to Mister Crosbie and his girl. Shot them both, stuffed them into the trunk, and then went into this guy's house and blew his head off.'

229

'And? Could the old man in the house have killed these two?'

'It don't look good for that. For one thing the old guy has a bullet in his knee. From a big calibre. Then there's a .357 revolver in the trunk with these two, so maybe Crosbie here could have shot the old man with that; but that means somehow the old man shot Crosbie and this girl, picked them up and threw them into the trunk, then walked back to his house and killed himself. Don't reckon to that.'

'Bullets?'

'Don't know, but the entry wounds on these two are pretty small, as is the head shot on the old man. You can see for yourself that there's no exit.'

'What about the old man.'

'Be my guest. But his leg's bad.'

Frank and Debbie walked to the bungalow and nodded to the officer at the door. There was no need to enter. The flies and the smell of blood were repulsive already.

'See what I mean about the leg,' the detective said. He shook his head. 'The old man copped a slug in here, I'd say. Bullet was through and through, taking most of his thighbone with it. He'd have died soon from that anyhow.'

'So you don't believe the story.'

'No. I think another guy shot the two in the trunk, put them inside and drove here with them. Once here, he shot the old man for some reason, and then blew his head off.'

'Why?'

'You tell me. But there were some kids down the road said a big man in a suit was here. They called us because they heard shots. He came here in that car, alone, and then walked in here.'

'What about afterwards?'

'Kids saw him walk out and back towards downtown,' the officer said, jerking his thumb to point.

'Name?'

'Yeah. Like they'd have asked,' the detective grinned.

'What else?'

'There was a gun in here. A small .357 – two inch barrel, blued, all normal. Except it's got no maker numbers on it. Serial or anything.'

'Ah.'

'Yeah. He was a pro all right.'

Frank nodded.

'OK. Thanks for this.'

He walked out to the car and glanced in at the trunk again.

Debbie joined him. 'You reckon this was your guy?'

'Where'd he get a gun that fast? No, I think this was done by someone else. But...'

He had seen a small group of teens watching. One was on a pushbike, while the others loitered. One appeared to be in some pain, but none made any move to leave when Frank walked over to them.

'Hi.'

There was no answering welcome.

Frank jerked his thumb over his shoulder.

'You knew this guy?'

'It was old Jonah. We all knew him.'

'That was his name, right?'

The boy with the sullen expression nodded. His voice was rough when he said, 'How'd we know? That's what everyone called him. Jonah Lewis.'

'Did you see the guy come here who killed Jonah?'

'Why?'

'Because if you deny it you'll be arrested and spend the next week in gaol,' Frank said, as he showed his FBI badge.

'Why you here? This ain't federal.'

'There's an Englishman I want to talk to. A foreigner makes it more interesting to me.'

'You mean Sumner or the other one?' This was from a shorter boy.

'Who is Sumner?'

'Man used to live there with Jonah. He ain't here today; he'll be up the Safari or somewhere playin' poker.'

'And who was this other one?'

'Don't know,' the hoarse boy said, 'but he fucked us up.'

Gradually, Frank managed to elicit a description, and he looked at Debbie as he showed them the photo of Jack and they all nodded.

'His hair's wrong, though,' one said. 'He was fair.'

'Fair, huh? What did he do to you lot?'

'He came here, he spoke to old Jonah, and then came out here and beat up on us,' the hoarse boy said.

'You see him drive up?'

'Yeah. A rental, I reckon.'

Frank shot him a look.

'Not that car?' he asked, pointing.

'No, that was another guy, later.'

231

'Who? A friend of Jonah's?'

'No. Just a man in a suit. Like you.'

Frank nodded. Then, 'Debbie, we're going off to the Sahara.'

'Yeah. Better hurry, too,' she grunted as they ran side by side to the car.

'Yeah. I reckon someone else is already looking for Jack,' Frank said.

*

19.31 Las Vegas; 03.31 London

Jack managed to tempt Sumner away from the table, and the two walked to a bar farther inside the casino. Sumner wiped his face with a handkerchief, and now sat shaking his head, immersed in sad memories.

'What are you doing here, Sumner? Really?' Jack asked.

Sumner shrugged.

'I used to know what I was, what I existed for, when I was in the Army. I had a reason to wake up in the mornings. I did all I could to help my lads, and I understood the chain of command so I could protect them as well as the public. Because that was what we were there for, to look after the people of Iraq and Afghanistan, and those here, and at home. But when things started to go a bit sour, well, we couldn't help but look at ourselves again and wonder.'

'You tried to help others.'

'Someone had to. You know, when I looked at my hometown, Salisbury, I found that of all the men sleeping rough, half of them were from the Army. Half of them! All the guys who'd put their lives at risk, soon as they came home, they were forgotten. What sort of country does that to its men and women?'

Jack motioned to the barista, a woman in her thirties who looked as though she should have been working as a model, not here serving tired men in a tired hotel. She had a smile as clean and fresh as the desert sky. He ordered two double-shots of espresso and sat on a stool with Sumner beside him.

'So, how did you meet Danny?'

'In Iraq, you mean? We used to wander about the place – as intel officers we would be thrown from one place to another, generally affiliated to one or other regiments while they went into a town to search for terrorists. Occasionally we'd end up together and swap stories like you do. I didn't see him for some years after this,' he added ruefully nodding towards his empty sleeve.

232

'How did that happen?'

'My stupidity. I was wandering about the Green Zone one evening in 2003, and a car drove past me too fast. Well, I heard the crunch when it crashed a few moments later. There were mercs all over the place then, ruddy fools who thought that they were God's gift because they were paid double what the squaddies were, and drove like berks the whole time. It was they who caused half our problems because they would go shooting people. Nerves, I suppose. But they created most of our enemies over there.'

'They crashed?'

'That's what I thought. I just went, "Wankers" to myself, and trotted off to see if I could help them. And there they were, in a ditch with smoke coming from the radiator, and I went on to get them out, if I could, before their truck caught fire. Well, cars and trucks always blow up on films, don't they? Trouble was, the truck didn't blow up. I did. Some bastard had made the truck crash by blowing a small bomb under it, and when I got too close, another bomb went off near me. Apparently it took my arm off in a flash, if you see what I mean, and almost completely undressed me. When the Gurkhas found me a couple of minutes later, I was trying to cover my shame with shreds of uniform I found lying about me. Not good. Anyway, I was brought back, and that was that.'

'Which was when you tried to start your charity?'

'Sort of. I met a chap who wanted to invest, and I shoved all my money into it to try to help the lads – especially the Gurkhas. Always had a soft spot for them.'

'How did you get the money together?'

'Ah.' He looked at Jack with a twisted smile. 'It always comes down to the money, doesn't it? There was a fellow offered it to me, like I said. An American donor.'

'Why'd an American help a British charity?'

'He was a veteran from Vietnam, and he had lost his father in Korea. He said he always admired the way that the Gloucesters died and admired the British martial spirit.'

'He didn't see much of that in Vietnam,' Jack commented. 'Who was he?'

'A man called Brian Peachfield.'

The Brain, Jack remembered from the journal. He'd wondered if that might be the nickname of a man called *Brian*.

'Why?'

233

'That was what I wondered, too. At first I thought he was a pleasant fellow who was keen to support our troops. He came along and suggested he could help me. I hadn't thought about it too seriously. At the time I was in Headley Court with rehab on my legs, because they'd been pretty badly knocked about too. It was while I was there and heard about some of the facilities that I decided I should do my own level best to help, which is why I started investigating fund raising. Originally with the other charities, but then... well... my drinking was getting a little out of hand, and they all turned me down. So that was why I began to look at setting up my own charity. I mentioned it among some of my mates, and generally it was thought not a bad idea.'

'How did this man Peachfield hear of it? Was he involved from the start?'

'Yes – I couldn't have started without him. He was keen. He told me he'd heard it from some other officer – don't know who – and that he'd like to help out. Must have been a businessman who had a stash. Either that or he was a banker filled with shame at his disgraceful bonuses,' he said drily. 'Anyway, he deposited thirty thousand quid in my bank to get things moving, and did they ever! We started from a small end of terrace house in Kenley next to a railway line that he managed to rent for me, and within three months by using the internet to market, I had nearly a quarter of a million. It was brilliant!' he said reminiscently. 'I was looking at the cash and spending it all in my head. And then I had the idea of rehab on the move, sort of thing, for the guys who had already come most of the way through their pain, and I was planning skiing trips, walking on the road to Santiago de Compostela, a trek to Machu Picchu – you name it, I was thinking of it.'

'What happened?' Jack asked.

He was keen to return to Danny Lewin, but there was a remorseless pace to the story now that Sumner had begun, and Jack guessed he would have to tell his tale as he wanted before Jack could press him on Lewin again.

'Look at me! I'm no bloody finance wizard, I realise that, but even to me it was obvious something was screwy. One of the lads had an accident on a trip and died, and while we were sorting the finances afterwards we found a hole. Chunks of money had gone walkabout. It was so frustrating.'

'So you did what?'

'What could I do? I did what I thought was best. I spoke to Brian and asked him for more, but the recession was starting to bite, and he put me off. He reckoned my best bet was to speak with a friend of his. Which is where Danny comes in, too.'

*

19.32 Las Vegas; 03.32 London

Stilson pulled up outside the Sahara and checked the parking lot. He really hated driving this piece of shit. He felt as though the seats and ceiling were leaking foul fumes that were infecting his lungs: putrid, disgusting, nasty. Those were the words that summed up this vehicle.

He had dumped the two bodies into Bing's own sedan. He couldn't very well leave them in his rental. But having driven to the old man's bungalow, he had hoped to find Sumner and kill him and the old man and make a good crime scene with Bing's revolver. Nobody would miss Bing. The LVPD loathed him, because they knew he was providing guns for many of the Mafiosi in the city. No he wouldn't be missed. And neither would a druggie woman, or a pensioner without a dime to his name. The only man who could have got somebody's interest would have been Sumner, but he was a drunk and down-and-out now, so no one would worry too much about his death either. It had been perfect as a plan.

Not now. Since Sumner wasn't there, all he could do was wind things up quickly, kill the old asshole and get out of there. He'd walked fast and caught a cab a few blocks away to get back to his rental, and now here he was, at this ancient casino, to find Sumner. Perhaps he could strangle Sumner in the washrooms. Make it seem like a sex perversion death. It was the right way for a man like him to die – drunk and alone.

He wasn't comfortable, though. He didn't like bad luck, and it appeared to be dogging him today. Things were growing a little too dangerous. He had left his throw-down piece in the old asshole's bungalow, together with the old man's .38, so all he had left now that was untraceable was the Springfield .45. He couldn't use his Glock – it was too easily checked, and ballistics could work wonders with a used slug. Still, at least there was no apparent connection between him and the old bastard or Bing. That was the beauty of being a professional who killed those he was instructed to. It was so easy to make a hit and walk. The cops spent all their time trying to find a link

235

to provide a motive. When there was none, it made their task impossible.

Stilson had to remove Sumner somehow. Best, probably, for him just to disappear. If Stilson could get him into the car and drive off, that would be fine. There were lots of places in the desert to lose a man. Alternatively, there was always the option of throttling him in the washrooms.

The old man had said Stilson's vice was the cards. Stilson disliked doing it, but he couldn't take risks. He took his Glock and its holster from behind his hip and placed them carefully under his seat. First place a thief would look after the glove compartment, but he couldn't help that. He shut the door, locked it, and walked to the entrance. Weaving through the slot machines in case Sumner was there, he passed through and into the main card dealing area. There he saw the poker players, and he drew up a stool at a slot machine and began to push coins into it, his eyes watching the players. A large-breasted woman with a tray appeared with a bright, manufactured smile, and he asked for a soda.

He knew he may be here a while.

*

19.41 Las Vegas; 03.41 London

Jack sipped coffee.

'How does that come back to Danny?'

'It happened like this: Peachfield reckoned I needed a financial techie guru to advise me. This fellow saw in a flash what was happening...'

'This is your computer whizz-kid, yeah?'

'Yes. Jimmy.'

'What was his name?'

'Jimmy McNeill.'

'*Jesus*!' Jack stared.

'Do you know him?'

'I did,' Jack said, thinking back to a scene in his mind: his wife, Claire, in Jimmy's arms in the kitchen of her house in Devon, her body arched back, her pelvis thrust against his, her throat bare and open to Jimmy's kisses. Jimmy, the handsome honey-trap, the...

'Jimmy was my financial whizz. Brian Peachfield put me on to Jimmy, and it stopped the money gushing from the accounts, but it was a bit late. Someone in Ukraine or somewhere had got a software package onto our computer that meant all our details were copied to them. God knows how. I was at my wit's end. From a small fortune the charity had gone to nothing.'

'So the cash was all gone?'

'Everything. All I could do was wind up the charity. That was 2009. And then in 2010 I got a call.'

'Who was this, Roger?'

'Another American. He said he worked with some associates who thought they could use my skills. Ha! New to me, that. Didn't know I had any. Still, I spoke with this fellow on the phone...'

'His name?'

'None given. He told me that there was money for me if I would meet him. The job was helping America and Britain fight the good fight. Not quite how he put it, but that was his meaning. A week or two later, I had a ticket in the post. I met him in the Paradise Cafe restaurant at the Mirage. Never been to Vegas before, and I admit, it staggered me. I came with a little spending money, just two hundred pounds, and lost it all, but there was a short period when I was beginning to do quite well. I have those moments every so often, you see,' he added.

Jack knew. Many people did. It was why casinos made so much money. The brief flaring of hope triumphing over reality. That was what kept gamblers returning for more.

'What was his offer?'

'He told me he represented a consortium which had decided that since Guantanamo Bay was to close and the troops were coming out of 'Stan, there was a need for a non-governmental body to take over certain responsibilities.'

'What does that mean?'

'In short, pirates. Mercs. You have a government that thinks it knows a man or two who has information, and you kidnap them. Oh, in official terms it got to be known as "rendition", but it's kidnapping. Their idea was to kidnap their suspects, and fly them to Uzbekistan, or Azerbaijan, or Pakistan, and then send expert interrogators to pull them apart and suck all the intel possible from their marrow,' Sumner said, but now his voice was closed. All enthusiasm was gone. He drained his coffee, but made no effort to rise and leave.

'So you told him—'

'To fuck off. I am no merc, and I am not a torturer. That's what he wanted, really. Someone who'd be prepared to use cattle prods, stun guns, electrical wires, whips, coshes, water-boarding, stress –

anything. And I'm not that sort of a man. I did what I had to when there were rules, when there were boundaries. These bastards were talking about capturing people and flying them halfway around the world. And what then? Uzbeks'd torture them, I'd get all the data from them, and then the poor bastards would remain there. Couldn't exactly take them home, could we? So, for all I know, I'd have become the last European to see these fellows before they were condemned to life in prison or to a hanging. I'm not going to do that, I said. He asked where my boundaries would be, and I said "you've already passed them, matey." And that was pretty much that.'

'Except for Danny.'

'Yes. Except for Danny.'

'How did he fit in?'

'Well, he and I happened to bump into each other in Manchester. He looked terrible, *terrible*. Thin as a straw, pathetically guilty, and anxious the whole time. He'd had a pretty torrid time after he left the military. And then they nicked him for trying to acquire a pistol. I mean, he'd carried one every day for years, and soon as he came back, he wasn't allowed to protect himself! He did apply, and the police said it was illegal for him to have one at all, so he asked for protection from armed police and they said he didn't merit it in their opinion. Bloody cretins! Anyway, he wanted to get away and he needed money, too.'

'So you put him onto this guy?'

Sumner was quiet for a minute. He fiddled with the cup's lid, tearing little strips of white plastic from it, dropping each into his now empty cardboard cup. Jack held his tongue. He had seen men in this mood before. There was something he wanted to get off his chest, but it was painful even now. He was ashamed, Jack guessed.

'I had debts, you know? And I wanted to get cash for the charity. Did you see what I called it? The Heroes Rehabilitation Trust – HRT. I didn't realise HRT could mean Hormone Replacement Therapy until some while afterwards. Never had need to think of such things when you're only in your thirties, do you? But I did want some money. Like Danny.'

'So although you refused to participate, you said you'd mention the idea to others?'

'No, only that I'd give his number to people if they were on their uppers like I had been. And when I saw Danny, well, I thought it could help him.'

238

Jack nodded. Sumner's suggestion had almost certainly saved his life at that time. The 'Associates' would not have been keen to leave a man with knowledge of their plans alive and well to spread the news, but if he was sworn to secrecy and ready and willing to act as their unofficial recruiter, perhaps they would have been more comfortable. In any case, the fact that he was an experienced interrogation officer meant he was used to keeping secrets – sometimes very dark secrets. He was perhaps more trustworthy than others could have guessed.

'So you put Danny on to this guy.'

'Yes. And Danny was offered a place to recover in Alaska. He told me about it.'

'I see.'

'The funny thing is, I saw the man again.'

Jack looked at him.

'Who?'

'The man who tried to hire me. It didn't occur to me that he'd actually live here in Vegas, but I've seen him here a few times. He's in charge of security at the Mirage. A fellow called Peter Sorensen.'

'Has he recognised you?'

Sumner looked at him.

'If he had, I think I would have left town. I don't somehow think that a man who's tried to hire me for something that secret would make a good friend.'

'That's why you come here, then?'

Sumner looked at him very sharply, and Jack felt that there was steel in those eyes even with his shabby clothing and surroundings.

'No, Jack. I come here because I am broke and a drunk. I have just enough self-respect left to try to remain a little above the bums in this place, but that's all. I have no arm, no job, and no hope. I have just a little money left, and the day I cash my last chips, I'll shoot myself. I have an old revolver to ensure I do that properly. That's why I'll stay here in the US. So much easier to acquire guns than England.'

'Really?'

'You doubt me? There's a programme on which a minor celeb learns all kinds of sad details about his or her ancestors. In this case it was a man whose father had fought with the Highlanders or some similar regiment out in Burma. You know of that war? It was foul. Really foul. This fellow clearly suffered. He had shrapnel wounds that left him badly injured, and he'd fought in two of the worst battles

239

in the Jap wars. Afterwards he came home, but couldn't adjust. So after a while he went out to Malaya and that was where he died. And what the family never learned was, he blew his brains out. You see, he'd lost all his mates in the war. The only people who could understand him were dead. So he played Russian Roulette each weekend, until one day he was finished.'

'You wouldn't do that, would you?'

'Oh, yes. When there's no more money, why not play the final game? It's a game that shows who's won rather more explicitly than any other, I would think. Wouldn't you?'

*

19.48 Las Vegas; 03.48 London

The Strip was full of traffic again as Frank and Debbie tried to make their way across the city to the Sahara. There were calls going out on the radio, but Frank was determined to get up there before the cops. He wanted to get Jack and hold him for himself.

'Come on!' he hissed.

'Don't take it so personal, Frank,' Debbie said. She was staring across at him.

'It's not personal. I just want to get the guy,' Frank said.

'Weird, huh. The guy in LVPD recognising one of the two in the Gas Park shots.'

Frank negotiated a space around a electric pink Hummer stretched limo.

'Did he give me the finger?'

'He's in behind a black windshield, Frank. How'd I know? Did you hear me?'

'Yes, I heard you. Yes, it's weird. The guy was a hitman, though, and a few of them do come from the military, I guess.'

'I guess,' she said, but her eyes were narrowed as she continued thinking.

'What?' he demanded, his foot hitting the brakes just as they were about to hit a truck. 'Shit!'

'No prints, no DNA, no ID of any sort. You said the only folks with the power to remove all that data about someone would be someone in a big agency, and now we learn he was with the boys in Iraq. So he could have been intelligence out there. Which would mean he could have had his ID wiped by folks in the government. Like you said.'

'That's just paranoia.'

'Just because I'm paranoid doesn't mean they aren't out to get me,' she said, but without smiling. 'I want to run a check on this Ian McDonnell who could have been in the Abu Ghraib.'

'You do that,' he said, swearing under his breath as a Chrysler pulled out in front of him.

'The cop in there was really convincing.'

'Yeah. I agree with you there,' Frank said. 'I just hope Sumner is still there when we arrive.'

'I just hope we get there this year,' Debbie said, looking at the traffic ahead.

*

19.59 Las Vegas; 03.59 London

Jack questioned Sumner a little more, checking on the description of Peter Sorensen, the man at the Mirage.

'Heavy build. Looks like one of those fellows who spent all his teenage years pumping iron and drinking ridiculous concoctions designed to make his muscles look even bigger. Fair to brown hair, which could be faded because of the sun out here. Always wears a white shirt, short-sleeved, with dark slacks, black shoes, a black belt, and very flash designer Ray Bans when he's outside. Indoors he always has a jacket on, just a lightweight thing, but enough to cover his pistol. Like so many of the security men over here, he isn't dressed without his gun.'

'Face?'

'Square, and he has a moustache with just a trace of grey in it. Wide hazel eyes, and he has a broken nose. Looks the sort who keeps it to brag about being in a fight,' Sumner added with contempt. He glanced down at his own arm momentarily.

'Thanks for that,' Jack said. 'You want another coffee?'

Sumner pulled a grimace.

'No, I'm fine, thanks.' He stood. 'I need a leak after that stuff. It's the problem with caffeine, you see. My body is a temple, and I worship it with lavish quantities of bourbon. If you'll excuse me, I'll go for a piss, then back to my table.'

'Yeah, sure.'

'Just one thing, though. Danny, you said you thought someone put a bullet in his head for him. Are you sure of that?'

'No. He could have shot himself, but it didn't look like it to me.'

'In Alaska?'

241

'A town called Whittier.'

'Never heard of it. What was he doing there?'

'He had a diary. He said that they'd paid for him to go out there. He was being put up in a log cabin way out in the middle of nowhere. They didn't suggest it to you?'

Sumner shook his head.

'I didn't think they were the kind to let me know a secret if I didn't need to, so once I got to the "Thanks, but no thanks" stage, I backed off before they decided I was a threat.'

'Could be you made the smarter move.'

'Yes,' Sumner said, with a fretful anxiety in his eyes again. 'But I led him to his death. That's the long and the short of it.'

Jack said nothing more as Sumner shook his head again, and then stood and made his way towards the toilets. He was steady on his feet, and Jack was impressed. He'd been drinking solidly, from his appearance, and the fact that he was functioning indicated to Jack that his liver was inured to the punishment.

He didn't see the man who followed Sumner into the toilets.

*

20.06 Las Vegas; 04.06 London

The toilets were not crowded yet at this time of day. Stilson walked in and saw Sumner with his back to him at a urinal. There were mirrors in front of each, but Sumner was not looking behind him. He was studying his own reflection.

There must have been thousands came in here over the years, with exactly that same look, Stilson thought to himself, thousands who realised after a late night that they no longer owned their cars, their houses, or even their mobile phones. All lost. It happened so often.

But this one was different.

At the urinals there were two other men, murmuring a conversation as they emptied their bladders. They zipped up and walked out without glancing at Stilson.

A large bin was under the paper towel dispenser. It was a fair weight, and Stilson moved it to the door, jamming it. When he turned he saw that Sumner's eyes were on him.

'So you want me now?' he said simply.

Stilson said nothing, approaching cautiously but with speed.

'Wait until I've at least finished my piss!' Sumner said.

They were his last words. Stilson hit him at the base of his skull with a fist. Sumner jerked forwards, his head cracking on the mirror, and Stilson pushed him to the floor. He put his knees on Sumner's back, his left elbow around his throat, right hand on his skull, and jerked and twisted. It took little effort. He pulled the body into a cubicle, pulled Sumner's trousers down round his ankles, and left him propped on the toilet. Shutting the door he turned the vacant sign to engaged by inserting the blade of his pocketknife into the slotted screw. Then he pulled the garbage bin away from the door, washed his hands thoroughly, and exited.

At the entrance a series of figures appeared: two moved off to the left, another couple to the right, while three stood in the middle of the entranceway, staring into the main slot machine hall. Stilson saw a security guard march towards the men, and saw Frank Rand pull out a wallet and show something. There was a gleam of metal. It must have been a badge, and that meant police or FBI. Then he saw four uniformed officers hurrying in, the man with the wallet pointing them along one side of the hall.

Stilson wanted nothing to do with police of any sort. Without breaking step, he turned and marched away to the right, towards the lifts.

*

20.11 Las Vegas; 04.11 London

It was the barista who saw the cops entering.

'Aw, fuck! What do they want here?'

Jack turned and caught a glimpse of two officers, both with their hands near their pistols.

'Do they often come in?'

'No. Usually we have to call 'em because of some punter acting like a dick. Sorry, present company etcetera, etcetera.'

'That's fine. Tell you what, how about another shot? A single, this time.'

'Sure, honey. You wait there.'

She busied herself at the machine, emptying the old puck, flicking the lever on the grinder to dispense just the right amount of coffee, tamping it hard, leaving the surface smooth and flat, and then locking it on the coffee machine. She pressed the button, and steam began to rise as the water was forced through the coffee at high pressure. And all the while Jack's eyes were fixed on her movements, smiling at her as she caught his gaze. She could not realise that the polished metal of her espresso machine was his mirror. He was watching four officers moving through the lines of slot machines behind him. And then he saw a face he recognised – an African American face from Anchorage.

'Here you go.'

'Thanks,' he said, and dropped a note on the counter.

'Hey, thanks!' she said with notably more enthusiasm as he rose and picked up his cup. 'You have a nice day, y' hear?'

'You too,' he smiled, and moved off before Frank Rand could see him.

*

20.13 Las Vegas; 04.13 London

Jack walked quickly but without urgency, sipping from the hot coffee as he went out towards the back of the complex. From a quick look around he reckoned he could understand the casino's layout. Large main hall here, bars and restaurants at the back where guests had to pass through the slot machine hall to reach them, and he was convinced that the lifts would be out here too. He finished his coffee on the way, and dumped the cup in a bin.

He was right. There was a set of lifts, a door next to them. This gave onto the stairs. Quickly, he pressed the buttons to call the lifts. There was one already waiting, with the doors open. He reached in, pressed the button for the top floor, and slipped back out as the lift's warning pinged and the doors closed. By the time it was shut, he was already in the service stairwell. He heard the sound of running feet, and he took the stairs two at a time to the first floor, and darted out into the corridor. In the staircase he could hear feet pounding up, as officers sprinted to catch him at the top floor. Jack looked about him and strode along the passage looking for another staircase. Soon he found a smoke alarm. Further up the corridor he saw a cleaner's trolley, with dirty linen bags, clean linen, and complimentary soaps and shampoos. He walked to the trolley and saw that there was a cardboard box full of books of complimentary matches with the casino's name and logo in silver. He took two, and walked to the alarm sensor. Striking one match, he let it flare, then lit both books and held the flames under the sensor. It took a moment or two, and then a loud klaxon sounded. Instantly he heard a scream and, as he blew out the matches and dropped the still-hot embers into the trolley, people began to hurry from their rooms. He was soon being swept along in a crush of people, taking off his jacket and bundling it as he went, and smearing his hair down flat to emphasise the widow's peak.

Outside there were more people, all hurrying to the car park, and Jack pushed and shoved until he was at the front of the queues of men and women, ignoring the shouts and demands to know what was happening. He remained, watching carefully, as the police arrived and forced the crowds back, followed by the massive red fire trucks with their lights flashing and sirens wailing and honking.

Jack walked to his car and started the engine as the last of the police and casino staff left. There was so much security in these places that staff always assumed a fire alert was actually a diversion for thieves, so they would always lock up all the chips and cash before evacuating the building. Jack was impressed that they had succeeded in their lockdown procedures in such a short period.

The Mirage was at the opposite end of the Strip. He made a quick decision, drove out of the car park, and headed back down towards the Bellagio. As he did, he saw a car parked at the side of the road with two men inside. They had the look of Federal agents, with their suits and short hair. Jack averted his face slightly, thinking that they must be hunting him, but, as he did so, he saw one of them glance in his direction. He did not make any connection with Jack, clearly, because he turned back to stare at the casino, eyes narrowed, and then pointed. His companion leaned forward, nodding, both men absorbed by something or someone at the casino entrance.

Jack drove on by. These two weren't looking for him, then. When he glanced back, he saw a group at the main doors, Frank Rand among them.

*

20.14 Las Vegas; 04.14 London

Frank Rand stood outside the Sahara with a sense of rising frustration. There had been a moment there when he had thought that they would have him. He could have sworn that the man at the coffee bar had been Jack, but when the alarms went off it blew his chances. The girl serving in the bar was somewhere out here with the milling crowd, but there was no way of telling how long it would be before he could question her or show her a copy of the mugshot. *Damn*! He had been so close, he reckoned. And now this fire alarm meant that Jack would be far away before Frank could even check to see whether it was him here.

'Does this mean we've lost him, you reckon?' Debbie asked with a grunt and she joined him. She had been questioning all the staff she could find, but now that LVPD officers were taking over she was

245

getting in their way. 'Too hot to be interviewing people here,' she said in answer to his unspoken question.

'For now, I guess,' Frank said. 'But we can still get Sumner, with luck. He's bound to be in here somewhere. Just keep looking for him.'

'I have done, and the cops are doing all they can,' she said. 'You never know. Maybe we'll get him.'

Frank was about to respond when he noticed a police officer at the doorway to the gentlemen's washroom.

'What's his problem?' Frank asked.

The man was waving urgently to two other officers, and the three returned to the toilets in a hurry. Frank glanced at Debbie.

'I suppose I could send you in there.'

'Wouldn't be my first time in a John,' she said.

'I think I'd better go too, in case of upsetting them,' Frank said.

He led the way through the slot machines to the washrooms. There he pulled out his ID for the officers.

'What is it?'

'A guy in here. Must have overdosed or had a heart attack or something,' said the officer whom Frank had noticed.

Frank nodded to the closed door.

'Let's see.'

Another officer stepped forward and pounded on the door. Frank knew that they would be reluctant to barge straight in, not because the man could be embarrassed, but because it could be a drug addict brandishing a hypodermic. There was no answer, and the officer took a step back, and was about to kick the door, when Frank held up his hand. He had a dime on him, and he used that to turn the screw, opening the door. He pushed the door wide.

'That answers that,' Debbie said, taking in the sight of Sumner's slackly drooling mouth as the officer reached in tentatively and tested for a pulse.

'He have a heart attack?' one of the other officers asked.

'I don't think a heart attack would make his head go like that,' Debbie said caustically. 'Look at him. You think he's managed to break his neck while sitting on the John? Doesn't ring quite true to me.'

'Why'd he kill this guy and then set off the alarms, then? Don't make sense to kill him, set him in here to make him look like he's takin' a dump and then call attention to it,' an officer muttered.

'True,' Frank said decisively. 'Debbie, outside.'

When they were alone, Debbie turned to him.

'What?'

'I could have sworn I saw Jack Case in there as we walked in. He was over at the coffee bar, I think.'

'You think he could've killed this guy?'

'Could be. I just don't make him out as a murderer,' Frank said. 'Why'd he kill this Sumner? Makes no sense to me.'

'If it wasn't him, who was it? He's been around two places today where we've found dead bodies, if you're right,' Debbie said. 'You know, I don't like coincidences. They don't happen much in real life, I reckon.'

'Neither do I,' Frank admitted.

'Well, first thing is, find the barista you think could've served him his coffee, and see whether she recognises his face. If she does, we got confirmation it was him there, then we can start to check whether he went to the John and killed Sumner.'

'Yeah,' Frank said.

'And meanwhile, we can see what we can get on Sumner himself. And this Ian McDonnell. I'm interested in this guy.'

*

20.43 Las Vegas; 04.43 London

Jack was soon back at the Bellagio, and dropped his car off at the rental area. From there he walked up to the main lobby area, where he paused a moment before striding out to the casino hall. At the other side there were shops, he remembered.

Before long he was back in his room with a fresh blue check shirt in and a sports jacket. He studied himself in the mirror and wished he had some reversible clothes, perhaps a set of false spectacles, anything. To be walking about without disguise made him feel exceptionally vulnerable. In the end, he washed his hair and left it to dry without a parting in the hope that it would make a little difference. With a splash of eau de cologne from the Giorgio Armani shop, he felt ready for his next effort. He looked about him, then walked from the room.

The Mirage was another massive, imposing resort and casino complex like the Bellagio. In front of the huge buildings there was a simulation of a massive volcano, and it was beginning to erupt as Jack walked past to the entrance. He did not look as it rumbled and

247

lava appeared to roll down the sides. His eyes were on the two wings of the vast casino in front and above him.

He had brought five hundred dollars rolled into a tube in his trouser pocket, and, as he entered the front entrance, he paused and took his bearings.

The whole hotel was based on the idea of a Polynesian paradise, but the decorations were of no interest to him. He walked through, taking no notice of the aquarium behind the reception desk, and made his way straight to the gaming area beyond the atrium. There were rows of the omnipresent slot machines and, as he wandered about the room, he found the tables. He stood watching the players for a while, his hand playing with the notes in his pocket. Soon he had the measure of the nearer tables, he reckoned, and he walked to the casino's cage in the middle of the room. There he changed all his dollars into chips and two rolls of coins. Then he returned to the tables, where he sat playing Blackjack.

A waitress appeared and offered him a complimentary drink, and Jack looked up, blinking and smiling with his best American accent.

'Sorry, honey?'

'You want a drink, sir?'

'I'd surely love that. A bourbon, please.'

She smiled and was soon back with the drink. Jack took it with a smile and returned to studying the play of the others around the table until at last he saw Peter Sorensen.

*

21.38 Las Vegas; 05.38 London

Frank Rand was beginning to feel that he was getting somewhere. As Debbie walked into his borrowed office on the fourth floor of the LVPD building, he looked up hopefully.

'Yes?'

'Yes!' she grinned. 'Got him.'

'Let me see,' he said, reaching for her legal pad.

'Oh, no! You got to wait until I present it properly,' she said slyly.

'OK, just give.'

'Mr Ian McDowell was, as you were told, in the army. I checked with the army, and they said "Nope" he wasn't nothin' to do with them. So I looked at the Pentagon and drew a blank. So I checked with Veterans and…'

'Do you mind cutting to the chase, Miss?' Frank said sarcastically.

248

'Gettin' there, Frank. So I went to the NSA, to Home Land Security, to the CIA, hell, I even double-checked with our own records teams in case the SOB had joined us too, but nothing. No record of him exists. I went back to criminal records, nothin'. Went to the army CRC, Crime Records Centre, but nothing there either. Absolutely nothing. This guy didn't exist.'

'Fine. So let's get on to something else.'

Her grin broadened.

'So, I thought, these assholes are just testing this little girl, and I thought I was sick of taking bullshit. First, I reckoned maybe we were all wrong, so I looked in the army records to see if I had his name wrong. There's the Scots way to spell it, you know, with a second "I", like "Iain"?'

'I know.'

'But that was no good. So then I started thinking about trying to get another name. Like his first name wasn't actually "Ian", but was something else.'

'Debbie, for Christ's sake get on with it!'

'Just a little longer, boss. So then I went back and tried that. Again, still no matches. So that's when I got clever.'

'Debbie!'

She saw his mood and quickly decided to obey.

'OK, boss. I went the other way and looked at all the records to do with Abu Ghraib, and there, in the middle of all those reports, I found him.'

'What?'

Frank was already out of his seat and reaching for her notes.

'He was a WO1. That's as high as you get before you start getting keys to the officer's mess. Senior Warrant Officer in charge of some intelligence group at the prison. Couldn't learn too much about exactly what he was doin' there, but I reckon it was something to do with screening the prisoners. They must have had a whole load of problems trying to learn who was what down there.'

Frank's face was screwed up in consternation as he read her notes.

'But who'd erase his records? What the fuck was he doing?'

'Look down there, boss. You're missing the best bit,' she said, pointing.

'He is dead? We know that already, Debbie. His head got stove in by Case hitting him on a truck.'

249

'Look there, boss,' she said, jabbing with her finger. 'The date of his death. There were riots in Abu Ghraib because of the food. Prisoners were given rancid food with cockroaches in it, and rat droppings, the lot. And there wasn't enough, according to the reports from the Pentagon. One thing led to another, the prisoners rioted, and some guards were injured. One, apparently, was a certain WO1 McDonnell. Afterwards, Pentagon officials said, he should be given a posthumous medal for his defence. Said he stood up to a group of seven Iraqis when he'd run out of ammo. Another report said he was beaten up pretty bad, and died later in hospital.'

'So he's a hero and his records got trashed?'

'I don't think so! Look here.'

She brought out a photocopied sheet and passed it to him. It showed a photo.

'What's this?'

'Found it on the web with the stuff from Wikileaks. Yeah, I know, they're not nice people, but hey – maybe this time they're doing some good. And what they show is, this picture. And the caption reads: "Dick Farrer, Jimmy Borner, Ian McDowell, F. Peter Sorensen, and Stan Dewer".'

'Intelligence?' he read.

'I think that means he was paid to help interrogate prisoners, boss, and that the records are bullshit. This guy was still alive until yesterday when Case killed him. Which also leads me to question just why it was that the guy was after Case in the first place.'

'What do you mean?'

'I mean, I can only assume this guy was on an agency payroll of some kind. How else would he get clearance for a new life, with his past wiped clean from all the US government computers?'

'That means an agency has an interest in seeing Case killed.'

'Yeah. And a powerful one, too,' Debbie agreed.

*

21.40 Las Vegas; 05.40 London

He was still there at the Blackjack table when Jack finally saw Sorensen.

It was easy to recognise the man. He walked in as though he owned the place. Standing at the top of a small flight of stairs from whence he could view most of the tables, he eyed each of the dealers and punters with wide-set hazel eyes that missed nothing. Jack saw them flick to him, and then away, as though considering Jack to be of little

250

interest – just another semi-drunk who was here to lose a few hundred bucks.

Peter Sorensen did have a heavy build, just as Sumner said. His shoulders were so wide that he could have scraped along both walls in a corridor. In his pale cream jacket of some light material, he looked even bigger. His muscles were so pronounced that his arms swung well away from his torso as he walked. His neck was thick, and although he appeared to have little spare flesh on his belly, there was a good roll of fat around his collar, which made his head looked oddly small in comparison, even with his square jaw which was perpetually chewing gum. He had fair-ish hair, but it was less because of the sun and more to do with his age, Jack estimated. He was wearing a white shirt with a blue and red striped tie, and was smart in his dark slacks and black shoes.

Looking at him, Sumner's words came back to him. 'Indoors he always has a jacket on, just a lightweight thing, but enough to cover his pistol. He isn't dressed without his gun.'

Jack looked over the jacket. With men who walked like that, their arms swinging about their body, never scraping the hips, he often assumed that there was a gun in a shoulder holster. In this case, he reckoned the man's gun was on his hip, or just behind it, rather than under the shoulder. As he walked, it was obvious that Sorensen had weight in the right outer pocket of his jacket. From Jack's experience, that would mean a gunman who might need to draw his pistol quickly, flicking the jacket away before reaching beneath to grab the gun.

His gait was slow and deliberate, but watching him Jack saw that he was very precise too. This was not a man who was ponderously heavy, but a man who was light on his feet like a boxer – or a martial artist. He'd be tough to take down if he wanted to fight. And the fact that he had a gun on his belt too didn't bode well for Jack's chances. It was enough to make Jack scowl ungraciously at his cards. He asked for another, then a fourth, and declared himself 'Bust!' with an expression of self-disgust. He rose, drained his drink, and moved off idly towards the high pay-out slots behind the cage.

He took his seat at the end of a row, leaning on an elbow while he studied the machine. Beyond the flashing lights and spinning wheels, he could see Sorensen standing at the cage, talking to two cashiers. The big man moved on, and Jack saw his hand go to his cheek,

251

scratching it, as he strolled. He turned his back to Jack, and Jack watched with narrowed eyes.

Too late he realised that Sorensen had a microphone in his sleeve or held in his hand. His ear had a coiled, clear plastic tube running down beneath his jacket, and he was in constant contact with the men who sat in a room somewhere near watching the TV screens that studied the people down in the gambling room all the time.

Jack was about to rise when two men appeared beside him.

'Sir, we would like you to come with us,' one said.

Neither was openly carrying a weapon, but there was no doubt that they could fight if pushed. Jack maintained his slightly baffled demeanour, smiling, saying, 'Sure. Lemme just get my…' He grabbed his money from the top of the slot machine, which included one roll of coins unused, and dropped them all in his pocket. 'I've not had much luck, anyway,' he grumbled to himself as the two led him through to the elevator lobby. There he was taken to a small door beside the elevators marked 'Staff Only', where a swipe card opened the door.

'What do you want, anyhow?' he asked.

'You were being watched,' one of the men said.

'So you saw me losing? Is that a crime? I thought it was the whole idea.'

'Funny,' said the man and then, noticing that Jack was falling away slightly added, 'Hey, come on!'

Jack was over towards the wall now, glancing up at the ceiling all around, and the guard frowned, reaching for him. Jack allowed him to take his arm, and he was pulled onwards. The man propelled him slightly forward, pushing him in the small of the back, and Jack stumbled.

'Ah, shit,' one said.

Jack fell forward, both hands supporting his weight, and jackknifed. He bent his arms, his legs, his back, and then straightened explosively. His feet caught the nearer guard on the chin and nose, and the man's head snapped back as he was thrown to the floor. His companion swore and grabbed for Jack, but Jack was already on his feet, and his left foot snapped out and caught the guard in the belly. His breath left his body with an explosive grunt. Jack quickly chopped the first guy over the back of the neck, who collapsed to the ground. The second was gasping for air as Jack ripped the radio transmitter from his back pocket, tugging the wires free. The wrist

252

mic came away easily, but he had to pull the coiled plastic tube free from the man's ear.

The man tried to grab Jack by the leg, and he kicked out, hitting the man on the throat. He fell away again, clasping his throat, desperate for air.

Jack walked back the way they had come. He took off his jacket on the way and bundled it, throwing it quickly over his left shoulder. At the door, he looked out through the small spyhole before pressing the door release button and walking out into the elevator hall. He passed through it quickly, and on to the casino, his head down. There was no chance of speaking to Sorensen here, he reasoned, not now. Better to find out where Sorensen lived and question him there. First, he had to escape this place. He screwed the headphone into his ear as he walked on past the slots and tables of green and red baize, under the bright yellowish lighting out to the entranceway. He didn't see Sorensen in the main gambling floor, and he prayed that his jacket would prevent people from seeing his face.

He was almost at the door, when he saw Sorensen again. He was out near the entrance itself, walking back to the casino with an equally big companion. Jack turned right, towards the south entrance, and into the California Pizza Kitchen, where he stood for a second gazing about him blankly, before turning back and walking out from the casino. He began to walk along the pavement, staring at the volcano, joining other partygoers who were waiting for the next eruption. Lots of men and women were there, leaning against railings, and he became a part of the happy throng as he unobtrusively covered the bud in his ear and listened to the radio.

The static was bad out here, but he could make out voices calling commands, the sound of angry men shouting, orders to check the main hall, the cage, the high rolling tables, everywhere until they caught 'That son of a bitch!'

Smiling, he watched the volcano as it began its theatrics, and afterwards he slowly moved away.

He needed a computer or local directory. There should be something he could use at the Bellagio.

*

21.46 Las Vegas; 05.46 London

Frank Rand's call to Houlican had not been pleasant.

'What the fuck are you talking about, the guy could have been an agency man? He was a hood, Frank.'

253

'He was dressed up like an agent. Think about it, the haircut, the suit – all the marks of an agent, Bill.'

He could imagine his boss standing at that. His finger would jab at the desktop – short, stubby gestures that demonstrated his temper.

'No, Frank! You listen to me! You've been dragging your sorry ass around after a series of bodies, man – first the one you say died after he was shot in the tunnel at Whittier, then the two at Seattle with the Englishman, now three, no, four more in Vegas, and you have no answer to the question: where's the fucker responsible? We know it was this Brit, this guy Jack Case, but you're fannying about with theories about others…'

'The dead Brit in Seattle was attacked by the two agents. We have evidence; we have witnesses. Case acted in self-defence,' Frank protested.

'What about the others, uh? The Brit, Sumner? What about the old man whose only crime was, he was at the house when Case wanted Sumner? And those youngsters he beat up on? Come on, Frank, you're losing perspective here.'

'Sir, with respect, I think you've lost the big picture. This guy Case seems more likely to be the victim here, far as I can see. And I am seriously worried that the guys trying to kill him are with a US government agency. For Christ's sake, Bill, give me some help here, will you?'

'I will report your concerns, if you are serious and can send me your comments. One page at first. A summary, right? And then, a full and comprehensive document that will give me the full story. Why you don't think he was responsible, why he's innocent, and why you reckon an agency could be involved. Who, why, when and where and how. Got that? Until I've got that lot, I am running with the other possibility, which is we have a crazy running around and killing people.'

'Sir, I…' Frank saw Debbie walk in waving sheets of photocopied paper. 'Can you hold just a minute, sir?'

Debbie was blank-faced.

'They questioned the barista at the coffee shop. She is definite: Sumner was there with Case.'

'Shit!' Frank groaned.

'Wait! Sumner left and she saw him go to the John. Case was still there, up till the moment our boys turned up, and then he walked away, back to the main hotel.'

254

'Not towards Sumner and the toilets?'

'Nope. He went away. Coupl'a minutes later, all hell broke loose, she says, and she missed the rest of her shift. Not Case. No way.'

Rand took a deep breath.

'Sir? We just had confirmation that the Brit, Sumner, couldn't have been killed by Case. Very definite, very positive ID of Case still being around when Sumner walked off. He's innocent.'

'Then who killed the prick?'

'Sir, all I'm asking is, just don't make this a manhunt for Case yet. That's all I'm asking. You do that, some trigger-happy cop will blow him away and that'll wreck our chances of getting to the truth.'

'I couldn't give a good Goddam about the truth. I just want this crap off my desk, Agent Rand. Got that?'

'Yes, sir. But the truth is that if he gets shot, we'll end up with more paperwork than a publisher. He's a Brit. If the papers hear we shot a Brit and he was innocent, we'd all be in the shit.'

'They wouldn't find out.'

Rand tilted his head.

'Did Rodney King get out? Did…'

'All right. You made your point.'

Rand listened as the line went quiet for a minute.

'OK, Rand. Find him. Question him. But at least fucking find him. We can listen to his story then.'

Rand put the receiver down. Debbie looked at him enquiringly.

'Well?'

'We are now supposed to find this guy – Case – and arrest him. Quietly, without fuss, so that we can question him.'

'Oh. So, what, we've been sitting on our fannys all day waiting for his command to find Case? What an asshole!'

'Debbie, that's fine. You use all the invective you want against him, and I won't stop you. But the main thing just now is that we still don't know what he's up to, or why these other guys are after him. And I am beginning to think I haven't the faintest idea how to.'

She rubbed the back of her neck.

'This guy Sumner. Case was talking to him a lot over coffee, according to the Barista.'

'Angry? Aggressive talks?'

'Nope. Like old buddies.'

Frank nodded.

'If that's so, maybe they used to work together? We think Case was probably a spy of some sort, so maybe Sumner was too. Case may be trying to figure out who killed Danny Lewin, and that may mean the link is there. Lewin, Sumner, Case. Lewin was military intelligence. Could Sumner have been?'

He looked over at her, frowning.

'It'd make sense,' she said. There was a note of disapproval in her voice as she continued. 'Some guys give up after PTS. I've seen men from my college who were bright, clever, the lot, and after they came back from Iraq they were different. They saw things, did things, they shouldn't've. Knew one, he was only a boy, who came back and on his first day home, he heard a truck going over a metal plate. You know, they're doing roadworks, and shoved a steel plate over the hole? This guy, he heard the bang, and dove under the nearest stoop. Took them ages to get him out again. He was crying and, oh, it was terrible. I know a few who went to the tables to gamble soon as they could. Wouldn't surprise me if this Sumner was like that. He was known to the barista there at the Sahara, after all. She said he was there most days.'

'OK, go check,' Frank said. 'And while you do that, I'll see what I can find out about the two in the car's trunk. What they were doing there, I don't know.'

*

22.34 Las Vegas; 06.34 London

Jack had put on a dark T-shirt. It was a tight fit over his belly, but he pulled it over his head and tucked it into his dark slacks. Hopefully there would be little need for heavy shoes, he thought.

The hotel had a small computer room, but it was clearly not designed for extensive work. Businessmen were expected to have their own computers, not to want to use a hotel system. The machine itself was antiquated, oddly out of place among the splendours of the Bellagio, and lay in a poky little room on the first floor. Still, it was adequate for his needs, and Jack settled in front of it, entering a request for telephone directories in Vegas. There wasn't one, and Jack swore to himself at the thought that the man could have gone ex-directory. He wondered for a moment whether there was a way to hack into the telephone company computers, but dismissed it. He had no computer skills, let alone his own computer – it wasn't remotely possible.

Instead, he thought he'd try a different tack. He dialled the number for the Mirage and said he was calling from Triple K Kable Security Systems. He wanted to have the name of the man in charge of security so he could write to introduce new products.

'Sorry, sir, but we don't take unsolicited calls from salespeople.'

'That's fine. I wouldn't expect you to. But I have Mr Sorensen's name already. I only wanted his correct initials so I can address the letter OK. He can always throw it into the wastebasket if he wants nothing to do with us, but at least I'll have done my job. You know how it is.'

'Yeah, sure. And it will end in the basket, you know? Don't expect miracles from him.'

'Hey, my boss just wants the job done by the numbers.'

'Right. OK, then. His full name is F. Peter Sorensen.'

'Know what the "F" is for?'

'Fred, I think. But he never uses it. He's always Peter.'

'Oh, I see.'

With thanks, he closed the line and checked on the screen again. There was only one F. P. Sorensen, and when he looked on the map of the city, he soon found the road. Heatherley was easy to find.

Jack picked up his bag and shoved in some small items before setting off. He wanted to learn all he could about Sorensen, and he had an idea that the man's house could hold some relevant secrets.

*

22.41 Las Vegas; 06.41 London

Stilson was glad to have escaped the police at the Sahara. Now he was determined to finish his jobs here and get away. The city would soon become a dangerous place for him, and he had no intention of being discovered.

He knew the way he was going. It would mean a late night, but there was no way around that. He must go somewhere and rest up, then return very early in the morning. It was the problem with Vegas, he always found. This was truly the city that didn't sleep. As soon as the night fell, the whole place woke up. That was especially true of security managers in a casino. Sorensen wouldn't be home before four at the earliest. No point being there to meet him. Better to drive out here and doze and get back early to find him.

The place he was going to was at the edge of the city out towards the east, in a road called Heatherley. The houses here were sumptuous. They were the kind of places a middle-ranking White

257

House official would look to, thinking to get a little of the genuine Vegas atmosphere, while not wanting the kids to see the adverts for whores that stayed stuck in the chain-link fences all around the Strip. These houses smelled of money, but not too much. They were not the sorts of houses the professional gamblers would go to. They'd stay in trailer parks or rented apartments until the big one came in (if it ever did) at which point they'd bypass Heatherley and move to a ranch or one of the serious apartment blocks overlooking the Strip.

Stilson knew this house. It was a really good size, with a bronze roof, Mexican styling, and three immense Yukkas in a line overlooking the brick driveway. Beside the front door there was a little gravelled area, with a fountain, to show that the guy had money and access to water. Big deal. Stilson could see from here that he'd upgraded his security, too. It wasn't too uncommon for a man like him to get a cheap deal on his home cameras, once he'd helped get the casino deal for the security company. Stilson knew that the security here was very good. He knew that more cameras covered every angle on the house, that they covered the side walls, the doors, windows, even the rear yard's fencing. And of course the gravel to the sides and at the front served the secondary purpose of making anyone's steps audible. Then there were metal grilles on the windows and the door, which had a reinforced steel plate in the middle. This was a secure house for a bachelor.

Selecting 'Drive', Stilson took the car away, round the corner, and then north on Hubbell, and before long he was out of the city itself and driving up into the hills. The Lake Mead Road climbed up the side and to the north of Frenchman Mountain, and then he was up in the valley area.

He remembered all this. It was the land where his father had lived and died – a dry, harsh, unforgiving land. And Ed Stilson had been a tough, unforgiving old bastard, ideally suited for the land. He owned a chunk of the action down there in the plain, but when some businessmen told him they were going to take his land, he ought to have taken the cash they offered, not stood calling them sons-a-bitches and mothers who'd play a trick for a dime. That sort of language was all right to Ed Stilson, because he lived on his own pretty much, with only his little son to help him.

They returned that night, with Molotov cocktails and rifles, and old Ed Stilson learned the cost of digging his heels into the Nevada dirt.

He dug them in all right. All the way six feet under. Silly son of a bitch.

Stilson was searching for a particular place out here. It was the place where he brought his first girlfriend, the daughter of a stripper at the old Tropicana, for a blowjob. She seemed happy to oblige. Probably thought it was the natural way for a girl to reward her man after seeing her mother do the same for various customers every week.

He found the turnoff on the left, and took the mountain road up and up until he came out on the dusty trail that led off over the top of the next ridge, and here at last the full vista lay before him – the sprawling metropolis of Las Vegas. He had been born here, he had paid for his first whore here, and he had shot his first man here. He hated the place.

And loved it.

*

23.45 Las Vegas; 07.45 London

Walking the street before Heatherley, Jack moved quietly and cautiously. His abiding fear was that he might be seen and reported to the police, so he walked along slowly, but with purpose. Not a dangerous burglar, but a man tired after a long day at work, whose car had broken down, and who was forced to walk homewards with his rucksack full of work for the following morning.

He had driven to a mall before coming here. There, he found a small security store that specialised in preventing industrial espionage. He told the young salesman that he ran a computer security company, but that reports of meetings he had held with a client were in the papers. That meant he was worried that his meetings room had been bugged and that there could be a video camera installed to spy on his meetings. Was there any way to locate video cameras and stop them broadcasting data?

After listening to his concerns, the salesman had been fascinated by the problem and began to riffle through magazines and sales catalogues, eventually presenting Jack with a small box the size of a walkie-talkie. He said if there was a video in his room, this receiver could check the picture it was sending. It meant he could line up the picture with the room, so he could locate the bug more easily, and if he wished, there was some equipment that should prevent any company spies from learning anything: jamming systems that

259

prevented wifi transmission of signals. Most modern videos were wireless, and those jammers would work fine, he said.

He drove off with his purchases and filled up at a garage a couple of blocks further on. He bought two canisters of instant foam for filling flat tyres and a small LED torch, before carrying on to within a mile from Heatherley, where he parked his rental before walking the last stage to make sure that he got a clear feel for the neighbourhood. So far, he was confident that this was a good area. The cars were often BMWs or Mercedes, with a fair number of Jaguars, as well as the normal Chryslers, GMs and Fords. Few appeared to have any dents. The houses themselves were good, substantial looking places with stone walls and cool tiled roofs. It was the sort of place Jack would have liked to live. Warm all year round, it would suit him after the cold of Dartmoor, he thought, but then pushed all thoughts of Devon away. He had to concentrate.

The house was set well back from the road, and had electric gates. Jack wandered past, giving it barely a glance. His attention on this pass was all for the other houses in the street. It was a pleasant, wealthy road with plenty of houses. The real estate developers had squeezed as many buildings into the road as possible. However, he saw that three Yukka plants and a low hedge a little further along blocked the view of the houses opposite. It was here that he took a rest. There was no one looking that he could see. He slipped into a shadow, away from the street lighting, and stopped, listening. Apart from the rumble of traffic on the freeways, there was nothing to disturb him. He moved to the wall and stood again, listening. There was a camera, he saw, set high on the wall, which gave a full view of the gates and the inner walls. Inside, he knew there must be more. That wasn't his concern at present.

He opened his rucksack, took out the video signal jammers, and set them on the ground near him. With the video interceptor he scanned for local wireless video, and soon located the camera above him by the transmitted signal. He took one of the signal jammers and turned it on. The tiny LED lights flickered for a few moments, and then the three lights were steady. As they became fixed, the picture on his interceptor became snowy, and then faded to a mess of white static. He threw his rucksack over his back again, and with the interceptor and jammer in his pocket, he looked about him quickly, and then sprang up to the top of the wall. It took some scrabbling, but at last he was on the wall. He left the signal jammer there, and sprang down the other side. The monitor still showed that the signals were jammed, and, as the store's salesman had assured him that they would work over wide spaces, he was fairly happy that he was safe from being filmed, but he was keen not to run risks. He went over the gravel in a hurry, and soon he was at the wall, staring up at the alarm bell housing. From his pack he took one of the aerosols for a flat tyre. Bringing a large pot that held a shrub over to beneath the alarm, he stood on it and injected the quick-expanding foam in through the alarm's grille . As soon as it started to escape, he moved the nozzle to a new opening and squirted again until the housing was full. Then he quickly wiped away all the excess so his work was unnoticeable, and moved the plant pot back to where he had found it. He walked around the back of the house, checking with his video that the jammers were still working. There was no second bell housing at the rear of his house.

It was time to get inside.

It was a source of amusement to the locksmiths at the little Hertfordshire manor house where the Service sent its recruits to learn breaking and entering, that so many people would install the most expensive, strong, and effective locks on their front doors, and use progressively less secure fastenings on others. Here, Sorensen had two strong Chubb locks on the front door. His back door used one, and the lock to the garage door only had a standard five lever.

Jack pulled on latex gloves that he had bought at a drugstore. Breaking the lock took only a few moments, and then Jack was inside, his second jammer in his hand as he stared up at the video cameras inside the house. He took out his video interceptor and checked it. There was still no signal.

The garage door led into a utility area, and it was here that he saw the alarm with the flashing red LED. He had expected that there would be something, but when he looked at this, he was relieved he had stopped the bell. If he hadn't, it would be ringing constantly now.

He moved quickly and methodically through the house. There was no evidence of feminine influence in any of the rooms. The whole house was rigorously masculine in decoration and tidiness. Jack hoped he was right. He didn't want the complication of a woman suddenly appearing.

The utility room took him through to a small but well-appointed kitchen, with dark granite worktops and plenty of oak cupboards. Beyond that was a large, open sitting room with a dining table at the nearer side, and a fifty-inch plasma screen on the wall, with a pair of soft leather sofas facing it. Behind them there was a large, old-fashioned desk, and he crossed the cool, tiled floor to it. He opened the drawers, peered inside, and felt around in them with his gloved hands. Nothing there.

As he felt underneath the desk, he found a steel box. It was clearly a pistol safe, and he studied it for a moment. There was some form of touch-sensitive lock with four buttons, and he lay under the desk for a while, studying it with his torch, but he could not make sense of it, and gave up.

Instead he carried on up the stairs, checking the video interceptor periodically as he went. There was no sign of a safe or other security measure up here, but he did find a set of old storage boxes in a small bedroom. One was full of records and photos from Sorensen's time in Iraq. He went through that quickly, glancing at the photos, but for the most part skimming documents. Most seemed to relate to possible corruption charges and, from the look of the discharge papers, Sorensen was not covered in glory at the end of his military career. Jack perused his working record, and lost all sense of time.

He was still there reading, when he heard the sound of the gates creaking open. Moving quickly, he went to the window and peered out carefully, his torch off. The gates to the driveway were sliding back, and a Mercedes coupe was rolling up the gravel. The lights swept around the house.

Sorensen was home early.

*

23.49 Las Vegas; 07.49 London

Debbie was at the computer terminal, staring at it with bleary eyes, when she paused and stretched.

In all her years at the agency, the one rule she'd always stuck to had been this: never, at any time, would she ever look on another agent as a possible bedfellow.

It never worked. The women in the partnership, if they were better or worse didn't matter, they would be moved. The guys were safe enough. Testosterone meant stability in the FBI. Besides it was better that way, sometimes. If a girl stayed in the same unit, there could be friction. She would have a reputation in no time: the office bike, if they thought she slept around, the office dyke if she didn't. And Debbie had seen it before: one guy had propositioned a girl in her third year in Atlanta, and when she turned him down, rumours began to circulate. The men would nod and wink if she showed friendship with other women in the unit. She wasn't gay, so far as Debbie knew, but that wouldn't stop the talk.

If a woman did take another agent home, and stayed with only the one guy, the other members of the team could become too protective, and that was often worse. It could mean that lives could be put at risk. It wasn't worth it, not on any level. The men would occasionally get promoted, but if a woman was to hang about, she could cause problems.

It all made sense. She knew it. Among equals it was fair enough. But when there was the added spice of different ranks involved, that just made it a whole lot more complex. Then instead of simple jealousy, there was the suggestion that the girl was sleeping her way to the top. And Debbie would never tolerate rumours of that sort. No. Better to be thought of as a cold, heartless bitch.

But it was hard, sometimes.

She sighed and stared at the screen again, and something caught her eye as she looked through her notes.

It was among the photos on the screen – the picture that she had shown Frank earlier. Now she frowned slightly as she looked at the photo of the guards at the prison. Perhaps there was another link here. She began to search back through her reports. There was one that detailed the death of McDonnell and also gave the names of other men from the prison. Several were shown to have left the military afterwards. She took their names and scribbled them down before searching for their present occupations and locations. It took her more than an hour of searching through the different databases. Only one had been logged as a felon, and he was on death row after shooting an old woman in Philadelphia while trying to rob her to feed his drug habit. Then her eye caught another man.

An expert in security systems, in comms, and in interrogation. He had been with McDonnell in Abu Ghraib, and soon after the riots, he had quit the army and moved to here, to Vegas.

She felt that rush of excitement as she took down his details. When she checked his employment history, she saw that he was in charge of security now at the Mirage. And then she looked back at the picture, and saw that his face was there, right next to McDonnell's.

'Shit! Frank!' she called, and hurried through to his office.

*

00.14 Las Vegas; 08.14 London

Outside the Mercedes cut its lights and remained stationary while the gates slid shut behind it. The driver remained in his car, and the vehicle moved and wobbled as he moved in his seat. By the time he opened the Mercedes' door, gun drawn, Jack was downstairs.

The door thumped shut. All the outside security lights were on, and Jack heard steps on the gravel. He moved to the side, behind the front door as it opened. A pair of keys were inserted into the strong locks on the door, and then the door swung wide. Jack stiffened, torch gripped in his fist, left hand a little in front of his right, as the heavy figure of Peter Sorensen appeared. He flicked the light switch with his left hand.

Jack moved. He grabbed the pistol in his left hand, grasping the slide tightly, his thumb going inside the trigger guard. The gun barked once, and he felt the slide jerk, but it couldn't action with his hand exerting so much pressure. Now it had fired once, he was happier. The slide had not actioned. The chamber still held the empty cartridge case. With his right hand, he jabbed twice at Sorensen's throat, but he had already dropped his chin, and Jack's blows met only bone. Changing his position, Jack tried to throw Sorensen, but the man was too strong and, although he had been surprised, he had already recovered. His fingers scrabbled at Jack's face. Jack had to duck to protect his eyes, both men grunting and gasping. The pistol was turning towards Jack, and he had a momentary fear, but then he let go of the gun. It was pointing at him, Sorensen snarling in delight as he pulled the trigger.

Nothing happened.

Jack kicked out. His boot's sole scraped down the front of Sorensen's shin, from knee to ankle, and the man gave a cry of agony, his body curling in pain, and Jack hit him twice, quickly, behind the ear, with a clubbed fist. He took the handgun, whipped off Sorensen's tie and quickly bound his hands. Then he kicked the door closed and racked the pistol again. It threw out the empty cartridge case, which tinkled on the tiles with a cheery ring, and he pressed the safety upwards. It was a small-calibre Colt auto, a .380, and he checked that the magazine was almost full before stuffing it into his belt in the small of his back. Then he took off Sorensen's belt and wrapped it about his ankles, fixing the loose end to a pipe by the wall. He tied it as best he could to keep Sorensen's legs still, and fetched a stool from the kitchen. He sat and waited for Sorensen to come round.

It did not take long. Sorensen peered about him blearily.

'You're the prick beat up my guys at the Mirage.'

'I didn't want to be questioned.'

'Who are you?'

'I am finding out why you wanted to hire a friend of mine,' Jack said.

'Fuck you!'

'You tried to recruit Roger Sumner, and he gave you Danny Lewin. I want to know what you were doing with them.'

'Me? Why'd I want anything to do with them?'

'Because they were intelligence officers with specific skills,' Jack guessed.

'You know dick, don't you? Well, you're in a whole barrel load of shit, man. You broke into my house, that's a serious felony in Nevada. And you don't have the faintest idea who you're dealing with.'

'The CIA,' Jack said.

'You think they'd be able to mount a covert op this serious? Man, you're more of a moron than I'd've thought.'

'Why don't you tell me, then?'

'Fuck you! I'm telling you nothing.'

'You've been on active service. So have I. I spent time in Ireland during the "Troubles". You saw a lot of men badly injured there – crippled. Ever seen what happens to a man who has his knees shot off? A shot through the back of the knee is just enormously painful, but a man will recover most movement in time. But the other way, from the front, now that's different – you get all sorts of bone fragments being blown back into the joint, and the kneecap itself is shattered to nothing. That is really, really painful. From what I've seen, the wound never really heals. You have to get a new knee.'

'Fuck off!'

'You've killed two British agents, dickhead. I'm a British agent, and I have authority to kill anyone doesn't help me. I am allowed to play first.'

Sorensen's eyes were wide now, but there was belief in them.

'You can't! You don't know who you'd be upsetting.'

'Suppose you tell me.'

'I'm still on the active list for the CIA. They'd be interested.'

'Not good enough.'

'The Mafia. They own this city. I'm—'

'Bullshit. They have no interest in a security manager, and I will bet my arse they have no interest in two intelligence officers.'

Sorensen squirmed as Jack approached him with the gun held out, muzzle pointing at his knee.

'I won't shoot your right one first. It'll be the left. Not that it'll make a huge difference.'

'Why are you here? I'm nothing to do with it, I'm just the messenger.'

'Prove it.'

'How the hell do I prove it?'

'Papers. The trail.'

'There isn't a trail, for fuck's sake!'

'Wrong answer.'

Jack went to the sofa and brought a cushion back with him. 'Amazing how well these can stifle the sound of a gunshot.'

He placed the cushion on his knee and set the gun over it, before looking at Sorensen questioningly.

He curled his lip.

'Fuck you! You wouldn't!'

Jack shrugged and fired. The shot was much quieter, but the noise made by Sorensen was shocking. He roared and screamed, and Jack was startled enough to pull the cushion aside and look. There was a slight flesh wound, but nothing more. 'I missed,' he said regretfully, and replaced the cushion.

'All right! Stop! I'll tell you!'

'Talk.'

'I was the messenger. I was in Iraq with Sumner and some others. We all kept ourselves to ourselves. But when I came back, there was this man who wanted me to find him men.'

'Why not you?'

He screwed the pistol harder into the cushion, and Sorensen winced.

'I was never a fuckin' intel officer. I was a guard, right? These others, they were trained.'

'Trained in what?'

'Torture. That's what they wanted: *torturers*. So they had me catch two of them, and then reel them in.'

*

00.39 Las Vegas; 08.39 London

Stilson came to with a snort, and was instantly wide awake. The years working with the Agency in so many different countries gave him that immediate wakefulness. It was natural to him to be fully alert as soon as his eyes were open, no matter what the time of the day, no matter how tired he might be.

He stared all about him. In the cool of the night, he could see moderately well by the sickle moon. There was enough light in the sky to illuminate the desolate hills about him. Only when he was convinced that there was nobody around watching him, did he risk his eyes' sensitivity by looking out over the city before him.

It grew every year. The middle of it was renewed every few decades, the older casinos falling by the wayside as newer ones took the bulk of the revenues, they themselves falling prey to still newer ones, but here on the fringes new houses went up every year, encroaching further and further towards the hills as more men and women arrived, keen to earn money. It was similar to LA. People just arrived, assuming they'd make their fortune, and most often, as Stilson knew, they would fail. The women would try so hard to stay straight, many of them, but after the first flush of their looks were fading and too many men with money kept propositioning them, they'd succumb for the price of a good meal, for the Versace dress, or a new car, and before long they'd be supporting themselves in a new way, advertising their bodies on the chain-link fences all over town. The men would try poker, and lose. And lose again. Because that was how casinos made their money. And the men would gradually fall into that well of despair and self-loathing from which so few escaped. And then they would lose again, but this time it was everything. Alcohol and cocaine were the oils that maintained the downward rush of men and women who were born to take the down escalator of life.

He had escaped it by joining the Agency and leaving town. The men who had killed his father and taken his land were mostly dead now. But they had shown him the simple truth: no one was safe in this world, and especially not in a town like Vegas. As he had shown the man behind Ed Stilson's murder. That man's body was still out in the desert, and if anyone found him, they'd find a nice, neat .45 calibre hole in the back of his head. They may even find the slug rattling around inside the skull. It didn't worry Stilson. The gun he used to kill the guy had been his old man's wartime Colt. Seemed like justice to use Ed Stilson Senior's gun on the bastards who killed him.

The engine started first time, and he eased the car out onto the road that led down the pass towards Vegas again. Only ten miles or so to Sorensen's house. He should be there shortly before Sorensen arrived back from work. He could finish things and be out of Vegas again within the hour, then he'd drive to Seattle and take a flight back east.

When his phone rang, he frowned. It was not normal practise to have calls at this time of day. There were few phone calls in the early morning, which meant it was faster and easier for Echelon to identify any keys. It never used to be a problem, because Echelon had been specifically designed for foreign communications intelligence, but since George W Bush's presidency, new laws allowed almost any calls to be intercepted anywhere on American soil too.

He picked up his phone and pressed the receive button, and at once heard Peter Amiss's voice.

'Go secure, please.'

Stilson pressed the button, and there was the usual fifteen to twenty seconds of static, before Amiss's voice returned.

'Can you hear me?'

'Yes, sir.'

'Stilson, we have a problem. Our comms analyst tells me that there are two FBI agents outside Sorensen's house. Also, someone has made a connection to McDonnell. Have you been to Sorensen's yet?'

'No. I'm still on my way.'

'Are you close?'

'Fairly. About six miles away.'

'What do you wish to do? Abort or continue?'

Stilson reflected.

'We cannot afford to run any risks. I'll continue. We have no need for Sorensen any more and if they can confront him with McDonnell's name or someone else, he may break. It's not worth the risk.'

There was a pause on the other end. Then, 'It's a shame. He has been a useful man to us.'

'We don't have time for lengthy evaluations and risk analysis. If we had more data, I'd say yes. But, as it is, we don't have time. I'd say we should still take him out.'

'I see.'

'Don't worry. I'll deal with Sorensen.'

'And the FBI agents?'

'I have had two of our men tailing them for the last few days. I'll call them now, get them to remove the Feebies.'

*

00.41 Las Vegas; 08.41 London

Like so many, once Sorensen started, he found confidence in his story, as though he had recruited Jack as his own accomplice.

'They contacted me through another guy I knew: Ed Stilson, a guy used to work in Iraq with the NSA. But the orders came from above. He was just the bag-carrier.'

'What did they want torturers for?'

'Why do you think?'

Jack shook his head.

'This is the CIA? NSA? Who was recruiting them?'

'I don't know. The only thing I heard, they called themselves the Deputies. The Deputies General, I think.'

'What does that mean?'

'How should I know? They were just ex-army or CIA guys.'

'Are you with them, Peter?'

'No! I was only there to recruit some of the guys, that's all. I knew them, so I guess they thought they could use me, it'd give them a degree of separation. I wasn't supposed to know about the main group.'

'How did you find out?'

'I heard Stilson talking to his boss. He mentioned this "Deputies" thing.'

'Who was he talking to?'

'Come on, gimme a break!'

Without hesitation, Jack put the cushion back on his knee and fired. The gun jerked, and this time Sorensen's head flopped back. He was out cold. Jack fetched a glass of water and emptied it over his head.

'You don't understand, Mr Sorensen,' he said, as Sorensen puked bile on the floor by his head. 'I am very serious. Two friends of mine from my Service are dead, and you appear to know who killed them and why. I want to know everything you have, because otherwise you will be crippled or dead by the time I leave here. Understand me?'

Sorensen nodded dully, staring wide-eyed down at the cushion. Jack did not move it. He didn't want to see what he had done. If he did, he'd throw up too, and he couldn't let Sorensen see his weakness. Sorensen was sobbing now, shivering like a man with a fever.

269

'I don't know. I don't know. It was someone high, that's all. They mentioned some place – place I never heard of.'

'Where?'

'It's called the Dollar building or something. I heard that much. Thought it was weird, calling it that. Heard of a Golden Dollar, all sorts, never a "Dollar".'

It made Jack frown.

'The Dollar? Are you sure they weren't talking about getting money in? Dollars?'

'It was the Dollar or something… Jesus, I need a hospital.'

'Shut up or you'll never need one again,' Jack said. 'I don't have time. Who else do you know in this Deputies General?'

'No one, I swear it! No, don't shoot me again, Christ, just leave me!'

Jack hefted the pistol and held it over his other knee.

Sorensen stared with fascinated horror.

'No… no,' he whispered.

'I have to know it all,' Jack said.

'All right. Amiss. The deputy director of the Agency. It was him. He was always Stilson's boss, all the way back. It was him.'

'Is there anything else?'

'Nothing! Nothing, I swear!'

Jack tried asking other questions, but got no nearer an answer. Either Sorensen was brave enough to risk being shot again, or he was telling the truth, and Jack was about past caring either way. There was a trickle of blood running from under his leg now, and Jack felt truly sickened. He'd never been involved in interrogations before, not violent ones. His methodology was to ask one question at a time and repeat it until something slipped out. In his dealings with his spies, that was all he had needed. To tear a tiny hole in the cover story they had created, and begin to draw out the truth. Most of them were so deeply involved in their professional bonds of secrecy that they would not willingly open up even to him, their handler.

This was different. There was the smell of sweat – his own as well as Sorensen's – a foul odour where Sorensen had soiled himself, and the tinny, metallic tang of blood. Jack had deliberately avoided shooting bone, which was why he had thrust down so hard, to make sure he was firing into flesh, but there was always the risk that when he fired, the gun had jerked… perhaps he had crippled this guy.

270

Sorensen may never walk straight again. That thought was enough to make the gorge rise in his throat.

'Don't call the police for a half hour. You understand me?'

'Yes.'

'Anyone know you are here?'

'I was called. I said I was coming back.'

'Why?'

'The alarm guys called me. The alarm. It rang at the call centre. But when they checked with my neighbours, there was no bell – so they thought it was a fault. They called me to come and reset.'

'They don't send their own guards?'

'Not at the rate I pay.'

Jack nodded.

'Next time, I'd pay the higher rate. You may get a security guy shot instead of yourself.'

'Fuck off,' Sorensen said.

His face was white, but the blood was not pouring from him in a way that looked life-threatening. Jack felt it was more likely the man was suffering from shock.

Jack stuffed the Colt back into his belt. When he pulled Sorensen's belt off, a magazine holster had fallen free with one full magazine in it. Jack picked it up and put it in his pocket, then opened the front door and slipped outside. He crossed the gravel to the wall and peered around before springing up to the top and climbing over to fall to the ground behind the Yukkas.

He was about to stand and walk away, when he heard a car approach. It was a large Ford, and as he peered through the leaves of the Yukka, he saw Frank Rand and a woman in the passenger seat. They stopped, and Jack set his teeth in silent, grim irritation as the car's engine turned off. He could not move with them there. They would be sure to see him.

And then he saw the other car slowly draw up behind Rand, a few tens of yards away. Something made it appear odd, and then he realised that it had no lights on, not even sidelights.

*

00.53 Las Vegas; 08.53 London

Frank Rand pushed his long back into the soft leather of the seating, and fiddled with the headrest, trying to get comfortable.

'Shit, I hate working through the night.'

Debbie snorted, resting her elbow on the door and yawning.

271

'Don't you worry, Frank. If you don't like it, I guess Houlican would be happy to take away your future duties without a problem. Either that, or he'd give you the choice. Put you onto every scummy surveillance overnight until you throw the badge in his face.'

Frank sneered at her.

'Don't you ever let up?'

'Nope. Shuddup and have a snooze. It's what you need,' she said without taking her eyes from the driveway. 'Hey, is that his car?'

'What?' Frank opened his eyes and peered. 'A Merc. Could be. What's the plate?'

She began to leaf through pages on her notepad, but even as she started, Frank's phone rang. He grabbed at it.

'Frank Rand?'

'Mister Rand. Remember me? Last time we met we were opposite each other at a bar table in Anchorage.'

For a moment his mind was blank, then he glanced at Debbie, nudged her, and gestured to his phone.

'Mister Hansen. Or do you prefer Mister Case, Jack?'

'Do you prefer to remain alive?'

Frank's jaw clenched.

'I dislike being threatened. If that's all you got to say, I can give you a short answer, Case. You try to—'

'Not me! Look in your mirrors, agent.'

Frank's eyes automatically did as he was told. In his wing mirror he saw a man walking nonchalantly towards the car, a hand concealed beneath his coat. The other mirror showed a second man, his gun hand too was hidden but, as Frank watched, both men drew their hands out into the open, guns ready and pointing towards him and Debbie.

He dropped the phone, said, 'Debbie, *move!*' and was about to throw himself from the car when he realised it was too late.

His hand was on the door, his right reaching for his Glock, when he saw the barrel of the gun at his temple. He looked up, but in the eyes there was nothing but cold determination.

'Shit, Debbie, I'm…'

He had been going to apologise. It was senseless, a waste of her life to die out here for no reason, but even as he prepared to say so, there was a flare of light from the gun, and he winced and snapped his eyes shut, expecting the bullet in his head at any moment, but then the car jerked and rocked, and he heard Debbie swear. He looked at her in

272

time to see the man her side slide down the side of the car. He left a smear of blood against the window as he went. Frank turned to the man with the gun at his head, but he was gone, slumped against the low wall of a garden, eyes wide.

He had his Glock and pulled it out and up as he pulled the door wide, shouting, 'FBI, drop the weapon!'

There was no answer. The man was moving, just, his empty hand jerking up towards his chest, and then Frank saw over his gun sights that the downed man had a spreading stain on his shirt. The hand twitched, and then gently drifted back down to settle in his lap. His leg shuddered, once, then again, and his head slowly eased down to rest on his shoulder, his eyes fixed on Frank with total surprise.

Frank walked to him, his gun out and pointing at the fucking jerk, and in his mind he heard his armourer's firm but calm voice saying, '*Foresight, squeeze, foresight, squeeze, don't jerk it!*' and there was a loud rushing in his ears as adrenaline fizzed in his blood like cocaine, and the urge to shoot the fucker was almost unbearable…

'Debbie? You OK?'

'Yeah, I'm all right.'

Frank turned, and there, he saw Jack Case standing the other side of the car.

'You're making a habit of getting shot at, you know.'

'Yeah. I know. Drop the gun, Jack.'

Jack turned and pulled on his backpack, stuffing the small pistol into his belt as he walked.

Frank shouted.

'Hey, where d'you think you're going?'

'I saved your life,' Jack said without turning. 'If I stay here, I'm likely to end up as dead as those two. I've been set up from the moment I landed in the US.'

Frank lifted his Glock.

'Stop! Don't make me shoot you!'

'That would be taking ingratitude to a new level,' Jack said forcefully. He felt weary, so tired he could sleep for a week. The smell of blood and urine was still in his nostrils, and he shivered suddenly as a wave of cold fear washed down his back. He lifted his hands and faced Frank.

'Someone is after me, Frank. They tried to shoot *you* just now. What more proof do you need? If you take me anywhere, I'll be killed.'

'*Who* is it?'

'I'm trying to find out. The answer is in a place in Virginia, apparently.'

'Where? Virginia's a big place.'

Jack cocked an eyebrow.

'A man called Deputy Director Amiss.'

'You are kidding me!' Rand said. 'He's no more likely to be behind this than the President himself, Jack. Someone's been bullshitting you.'

'Yeah. I've not been taking bollocks from everyone since I landed in the States, Frank. I dreamed it all up.' Jack eyed him. 'You're on their hit list too, now. That's why those two were after you.'

'Who are they?' Debbie demanded. 'Why're they after us?'

'Don't know. But they look the same as the two in Seattle, don't you reckon? Did you get who they were?'

'There was no ID on them.'

'What would you take in a bet that these guys don't either?'

Frank looked at the nearer of the two bodies.

'Why'd they shoot me?'

'You've been behind me every step, haven't you?' Jack said. 'And these guys were behind you. How did they know where you'd be? They follow you, or did they have a beacon on the car?'

Debbie was just behind Frank. She pushed Frank's gun until it was pointing away from Jack.

'Thank you, sir. Appreciate your help. Now it's time to figure out this shit. You come with us and we'll get this all sorted and have you back in England in no time.'

'No. You have to shoot me to stop me, Frank,' Jack said. He had his hands in the air still, but he was taking steps back. In the distance there was the sound of sirens. 'These guys were in an agency of some sort. I can't take the risk that they're "friendly",' he added sarcastically. 'I have to get away from here.'

'Look, wait a minute,' Frank said, as the sirens were grew nearer. 'OK, then, we'll sort this somehow. You just have to come in and—'

'I am not going to be taken into custody,' Jack stated. 'Shoot if you're going to, Frank.'

Frank felt his finger tighten on the trigger. He felt sweat break out under his arms, felt the first pressure of the trigger taken up, and then he heard Jack's voice.

'I saved you, Frank. You need to remember that before you fire.'

'Oh, fuck,' Frank muttered, and his gun dropped to point at the ground. 'Come on, Debbie. Let's get things sorted.'

'What about him, Frank?' she demanded, pointing at the figure disappearing into the shadows.

'We didn't see him, Debbie. Understand me? We didn't just have that conversation.'

'Sir, I don't know that—'

'Fine. You tell Houlican what you want, agent. Me, I'm not prepared to risk his life. He just saved us both. So you get on to the airport and sort out a plane for us while I see if these pricks are carrying ID.'

*

01.02 Las Vegas; 09.02 London

Stilson passed by less than five minutes later and, as he passed, he swore quietly under his breath. Soon as he was parked a couple of miles away in a suburban street, he picked up the STU-III and called Amiss.

'Go secure,' he said.

'Yes?' Amiss's voice was not sleepy. It was four in the morning, Stilson told himself, looking at the car's clock, and the guy was as wide awake as he was at noon.

'I don't know what happened. By the time I got to Sorensen's house, there were police all over the place. My boys were there, I think. I saw their car. I don't know what's happened to them... or to Sorensen.'

'That is highly unsatisfactory,' Amiss said.

Stilson pulled the phone from his face and stared at it.

'Yes. It is,' he said. 'I need you to find out where Sorensen is, so I can get to him. I don't want him shooting his mouth off, if they got to him. Call me back.'

He put the phone down and waited. It took seven minutes by his watch.

'Yes?' he responded when both phones were synchronised.

'He is in the hospital. Apparently he was knee-capped by this damned Brit, and two men were shot dead while trying to attack FBI agents. That explains the others. Sorensen may have told the Brit about us, I expect. You must get him removed. He is an embarrassment we can well do without. And when you have that sorted, get back here. I will need your help.'

'All right.'

02.50 Las Vegas; 10.50 London

Back at the Bellagio, Jack walked into his room and stared about him. His rucksack was in his hand, and he let it slip to the floor now, feeling the tension in his whole frame. The scene in that room was with him still – the smell of urine and blood and sweat from Sorensen, and his own sweat as he tried not to show his horror at what he was doing.

He was no torturer. Nor a murderer. But today he had killed two men. Two more yesterday. Who were they, the two trying to get the jump on Frank Rand and his companion? Just two more faceless soldiers, like the two who'd killed Stephen Orme, probably like the ones who'd killed Danny Lewin. How many more of them were there?

But through all his thoughts he could see the face of Sorensen – his white face as Jack had shot his leg. No matter that Jack was trying not to injure him badly, Sorensen wouldn't care about that. He was just a small cog in a machine, and now Jack had set his face against the world by attacking him.

He felt a growing nausea and hurried through to the bathroom, where he rested with a hand at either side of the sink, staring at himself in the mirror.

His eyes were bloodshot now – tired, like the rest of him. But this was worse than usual. Even when he had killed before, that had been necessary. The violence had been essential. This was worse, much worse, and he was so exhausted because he was suffering the reaction. Shooting Sorensen was torture. By that act he had been reduced to the level of a Nazi or a Soviet. No better than one of those from whom he had sworn to defend his country.

Now, for the first time, he really understood what Lewin had gone through. He would never lose that feeling.

A violent retch made him close his eyes and bend his head to the sink. It felt as though it would never end, as his stomach heaved and contracted, but he had eaten so little in the last day and a half, there was nothing to bring up. He forced himself to calm down, sliding down the wall of the bathroom, keeping his back flat against the wall, head resting against it, his palms in his lap, until the shivering and anxiety left him, and he could feel his rapidly beating heart calm a little, his panting slow down and deepen.

He would not give in to this fear. Nor would he succumb to terror or self-recrimination. He wasn't some murdering machine, and the fact that he had taken extreme action to get what he needed from Sorensen didn't make him evil. It made him desperate – desperate to get back home and to put an end to this.

Getting to his feet, he walked through to his bedroom and stared at his bag. He had stowed the little Colt .380 in his backpack, and now he took it out and sat at the desk.

It was some years since he had stripped a Colt and cleaned it, and now he went through the process, pulling the slide back to throw out the cartridge from the breech and locking it open. Ejecting the magazine, he pulled the slide and let it run forward, snapping the hammer down. He pressed the button under the barrel and rotated the bushing to loosen the recoil spring, and pulled the pin from the side so the barrel and slide assembly could come off, and tugged the springs and barrel from it. Cleaning it with Kleenex from the bathroom took him some time, and when he was done, he methodically put it all together again. Not ideal, he considered, because it was dry and could have done with some oil, but it would do. And it had served its purpose. He felt a lot better for the concentration.

He sat back. The bed beckoned but he dare not lie down. If he did, sleep would bring back the sight of Sorensen's face, his leg, the sound of his scream, the smell of his body, and his terror. Jack had killed before, but there were reasons then. Torture was different. It left him feeling shabby, befouled. He could not lie down; in preference Jack went to the bathroom, stripped, and took a shower. Today he had it almost scalding hot, and then turned the dial to cold, and stood it as long as he could, feeling the water take the dirt and horror away. And as it went, he found himself thinking with a new clarity of mind. He could feel his purpose returning as he rubbed his arms and chest against the cold.

He would have to prepare for the next stage.

Someone from Virginia had tried to see him killed. They had attacked him and had murdered Sumner and Lewin.

They would pay.

*

07.14 Las Vegas; 15.14 London

Jack did not go to bed that night. Instead he went through his clothes and picked out all those he thought Rand might have seen. He

277

put them into a bag, then went downstairs and out into the Strip. There was a dumpster bin a block or two away, and he shoved the clothes inside before returning to the casino. He ate pizza overlooking the fountains and tried to fix the memory of the place in his mind. Back in his room he renewed his widow's peak as he shaved, and pulled on a clean T-shirt and trousers. Soon he had packed again, and left, taking the stairs to the ground floor. There he paid off his room with cash.

'I got lucky,' he said with a smile.

The girl at the desk smiled back as though she truly felt pleased on his behalf, and soon Jack was outside throwing his bags into the trunk of his rental. He still had the little pistol in the small of his back under his jacket, but when he sat in the car, he removed it and stuck it beside his seat before strapping on his seat belt. He had a long journey, and didn't want to be uncomfortable.

As he pulled out of the car park and onto the Strip, his phone rang.

It was an alien sound. He stared at it for a moment, his heart lurching. Nobody knew this number. His Blackberry was the only phone he had where others knew the number, not this throwaway one. With some trepidation he picked it up and answered the call.

'Yes?'

'Hello, this is Frank Rand.'

'How did you get this number?' Jack asked with genuine surprise.

'You called me last night, remember? There is such a thing as call-back.'

'Oh, yes.' Cursing himself, he realised he had not turned his new phone off again after the shooting. He was losing his touch.

'You left Sorensen in a bad way.'

'I had to find out. It was the only way in a short timescale.'

He sounded defensive even to himself.

'Look, Jack, can we try to sort this all out? I'm sure there's a misunderstanding here.'

'Are you recording this call?' Jack said.

'No. And before you ask, neither am I tracing you. I want to talk, Jack.'

'I have a lot to do today.'

'Right. And damn the idea that I could help.'

'What could you do that I can't alone?'

There was a pause, a slight hesitation. Then, 'I might be able to help you to speak with Amiss.'

278

08.29 Las Vegas; 16.29 London

The hospital was bright, busy, and full when Stilson entered it that morning. He had a large bunch of flowers and, as he stood aside to let two hurrying nurses with a trolley go past, he saw a cleaner sweeping the floor.

'Hi, can you tell me where the trauma centre is? An employee of my company was shot last night and brought in.'

'Sure, head down to the end of that corridor and take the elevator. It's all signposted.'

'Ah, thanks,' Stilson said, and followed the directions.

This was a new hospital. Although Sorensen could have demanded to be taken to a more expensive facility, Stilson knew this had the reputation of the best hospital for trauma. They had the American College of the Surgeon's highest ranking for the work they did with their thousands of patients every year, and Stilson was sure that Sorensen would have demanded to be brought here. Whether he had or not, Amiss assured him that his name was logged on Echelon as being taken there in the ambulance.

Stilson looked through the windows into the trauma rooms. There were many ICU beds, and another set of rooms with resuscitation beds, but he was guessing that Sorensen wouldn't be in any of them.

At the end of the corridor he saw a police officer waiting at the door. Immediately Stilson dialled Roy Sandford's number.

'Yes, there's a police officer at the door. Right.'

Sandford had a list of the officers who were on duty, and he had already isolated Officer Martinez as being responsible for Sorensen's safety. Stilson closed his phone just as Martinez answered his own. He looked startled as Sandford told him that a truck had run into his parked black and white, and, shutting off the call, the policeman pelted along the hallway and out the fire doors at the far end. Stilson continued on and opened the door he'd guarded.

Sorensen looked dreadful. His face was waxen, pale, and drawn. There was a drip in his left arm, and he had an oxygen tube in his nose. A livid bruise on the side of his head made his features look unbalanced as he opened one swollen eye and stared at Stilson.

'You all right?' Stilson said, looking around for somewhere to put the flowers.

'I guess,' Sorensen rasped. His voice was rough, and he looked a little disorientated as he narrowed his eyes, peering at Stilson.

279

'I had to come and make sure you were OK, that you hadn't told the guy anything.'

'I didn't.'

'He tortured you, though?'

'Yeah. He was asking about the two. Sumner and Lewin, and what they were wanted for, and he shot me, the bastard. In the knee.'

'This one?' Stilson said, looking down at the lump under the bedclothes.

'Yeah,' Sorensen said.

'But you told him nothing? What sort of nothing did you tell him?'

'Nothing,' Sorensen said. The big man shivered. 'Look, Ed, I wouldn't give anything away, man. It's just not me, man.'

'I knew you were a fool, but I always kept any real information away from you because of that,' Stilson said. 'You never could hold a secret, could you?'

'Look, Ed, I...'

Stilson had his hand on the bedclothes and he lifted them away now. Over Sorensen's knees was a kind of table to stop the bedding from falling on his knees and hurting them. 'You were shot up, weren't you,' he murmured gently.

'Yeah.'

'Must have hurt, being shot in the knee.'

'Ed, I...'

Sorensen held up his hand, listening.

'What is it?'

'Nothing,' Stilson said, and then smiled. He suddenly slammed his hand over Sorensen's mouth, while he punched hard on the injured knee. Sorensen rose, eyes popping with agony and hands in the air, as the searing pain rushed through his entire body. It was like a fire that screamed through his veins, scorching every cell of his being, until all that was left was a shuddering torture.

Stilson eyed the reaction, and when the man's frame collapsed back on the bed, he struck once more.

This time Sorensen's eyes rolled up into his head, and although his body tried to spring from the bed, he soon flopped back. Stilson nodded to himself, and took his hand away from Sorensen's mouth. It was quiet here in the room, and Sorensen's stertorous breathing was oddly deafening.

The man was weak. It meant nothing to Stilson, of course. He was used to seeing people in pain and dying. He had killed enough men here in Vegas when he was taking revenge for their killing of his father, and those deaths had shown him that he was unaffected by the suffering of others. There were some he may have cared about. He would have thought he would have found dealing with Sorensen quite difficult, because the man had been part of Stilson's unit out in Iraq, but in reality it just meant Sorensen was more interesting as a subject. Those Iraqis were nothing. They'd been shown to be willing to hurt America, because of their distorted, dysfunctional religion, and so he had taken all measures to prevent their being able to attack.

Sorensen, though, he was more interesting.

Stilson sat on the edge of the bed patiently, and took a little bottle from his pocket. He unscrewed the lid and held the bottle to Sorensen's nose. The smelling salts soon worked their magic, and Sorensen rallied. His eyes returned, his eyelids fluttering, and his breath came in grunts of anguish.

'You all right again? Now, I'll ask you again, and keep hitting your leg and asking until to tell me what I want to know. You know me, Peter. You know me well. And you know I'll do it.'

The broken man nodded.

'Good. Did you tell the Brit about the Deputies General of the Empire of East and West?'

'No! I…'

Stilson held up his hand.

'Did you tell him about me, did you tell him about Deputy Director Amiss, and did you tell him about the plans?'

'I told him nothing! How could I, Ed? I don't know anything?'

'What about the facility?'

'What, the Dollar?'

'You did hear about that, then? Did you tell him about that too?'

'No!'

Stilson stood and made as though to smother Sorensen again.

'NO! All right, I told him about you, yes, but only that you were involved a little out there, nothing about here.'

'And the facility? Our plans?'

'No. Nothing!' Sorensen said, staring at Stilson's hands, fearing another assault on his ruined knee.

'OK, good,' Stilson said. He patted Sorensen's chest gently. 'Sorry I had to do that, Peter, but I had to be sure.'

Sorensen nodded, but there was hatred in his eyes. Stilson smiled, but then he reached forward, pulled the pillow from behind

281

Sorensen's head, and rammed it over his face, both hands on top, holding it over Sorensen's mouth and nose, pressing firmly, and waiting until the fighting arms sagged, the legs stopped their twitching and kicking, and the torso ceased bucking and rocking.

He waited a little longer, and then replaced the pillow, closing Sorensen's staring eyes, and returned the cage over his knee, settling the blankets and sheets once more.

Picking up the flowers once more, he left the room and strolled along the corridor.

He would tell Amiss that another problem was removed. But the Brit had learned far too much, and he was the worst threat to the Deputies' plans. He must be dealt with.

Stilson wouldn't entrust this one to anybody else. He would take care of Jack Case himself.

*

09.21 Las Vegas; 17.21 London

Sunset Park was a broad area that covered thousands of acres. As Jack pulled in to the car park off South Easter Avenue, he studied the area in front of him with the eye of an old Russia hand.

The cover was good for him, but also for any assassin. The landscape here was grassy, with that thin harsh grass that appeared to survive even in the desert heat, but with bushes and stunted trees dotted about the place. He could see a huge area for playing baseball with four separate baseball fields set about one central hub. There was the glitter of water further away.

He left the car, locked it, and walked slowly down to the water's edge, hands in pockets, the picture of calm idleness, but inside he was buzzing like he was on speed. The rush of excitement had not left him since he took Rand's call.

Here he saw that the lake was vast. In the centre was an island, and he saw what looked like some Easter Island heads set out. Even here, he thought, the people of Las Vegas had to invent more. The park was obviously man-made, and he assumed the lake would be too, but he longed for a little simplicity – for the lush green dampness of Dartmoor. All this heat made him feel dry and half dead.

He took the loop-road that led around the water, his eyes on the look out for a flash that could betray a telescopic sight, or a man in an unnatural posture, a woman with a pushchair that looked too light for a baby – anything – but there was nothing obvious.

It felt like the good old, bad old days at Gorky. There he had experienced the sheer terrifying excitement of never knowing when a Russian KGB agent would leap from a bush. He had conducted so many meetings there that he had grown to know it as well as if it were his own garden. The thrill was always there, but so was the fear, whenever he visited it.

And today it was the same. Here, in this open space, he felt the conviction that any one of the thousands of windows overlooking this park could be housing a pair of men with spotting scope and sniper rifle. A number could be standing near with parabolic dishes ready to make a sound intensified recording of anything he said, a long lens could be ready to take photos. With the lack of cover, he was a sitting duck.

As he came to this conclusion, he reached the edge of the lake, and stood aside for a pair of young female joggers, both with tight Lycra suits. He took the opportunity to turn and stare after them, but in reality he was not watching their bodies, but casting about for surveillance teams – still nothing obvious. He was halfway to a children's play area, and he carried on along the shoreline towards it.

A jet ski whined its way past on the lake, and he wished he was there on the water. Then, as he had the thought, he saw one person who was out of place.

She was short, unprepossessing, and he recognised her instantly from the very early morning. At the moment, Debbie was sitting on a bench overlooking the water with the expression of someone who had bitten into an apple only to find half a maggot wriggling.

'Morning,' he said.

'Yeah. Hi. Again.'

'Where is he?'

She jerked her head back towards the baseball pitches.

'Waitin' for you.'

He nodded, and was about to walk to meet Frank, when she said, 'I didn't want to come here. I wanted to call you in. But he's right. You saved our lives last night. Makes you sort of on our side, I guess.'

'Thanks. It'd be good to think I wasn't entirely alone,' Jack said, and saw her pull a reluctant grin.

He walked off across the grass to the main path that ran northwards. A way up there, a left took him onto a path that ran to the centre of the four pitches and, as he walked, he saw a man sitting on the white benches overlooking the nearer pitch. He strolled along to the seating and climbed up to the fourth level bench where Frank Rand was sitting, clutching a large coffee cup in his hands.

'Morning,' Jack said again.

'Hello, Mister Case,' Frank said. 'I guess we can be on real name terms now, eh?'

'I'm happy for that. What do you want?'

'When I spoke to you, I wanted to make sure what you were on about,' Frank said. His eyes were all over the land before them. 'You got to appreciate this: I am really out on a limb. I will be fired when they learn what I'm doing. That's why I refused to let Debbie in on what I'm going to say to you.'

'You'll be fired? For what?'

Frank looked at him.

'Mainly for meeting with a man listed as a suspect in several murders. I ought to be arresting you and taking you in.'

'And instead?'

'Instead I'm going to talk to you and discuss what the fuck is going on,' Frank sighed. 'Do you have any idea?'

'I think that someone is planning some kind of covert operation, and that they're bringing people in to help.'

'That's what they were doing with Lewin?'

'Yes. He was a trained intelligence officer. But what Sorensen told me was, that they were bringing in one type in particular: trained inquisitors – torturers.'

'I don't like torture, and I didn't like what you did to Sorensen,' Frank said, and his voice was very cold.

'He wouldn't talk without me making him. Without doing that to him, I'd not have got anything. He was very scared of another guy. Someone called Stilson. Said this man was an associate to Amiss, who he said was Deputy Director of the CIA as well as leading this Deputies General.'

'Deputies General?'

'That's what he said they were called.'

'OK.' Frank sipped his coffee and pulled a face. 'I hate it cold,' he muttered and set it on the bench beside him. 'What do you plan to do, fly out to Virginia and knock on his door?'

'I was thinking more in terms of following him when I could and seeing what I could learn.'

'Oh. And what do you think you'll learn by getting arrested? Because you will, Jack. He's Deputy Director. He has his own secret service protection group round him all the time. You'll never get within a hundred yards.' Frank said, as his phone rang. He pulled it out, still holding Jack's gaze. 'Frank Rand. Yup. What? When?'

Jack stared at Frank blankly as he muttered a few more comments and shut off the call.

'So, Jack. Can you guess who that was about?'

'No.'

'You didn't know Sorensen was killed this morning?'

*

08.39 Whittier; 17.39 London

Chief Burns walked into the bar with his crutch and glared at Suzie. 'Don't make a fuss!'

Suzie smiled and carried on walking round the bar, helping him to his stool and setting his crutch beside him.

'Calm down, Tony. I do this for all my customers.'

There was a snigger and Burns turned to give the table behind him a long, steady glower. Three fishermen at the table nonchalantly drank their coffees, chatting quietly to each other and studiously ignored the chief.

'Good to see you back, Tony,' Suzie said.

'Glad to be back, honey. Thanks.'

She smiled and brought him a coffee.

'This is on the house.'

'I'll have to get myself blown up more often,' he said.

Suzie smiled thinly. She had thought her heart was going to burst when she had heard that Chief Burns and the Brit were in the Station when it blew up.

'Is there any news on the building, and why the gas tanks blew?'

'No. Probably never will be, either,' he said. He looked over at the window as he ordered eggs and toast. Suzie went out and began preparing his breakfast. 'What's going on out there?'

Suzie came back and followed his look. 'Hadn't you heard? There's more men up there to make the Bucky safer. There's a gang of men up there now, installing new security fences and boarding the doors and windows.'

''Bout time,' Chief Burns muttered. 'I don't want another death up there. It was the first time I had to tell a mother her boy was dead.'

'It must have been hard, Chief.'

'Yeah,' he said. 'A boy like that, just wiped out in a moment. It was very hard.'

285

'Still, perhaps they'll figure out what to do with the joint in a year or two.'

'We can hope,' he said.

She went out, and soon she was back with a plate of eggs, toast, and some good, crisp bacon, cooked how he liked it. She refilled his mug while he ate.

'Kasey's still walking about,' she said.

'Yeah?' Chief Burns said. Looking out through the window, he gazed at the building in the distance. 'God, I hate that place. If we could only blow it up.'

'Not with all that asbestos inside, thanks,' Suzie said. 'They'll hopefully make it safe, anyhow. Keep the asbestos inside, and have some real defences against kids getting in again.'

Chief Burns grunted his agreement. The idea of all that asbestos rising from the remains of the Bucky didn't bear thinking about. He finished his coffee and eggs, and retrieved his crutch.

'You seen Kasey today?'

'Yes. She's probably at the usual. You know where she always goes.'

'Yeah. I guess.'

'It's a shame, I know, Chief, but there's nothing we can do to help her.'

'Maybe not,' Chief Burns said. He stood and hopped to the door. 'Reckon she deserves us trying, though. I don't like to think of her out there when the weather's drawing in.'

He pulled the door wide with a little effort and made his way through. Leaving the bar, he stared up the roadway into the distance. He could see Kasey by the light of a window, and he glanced down at the roadway. At least there was no ice yet. It was early enough in the year for there to be only puddles.

He laboriously made his way to her.

'Hi, Kasey. What're you doing out here at this time of day? It's getting cold, isn't it?'

'I just wanted to see if I could hear him,' she said, leaning forward, her lips parted with the concentration.

'Honey, he's gone,' Burns said. He had no kids of his own. Never met a woman he had wanted to settle with, except maybe Suzie. He forced that thought from his mind and smiled down at Kasey. 'Come on, let's get you home, eh?'

She submitted to his request for aid, and soon he had his arm about her shoulder for support as they walked back.

'I've heard him before, you know,' she said in a light and conversational tone.

'Yeah? You been playing with a weejie board or something?'

'Ouija,' she corrected him mildly. 'No. I've heard him up there. There have been times, when it's real quiet, and the sea is hushed, when you can hear him in there. He's sad. I want to get the priest to visit and give him peace, you know?' She turned to Burns, and suddenly she was sobbing. 'I just hate the thought of him being there, all alone, so sad… I want him saved.'

*

09.40 Las Vegas; 17.40 London

'No, I had no idea,' Jack said levelly. 'Are you concerned that I was involved? When was he killed?'

'The fuck should I know? That was the LVPD telling me as a courtesy because they knew I'd been there at his house last night. What happened?'

Jack took a breath.

'I'll say this once, Frank, because you're bright enough to understand English. I don't know where he was killed, when he was killed, nor who killed him. If I had been going to do that, I'd have done it this morning. I didn't need to escape from his house, save you from being murdered, and then go to his hospital to shoot him there. I could have finished him off, if I'd wanted to, last night. So don't try to fix this killing on me.'

'You shot him in the legs.'

'Yes. And stopped there. I wasn't going to do that much, but I had to get him to answer me.' He stopped and looked at Frank very directly. 'When I got back I spent the night throwing up. I'm not used to this kind of work, Frank. I'm an analyst, not a bloody killer!'

'Really? But your friends in England told us different.'

'Eh? What do you mean?'

'That you're suspected in a murder.' Frank pulled a notebook from his pocket. 'Guy called James McNeill?'

Jack clenched his jaw and looked away. 'They never said that to me,' he said. 'My wife left me and set up with Jimmy. He was a colleague from work. He went out riding, and fell from his horse in a river and drowned. End of story. After that she came back to me.'

287

'You do it?'

Jack looked at him.

'He died in bloody Devon. I was in my London flat. That's two hundred miles across England. It's not like driving two hundred miles over Texas – England is crowded. It's a four-hour plus journey, to get from London down to the moors. I wasn't there, no.'

'Sorry,' Frank said. He looked away and frowned. 'But someone is setting you up, Jack. You come over here, and in a few hours we have reports that your own boys suspect you of murdering some guy? And you're shot at all the way from Whittier to Seattle.'

'And someone tried to blow me up, and now they're trying to set me up with a murder charge here, too,' Jack said.

'Is there anything you can tell me?'

Jack glanced at him. He instinctively liked Frank, but that did not affect his professional judgement. He had spent all his life maintaining secrets: sharing them was entirely against his nature. But he would need friends if he was to achieve what he needed. He had to get to this man, Amiss, and he had to clear his name if he was going to return to England.

'All right,' he said. 'It started with Lewin, as far as I was concerned. He came here because he wanted somewhere safe.'

Frank listened without expression as Jack spoke of the journal Lewin had written, then as Jack spoke of the men in the boat and the shooting of Orme, he shrugged.

'Yeah, we guessed that much.'

'Those guys. Where were they from?'

Frank pulled a face.

'We never knew. They were not listed anywhere. In fact, Debbie down there reckoned they had to be government agents of some sort.'

'What does that mean?'

'Look, I'm a Feebie, right? FBI. There are plenty of guys stomping all over my turf now, from the Bureau of Alcohol, Tobacco and Firearms, to the CIA and Department of Homeland Security. Time was, I had the home turf, the US, while the CIA had everywhere else. Now, the lines are sort of smudgy. They can mount some operations over here, if they get sanction.'

'But if they need approval, they wouldn't go in without ID on them,' Jack said.

'No. That's what makes these guys a bit more interesting. They had nothing.' Frank looked at him. 'Nor did the two you shot last night. They had no ID at all on them. Not even a credit card.'

'Which implies that they have some senior powers working with them,' Jack said.

'I think you'll get on well with Debbie,' Frank said. 'She likes to make mental leaps like that too. Yeah, it's what she said. They had to have government authority behind them to get their IDs wiped. There's more, though. One of the guys who took a shot at you in Seattle – he was called Ian McDonnell. A Sergeant in Iraq. But he was supposed to have died out there. So someone with authority wiped his records – or removed them. According to the Army and Veterans, the lot of them, he died years ago. You killed a ghost.'

'And this morning I killed two more,' Jack said.

'Is that a hint that I should appreciate you more?'

'No. It was an assessment of your ability to get anything on them. Do you have anything on those two – or on the other one in Seattle?'

'Not yet,' Frank admitted. 'They don't seem to exist on any of our usual databases.'

'They won't. If they were with the CIA or something similar, there are computer specialists who can go through and remove every aspect of their lives.'

'So what do you think we should do?'

'I have to get to Virginia and see if I can find out anything about this "Deputies General" mob.'

'How do you think you'll be able to do that? Without an agency, without the help of your own guys, and against all the men the CIA can field against you? It'd be a miracle for you to learn anything before you were found. And killed.'

'What else do you think I can do?'

'Lie low. Give me a chance to see what I can learn for you. You'll be better off keeping your head down.'

'And you'll be able to get warrants to arrest Amiss? Or you'll be able to get into his office and search his desk and safe without help?'

'I'd be more likely to do it than you,' Frank said.

'Really?' Jack said. He leaned back, both elbows behind him. 'Have you had training in breaking and entering, in how to crack safes, in how to look for alarms and…'

'You'll be on your own.'

289

'Yes. Which is what I've been trained for,' Jack said. 'It's what they teach us. How to get in and out quickly, how to gather intelligence, and always at arm's length.'

'Like I said, you think you can do that with all the US agencies looking for you?'

Jack looked at him.

'I managed it in Russia with the whole of the KGB looking for me.'

Frank puffed out his cheeks, shaking his head slowly.

'You'll need help if you mean to get to Virginia.'

'I will, yes.'

Frank eyed him for a long time without blinking. Then, 'Oh, shit! OK.'

*

17.55 Washington DC; 22.55 London

Arriving at the Ronald Reagan International airport, Stilson felt the strain of the last few days leave him. He stepped from the airport into a cab and rode along the George Washington Memorial Parkway all the way to the turn off for Langley. He had a small house in West McLean, and he had the driver drop him off at the door. The CIA had a company account with this cab firm, and he signed the record for the driver before waving him off.

Stilson unlocked the door, shut off the alarm system, and went to his bedroom. He carefully hung his suit on a hanger before going to the bathroom and preparing himself for a shower. He felt grubby after the last day. Over twenty-four hours without sleep had left him with the conviction that there was grit all over his skin. A long, hot shower was enough to banish the discomfort. He shaved, tidied his hair, dressed in a fresh grey two-piece, and was back downstairs in less than half an hour with his Glock checked and reloaded. He believed in preventing malfunctions by cleaning and testing his firearms at every opportunity. The Springfield .45 he had left in his wardrobe. It may become useful at some time in the future.

The traffic from here to the George W. Bush Centre where the CIA was based was usually atrocious. Today, he took the turn before the Agency headquarters and drove in among the trees.

It was a large house, and he took the sweeping drive slowly. Amiss hated hearing his gravel being torn up by young tearaways, he knew, and it had cost two or three men their careers when they braked too suddenly outside Amiss's door.

When he had parked, he nodded to the security camera by the door. The guards would be watching him. As he rang the bell, he knew that he would be surveyed from several angles. As soon as the door opened he stepped inside. In the wide marble-flagged hallway, there were two desks, one at either side of the front door. On the left were two men, standing well apart, with a series of television screens in front of them. To the right, with a third armed guard behind her, sat an unsmiling receptionist – a harsh-faced brunette with rectangular brown glasses. She stared at his ID card, as though she doubted its veracity, before she scanned it and then held up a small camera to record and validate his iris. Finally, she had him press his thumb against a small block. With iris and thumbprint checked and confirmed with a quiet bleep, she agreed to let him pass. The man behind her visibly eased as she turned back to her computer screen.

Stilson entered the library. Amiss was sitting at the far end of the room with a man whom Stilson knew. Tullman, the deputy director (operations) at the NSA. Stilson knew Tullman by reputation. He was another career operative who had come up from military intelligence, like Amiss himself. He was a little younger, but he was known for his clear-sighted analysis of any threats facing America, and his determination to do all he could to protect her was undoubted. He had helped the President a great deal after 9/11.

'Mister Stilson, this is Mister Tullman. You may speak in front of him with perfect confidence. What is said in this room stays in this room.'

'Good,' Stilson said. He knew that behind the panelling of the room there was a mesh of copper wires forming a barrier to electronic spying. The computers here were all NSA-checked weekly for security. There were line filters and scramblers fitted so no one could listen in or view what he was seeing on his screen, there was film over the windows to prevent a laser listening device, as well as bullet-proof secondary glazing, and every room in the building was regularly swept for bugs. The telephones were all STU-III handsets that could not be remotely turned on like other telephones. Only a few houses in America would have such sophisticated defences.

'Your mission was successful?' Amiss asked.

'No. The Brit escaped.'

'I see.' Amiss's expression clouded. 'What of the other two?'

'Sumner and Sorensen won't talk.'

'Who is this man?' Tullman asked quietly.

Amiss opened a drawer and pulled out a manila file, which he passed to Tullman.

'He is a spy. Our fellows knew him in Berlin in the 1990s, where he had a very good reputation. When the Brits decided that money was restricted, they concluded they must close a number of their networks, and Case's were amongst them. Result: a paltry saving of a few thousands of pounds a year, and the loss of all effective humint from the Soviet bloc. It was a great coup for democracy! Since then, he has apparently been held to a number of poor, end of service tasks. Nothing significant, and nothing with international impacts.'

Tullman nodded as he leafed through the file.

'This man should be little problem. I don't understand how he has come to threaten us.'

'He appears to be extremely fortunate,' Amiss said coolly.

'Well, luck comes and goes,' Tullman said, as he placed the file back on Amiss's desk. 'We have the bigger battalions on our side.'

Amiss nodded, bent his head and clasped his hands. Tullman followed suit, and Stilson copied them. But he was not thinking of God or offering up prayers. He knew that was a ridiculous affectation; he preferred to count on his own abilities rather than apportion success to a series of mythical beings. Nothing in his life had prepared him to believe in an omnipotent God, whether he was called God, Yahweh, or Allah. They were all smoke and mirrors designed to confuse tribes from the Iron Age. Stilson just couldn't get how it was that bright guys like these two could believe so devotedly in this supreme being.

Him, he preferred to trust to his handgun and his speed at firing.

*

22.56 London

Karen Skoyles was in her apartment when she received the call.

'You need to look at Twitter, Karen. Right now,' Starck said.

There was something in his voice that made her heart give a leap. She crossed the floor to the table and opened her laptop, logging on to her Twitter account and shaking her head.

'What am I looking for?'

'Just look at the trends, Karen. Do you know anything about this?'

Karen stared at the top ten trends on her page. The fourth and seventh were *rendition and *USkidnap.

'What the…?'

'Seems there is a fellow who's been snatched, Karen. One of the men held under control orders. Do you know anything about it?' Starck asked.

There was a note of glee in his tone. Karen gritted her teeth.

'I want this to go.'

'And how exactly do you expect me to stop this? It's viral, Karen. There are comments flying around the internet from... From Reykjavik to Jo'burg and beyond. I don't think that the Service has enough manpower to visit all of these people.'

Karen swore and hit the off switch. It was that bitch, Sara al Malik. Karen should have seen to it that she was removed somehow. Made to keep her mouth shut. Perhaps it wasn't too late. She had promoted this, must have, so she could be threatened with having her children taken into custody, maybe have her arrested for breaching the terms of her husband's custody.

But it was her husband's custody. With him gone, it would look odd prosecuting her. Karen strode about her room. When she sat again and saw the refreshed Twitter screen, *USkidnap had risen to sixth in the trends.

'*Fuck*!' she screamed, and hurled her mug at the wall. It smashed, the coffee hurled in a stain over the white paint.

Karen could do nothing. If Sara was silenced, the conspiracy theorists would all be out in force in moments.

But the publicity would destroy her career. And there was nothing she could do about it.

Saturday 24th September

19.48 Washington DC; 00.48

Frank walked through the doors at the airport with a real sense of queasiness –

this was the first time he had broken his country's laws since he'd been a teenager. Then, a young black guy growing in a project in New Jersey, he'd not had much of a chance. The likelihood was, he'd be taking a quick trip to a gaol before long, and he'd taken to thieving.

'You all right?' he asked Jack as they left the main doors and stood in line.

'I'm fine,' Jack said. He was glancing about him, his eyes flitting quickly from the two men managing the cab rank, to the men queuing in front of them, to the drivers of the cabs. His eyes remained fixed on the cars and their drivers. 'You ever feel like your whole life was bringing you to a destiny where you'd just end up being a target?'

'I used to be a bit like that when I was a kid,' Frank admitted.

'What happened?'

'My kid brother died,' Frank said shortly. 'It changes your outlook. Before that I was an asshole, but him and me were a pretty good team. Then we did something dumb and stole a car from a drug dealer, and got beat up.'

Jack watched him.

'I joined the police department after that. Managed to pass the test, but Gerry, he didn't reckon the same as me. He wanted to get his own way in the world, so he joined the gang that had beaten him up. He was dead in less than a year. They told him to go kill a guy who'd upset their boss, and he tried to. But he was so damn young. Never had much idea. The target saw him coming and blew him away. Two shots. Bam bam.'

Jack frowned.

'Sorry to hear that.'

'Plenty of others have similar experiences, I guess. It made me determined to go get other gangs and break them.'

'But you aren't fighting gangs now.'

'You reckon?' His phone rang, and Frank answered it quickly. 'Yeah?'

He listened, and then closed the call. 'Debbie has been through the area and can't see anyone on our backs.'

'Where is she?' Jack asked without turning.

'About thirty yards up on the right at the next exit.'

'Good. I wouldn't want to think she was too far away.'

Frank smiled.

'I've seen her hit a target at more than two hundred yards with her little twenty-seven.'

'So long as you're sure,' Jack said.

A cab drew up, and Jack peered in.

Frank gave a dry smile.

'If you're worried, let me just say I've had no involvement here. This ain't Seattle.'

'Good,' Jack chuckled drily.

He climbed inside and Frank followed him while the driver stored their luggage in the trunk.

'What now?' Frank asked.

'You know what I plan to do. I need a car and some gear. Then I can get on with it.'

Frank nodded.

'OK. If you're sure.'

'What about you? Those two were after you, not me, in Vegas.'

Frank nodded, and his face was set.

'I know that.'

'What will you do, then?'

'That's why I wanted to come here,' he said. 'I have friends who won't mind helping.'

'Officially?'

'No. Very unofficially. They understand the problem I got.'

'So long as you're sure they're on your side, Frank.'

'Yeah,' Frank chuckled. 'Not too sure how to check that just now.'

Jack turned and peered at the line of waiting people. As he watched, Debbie appeared and flashed her badge. In a moment she was in a cab and behind them as they entered the freeway.

Frank gave a short grin.

'What? You didn't think she'd make it?'

'I had no doubt she'd make it, actually,' Jack admitted. 'I just wanted to see if anyone dared try to stop her.'

*

19.52 Langley, Virginia; 00.52 London

Stilson sat as Amiss and the others spoke. He knew his place. His was no more a position of authority than any servant's. These men commanded, and it was his duty to obey. At half seven the rest of the committee had arrived. Three more men so that the management would never have the mess of a 50:50 split vote. The total present must always be an odd number.

'They are on their way?' Tullman said.

The short, dumpy man sitting over at the far right answered. He was called Will Barnard, and he worked with the CIA. It was said he had been one of the founders of Air America in his youth. Now he ran airplanes again.

'Yes. Bouvier is already here. He's been stored safely in the park for softening. Al Malik is there too. We have three more in transit, but we're being cautious about the shipments.'

'Rendition was a lot easier,' said a taller, paunchy man, whom Stilson knew as Louis Keen. He was based with the Security Service in the White House.

Amiss pulled the corners of his mouth down. 'Yes. It was faster. But since the Brits have started complaining, we've had to stop using that route.'

'There are still plenty of other options,' Barnard said.

'I don't need to know,' Tullman said. 'When do we begin on them?'

'Tomorrow. There's no need to hurry matters. We'll get on with the initial questioning, soften them up, and proceed accordingly.'

'Fine.'

The third member of the committee was a lanky, leathery-faced old man with a shock of yellowish white hair. He had faded blue eyes that contained a deal of sadness, Stilson thought. He was from the operations team that had set up Guantanamo and other interrogation camps around the world. Nominally he had reported along the army intelligence structure, but now he was a freelance. Brian Gutterson spoke with a mid-western drawl. 'So long's we can get to work soon. My boys are desperate to see what they c'n get.'

'They will be able to start very soon,' Amiss said.

Within two hours the main business was complete. The money allocated for the interrogation suites was adequate, the food supply sorted, and now that the building had been prepared, the first inmates were on their way. The next stage of capture and rendition was talked about, and then the meeting moved to total numbers which could be disposed of, once their intelligence value was diminished, and then after some updates on transport, Amiss looked about him at the Committee.

'Gentlemen, there is one other item I'd like to bring up.'

The four men were silent, waiting expectantly.

'I have been considering another member of our Order. He is not a Mason, but he has the faith. I have used him professionally, and he would appear to be honest and have the integrity we need.'

'Who is he?' Tullman asked.

'You've seen him. He is Roy Sandford, a communications technician from the Echelon coordination unit. He is bright, and very competent with his job. He can scan communications and help us with surveillance when we have need. He has religious convictions, too. Do I have your agreement to approach him?'

The men exchanged glances. Tullman nodded, and gradually the others followed suit.

'In that case, I shall speak with him as soon as I can. We can induct him as an epopt at our next meeting. He can join the lowest level of initiates until he has been tested. Bearing in mind our schedule now, I propose we should hold that tomorrow.'

His suggestion was approved and the meeting was wound up. The men rose and gathered up their notepads and pens, but Amiss remained in his seat.

'Thank you, gentlemen. Mister Stilson, would you mind waiting with me for a short while?' Amiss said.

'That's fine, sir.'

Amiss rose as Tullman and the others walked from the room, and then looked at Stilson.

'Do you think that there are any precautions I should take?'

'I believe you ought to be safe enough. The Brit surprised me in Vegas, and managed to speak to Sumner before I could remove him. Still, if it were not for the FBI agent, I would have got to him, I think.'

'I am concerned. I have been told that the FBI operative is on his way back here. He may be here already. Why would he be coming to Virginia?'

'You want me to see if I can remove him too?'

'I think that it could be a sensible precaution. Perhaps this time you will use more competent men than those you delegated in Vegas?'

'Very well, sir.'

'But first, watch him. If he has returned, I would like to know whether he has any news of this Brit. After all, he was staking out Sorensen's house when the Brit was inside.'

'That was my inference.'

'OK. Watch him. I'll have him under covert surveillance too, and we'll see if we get anything.'

*

09.52 Langley; 14.52 London

Jack felt a great deal better that morning as he checked through his bag and counted the remains of the money he had taken from Orme's safe. There was over three thousand dollars left, and he set them down on his motel bed. Frank had dropped him off here the night before, at a motel out near the Maryland/Virginia border. At the time, Jack had been so exhausted after the last days of running and danger that he had been almost incapable of noting the details. Frank ran inside the reception area, and then walked Jack to one of the motel rooms after checking him in. It was a great relief to Jack to be left in a clean room with a bed. As soon as he had stripped and showered, he lay down and fell asleep.

He woke to find that men had broken into his room. Someone was behind him, and he was being held down while Danny Lewin set a cushion over his legs and then slowly brought out a pistol, held it over the cushion, and fired, all the while smiling with a sympathetic expression fitted to his face. Jack writhed as he felt the bullet crash into the bones of his knee, and he screamed out loud, but there was nothing he could do to move Lewin, and Lewin shook his head sadly as the agony from his smashed kneecap flared and throbbed, and the blood seeped out to soak the mattress. Lewin moved the gun to Jack's other knee, and Jack tried to plead with him to stop, but something stopped him from being able to speak. The report of the pistol was so loud that Jack sprang up, throwing off the man who was holding him down, and Lewin disappeared. Jack's knees were constrained by the bedclothes, which had wrapped themselves about his knees, and his mind cleared as he remembered where he was.

It was with a pounding heart that he rolled free of the sheets and sat on the edge of the bed, and rested his head in his hands. The nightmare had been so vivid that he scarcely dared look at his knees in case he would see the holes in them. But there was nothing. It was only a dream.

298

After Rand dropped him here, he had told Jack to be ready this morning. He would come back as soon as he could. For now, Jack must prepare.

He took the .380 and stripped and cleaned it again, checking that the link mechanism was secure, that the feed ramp was clean and polished, and the ejector was not clogged, before putting it all back together again. There was only one magazine left – he had emptied the first when he rescued Frank and Debbie outside Sorensen's house. He would have to buy some more. Best locate a gun shop for some oil and ammunition, he thought.

He split his clothes into two piles. One shirt and a spare pair of socks went into his backpack. He stuffed the pistol into it, wrapped in a second shirt, then put his book in on top. He split up the money. Some went into the front pockets of his trousers, five hundred he crammed into his wallet, which he zipped up in his inside jacket pocket, and the remainder went into the backpack. He didn't want to lose any of it.

As he was finishing, there was a knock at his door. He squinted through the security peephole to see Frank and Debbie standing outside.

'Morning, Jack,' Frank said.

Jack stood aside for them. Debbie looked about her as she walked in with a sneer as though she had nothing but contempt for Jack and his predicament.

'Are you sure you want to go through with this?' Frank said, as he took his seat on a chair.

'I want to find out what has happened and who's trying to get me killed,' Jack said. 'Don't you?'

'What we think doesn't seem to matter, now, does it?' Debbie said caustically. 'If we mattered, you'd be in a safe location in Seattle with twenty-four hour guards from the FBI and Frank wouldn't be risking his badge to help you over here.'

'I don't want to get him into trouble,' Jack said. 'This isn't his fight. It's mine.'

Frank shrugged.

'Since they tried to shoot me and Debbie, I reckon it's our fight too,' he said.

Debbie shook her head.

'You two are determined to get yourselves killed.'

Jack ignored her.

'I have to find out all I can about this guy Amiss.'

'Here's a picture,' Frank said, passing him a manila envelope.

Jack opened it to see pictures of a man in uniform, smiling, in front of a building flying the US flag. Under that was a photo of Amiss sternly saluting, dressed in drab olive. A third had him in what could have been Vietnam, in his shirtsleeves.

'Who's this?' Jack asked pointing to a picture of Amiss with a taller, slimmer officer. He was smiling, and had curiously unemotional eyes even for a photo.

'That was him in Grenada, with a guy called Peachfield. They ran the interrogation centre there, after the invasion.'

The next showed Amiss older, in a dark suit standing next to a lean man with a square face, both shaking hands.

'That's him with the head of the CIA after the Contra enquiries. They tried to get him to testify against various folks, but he refused absolutely,' Frank said.

'Where was this?'

Frank took the picture and gazed at it for a moment.

'Don't know. It looks like a church, doesn't it?'

Debbie tutted and took the picture.

'It's Saint David's out at West McLean.'

'Never seen it,' Frank said.

'I used to go to the Baptist church up the road from there,' Debbie said.

'What about this picture?' Jack asked, waving a picture of Amiss with another man. Prominent behind them was the tall spike of the Washington Monument.

'That guy is second in charge of the NSA. He's called Tullman,' Frank said.

'Why have the photo there?'

'It's the centre of our government,' Frank said. 'Maybe they had meetings with senators that day and met up for a photoshoot after? You often have politicians and soldiers wanting to have their pictures taken with the country's greatest landmarks in the background.'

'I suppose so,' Jack said.

*

10.31 Langley; 15.31 London

Roy Sandford had been in the office for almost three hours when the call came through, and he immediately left his screen and hurried along the corridor to Amiss's room. Once again, the room was dark compared with the corridor, and Amiss stared at him at the door as though wondering why Roy had come. Then the door's lock clicked and he was inside.

'Sir?'

He saw that the deputy director's assistant Stilson was in the room, standing at the back, resting his backside on a sideboard, but then his eyes went back to the deputy.

'I have been most impressed with you, Roy. Your commitment in the last week or so has been good, and it's been noticed.'

Amiss motioned him in and Sandford entered, letting the door shut quietly behind him. At a gesture he realised, to his surprise, he was required to sit. He took the seat nearest the desk and sat upright. The only time he'd heard of people being called in here were the times when they'd been given a ball-roasting, and a prickly sweat broke out over his body as he waited for the inevitable sneering rebukes. The first words must have been nothing more than a softening up.

'Yes, Roy. I have been impressed. Tell me,' Amiss said, pulling a file from a drawer, 'you were at MIT, I believe?'

'Yes, sir.'

'And since joining us you've had no regrets?'

'No, sir.'

'Many would think that sitting on the Echelon liaison desk would be galling. You have been there some while.'

'Sir, I like it. I think I'm good at communications surveillance.'

'That is what I like, Roy.' Amiss turned a page and studied two pages side-by-side. 'And I like the quick work you made in Seattle, arranging for the software to turn on the British spy's telephone.'

'I'm afraid I didn't get him, though,' Sandford admitted.

'We shall. With the help of agents like you, we shall,' Amiss said. He stood and walked around his desk, sitting in the armchair beside Sandford. 'But the best agents need to be closer in the loop.'

'Sir?'

Amiss leaned forward.

'Do you love your country?'

'Of course, sir.'

'Is there any loyalty superior to that love?'

Roy licked his lips, unsure of how to respond.

'Sir, I...' And then inspiration struck. He remembered all the comments about Amiss's crucifix behind his desk, and he squashed the urge to glance at it with only a supreme effort. 'Only my duty to God, sir.'

'That,' Amiss said, glancing over his shoulder to Stilson, 'is a good answer, Roy.'

Stilson rose and left the room without speaking, and when the door had clicked shut behind him, Amiss continued.

'You see, the nation is at great risk. We all know the dangers of terrorism. But terrorism is nothing. It's a sop to the collective spirit of the country. What, so a bunch of guerrillas could get to New York and shoot a hundred people? Two hundred? Three? So what? They'll get killed and we'll have three hundred more Americans born in under an hour. The actual impact would be negligible. But the fact that we tell the citizens about it, that means they feel involved. They keep alert to the threat. That is not the real danger, though.'

He shook his head. 'The real danger, Roy, is the danger from rogue states with nukes. If Pakistan becomes more determined to follow the route of Muslim fanaticism, it would be alarming; but we already have the risk of nukes from North Korea, from Iran, and from any other disaffected little states with Russian know-how. We are living in an age of enormous power and danger, Roy. At any time, any of these states could decide to launch attacks. Just think: if someone managed to get some nukes into the US, one in, say, New York, one in LA, one in Washington. Not megaton bombs – just dirty bombs that would blow and pollute hundreds or thousands of square miles. That would be a real threat. The worst threat.'

'Yes, sir.'

'It is why some of us in the intelligence community grew alarmed at the risks when our new president arrived. It was obvious that he was an appeaser, Roy, and a risk to our security. He wanted to stop finding our enemies and bringing them to book. He ordered the closure of Guantanamo Bay and other facilities. Some of us felt he was wrong to do that. So we organised ourselves to do what our consciences told us.'

'I see.'

'We came together, Roy, to protect our great country. Roy, I would like to ask you: would you join us?'

'Yes, sir.'

'It means commitment, Roy. It means agreeing never to divulge what you have learned. It means absolute sincerity with us at all times

302

– immediate, unswerving obedience; devotion, even. Do you think you can hold to that kind of a bargain, Roy?'

'Yes, sir.'

'Some people would say this was a bargain with the devil, you know, sealing a deal like this. You have to be absolutely convinced in your own mind, before God, that you are prepared to adhere to our strict rules. You see, it's not with the devil that you're sealing this pact: it's with God. God and your country.'

*

14.21 Quantico; 19.21 London

Debbie watched as Frank came through the doors at the local office and fell into step beside him as he strode across the blacktop towards the car park.

'And?' she said.

'I don't know what the fuck's going on,' Rand said. 'I just had a call from Houlican telling me that unless I can pull Jack down by close of play today, he's going to have Jack's face spread over every available site in the US. He'll personally upload Jack's mugshot to the FBI's Most Wanted pages.'

'So you didn't tell him we're working with him,' Debbie said. She looked up at him. 'Frank, look, I don't know how you feel about this, but I feel pretty lonely.'

'How can you feel like that when there's him and me to look after you?'

'Funny. Very funny. But there were two guys tried to kill us. This isn't a game, Frank. I'd be a whole lot happier if I knew the rest of the Bureau was behind me. Just now, I'm feeling like I have a bullseye target on my back saying, "Aim here, guys", and it's not making me happy.'

'I know that feeling,' Frank said.

They had reached his car, and he opened the door.

'I mean, if they are still serious about getting us, how about a bomb in the car?'

'They wouldn't,' Frank said.

'Why not?'

'Because it's too damn messy. Especially here, in the main car park of an FBI office, Debbie.'

'Pretty obvious to try to shoot us in a Vegas suburb.'

Frank eyed her. Then he crouched down and looked carefully all over the underside of the car, checking the wheel arches, reaching

303

round behind the tyres to ensure there was nothing inside the wheels. It took him fifteen minutes to ensure the vehicle was safe, and then he grabbed some Kleenex and wiped his hands.

'Happy?'

She was already in the passenger seat. But he noticed that she reached beneath her to make sure that there was nothing under the chair.

'Yeah.'

'Because you were here all the time. You'd have seen someone getting to the car.'

'I know. But I'm getting kind of paranoid,' she admitted without looking at him. 'I don't like this.'

'Look,' he said, as he sat down and pushed the ignition home. 'They tried to kill us in Vegas, yeah, but now we're aware of them. OK?'

'How can you be so sure?'

'Because I have three friends with us now.'

'Who?'

Frank glanced at her.

'I spent a lot of time trying to get on with the FBI, you know?'

'You've done well, Frank.'

'But I flunked one set of tests – twice. Both times down here.'

She frowned.

'Doing what?'

'I wanted to be on the Hostage Rescue Team. And both times I blew it,' he said harshly. 'But I'm not alone,' he added defensively. 'There's, what, eleven hundred men and women in the FBI, right? And only two hundred have ever made it to the HRT.'

'It's the hardest course we got,' she said.

'The start was the "Yellow Brick Road",' he reminisced as he drove from Quantico's car park. 'It's a bitch, too. Full packs, with guns, and we had to run seven and a half miles after it. The obstacle part had all those things you like when you're a new recruit: ropes, jumps, climbs, the lot. I succeeded there. But next there was the Quigley. That was a real bitch. Climbing log ladders that just kept on going up, sitting with our legs over a four-storey drop, swimming through a sewer…'

'A sewer?'

'A sewer,' he said, and a corner of his mouth lifted at the memory. 'But the part I failed, twice, was the one after that lot. We were given blacked-out gas masks and shoved into the underground heating ducts in Quantico. Had to get from one end to the other. And I tell you, Debbie, I've never liked small spaces. I tried it twice, but couldn't do it.'

'Well, that's not something you have to do every day,' she said, watching him now.

'No. And it's lucky. Because if I had to, I'd blow my head off rather than go down those ducts again,' he said.

'What's that got to do with us here and now?' she demanded.

'We got three guys who're going to help us. They're all HRT, and friends of mine. If anyone can make sure our asses are covered, it's these guys.'

Sunday 25th September

19.14 Langley; 00.14 London

Jack was waiting when the call came through. He had packed and prepared after a visit to a local store, and now he had a pair of binoculars in his backpack, along with some energy bars and a sports bottle filled with water.

He left the motel room and hesitated when he saw that there were three cars outside. Frank was in the front car, but behind him were two more with men clad in dark clothing with identical short haircuts.

'Jack, it's all right. Come on over.'

Jack climbed into the seat behind Frank, nodding to the pale and uncommunicative Debbie.

'I thought we were going to keep everything quiet?' he said.

'We were,' Frank said. 'But Debbie and I were nervous, so we've got friends of mine to watch our backs. They're all instructors from Quantico. And they're friends of mine.'

'Yeah?'

'They're about the best you'll find in the world, Jack,' Frank said. 'And they'll keep quiet. They just enjoy the buzz.'

Jack mused over that as they drove on. There was a small bridge over a stream, and then they were into woods.

'He's got a big house for a guy living on his own,' Frank said. 'It's got a large set of grounds round it, and it's all secure. There are all kinds of static defence, from cameras and barbwire to electronic listening devices every few yards. That's the perimeter. As you get closer in, the security increases – with enhanced light cameras, motion detectors, the works.'

'What about remote surveillance?'

'He's right in among the trees. Impossible to view the property from any range. Can't get close enough for a laser listener to poke at the windows. Not that it'd do much good if you could. The glass is triple-glazed and has a film on the outer to stop vibration from voices.'

'What can we do, then?'

'First, we'll circle round the compound, and then we'll see if there's anything you think you can do.'

306

Jack nodded, and soon they were rolling along a quiet roadway in woods. The trees were still in their full foliage, and trying to view between them was next to impossible.

'He's in there?' Jack said.

'Yes. Not that you could tell it too easily. His house is a good few hundred yards from here.' Rand turned to the right at a T-junction, the car smoothly pulled away, and they moved on past more trees and then a wall. 'This wall continues all around his property. It's topped with broken glass, and there are steel spikes at sections, too. Try sitting on that lot, and you'll regret it in a hurry!'

Jack eyed the wall with a growing sense of the impossibility of the mission.

'Right. Keep on going, and let's see if there's even a remote chance of getting inside the perimeter without being spotted.'

Frank shrugged, and Debbie stared out to the left as though desperate to conceal her frustration. It was clear that she had no faith in Jack's ability to get inside. The whole concept should be aborted.

Jack could sense her resentment, but ignored her. He was determined to get inside somehow.

'There's a car there,' he said, pointing ahead.

'It's my buddies,' Frank said. 'I've had video cameras installed at every entrance. The operators in the car here have feeds that are motion-activated. If someone goes in or out, he'll know. If it's interesting, he can follow.'

'I see.'

'Just what do you think you are going to do?' Debbie said, still staring out the window, her back stiff. 'You want to keep on driving round and round here on the off-chance you see a tunnel under the wall? Or you waiting to see if there's a ladder, with a sign sayin', "over here, guys, it's safe"?'

'Amiss is somehow connected to Lewin, and that means he may know something about the men who killed Lewin, and the guys who tried to kill me and you two as well,' Jack said. 'Unless you have an idea how to break into the CIA headquarters and into his safe, I'd suggest getting into his house is about the only way to speak to him.'

She gave a short, sarcastic laugh.

'Yeah? And let's think: he's got five, six men in the house? Patrolling agents out in the garden? Dogs? Just how many guys can you take out on your way to him?'

'I don't know,' Jack said. 'But…'

He was saved by a two-tone bleep.

Debbie sneered as she picked up her phone.

'Yeah?'

There was a moment's silence while she listened, then she asked a couple of questions, nudged Frank, and whirled her hand twice in the air before jerking a thumb back the way they'd come.

'OK, on our way now!'

'What?' Frank demanded.

'Turn round, Frank. Amiss is in a car heading north.'

*

19.29 Langley; 00.29 London

Roy Sandford felt real good as he left home and strolled to his car. The car beeped as he pressed the alarm remote, and he looked back and saw her in the window. Her blouse fell open as she lifted a hand to wave, and he grinned as he climbed behind the wheel.

His apartment was a tip, but that didn't matter tonight. Janice (he must get used to calling her by her real name) was already there when he got back, and even as he threw his jacket over the chair and began to undress so he could have a shower, she was already tugging off her blouse and skirt, and then helped him to remove the rest of his clothes. The result was a fifteen-minute delay before he could climb into the shower, and that increased when she joined him in the small cubicle. It was very snug in there.

Yeah, leaving his apartment knowing Very Nice was waiting for him to get back was a great way to start the evening.

He had no idea what was about to happen. Some kind of interview panel was what he assumed, and he drove off to the location Amiss had given him with trepidation and a fluttering in his gut, but the anxiety was stilled by the memory of Very Nice's backside rubbing against his crotch in the shower, her hair bedraggled in the water, making her appear more wanton than ever. That was a lovely picture to hold in his mind.

The turnoff was not far from here. He took the road down into McLean, and very soon he was rolling along the smooth blacktop towards the chapel at the far end. He parked up, and stared at the little chapel. With a shrug, he left the car and pressed the button on his key fob to lock it and set the alarm. Tugging his jacket more neatly over his shoulders and buttoning it, he crossed the road and walked to the Chapel of St David's.

*

19.32 Langley; 00.32 London

'I know that guy,' Frank said, as he watched the slim figure cross the road. He snapped his fingers at Jack, who was watching through his binoculars.

Jack passed them over the seat, and Frank peered.

'Fuck me, Debbie. It's Roy Sandford.'

'I ain't…'

'All right, Debbie. What the fuck is he doing here meeting with Amiss, though? The prick was supposed to be our comms and intel support in Seattle, and now he's having cosy meets with Amiss?'

*

19.34 Langley; 00.34 London

Stilson met Roy Sandford in the door. Ed Stilson was still in his own suit, which was reassuring. It made the meeting place seem a little more normal. He had to admit, crossing the street to this old clapboard chapel had struck him as a little worrying, especially when he saw the strange symbol over the doorway. It was the old device of the dividers with a set square beneath, and he knew as well as anyone who'd ever read *The Da Vinci Code* that it meant the Masons.

Well, no one who'd ever lived in Washington or near it for more than a couple of weeks would have missed the fact that the Masons were all over the place. There were masonic symbols everywhere, and anyone who doubted it only had to look at a dollar bill. The all-seeing eye in the pyramid was something to do with them, too, he thought.

'Hi, Mr Stilson,' he said, holding out his hand.

Ed Stilson smiled, took his hand, and pointed him through the next door.

Roy walked to it, opened the door, and saw that the room beyond was in darkness. He was about to turn and ask Stilson where he should be going, when his hands were both grabbed. Before he could shout or fight to free himself, Stilson had a black velvet bag over his head, and the drawstrings were pulled tight. His wrists were held tightly at either side. Roy wanted to shriek, but he had a sudden clear recollection of the masonic symbol over the doorway, and he realised this must be an induction ceremony of some sort. It didn't stop his heart from thundering painfully, but he could control his breathing and avoid hyperventilation. He was led along what must have been a timber floor, and then the sound altered. He was on stone. He could feel the difference in texture of the ground and, as he went after the men pulling his wrists, he felt them go down slightly. A moment later, he found himself stumbling down some stairs. They must have been very broad and steep, and suddenly the hands on his wrists were gone, and when he reached out, he felt stone on either side – a narrow passageway.

He had the choice of ripping the bag from his head, turning and fleeing, or carrying on. At MIT he had been brought into a society at which there had been an induction ceremony, which had involved several women and a lot of beer. His fear dissipated a little at the memory, and then the recollection of Janice's very nice face in the shower as she reached up to kiss him in gratitude came back to him, and he thought of telling her all about this evening. That was enough to give him the incentive to continue. His hands brushed the wall on either side, and the stone became colder and damper to the touch. There were still stairs, but now they were closer together, and seemed to go winding round leftward. It put him in mind of the old castles he'd seen in pictures of Europe. He shrugged and carried on, and then there was no wall on either side, and he stood still, reaching out blindly to see if there was anything near him.

His feet tapped at the floor before him. There was a coolness in the air and, although he could hear nothing, he had the impression of height and space all around. It was strange and scary. He kept walking, hands outstretched, trying to find a wall, anything.

'Stop!'

The voice almost made him jump out of his skin. Someone was very close to him, over to his left. He turned his head instinctively, but then his arms were gripped, and someone ripped the sack from his head, and he was in a large chamber. With astonishment, he gazed about him.

It was a cavern carved into the rock. Somehow he would have expected to see flaming torches set into wall niches, but instead there were electric lights strung out on either side, outdoor waterproof bulkhead lamps. But it was less that than the scene before him.

Directly in front of him was a large hole in the ground. At some point, he guessed, this had been a well. It had never been covered, and now, as he stared down into it, he could see sluggish black water moving at the bottom. The sight was enough to make his stomach lurch. He was only a step at most from falling into it. The thought made the sweat break out on his forehead.

'You are gazing into the pit.'

Looking up, he saw that all around were men dressed as monks, with their faces hidden behind hoods. A man stood on each side of him, while others were grouped at the far side of the hole in the ground. He guessed that the man directly opposite him was Amiss, but it was only a guess, while at either side of Amiss himself were two more men. From the build, he thought the man on Amiss's right was probably Tullman.

'The pit is the resting place for anyone who betrays us,' Amiss said. 'We are the Council of the Deputies General of the Empire of the East and West. We all believe in one Supreme Being, and in the sacred duty of all to follow Him. We work ceaselessly to aid Him in His works. Will you join us?'

'Yes,' Roy said.

This was stupid, but incredible. These old guys were like Masons, then, but not Masons. He was honoured that Amiss had thought to invite him in as well. It was like an old work colleague inviting a new recruit into his club.

'You will learn secrets while you are with us, Roy. You will gradually rise through the levels. At first you will be a novice, an Epopt, until you can advance. You will have many duties. You must obey and work always to the benefit of the Council.'

'Yes, sir.'

'And if you flag, if you falter, if you fail, there is no shame. So long as you have striven with all your power.' Amiss's hands had been clasped. Now he held them open, as though somehow embracing the pit before them all. 'But if you desert us, betray us, attempt to destroy us, we will seek you out and we will ensure your ruin, your devastation and death. Your body will be cast into the pit before you here; your soul will be cast into the outer darkness. And your memory, your history, all will be lost forever. It will be as though you never lived. You will be utterly erased.'

There was a strange feeling as he heard that. Roy felt as if he was in the presence of a senior priest, and that the word of God was being invoked. It was the same as when he had been confirmed and the Bishop had laid his hands on Roy's head. The same sort of odd tingle in his scalp, the same hypersensitivity to all about him.

'Do you join us?'

'Yes.'

'Then we shall pray,' Amiss said.

*

311

Jack was sitting in the back of the car with his elbows resting on the backs of both front seats.

'What is going on in there?'

'It's a chapel,' Debbie said scathingly. 'They're probably praying.'

'Why are there no lights on, then?' Jack demanded.

'Look, Jack, I don't give a shit, OK?' Debbie said. 'Frank, let's get out of here. I don't like this at all, and you know that. I want to get back to my nice, comfortable desk at Seattle where I know what is happening, and not have to follow the deputy director of the CIA any more. All we're doing here is frigging about, and I don't want to play any more. You got that? If we're still here with this Brit shit-for-brains tomorrow, we'll all be wanted along with him.'

'Debbie, we'll be OK,' Frank said. 'Look, we—'

'No, Frank. Houlican told you that if you pissed about he'd have your balls. I think he meant it. But you prefer to be out here, watching Amiss instead of doing your job.'

'I want to know if he had anything to do with ordering our murders,' Frank said.

'I'm missing something, I think,' Jack said. 'You've been ordered to bring me in or face discipline yourselves?'

'Yeah. Something like that,' Frank said.

'Shit!' Jack looked at the chapel. 'Look, I'm going to go take a look, in case there's something we can take away with us. That OK?'

'Just go,' Frank said, waving his hand and staring at Debbie.

*

19.50 Langley; 00.50 London

Amiss lifted his head after the prayers and glanced about him at the other members of the Council.

'We are an ancient body. We were created over two hundred and fifty years ago by warrant, and we have striven to support the aims and objectives of all those who believe in a Supreme Being and seek the better government of the world. We will not cease in our fight for the freedom and democratic principles that underlie our great nation. We reject those who seek to harm our nation, we spurn those who seek to destabilise our beliefs, and we will destroy those who seek to wage war upon us. We are the Council of the East and the West.'

He felt the cold satisfaction wash through his soul as he spoke the words again. His own belief had been rigid for many years now. This would be his twenty-fifth year in the Council, and he was proud that he had never once lapsed in his duties since the very first day. His faith was as strong now as on that first day when he was accepted as an Epopt.

'Never before has our duty been so important. Our purpose is to protect our nation from the many adversaries ranged against us. Only by our determination and our rigid inflexibility will we succeed. There are unpleasant choices to make, and a long road to travel before we can say that we have succeeded.'

He knew that too well.

'The battle is not only with those from abroad who would see us destroyed, but also with the enemies within. The people who seek to weaken the country so that we no longer have the ability to defend ourselves. We will not permit them to succeed!'

He held up his hands. 'We all know what we must do to prevent their attacks upon us. We must use all methods. Covert, overt, intelligence gathering of all forms, in order to thwart the enemies who threaten us and our way of life. Our religious way of life.'

Amiss looked at the other men about him. They all agreed. Yes, most, like him, were deeply convinced Christians, but there was one who was not. Gutterson was a Christian Scientist, so he believed in an alien locked in a mountain somewhere, so far as Amiss could understand it. He didn't care. Gutterson had the key attribute he was looking for: absolute and unswerving support of the United States. He would die for that cause, and Amiss demanded nothing more from his men.

'Roy Sandford. Step forward,' Amiss said, and did so himself.

The men all stood at the very edge of the well-pit, and Roy had to command himself not to look down. He could hear the slap and trickle of the water at the bottom of that shaft, and with the analytical part of his mind, he told himself that the water was moving down there. Any body thrown down would perhaps disappear forever. There was no telling where the underground stream would carry it. The thought made him shiver.

'Roy Sandford, do you believe in a Supreme Being?' Amiss demanded, his eyes glimmering in the lights.

'Yes, sir. I do,' Roy said, remembering Very Nice in the shower.

'Do you swear by your Supreme Being, that you will work to obey the Council of East and West, that you will strive constantly to serve this Council, and that you will willingly suffer any punishment this Council imposes if you fail in your duties?'

313

Roy had to stop a grin.

'Yes, sir. I do.'

It was a bit pathetic, really, he told himself. The old men here had their little masonic temple, they had their rites and their paraphernalia, all to make it seem more important than it really was. He wondered, for a moment, whether they were all deeply unhappy at home. Perhaps they had invented this charade in order to give themselves more of a veneer of control over their own lives.

He could understand it. They were all, if they were like Amiss, older, and the active events of their lives were over and done. In their homes, they could try to rule like tyrants, maybe, but the taste would be sour. Amiss had cut his teeth in Vietnam, others here were of the same era. And now they were all winding down to retirement. Still, who was he to complain, he told himself happily. If they wanted to have him join them, shake hands with the strange tickle of a little finger, and meet up like this once in a while, he wasn't going to stop them. Not if it meant he had a sudden ride on the up-elevator at work.

There was a nod from Amiss, and he looked at Roy with a curious expression.

'You swear this by your Supreme Being?'

'Yes, sir. I swear it.'

From behind him came a bleating noise. Jesus, Roy thought – they aren't going to slaughter a lamb, are they? He turned with a smile beginning to form on his lips, and there, behind him, he saw Stilson marching a young man towards him.

This was little more than a teenager, from the look of him. He had long, lank black hair, and the dark skin of a man from the subcontinent; perhaps he hailed from India or Afghanistan. He was naked from the belly up, and the only concession to his modesty was a pair of jockey shorts. He was bare-legged and barefoot.

On one side of his face there was the beginning of a beard, while on the other side, the beard was gone. In its place was a livid mark where the tissue was scorched away, and a weeping sore was all that remained. His right ear appeared to have been cut off, his torso was marked with bright crimson where he had been repeatedly cut, and he limped as though his toes were broken, hobbling painfully as Stilson propelled him onwards. As he reached the group Roy could smell his sweat, his terror, over the odour of faeces. The man stood with his head bowed and, as he stood there, Stilson took a switchblade knife and flicked it open. Holding it up so the victim could see it, Stilson smiled as the little man in his grip quailed and moaned, making that strange, terrified bleating again. Stilson slipped the blade under the waistband of the man's shorts, and cut them away.

Beneath his makeshift loincloth Roy could see how the man had been assaulted. The blackened organ was shrivelled and ruined.

'Amazing, isn't it?' Stilson said. 'A little electricity is all. But he sang the tune we needed when we plugged it in.'

Roy could not speak. He stared in horrified fascination. Surely this was a test. The man was an actor, that was all. He had not really suffered in the way that seemed so hideously genuine. This must be make-up. That was it. Soon they'd all laugh at the sight of his face. It was a test, a team-building exercise to make him feel what they had felt when they had joined. 'We all went through that, but Jesus, you should have seen your face!' they'd say, and slap each other on the back. They'd go and have drinks in the bar up the road, that was it. Nothing more to it than that. It was a test, and a joke.

The man was sniffling now, and gazing down, he moaned a high-pitched ululation of terror. Then he looked at Roy and said something in Pashtun. Roy's mouth fell open.

'Roy,' Amiss said. 'Push him down the shaft.'

Roy swallowed and stared at Amiss.

'But, sir? He...'

'Instant obedience is needed,' Amiss said. 'You must obey. Push him.'

Roy was incapable of lifting his arms. They remained at the side of his body, and he trembled slightly. He felt as though he might collapse at any moment. There was a roaring in his ears, and he could taste bile in his throat as he looked at Amiss. This was a joke. It had to be a joke. No one would really expect him to do this.

'This man, Roy, is a murderer,' Amiss said in his reasonable voice. 'He has plotted with friends to come to America and buy guns. His plan was to go with twenty more men to a hotel in Hawaii, in convention time, and kill all the delegates there. He plotted to bring guns and grenades there, to where Americans go to holiday, and kill as many as he possibly could. If he could, he would have brought over a nuclear weapon and killed everyone on the island. You understand me? This man deserves death.'

'Wh... Why here?' Roy managed.

'We brought him here because we knew he was planning something, but he wouldn't admit what his offences were to be. It was only when we had him strapped to a table and began to work on him that he confessed. It didn't take long, honestly. We are not barbaric. But when you fight ruthless killers, you must be ruthless too.' His voice hardened. 'This is your test, Roy. He would have killed you, me, Peter there, Ed, all of us, all our wives and children, all our friends and neighbours. Everyone. And now, if he isn't killed, he will win the hearts and minds of more. He will parade his injuries in front of television cameras and newspaper photographers. He will go to Wikileaks and reveal what we did to him. And afterwards, we shall be arrested and condemned for doing... what? For simply guarding our people. Our state, our way of life. Push him in, Roy. Kill him.'

The man looked up at Roy. His face was a mask of fear and, as Roy looked, a trickle of snot ran from his nostril. Roy couldn't help himself. He began to take a step away, and then he heard the sound of a gun clearing leather. No safety on a Glock, he reminded himself as he turned and squinted down the square slide of the gun. Nothing to click on or off to make the gun ready. No hammer to cock. Just draw it and it's ready.

A square inch of steel was at his temple, and he heard Ed Stilson murmur, 'I can do you, if you want. Don't carry out your order, and you'll be in there before him. He'll still die, but you'll die too. You want that?'

The Glock's barrel was cold. With a sudden cry that was almost a scream, Roy stepped forward, grabbed the man, and pushed. He gave an agonised wail, a shriek that was cut off as his head slammed against the bricked wall of the well, and then he was gone, and there was a silence, broken after what seemed half an hour, by the loud splash of his body striking the water. And then there was nothing.

No man, no victim. And no soul in Sandford's heart. All were gone.

*

20.32 Langley; 01.32 London

Jack walked around the little hedge that bounded the chapel, and stood a while watching in case there were guards. Soon, he saw them – two men over at the rear, both walking towards him. He slowly bent his knees and hid behind the hedge as the two came past, both in suits and one with a trailing spring of wire from his earpiece. Jack settled and waited, watching to see what their routine was. He timed them, and after they had walked round twice, he could see that they were professional. The first circuit took them seven minutes, the second only four. They were breaking their steps so as to confuse anyone watching.

He took a deep breath as they passed around the corner of the chapel, preparing to leap forward and go listen, but before he could, there was the sound of a door opening, and suddenly a small, chubby man came out from the door. It was clear he was expected, because the two guards came back and one stood with him while the other walked to the road, his jacket open to allow him to draw his pistol. He stood there at the roadside, taking into a mic in his hand, and a car flashed its lights as it approached. A large sedan drew up. The man climbed into the back, while the guard stood watching the road, and it pulled away quietly.

The same thing happened four more times. The last time, Jack recognised the man with the guard. Amiss stood at the roadside while his car purred to meet him, and a second sedan came and stopped behind him. The second guard moved to that car, while the man at the road waited patiently. Soon Jack heard locks and a chain, and then two more men left the Chapel. One was a young guy, who appeared to be walking with some difficulty, as though he was in trouble of some sort. The second appeared to be another heavy.

'You did well tonight, Roy,' Amiss said. His voice carried clearly on the cool evening air. He patted the younger man on the shoulder. 'Go home, get some rest, and tomorrow we begin the good fight anew.'

'I'll drive him home,' the second man said, and led Roy away.

*

20.46 Langley; 01.46 London

Frank was already starting the engine of his vehicle when Jack yanked the door wide and leaped inside. 'You see them?'

'Yes,' Frank said drily.

'The first car is Amiss, the second has his goons,' Jack said. 'That other car there,' he pointed, 'has a young guy in it.'

'I know,' Frank said as he drew away from the kerb. 'It was the guy used to be my comms specialist. Looks like he was happier working with me.'

He drew off after the car with Roy, and Debbie grunted as it turned off towards Langley.

'What's the betting he's going in to do some work?' she said caustically.

317

But he wasn't. The sedan they followed took them on past McLean itself and out the other side, and fortunately there was plenty of traffic about. It was not easy to trail the sedan, but Frank was a skilled driver and he managed to keep six cars behind, while Debbie called out any manoeuvres from her side. They were not there for long, but followed their target as it turned off into an estate with old houses that had been converted to apartments. It was outside one of these that the sedan stopped, and Frank continued on. Debbie already had a hand at her seatbelt when Frank turned off to the left and, as he slowed, she and Jack jerked the door handles and quickly hurled themselves out while Frank carried on up the road.

Debbie was crouching low. Jack touched her arm.

'Let's walk, honey,' he said.

'Don't fuckin' "honey" me!' she spat.

He put an arm about her waist. She removed it. He replaced it and squeezed. She put a hand threateningly over his crotch, and he grinned as he put his arm over her shoulder instead. With a muttered curse, she removed her hand and they continued out along the sidewalk.

The black sedan was there. Jack saw it was a Ford. The driver was at the door of an apartment block and, as Jack and Debbie passed, she reached up to him, and murmured, 'Gimme a kiss, asshole.'

He responded, knowing that all the while she was peering over his shoulder, and then she broke away, quickly wiping her mouth, and leading him along the road again. 'Got it. 538,' she said, as they turned right up the next street. As she walked, she sent the house number to Frank as a text message.

The sedan was already moving off, and Jack took Debbie to a tree. He had a suspicion that the driver would be looking out for any surveillance, and sure enough, a few minutes later, the sedan came back, very slowly and almost silently rolling past the house. The driver was looking all over for any people who shouldn't have been there, Jack knew, but in a moment the car was gone.

'What now?' Debbie said, as Jack reached behind his back for the pistol. He checked it was still in the little holster, and grinned.

'I'm just going to have a chat,' he said.

'No, don't be a fuckwit! You have no place here, no jurisdiction, nothin',' she protested.

'I have no jurisdiction.'

'He'll be in his rights to blow you away,' she said. 'Leave it to...'

'Who, Debbie? I'm on borrowed time as it is,' he pointed out.

'What d'you want to do, then? Kneecap him too?'

He clenched his jaw, and set off along the sidewalk. Behind him he could hear her grumbling to herself, and then she pattered along the pavement and joined him.

'All right, all right. Gimme a chance. I'm coming too.'

The path to the door of 538 was gravelled, and their steps sounded abnormally loud.

'Let me do this,' she said. She reached into her jacket and pulled out her ID badge, then held it up, open, while she rang the bell.

The light over the door was already on and, as Jack waited, he saw another light turn on inside the apartment, and then, when Debbie rang the bell again, a figure appeared behind frosted glass.

'Who is it?'

'That's not him, unless his voice went up several octaves,' Jack muttered.

Debbie snapped, 'Shaddup! Ma'am, I'm with the FBI. This is my ID. Can you let me in, please? I want to have a word with you and your man.'

'Can't you wait, come back tomorrow? Roy's not well.'

'This won't take long.'

With a rattle of the chain and snapping of bolts, the door opened and Jack found himself confronted by one of the most beautiful young women he had ever seen, clad only in a button-down man's shirt with a blue pinstripe. He desperately fought to keep his eyes above her chin.

'Well?' she asked once she had studied Debbie's badge.

'Where is Roy, Ma'am?'

'In the bathroom.'

'Are you his wife?'

'No. I'm his girlfriend, Janice O'Hagan.' She reached into the pocket of a jacket hanging on a peg and brought out her own wallet. 'CIA.'

'Good. Then you'll understand when I say this is a case of Homeland Security?' Debbie said. 'I need Roy right now.'

'Who're you to come in here demanding to see him...'

'I'm the one he was working with in Seattle, girl. We have some elements of that mission need addressing. OK? Just get him. And either get back to bed, or get some clothes on. You'll catch your death in that.'

319

With a filthy look, Janice left them.

'Take your eyes off her. I can hear them squeaking,' Debbie said.

*

20.58 Langley; 01.58 London

Roy Sandford wiped his mouth with a flannel as he rose from the toilet. In his mind he saw again that dark figure, he felt the Glock at his head, and he relived those split seconds when he reached forward and pushed the man down into the well. He heard the sickening crunch of bones as the man's head hit the wall, and then that distant splash. And with that, he leaned over the bowl again, heaving and retching like a poisoned man trying to bring up the foulness from his belly. But the poison wasn't in his belly, it was in his head, his heart, and his soul.

'Tell them I can't,' he whispered when Janice walked in.

She looked at him.

'Roy, they said it's something to do with Homeland Security. You know what that means. I can't just throw them out. What's happened to you?'

He wiped his face again, and then turned a ghastly smile to her.

'Nothing, Jan, *nothing*. Think it was something I ate, that's all.'

'You haven't eaten yet,' she said reasonably. 'Roy? You were going to your little masonic meeting, weren't you? And now you seem really... well, weird.'

'I'm all right,' he said again feebly. He stared at his face in the mirror over the sink. 'I just need some sleep, that's all.'

'They are waiting. You want me to stay with you?'

No. He wanted to be here with her, alone – and yes, he wanted her to go. He couldn't bear the thought that his guilt would become apparent to her. She stood in the doorway, and he stared at her abjectly. He hadn't joined the Agency to become a murderer. He had seen violence. Once, in Iraq, he had seen a car bomb take the leg off a friend, and he had kept his breakfast down even when he saw three marines catch the man they thought responsible, and kill him with their bayonets. That hadn't affected him, and he had known even then that if he had seen the man and could have got to him, he would have done the same. Just slaughtered the fucker for trying to kill him and the others. It was war, and who gives a fuck what the politicians say about it. War, that's all it was. You kill or get killed.

That man, though, with the injuries so plain upon his body, with the proof of torture all over him, he was innocent. That was what he had

320

said in Pashtun. Roy knew he was innocent. He had colluded in the murder of an innocent torture victim. And now he was tainted for life. His belly was empty, but he had to turn and retch again, trying to bring up something – anything.

'Roy, can I get you something?'

There was an edge to her voice now. She was getting restless and angry. He swallowed and tried to smile but his eyes filled with tears.

'Just wait for me, huh?'

'Have you done something?' She demanded, suspicion darkening her brows. 'Jesus, you haven't broken the Homeland Security laws, have you?'

'Christ, no,' he said, and began to sob.

*

21.12 Langley; 02.12 London

Jack was surprised to see a medium height man walk in, but Roy Sandford could have been shorter from the way he hunched himself over. His misery was all too plain.

Debbie was shocked, Jack saw.

'Jesus, Roy – what the fuck's happened to you?' she demanded. 'Come here and siddown. Tell us what's happened?'

'I can't,' he said, sniffing. Janice was at his side and, as he sat in his armchair, she took her place beside him. 'It's confidential.'

'That's not going to cut any ice, Roy,' she said. 'Look, you know who I am. We're investigating over here now. I want to know what happened to you tonight – in the chapel at McLean. We saw you there.'

'I can't talk about it,' he said, shaking his head.

'You went inside perfectly all right,' Jack said. 'But when you came out, you were…'

Roy seemed to notice him for the first time.

'You? Shit, Debbie, he's the fuckin' murderer! What are you doing bringing him here? Are you mad? Jesus!' he was clambering to his feet, moving away to stand behind the chair as though thinking Jack was going to launch himself over it at any moment. 'This is my private…'

'Shut up, Roy,' Debbie said. 'Things are different now. I need you to tell me what happened down there tonight.'

'I can't.'

'Then at least tell me who was there with you. It looked like Deputy Director Amiss.'

'Look, I can't tell you anything. You want to learn, you go ask him and see where you get. Don't you see? I cannot tell you a thing!'

*

21.15 Langley; 02.15 London

Jack and Debbie were back with Frank in a few minutes.

'Well?' Frank demanded as the doors closed.

'Nothing. He won't open his mouth for anyone. Ended up demanding that we fuck off or he'd call Amiss on the spot,' Debbie said succinctly.

'So what now?' Frank said. He glanced over his shoulder at Jack. 'Eh?'

'We wait a little,' Jack said. He had a clear view of the apartment over Frank's left shoulder, and now he was staring at the door. 'He may call his boss, he may call a friend. He may just settle down to screw his woman. But there's a possibility that he won't want to use a phone. He is an agent. He knows how easy it is to listen in to a call. If he's a problem, he may want to go meet his boss to tell him about us face-to-face.'

'What do you think, Debbie?'

Debbie looked at Frank and shrugged.

'You got somewhere better to go? In about three hours, Houlican's going to demand Jack's head on a platter, and he'll want to know what the fuck we've got if he ain't goin' to have Jack shot as armed and dangerous. So, if Jack wants to spend his time here, what the fuck? There's another thing, though. He was broken down. Know what I mean? Really broken down. Like he'd been beaten and kicked.'

'No explanation?' Frank said.

'What do you think?'

Jack hissed.

'There he is.'

Frank looked up to see the man stumbling down the pathway to the road. He walked to an old Saab and climbed inside. Soon the lights sparked and the car began to pull away from the sidewalk. It lurched as it started, as though he had jerked the clutch, and then was off up the road.

With his own car started, Frank watched as the Saab did a U-turn and headed back down the road towards them.

'Heads down,' he instructed, and waited until Sandford had passed them, before drawing out after him.

322

'I hope he's not going to the Agency,' Debbie said.

'Not likely. Not with the issues he has just now. If he was working legally, he'd just call his boss and tell him there was a problem. The fact he's looking to drive away means his boss doesn't want to hear anything over the phone, which means it's dangerous.'

'Or,' Debbie said, as they turned out onto the Dolley Madison Boulevard, 'it means that they know we could be chasing him, and they've decided to try to catch us.'

'Thanks,' Frank said.

The Saab took them north east on the dual carriageway, but went past the entrance to the CIA at Langley.

'Come on, Roy. Where are you taking us?' Frank said, as he punched a speed-dial number into his phone and was held it to his ear.

'Where is this?' Jack asked.

'We're heading toward the Chain Bridge Road,' Debbie said. Her eyes were narrowed as she kept her eyes on the Saab now five cars in front of them. 'That means we'll soon be in DC.'

'Who're you calling, Frank?' Jack asked.

Frank finished his call.

'Just told my friends where we are. One's coming up here to help, Tony Knussel. The other guys are staying with Amiss to watch him. Debbie, take my phone. Phone through to this number when we change our route. I need Tony to know exactly where we are going, OK?'

*

21.28 Langley; 02.28 London

The road was one Roy knew well. He'd commuted here when he was a very raw recruit and had been working on the protection of the communications of senators and government officials. The main job had been to design firewalls on the computer networks in use, and Roy had early on learned that any Senators who regularly viewed porn were to be quietly reported to his supervisor. Any information that could be used against a Senator was always to be kept on file. His supervisors believed in the maxim 'forewarned is forearmed' – if they were likely to be blackmailed by foreign powers, the CIA wanted to know about it first.

This route would take him in to the west of Washington DC, and from there he'd be able to cut down the Canal Road, which led him along the Chesapeake and Ohio Canal as it followed the Potomac.

There was a little bar near the Thompson Boat centre, overlooking the expensive vessels moored on the Potomac's banks, where Stilson had said to meet him. He had to tell Stilson what had happened just now with Debbie and Jack. Jesus! How could Jack have got in among the FBI? He was supposed to be wanted, a murderer, and now here he was, with Debbie! He had to tell Stilson.

The familiar surroundings of the bridge and the memories they evoked helped to calm his heart. He had been so scared – sickened and scared. The poor man he'd killed. It wasn't Amiss's fault, of course. He wasn't the man who'd tortured the poor soul. Amiss was at the head of an organisation, and it was natural that one or two men below him would be less than honourable compared with him. Amiss wouldn't have…

But Amiss had been there when Stilson held his Glock to Roy's head. Surely the deputy director wouldn't have allowed him to be killed there, right in front of him? Roy shuddered. The memory of the man's face screaming as he shoved him into that well would never be erased. He knew that. And Amiss had not blinked. He was used to death. Used to the sight of it. Fuck, in Vietnam he'd probably committed enough killings to be immune to this kind of weakness.

It was weakness. That was all. Once Roy had been up at the senior level for a bit, he'd be used to it too. A man had to be determined to protect the country.

He didn't know that he ever wanted to be used to it, though. He didn't want to feel this dirty ever again.

He glanced behind him as he pulled over to take a right to join the Canal Road, and noticed the sedan.

Roy Sandford was no expert at covert surveillance, but he had learned the basics, and when he looked in his mirror, there was something about the car three behind him, sticking out a little far, with a passenger craning her neck…

'Fuck! *Fuck*!' hissed, and his anxiety returned as he recognised the silhouette of Debbie.

In an instant his mind went into overdrive: They were chasing him now, with the English spy. How did he fit into this? Was he after Roy too, because they'd learned he was reporting to Amiss, or had they just lucked out when they saw the Chapel and saw Roy leave it? They'd said about the Chapel, hadn't they? Said it was where they saw him. Said they saw Amiss too. Did they mention Stilson?

There was a hoot behind him. He threw a look into the rear view. Yes, he could make out Frank Rand two vehicles behind. Shit!

He booted the engine just ahead of a car coming toward him. It screeched as the wheels locked; the driver was too shocked to even give him the finger as the Saab span a wheel and then flew on down right to the Canal Road. He pushed it on, the speedometer climbing rapidly, the Saab's old turbo whining, and his mind racing.

He saw a car ahead and thought: *can't ram it… a gap, overtake, make as much distance as possible between the Saab and the bastards back there. Keep going. Another car ahead, no space to get round… impossible… dangerous… space – boot it again.*

Then he heard the turbo scream, and felt a kick in the spine as it spun and squirted more gas into the cylinder. A Pontiac appeared around a curve, and then went back into the lane as the sweat sparked from the pores in his forehead and his back. His shirt felt wet already, and he had to wriggle his back against the car's seat to try to stop the rivulet reaching his waistband.

There was the left turn there, a long fork up to Reservoir Road, and he dithered until it was almost too late, before swinging the wheel and standing on the throttle to howl up the road. It wasn't a safe road – trees at either side, a grassy embankment, and, when he looked down, he was doing seventy. It was enough to scare him, and he almost took his foot off the pedal, but the quick glance behind him told him Rand was still with him, and he turned ahead with his scalp tightening in fear at the thought that he could be captured.

He was guilty of murder, after all.

There was a pothole. The shock absorber banged like a grenade going off. Up ahead was the reservoir, the Georgetown, and then he was hurtling past one junction, up the road a little further, and right on to MacArthur Boulevard, while a cacophony of horns and hooters surrounded him. There was a little corner, and he took it, sweeping round to follow the reservoir, swinging around slower cars all the way, past a slow truck, past a Lincoln, past a Jaguar, and darting in quickly to avoid a Jeep coming the other way, before pulling out again to overtake a battered old blue Ford, and then, while he was halfway past the Ford, he saw lights. Someone was pulling out from a side road, and they hadn't looked his way. Why would they? No one overtook on this little road. He pressed the horn, hoping the car could move. The car stopped, across his path, and he saw an old man inside with his mouth wide in a scream of terror, and Roy screamed, swerved, hit the Ford, heard the crunch of metal as he connected, and tried to push himself over, to avoid the car in his way. He shrieked as he covered his eyes just before the hideous moment of metal on metal...

*

21.48 Langley; 02.48 London

Frank winced as he saw the crash. There was a loud crunch which he could hear over the sound of his own racing engine. Then he saw the Saab lift, the left side rising up over the car it hit, shards of glass and metal exploding from the front wing as it lifted, and then it was over, still in mid-air, and turned onto its roof. Then it was hurtling forwards, upside down, and the remaining headlamp shone in his face and span away as the Saab rotated, sliding on its roof, gushes of sparks from the steel washing like fireworks over the blacktop, illuminating the scene.

He drew to a halt, attaching his blue, magnetic lamp on the roof to warn other drivers before popping the door and trotting to the stricken Saab.

It had stopped spinning, and was merely rocking slightly, front to back, balanced on the roof. A groan and whimper came from the driver's side and he looked down at the bloody face of Roy Sandford.

'Roy, you all right? Roy?'

He looked dreadful, hanging upside down from his seatbelt. His face was a mass of cuts from flying glass. The airbag had deflated already and lay like a giant punctured grey balloon, half out of the window, and all over its surface were the pinpricks of blood where he had hit it. The windshield was gone, and the laminated glass lay twisted and crackled all over in the road a short way behind them. The side window had shattered and it was those razor-like particles of glass flying into his face that slashed him so badly as the car rolled onto its roof.

'Roy, can you hear me?' Frank wondered whether to cut him loose from the belt, but daren't. If there was any damage to Roy's neck, it could be fatal. Better to wait until the ambulance arrived. Debbie had called it already.

'I couldn't help it,' Roy was saying. His voice was a mix of misery and agony. 'God, I didn't want to do it, but they made me!'

'Made you what, Roy?' Jack demanded. He had walked up behind Frank, and now he was crouched on one knee beside the injured driver.

326

'Made me kill him! They made me! I didn't want to, but Stilson said he'd shoot me if I didn't. He had a gun to my head! What could I do?'

'Why were they going to shoot you?' Jack asked.

'If I didn't push the man down the hole. The well. They said they'd kill me if I didn't. I had to prove myself to them, they said. I had to prove I could obey orders, prove I could kill for them. Do anything for them.'

'Who were they, Roy?' Frank asked.

'I can't tell you,' Roy moaned, his head moving from side to side.

'Amiss and who else?' Frank said. 'You've already told us about Stilson and Amiss. Who else?'

'They'll kill me too if I tell you,' Roy groaned. 'And they'll torture me, like they did him! I can't take that. I won't be tortured!'

'Who did they torture?' Frank asked.

'I don't know. I never saw him before. Just a guy from Afghanistan or somewhere. He spoke Pashtun, said he was innocent, but they made me push him down anyway.'

'In the chapel?'

'Underneath it,' he moaned. 'There's a chamber underneath, and a stream flows at the bottom of the well in the middle. They had me throw him down it, and he was washed away and drowned.'

'Calm down, Roy,' Frank said. 'We'll get you out of there soon. Where were you going?'

'To see Stilson. Explain about you guys coming and questioning me.'

'Where were you going to see him?'

'Thompson centre – the marina. There's a bar overlooking the boats called Bahama Bay. He said he'd see me there.'

'OK. Now hold on, Roy. You feeling OK? Just a little longer and we can get you out of there.'

'So what? What can you do to stop me being a fucking murderer?' Roy screamed.

He started fumbling, trying to release the belt, Frank thought, but Jack reached in and took away a pistol, which he passed to Frank.

'Give it back to me! I need it! Let me end it!'

'Roy, you aren't getting it. You've been taken for a ride by some bad characters. It's not your fault – it's them. With your help we can put them away,' Frank said.

'I can't help you with anything.'

'You can help have the worst offenders arrested, Roy. You aren't alone in this mess. There are too many people dying.'

'They want to protect us!'

'By killing me?' Frank said.

'What do you mean, killing you?'

'Amiss sent two men to kill me and Debbie. They nearly succeeded, Roy. It's gone too far. Amiss is murdering anyone who doesn't agree with him. That's why he set up Jack in the first place. Because Jack was close to the truth.'

'What do you mean?' Jack said.

'There must have been something about Lewin that was dangerous. Something Lewin knew.'

'He was recruited to help with torture,' Jack said.

'That's what he's doing,' Roy said. 'Catching people and bringing them here to find out all he can from them.'

'Well, Lewin was brought here to do it, and he refused,' Rand said.

'But he left proof of it,' Jack said.

'Yeah?' Roy said in a quieter voice.

Jack could hear a siren approaching.

'Look, Roy, you could save people's lives here. Innocent people's lives.'

'How can I do that?'

'Tell us what you heard: Who was there? What did they say? How can we get to them?'

'Yeah. OK. I'll tell you everything,' Roy mumbled.

There was a blare of sirens, and a pair of police cars arrived, with an ambulance immediately behind. Jack and Frank were pushed out the way as two paramedics arrived and squatted down at the side of the stricken vehicle, so the two men made their way back to the car. An officer held them up, but Frank showed him his badge, and held a short conversation with him. He was soon free and returned to the car, sitting in the driver's seat.

'OK, then, Mister Case. What is this about proof that Lewin left behind?'

*

22.18 Langley; 03.18 London

The bar was a mixture of old colonial woodwork and cocktails, with the kind of expensive artwork expected by the rich patrons who flocked here every Friday and weekend. Stilson looked about him with disdain at the oak furniture and the imitation sailing ship interior, with walkways and handrails like an old clipper. Flags adorned the walls, and bills of lading were framed on the walls. Above some tables were enormous barrels that had once held rum. The owner had paid a designer a small fortune to recreate a genuine Bahamian bar, and the result was as unlike the original as could be imagined. This was a rich man's meeting place, where the Washington Harbour weekend sailors came to pretend they still lived in an era of hemp and manila.

He was not comfortable tonight. Usually the atmosphere in this place would calm him down – the smell of mustiness around the old ropes, the cocktails and wine – but ever since Roy Sandford's call, he had been on edge. The man had sounded so scared. It was all he could do to shut him up and tell him to come here. It was bad tradecraft to give away the location on open telephones, but there was no time to arrange something more effective. Stilson wasn't going to go to Roy, not if his house was already under surveillance. And how long had it been? Stilson didn't like to think that his photo was already appearing on a police file somewhere. He valued his privacy.

Still no sign of the man. Where the fuck was Sandford? He'd called less than an hour after Stilson left him at his home, demanding an urgent meeting, mentioning the FBI, and Stilson had shut him up there, telling him to get here. But if he wasn't here soon, Stilson was going to walk from the place. It was late, and he didn't like this. It made him feel as though he was being set up.

He gave Roy until half past, and then he stood, finished his bourbon, and walked from the bar.

Outside the lights played over the cold waters of the Potomac. Opposite was the island on which the Theodore Roosevelt memorial stood, and the island stood dark against the sky. It was a fitting memorial to such a great leader, Stilson thought. He had great pride in his country, and the strong-willed men who had helped make it what it was today. Theodore Roosevelt had all the attributes of an American: brave, a fighter, but polite and smart too. He was the kind of man Stilson admired. He wouldn't have bent to terrorists. Just as he'd urged his nation to join war against Germany in 1915 and on, he'd have wanted to take the fight to those who threatened his country. Just like Amiss and the Committee. Just like Stilson himself.

But there were always those who would seek to derail a great project. They couldn't see the bigger picture. Stilson was here to protect his country, and he would do so, no matter what. If that meant torturing a few ragheads or shooting them from a drone, so be it. He wasn't going to let any assholes take over America without a fight.

He crossed the parking lot to his car, climbed in, and started the engine. Then he slowly drove away up 30th Street NW, and under the Whitehurst Freeway. He turned around a little further up, heading west, parallel to the harbour, and found a space on the street where he could stop and watch the harbour building from his seat. If Roy had spoken out, the cops would be here soon. Idly he turned on the police-band radio and listened to the squawks. Nothing to call people to the harbour – no warnings. And when he looked about, there were no vehicles racing this way. Only a mixture of parked cars, and he saw no heads in any of them. It looked as though he was clear.

*

22.21 Langley; 03.41 London

Frank listened carefully as Jack told him all about the journal and the list of names he had found at the back, the roll of clippings, the story of Lewin's life, and the self-hatred he had displayed in the book. By the time he had finished, Frank had drawn up and parked on a street overlooking a large building that proudly declared itself to be 'Washington Harbour'.

'That's it?' Frank asked.

'Yes. The journal was proof of Lewin's involvement in the torture of prisoners, both in Iraq and in other locations where he witnessed and advised on how to break men. When he grew convinced that it was a failed policy, he couldn't live with the implications.'

'And you, a British spy, are telling us all this?' Debbie demanded. 'Why the fuck should we believe you? If you were a real spy, you'd keep this kind of shit to yourself, wouldn't you?'

'If I hadn't been betrayed, yes. If the Service hadn't called you to tell you I was in fact a murderer, that would certainly be true,' Jack said. 'But since they've lied about me to you, I think my loyalty has been a little misguided, don't you? Besides, you two have been on their lists too. I saved you from two gunmen, remember. Did you ever get their ID?'

'You know we didn't,' Debbie muttered.

'Because they're linked to this mob as well. It's well funded because it's got the deputy head of the CIA in charge, and he can sign cheques, I guess? And who'd argue with a matter of Homeland Security after 9/11?'

330

'Enough!' Frank said. 'Jack, this is the place Sandford said he was to meet with Stilson. Washington Harbour.'

'What do you want to do now?' Debbie asked.

'Let me go and see if he's there,' Jack said, his hand on the latch.

'No. We'll wait here and keep a look out. I don't want to spook him,' Frank said. He had his telephone out already, and dialled. 'The guy may know your face, Jack. He'll probably know mine, if he was involved in deciding to have me shot.'

In a few minutes there was a tap at the window. Frank's friend from Hostage Rescue, Tony Knussel, was a tall, broad shouldered man of German extraction. He had appeared as Jack and Frank were returning to their vehicle from talking to Sandford, having followed them all the way there in an ancient-looking white Subaru Legacy estate. Tony climbed into the back seat, grumbling about the size of Frank's sedan, and then Frank explained about their chase after Sandford, the crash, and what had happened to Sandford already that evening. Tony nodded, chewing gum all the while.

'Shocking to think a guy could be killed like that,' Jack said, when Frank had stopped.

'There's been worse. A mob contract killer called Kuklinsky did people for fun. He trapped them, stuck them tied down in a cave where rats lived and left 'em there till they were eaten alive,' Tony said laconically. He sniffed, and added, 'Course, he came from New York.'

Tony looked at Frank.

'What you want to do, Frank? Your call.'

Frank agonised over it for a while.

'Tony, can you get out and check the car park? Stilson's car was a Blue Sedan. I'm pretty sure it was a Lincoln town car.'

'OK, but I reckon there'll be a few.'

'Yeah,' Frank agreed. This was a wealthy area, and there were all too many Cadillacs, Lincolns and more expensive European and Japanese cars. 'Let's just hope, eh?'

Tony left, climbed into his old Subaru, and drove off into the car park. Only a short while later they saw a dark Lincoln pull out from the car park and stop at the road's edge before pulling away. Immediately behind it was a white Subaru.

Frank's phone rang.

'Tony?'

331

'Tell you what, Frank. Duck. He's coming round behind you,' Tony said.

'Down!' Frank said, slumping in his own seat until his head was below the seat. 'Where now?'

'Oh, he's parked three vehicles behind you. I've gone on to the top of the road. I couldn't stop. He'd have seen me.'

'Good. Can you see him still?'

'I'm parked up about two hundred yards behind you in a side alley. I can see you, but I doubt he'll see me. There's enough trash around here to hide a tank.'

'Good. Tell me when he moves, will you? We'll get him from there.'

'You're the boss.'

'We'll trail him with us behind him first, then you. All right?'

*

22.41 Langley; 03.41 London

It was only later, as Stilson drove home listening to WASH-FM, that he picked up on the mention of a car accident. A Saab that had flipped over. The driver was in hospital, critically injured.

'Shit!' Stilson said. Still, the news shouldn't impact him too badly, nor the project.

He considered the plans and decided that all was fine to go ahead. When he reached his home, he picked up his STU-III phone and dialled Amiss.

'Sir, I'm afraid Sandford's had an accident from the sound of it,' he said, and told Amiss what had happened.

'I see. Will it impact our ability to continue?'

'Not so's I can see, no. If anything, we just have to move things on a bit. Take all the detainees over to the new facility now it's ready. And then we can begin to get all we can from them.'

'Very good. I'll give the order right away. And Mr Stilson?'

'Sir?'

'I think you should go there too. Perhaps a little time away from DC would do you good.'

Stilson nodded and chuckled as he signed off from the phone. He left his car and walked to his house to pack his bags. As he walked up his path, he heard a car. Looking up the road he saw a pair of cars – one dark, one white. The white one drew in almost half a block away, but the other carried on going. He eyed it suspiciously, and saw that it pulled into the kerb a hundred yards away. But no one got out.

332

The white Subaru driver was out of his car. He slammed the door, locked it, and then sauntered down the road without looking in Stilson's direction.

He pulled his front door open. He walked inside, slammed the door, and immediately turned to peer out between the drapes in the front. He saw the guy in the street carry on walking, all the way past the dark car, but the guys in that one stayed put. It was enough to make Stilson's hackles rise. The dark car must have a surveillance team. He was sure of it. Could be the police, could be the Feebies, he didn't know and he didn't care. He took the stairs at a run, opened his wardrobe doors, and grabbed for two boxes of ammunition. He had his Glock on his belt already, with two magazines fully loaded, and now he took two spare mags and threw them into a suitcase with his ammunition. He grabbed clothes at random, flung them into the case, zipped it up, and locked it, before pulling on a fresh jacket that gave him an easier draw. He tested it three times, flicking the bottom of the material aside, grabbing for his gun. It was all too easy. He was experienced.

He turned on the bedside lamp and then turned off the main light before carefully going down the stairs with his bag. Halfway down the stairs, he closed his eyes and rested them to acclimatize to the darkness, and he listened with his mouth open, straining to hear any strange sounds in the darkness. Satisfied, he continued down, stepping quietly on the soft carpet, until he reached the ground floor. There was still no sound to alarm him.

Crossing the floor, he walked to the window, and peered out. The dark car was still there, the man from the white one had disappeared, which was odd. Out of place. The man walked further up the road there, but if he wanted to park up, he could have parked his Subaru closer. Stilson stared into the street, and now every cell of his body was tingling as the adrenaline rushed through. He picked up his STU-III and called.

'I have been followed tonight,' he said when the phones had gone secure. 'There are agents in front of my house and another one's at the back.'

He returned to the front room from where he commanded a clear view of the street while he spoke. There was a security TV there, and he turned to a four-way view, two cameras at the rear, one at either side. When he flipped the rear cameras to infrared, he picked out the man there like a beacon, standing by a tree.

He could feel the expectation like a surge of energy, and he grinned wolfishly.

It was like being back at war.

*

22.52 Langley; 03.52 London

Jack glanced at the house and nudged Frank as the upper lights dimmed.

'See that?'

'It's late. So he's gone to bed.'

'You reckon?' Jack said. 'Somehow seems odd for him to come straight home and tip into bed. Doesn't it seem early to you?'

'He's an agent. I know Amiss is said to appreciate guys who get in early. He doesn't like to find his offices quiet,' Frank said with a shrug. 'So maybe this Stilson appreciates early nights too?'

'What are you going to do?' Jack demanded.

Frank was already on the phone.

'Speak to Houlican,' he muttered to Jack from the side of his mouth. 'It's up to him now. We're just holding this one down. That's why Tony's gone to the back, to make sure he doesn't try to escape.'

'I need to get out and stretch my legs,' Jack said.

'OK, but don't do anything dumb,' Frank said.

Jack sneered in reply and shut the door moderately quietly. He walked out along the road, with his collar up and his hands thrust into his pockets, scuffing the pavement as he went, like a tired worker on his way home. None of the gardens here had any cover, he saw. No separations like hedges or fences to conceal a man edging nearer a house. Jack kept on walking, crossing the road and taking a right up the next street. Here, once he was out of sight of the front of Stilson's house, he began to move more easily. Tony had come up here, and Jack was looking for him.

He found the HRT man at the top of the road leaning against a tree. Tony turned and spoke quietly.

'Hi, Jack. Any plans about what we do now?'

'I think Frank just wants to see what he does,' Jack said.

Tony sniffed.

'I have to admit, I don't like it,' he said. 'The whole idea of this is fucked. We're sure of our man. If Frank is ready we ought to arrest him.'

'Can't disagree with that,' Jack said. 'He's already implicated in taking hostages and torturing them, and if Sandford was telling the

334

truth, in having them murdered too. Frank's talking to his boss, so we ought to know before long what's happening.'

'Right.'

Tony's phone rang quietly, and he answered it.

'Yeah. What?' He threw a blank look at Jack, and then shot a glance over his shoulder towards the car where Frank and Debbie were sitting. 'No sign of him out here, no. What are you saying? Yeah. OK.'

Shutting off the phone, he said, 'Frank's boss wants a firecracker up his ass before he'll sanction anything. We're escalating it through my chain of command. You OK here for a while?'

'Yeah.'

'Just watch. Do not try to apprehend or get in anyone's way, OK? Just wait right here. I won't be long.'

Jack nodded. He turned and watched the back of the house with a frown on his face. Glancing over his shoulder, he saw the HRT agent walking back towards the car. He walked entirely naturally, with a loose gait that belied his power.

Leaning against a tree, Jack waited. Tony wandered all down the road, then quickly climbed into Jack and Debbie's car.

It was one of those situations Jack could understand all too easily. He, himself, had had situations before now where operations had been on a tightrope, and a quick discussion was needed to decide whether to continue or not. Frank and the others would be holding talks with Frank's boss, cajoling and pleading, while he pushed them for ever more information. Perhaps he would agree, perhaps he wouldn't.

Fifteen minutes by his watch. He heard vehicles moving about further up the roads, the distant rumble of traffic, but there was no light or sign that Stilson was awake. Perhaps he had gone to bed. His windows were all dark, the curtains drawn in the upstairs window, apart from a small triangle of blackness.

That was when Jack realised something was wrong. A short while ago there was no triangle there. It had been entirely covered with the curtains. Someone was there, watching him, he guessed.

He heard the car door slam, and saw Tony clamber from the car. Jack stood, and was about to call out, when he realised he had his phone. He grabbed it and dialled Frank.

'Frank, we're being watched, I think and...'

Suddenly the air was full of the sound of car engines racing. He saw three dark cars coming up the road behind Frank's. There was a blur, and he saw Tony draw his pistol. Jack was about to bolt after him, when he saw Frank and Debbie turn and stare at the approaching cars. The lead vehicle screeched to a halt, the door was thrown wide, and Jack saw the Uzi's barrel flame with white and yellow. Tony was already firing, but he didn't stand a chance in the open. Half a magazine ripped into his body, and his pistol flew through the air. By a miracle he didn't fall, but stood, his hands wide as though in an urgent plea, and then he slowly toppled to his knees, gradually falling forward to lie on his face.

Jack bellowed, reaching for his own gun, beginning to run to Tony, but even as he did so, There was a sickening crash of a blackjack against his skull.

He saw Frank's car draw away at speed, heading away off east, and Jack didn't care, because he felt the second thud-thud of metal against his skull, over his ear, and the shock of the blow seemed to start in his belly and roar out to encompass his whole being. He took two steps and fell, his face on the gravel, and the pistol was tugged from his hand. Then there was another club over his ear and he felt himself pitching headlong into Sandford's pit.

*

He was going to be sick.

Jack felt his belly roil and heave, a sweaty heat came from his stomach as he tried to open gummy eyes. The gravel under his cheek was painful, and when he moved he could feel the stones sticking into his flesh. Each small scratch and jab felt like a new piercing of his skin. He opened an eye a millimetre, and snapped it shut again as the light stabbed his senses, and his body convulsed.

'Aw, shit, the son of a…'

He opened an eye and blearily gazed around. There was no gravel, no pavement, and no road. He was on a couch of some sort. It moved – thrumming –and, as he came to, he could hear the rumble and whine of jet engines. A small jet. Perhaps a Lear or similar small private jet of some sort.

Trying to push himself up, he found his wrists were painfully constrained, and he could only stay there, staring at the vomit so near his nose. The stench was enough to make him begin to retch, and he was almost glad when someone kicked him in the belly. He curled up, taking his head away from that foul-smelling pool, and he did not mind the prick at his neck as the needle went in.

The oblivion that came afterwards was a relief.

*

10.30 Langley; 15.30 London

Amiss left his man at the door and continued on into the chapel.

It was good to see that Will Barnard and Louis Keen had already arrived. Brian Gutterson wasn't, of course. He had gone to the facility, as had Stilson. Brian Peachfield was already there. His position as head of intelligence for the Deputies made it essential that he should be there.

Last night had been a disaster. After so many months of careful planning, the whole damn thing was blowing up in their faces. The only good thing was that it should be possible to keep a cap on the affair. The facility was ideal, and unless they were enormously unlucky and a breach of security happened, they should be able to keep it that way.

He walked to the front of the chapel and bent his knee as he genuflected, then turned and walked to the front pew. There was no glance to either side as he sat. He had no need to look at Barnard or Keen. They knew him and he knew them. Their friendships had been burned and tested in the filth of the jungles and stinking villages of Vietnam.

Amiss could miss those times – So much solidarity amongst his companions, so much commitment and conviction. But that was before Philip Agee had gone back on his word as an agent, and broken ranks to tell the world that the CIA had been involved in torturing people. Of course the CIA had tortured people. Jesus, a man who was determined to protect his nation must sometimes go to extremes if he was going to protect innocents.

Some tried to use specious arguments to justify their actions. Amiss was not prepared to sink to that. There was no need. He knew his motivations: he was perfectly prepared to sacrifice any foreign national who might have any information that could help to prevent his country being violated by terrorists. It was that simple. Americans should not be harmed, but non-Americans were fair game. Whereas in the good old days of the sixties and seventies it was justifiable for CIA agents to get involved directly, in more recent years Amiss could understand that the public might be squeamish. That was why rendition was designed to allow suspects to be kidnapped and flown

337

thousands of miles to compliant states where the victims could be held, broken, and given the chance to divulge all they knew while under the watchful eye of CIA agents, with questions being prompted by those same agents. It was an irritation having that two-tier system, prolonging the delays. It would have been faster and easier if the interrogations could have been conducted nearer home, with all the technology that the CIA possessed, and with the CIA actually responsible for all the questioning, but the public didn't want to think that their own people were doing the breaking of the bodies. And the citizens' squeamishness meant that many of the prisoners were routinely killed as a result. Better to leave a couple of bodies in Uzbekistan than discover an embarrassingly ravaged prisoner turning up at Guantanamo.

But the new President ruined even that. When he vowed to close Gitmo and stop rendition, he destroyed one of the crucial arms of American defence. Didn't he realise that? *Dear God Almighty*, Amiss prayed, *Couldn't you have shown him*? But maybe not. It wasn't a part of His scheme to show a weak, vapid President from Illinois how to protect the nation. If the people of America were going to elect a Godless man like him, who supported abortion, and probably wasn't even a true Christian, they had only themselves to blame.

So it was that God had shown Amiss how to protect the people of his land. He must himself work to protect them, whether they liked his methods or not.

The Mass was deeply satisfying. He never failed to feel that awe and thrill as the priest spoke and, at this time of year in particular, he felt it still more deeply. The way that the lower sun cut through the windows and illuminated the whole of the interior, made him feel that the eye of God was here on him, on all of them, every time. It was a comforting thought.

After the Mass he walked through to the porch with the others, as they did every Sunday. He nodded to his guard, who stood at the doorway beside the pillars, looking more substantial than the white-painted round of timber. Amiss smiled and shook hands with the priest who had opened the door to the meeting place underneath the church itself.

Louis Keen and Will Barnard joined him a moment later. There was no need for their regalia today. All were in their suits.

'Problems?' Will Barnard asked.

'We have had a serious leak. The new boy, Sandford, was somehow compromised and died in a road traffic accident last night. It is a great shame. He showed promise,' Amiss said.

'How badly "compromised"?' Barnard said.

'It seems that a British agent, Jack Case, has somehow managed to get to understand a lot of our plans.'

'It was fucking Lewin, wasn't it?' Louis Keen spat. 'I knew that faggot Brit was no good! He was screwed from the start!'

'I cannot disagree,' Amiss said. 'But at the time he came highly recommended and we cannot turn up good operatives. It's not as if there is a professional body we can go to and ask for a man with the qualifications we need!'

'But the mission is not compromised?' Barnard said, eyeing Amiss keenly. 'Are we into damage limitation?'

'There's no need to think about fragging the captain, Will, if that's what you mean,' Amiss said easily. 'The Brit is being entertained by Ed Stilson at our main facility and we'll get all we need to from him.'

'What of the others?'

'I'm afraid there were two Seattle-based Feebies who were convinced by him.'

'You mean Rand and the woman who were supposed to be removed in Vegas?'

'Yes. They were threats then, and so they remain. But we will find them and remove them both.'

Keen looked about him at the chamber. 'We'd better. Because if we don't, we'll need to exercise our exit strategies.'

Barnard nodded and glanced at Keen. 'In that case, I think we should begin to plan for the worst. Remove all evidence from our sites here. Everything to be stored securely.'

Amiss nodded again.

'OK. And we need to make sure that our own covers are updated. Look at your alibis for the last few days and make sure that they're watertight. We don't know how far this could go.'

'What about you?' Keen asked. 'Are you remaining here?'

Amiss looked at him for a moment, his eyes hard.

'D'you think I'd run from my own country?'

*

10.46 Langley; 15.46 London

'How much longer?' Debbie asked.

After the sudden appearance of the police and men at the house, Frank had driven straight to Quantico. It took a short time to verify that Stilson's house was empty. Agents had hurried there, and a group had been sent to Amiss's house, only to discover that this too was deserted. Then a sharp-eyed agent had checked for flight plans, only to discover that Amiss's Learjet had taken off for Anchorage. A witness at the airport said that there was a man on a stretcher who was taken onto the plane. It wasn't Tony. Stilson's street was crawling with officers, ever since Tony's body had been found.

Anchorage. Frank and Debbie had quickly arranged for their own plane and had taken off from the small airport at Quantico, Frank all the while considering where Stilson could be heading. He had no doubt Stilson was on that Lear. But why Anchorage?

And then a comment Jack had made came back to him. It was something Sorensen had said when Jack was asking about the men he worked for. He said something about a 'Dollar' – a Dollar building. The FBI plane had satellite communications, and he fired up a laptop, searching for anything to do with Dollar in Anchorage. He found investment comments, mentions of golden opportunities, but nothing about a building. But he was sure that there was something there.

He tried Buck Alaska. There were pages about knives and hunting, pages about individuals, but nothing that seemed remotely relevant.

'What are you doing?' Debbie asked.

'This place, the "Dollar" building Sorensen mentioned to Jack. I'm wondering whether that could be there – maybe it's the place they're heading.'

She looked over his searches.

'Buck?'

'I'm just trying anything I can,' he said.

At Ted Stevens Airport there would be cars waiting to follow Stilson's plane when it landed, to see where it was heading. The local SWAT team would want to take Stilson, but Frank and HRT had discussed that and decided not to use them. Stilson's men had shown themselves competent already, but that wasn't the real reason. The HRT group wanted revenge. They wanted to get Tony's killers themselves.

Debbie had never seen Frank like this before, and she felt a strange dislocation, as though she had herself been kidnapped. The plane was filled with black-clad men who moved about quietly, carefully storing heavy-looking bags made of some black ballistic material. There

340

were seven of them, and she felt quite sure that these were more of Frank's friends from the Hostage Rescue Team. They were sombre, quiet and tense. A close-knit unit, they were grieving for Tony.

She said, 'Look up military. See if there's something there.'

He typed 'Buck Military Alaska' and one of the first pages had a piece on Whittier. 'The Buckner Building,' he breathed.

In a few minutes he had obtained detailed plans of the building from the army, and was studying a picture on his screen.

'They'll have the interrogation blocks underground, I reckon,' Frank said. He was looking at a building plan that he'd managed to print out from the plane's inkjet.

'It would keep things out of the way,' one of the men said in agreement. Two others were craning over Frank's neck as he studied photos, some from the sea, some close-up, and three from the air. All gave good indications of the location.

'Leave it to us, Frank,' the two said, and took the maps and pictures to another table behind them.

'You want to be with them, don't you?' Debbie said.

'Yeah,' Frank admitted. There was a look of wistfulness in his eyes as he turned back to the table. A coffee was sitting there, and he added a carton of cream and stirred it moodily. 'When I was new to the Bureau, it was the one thing I wanted above all else, to join the HRT. Now? I have to play second fiddle even though I am Assistant Special Agent in Charge in Seattle. I want to be there with them.'

'Yeah, sure,' she said. Not that the idea filled her with enthusiasm. She kept an eye on all the men with the wariness borne of suspicion.

Frank grinned.

'Another couple of hours to Anchorage, and then we'll get the cars and ride straight out.'

'And?'

'And then we'll get Jack out and kick the crap out of these pricks.'

*

08.12 Whittier; 17.12 London

Jack felt his head being jerked back just a moment before the water hit his face, and then he was choking and coughing, eyes closed, his head pounding from the blows he had taken. There was a sore bruised feeling in his neck and his arms, and he knew that he had been administered drugs to keep him quiet. That was more than likely the cause of the nausea too.

'Wake up, asshole!' was screamed, and a second bucket of water drenched him.

It was freezing cold. Sprawled on the concrete of a floor, it felt like he was only a little above freezing, and he was naked. He could feel the wash of air all around him on his soaking flesh. It was enough to send a shudder through his frame.

'Come on, you prick!' was shouted, and then there was a hand under each armpit, and he was hauled to his feet.

He had to open his eyes. His wrists hurt like hell. They were still gripped in the bracelets of some kind of handcuff, and he could feel something at his ankles too – probably shackles. Americans were very fond of that kind of thing still, he reminded himself. The sort of restraints that the British had long since outlawed were still in use in America. No doubt enterprising British firms were still vying for the business, just as the rope manufacturer was who sold hangman's ropes to the old colonial countries.

Jack was in a small cell. There were four-inch pipes running along the flaking paint of the ceiling overhead, and nearer he saw that the walls were concrete or cinder block. Any plaster than had once adorned them was long gone, and in its place was a mess of algae and decaying vegetation. But the lights worked, and he was dragged along the room to a heavy, green painted steel door with a peephole. Out through that, into a corridor with lights overhead – bulkhead lights with metal wire covers to protect them. There were doors on either side now, all green or grey.

He let his head sag, conserving the little energy he had. There was no need to act exhausted. It was all he could do to keep his eyes open. Whatever the drugs they'd shot into him were, they were potent.

He had to wake up. Take notice. Make himself alert. But he was so tired. All he wanted was to go to a bed somewhere and find a little peace. He'd sell his mother for the chance of a long sleep. No, he had to wake himself up. Take notice.

Two men, then – one either side. Guards, dressed in US army fatigues. Green T-shirts under green camo shirts, trousers of the same cloth tucked into boots. Haircuts in similar shaven Marine-type fuzz, and hard faces. These weren't guys who'd listen to a reasoned argument.

He let his head droop. A long corridor. Left turn at the end, and then another door – no, pair of doors. They were pushed wide, and he was in a large room. This was a work room, he saw. There were some plastic chairs set about the place, a table with three chairs at the far side, and a lamp. Nearer, was a metal chair's frame, beyond that a large metal tub filled with water. A table with restraints was set up on it for a man's torso, legs, biceps, and wrists. And near that were two large batteries, with wires attached and clamps on the other ends. They looked strong enough to shear through a man's skin.

Jack shivered again. He tried not to, but he knew what this room was for. It had been going to be Lewin's office, if Lewin had accepted. Now, it was the special preserve of someone else.

'Mister Case. Good to meet you at last.'

Jack managed to turn his head, and found himself being watched by a tall, heavy-set man.

'I think you know who I am,' the man said.

Suddenly Jack realised where he had seen this man before. It was the man in the Hilton's bar, the man all alone sitting there watching the game on TV.

'No,' Jack mumbled.

'My name is Brian,' he said. 'Brian Peachfield. You know my friend Mr Stilson. Ed, say hello.'

Stilson was leaning against the wall.

'I tried to have your colleague Danny join us here, but he wouldn't. Instead we had to sort out a way to keep him quiet. It was easy enough. A three-fifty-seven works fuckin' wonders as a silencer. But he did bring you to us, and that was a problem.'

'It was you who tried to kill me in the tunnel, at the cop shop, and in the hospital,' Jack said.

'It was my guys, yeah. You were very hard to kill, you know that?'

'Sorry to give you so much trouble,' Jack said, as his breath misted before his eyes, and he shivered again.

'Ah, you're cold. Take him to a seat. Tie him down,' Peachfield said.

Jack started to try to resist, but Stilson walked to him and took what looked like an effortless swing at his belly, and Jack couldn't help but double over. The pain was nothing compared with the hideous inability to breathe, and he was still desperately gasping as they shoved him down onto a metal-framed seat with a high back and cold steel seat. It was so cold that he felt like he was going to lose the flesh from his buttocks and balls wherever he touched it. Leather straps were tightened over his chest and, when he looked, the whole chair

343

was bolted to the floor. He wasn't going to escape from this in a hurry.

'Good,' Peachfield said. 'Now go fetch André for me.'

The two guards left the room, and Peachfield was quiet a moment. He looked at Stilson, then back at Jack.

'This may be instructive for you. What your colleagues like Lewin were doing out in Iraq and Afghanistan with our guys was not pleasant, but it was necessary. It led to the safety of your country, same as ours. Now, this is a kind of lesson for you, because what I want is to get you to tell me everything you know about us. I have to know what you know, and who you told, of course. We know that you've had some involvement with government agencies over here, and we would like to know who you've spoken to in there, how much you've told them, and when. After you've told us all that, we'll move on to the British services too.'

'Fuck you!'

'Well, I am pleased to see you have some fighting spirit. It means you'll feel the pain a lot more keenly. The guys who're already broken are far less helpful. More pain is difficult to impose. It was one of the ironic things that Danny Lewin used to talk about – the fact that an interrogator only had the one option – the threat of never-ending, constantly increasing pain. As soon as the subject realised that he'd hit the wall, that there was no worse sanction, the interrogator had lost. Can you imagine that? The number of subjects who realised that they'd got to the absolute limit of what the interrogator was capable of inflicting on them was quite large at first. That was when the rendition flights really took off, if you see what I mean. They started to move the really dangerous suspects from Iraq to all those countries where the systems were more lax than ours. And there, they knew that the boundaries of their pain were limitless.'

The door opened, and Jack saw a naked Asian man dragged in. He had wide, terrified eyes in his dark face and, as Jack watched, he saw the horror increase as he took in the steel chair frame in front of him.

'Set him up,' Peachfield said. 'This, you see,' he continued, 'is a refined form of torture that we had never used in America. Even in Vietnam it was unknown, but we learned of it in Damascus. It is called the "German Chair", because apparently it was the Stasi who showed the men of the Palestine Branch how to use it. The Palestine Branch is the main interrogation centre in Damascus, you see. In Palestine Street.'

As he spoke, the man was bound to the chair. The guards were quick and efficient. André was not placed sitting on the chair, but instead was positioned behind it, his back to the outside of the seat back. He was forced under the seat, his back stretched, with his arms brought either side of the seat back, so that his wrists could be tied to the front legs of the chair's frame, and then his legs were pulled back beneath the seat, ankles forced to straps hanging from the front, while his knees rested on the ground. His entire body was curled back on itself, and he wept and whimpered all the while. Jack could see that his body was a mass of bruises. There were marks on his upper body, on his legs, on the palms of his hands, and the soles of his feet.

'We prefer not to use the same tools as those in Damascus, though,' Peachfield said. He had a length of electrical cable in his hand now, a two-foot long section that was at least an inch and a half thick. Walking to Jack, he let it fall against Jack's shoulder. 'Feel that weight, eh? In the Palestinian Branch they beat their new guests with these for two weeks. No questions, just beatings. They're heavy enough to smash bones, but the men there are real professionals. They only damage muscles and soft tissue. Well, at first, anyway.'

The man was beginning to mutter now, and Jack was sure he was praying. In his eyes there was a pure terror that seemed to reach out and touch Jack with its evil chill. Jack had never known true petrified horror, but this sight was enough to make his muscles shake uncontrollably. It wasn't the cold: it was the knowledge that whatever agony was inflicted on this man, would soon be practised on him too.

*

09.45 Whittier; 18.45 London

There was a slight bump, nothing more, and the jet swept across the tarmac towards the main terminal at the Anchorage airport, but then, as it approached, it turned and ran around towards a separate hangar. As they approached it, Debbie could see that there were a number of unmarked cars there, and armed men standing in a huddle.

Frank was up and already at the door before it had opened. As soon as the stairs were extended, he was down them, and Debbie had to wait her turn as the black-clad men grabbed their heavy bags and followed him. Last in the line, she stood, disgruntled, and made her way down as well.

'I'm Special Agent in Charge, Harry Benning. I think we've met before, Frank. This here's Norm Baker, my ASAC.'

Benning was a middle-height man who looked like a sailor: broad, with heavy shoulders, and a bull-like neck. He watched the HRT men with pale amber eyes set in a lined, weather-beaten face. His assistant was taller by three inches, a lugubrious man with fair hair and an expression of longing in his sad brown eyes.

Frank spoke quickly about the Bucky and what he expected to find.

'Fine. You have my support, Frank. Whatever you want, let me or Norm know.'

As they all waited, a trio of Jeep Grand Cherokees rumbled towards them. They all halted and the men carefully stowed their equipment in the back before climbing in – two to one, three to another, and Frank and Debbie in the back of the third. She had scarcely closed her door before the Jeep was roaring off towards a chain-link gate, which opened and then the three vehicles were through and off on the road towards Whittier, a convoy of other vehicles trailing behind them.

*

09.47 Whittier; 18.47 London

André was in agony in minutes. The strain of that hideous position was enough to test a man's endurance to the limits, and he began muttering and wailing. Jack didn't understand: it sounded Arabic, but he didn't know where the man came from.

There was no one with them. The place was silent apart from the weeping and snivelling of André. Jack recalled the man's name now, and tried to speak to him in French, but there was hardly any way to reach the man through the waves of pain that flooded his mind and body. It took Jack a long time to simply get through to him, and even then André scarcely seemed able to comprehend what was being said to him. He just tried to lean back, to balance himself and save him from more pain.

His speech was broken with many gasps and groans, but Jack finally managed to understand roughly what he was saying.

'André, what are you doing here?'

'I was a PLO fighter, but the French offered me immunity if I would help them. I did, and I was living at peace, but then Americans came to capture me. Are you one of them? Tell them I don't know what they ask!'

'I'm not one of them. I'm English, and they are holding me like you. What do they ask you?'

'About fighters with bombs. But I know of none. There are none. How can I answer something I don't know? They ask about fighters

346

coming to America with guns to kill people in hotels. I don't know, I tell them, but they don't listen! They hit me, here, here, again, again, and they will not believe me. But I cannot tell them something I don't know!'

'No, no. I understand. Who is it who asks you all this? The man who was here just now?'

'Yes. Him and another. They question, question, question, and all the time their men beat me. They will kill me. I know this.'

'Where did they find you?'

'I was in France... ah, the pain is terrible!'

'What were you doing there?'

'I had offered to give myself up, and the French were always understanding to the PLO. They finally agreed, if I told them all I knew and swore never to aid an attack on France. Well, of course I agreed. And they took me in.'

'But these guys took you?'

'The French sold me! They must have done! They had given me a new name, put me in a place far from anywhere, where I should be safe, but no! I was taken, like this.'

'Why would they sell you, if they took you in?'

André was weeping. It was some time before he could answer.

'Because they decided I had lied? Because they wanted to be on better terms with the Americans? I don't know... I don't know...'

'Did you have in-depth questions from France?'

'Yes, yes. And from your English Service, too. There were Englishmen there asking me questions. Those Services always share, they always let others know...'

Jack nodded. Yes. They always did share. Whether the UK/USA partners or the European Services, all would share when there was little choice – and all would invariably keep snippets back. All Services wanted to maintain their own secrets and keep something in reserve for later trading.

'You say there were British officers there for your debriefing?'

'A man and a woman. Short, pretty lady. With brown hair, curly.'

'What of the man?'

'He was like *un vieux*. You know? Like a French colonial from Algeria? The sort who has lost his colour to Malaria, who has spent too much time close to the brandy bottle.'

Starck and Karen Skoyles, Jack told himself. They had both been there to question this man. Both knew of him.

347

'Why would you be wanted by the Americans?'

'I don't know. I don't know,' André said, shaking his head miserably.

'Is there anything you know that could interest the Americans?'

'I was only a fighter. I helped build bombs – nothing more. I don't know what I could say would help them. I don't know people in charge, nothing,' he wept.

Jack heard steps.

'Calm yourself, my friend. Remember who you are. Keep your hatred and pain away from you. Try to hide inside your head where they cannot hurt you.'

'Cannot hurt me? You have no knowledge of these things! There is nothing they cannot do to hurt. There is nowhere you can go where the pain won't cut into you! These men are animals! Beasts! They do not care about other people. Only themselves!'

The door opened and Peachfield was with them again. He smiled, pulled out some steel-framed spectacles from a shirt pocket, and set them on his nose, peering down with interest at André.

'I would think you're about ready,' he said, and nodded to the two men who had returned with him. He sat at the table and opened a file. 'Now, André, I'd like to read you a story.'

He leaned back, reading from a yellow sheet.

'In Guantanamo, there was a man called Abu Fazul Abdullah. Now he was one of those we thought of as a "nasty". He'd cut his own wife's throat for the chance of getting to heaven. And he hated America. We found him in Afghanistan. So he was a bad boy. We got him to Gitmo, and there we questioned him a load. Especially about the others in his force. And it took us time, but in the end we got some names. There was a guy called Maulana Fazlullah – and you. Now, Fazlullah, you know, was one of them who helped plan special missions. He was linked to al-Qaeda – and so was Abdullah. So there we have two links – and your name. And then we had another bit of luck. While we questioned this other kid, he gave us your name too. Said you were involved in acquiring weapons and materials for a new group.'

'No. Not me. I was given a place in France after I answered their questions, and they said I could leave the battle. I am nothing. I have no place. I never fought or…'

'Now, we know that isn't true, don't we? Hey? We know you were a keen fighter with the PLO in Beirut, and you were happy to kill Americans.'

'No, Israelis.'

'And Americans. We know that. You tried to blow up the World Trade Centre with a car bomb. You told of that in France, didn't you? Now all you got to do is admit it and we can go on to what you were buying and who for. Then you can go get some rest.'

'I had nothing to do with this! I am not a member of al-Qaeda! I fought Israelis, that is all!'

'Shame,' Peachfield said, motioning with his head.

One of the guards stepped forward. He had a pair of pliers in his hand, and he reached down to André's hands.

Peachfield watched closely, and Jack could see that there was a fresh excitement in his face. He was enjoying this. If he could, Jack guessed, he would be there himself, with the pliers.

'See, André, I got nothing against you personally. I don't want to have to break all your finger bones, say. But I will. Because I really want to know what you can tell me. And there is no limit to which I won't go to find out. Sooner you tell us all you can, sooner we all go home. OK. So, again, tell me who you were with, who you were buying for, why you wanted to kill Americans. Who else was in your team?'

'There was *no team*!' André shouted, spittle flying from his mouth.

Jack could see the panic in the man's eyes. He knew what was about to happen, but there was nothing he could do to prevent it. The torturers had only one logic, as Peachfield had told him: to keep increasing the pain until the subject gave them the answers they wanted to hear. But as Lewin had said in his journal, that had no bearing on the truth. Because in the end a torture victim had to surrender to the pain. He would always lie to try to prevent more anguish – and at that point the torturer would become convinced that his silence before had been due to intransigence or stubbornness, and would increase the torture.

There was no protection. No defence. Only pain and death.

The scream was loud and inhuman. It made Jack want to cover his ears. But he couldn't.

*

10.39 Whittier; 19.39 London

349

They had been racing all along the New Seward Highway since landing, and now, at last, Debbie saw that they were heading along the side of a mountain. She could see a railroad track and bridge a little over to the left, and then up ahead was the strange, triangular housing set into the rocks ahead.

'What is that?'

'The entrance to the tunnel. They had to have that kind of porch way. If there's an avalanche, it breaks over the steep roofline there and doesn't smother the tracks,' Frank said. He was on the radio to the lead car, and now there was a burst of static and a response. 'OK, let's get on through, then!'

The traffic in the tunnel had been stopped, apparently, and it was clear for them. Debbie watched as they approached the gaping entrance, and then they were inside, rushing along the concrete surface, the tyres thrumming on the irregular surface, and she could see the bare rock all about them.

'The army built this. Never saw the need for pretty cladding, I guess,' Frank said, grinning slightly at her expression.

'Yeah,' she said. The place was eerie. Ahead, she could make out a tiny pinprick of light. No more. 'That the exit?'

'Yeah, that's the other side,' Frank said. 'We'll be there in a short time.'

'What then? See the local cops and...'

'I don't think that would be sensible,' Frank said. He drew his Glock, finger off the trigger, and pulled the slide back a quarter-inch, peering into the breech at the cartridge case inside. He reholstered the gun. 'Amiss and the others have come here and set up shop. They could hardly do that without the people in the police department noticing. The Buckner Building is pretty big, but to get there all their supplies would have had to come through this tunnel here and the town. They could have brought stuff in from the sea, but even then it'd all be brought through the town. Everything. So unless the cops here are incredibly unimaginative, or maybe just stupid, they'd have noticed something being brought in. Which means they were at best condoning the arrival, at worst complicit. Either way, I don't think I want to let them know we're here to break open the building and rescue the poor souls from inside.'

'Right,' she said. 'But what if we need more firepower?'

Frank gave her a long-suffering look while the passenger in front threw a look back at her.

350

'Lady, d'you realise we've got more firepower in these three trucks than most African states have in their armies?'

*

The screams began to fade into sobs after the second finger, and Jack was straining at his restraints at the noise. He had lost his temper at other times, usually because of some slight he had been forced to endure, but nothing as concentrated or as vitriolic as this. The sight of a man being forced to endure unimaginable pain while others stood and observed was as shocking to him as the imagined tortures inflicted by Mengele at Auschwitz. It was inconceivable that such brutality could still be inflicted.

'Don't worry, Jack, your turn will come soon. It's best, though, to understand what we're going to do to you. It helps to fix your mind. You will endure the same regime as André here. And then we will see how long you can survive without giving us what we need to know. Of course, you will have gone through the basic training and the enhanced courses with the Special Forces at Hereford, won't you? Still, I think you'll find anything you learned up there with them will be as nothing compared with what I can achieve down here,' Peachfield said with a smile.

'You fucking wanker! Leave him alone!'

'You are determined. You want to replace him on the German Chair?'

'I'll fucking kill you if you try!' Jack said.

And he meant it. The rage had been building in him for the last hour and, now he saw Peachfield smile thinly at him, it was impossible to restrain himself. He wanted to grab Peachfield and knock him down, beat him with that length of cable, attach the electrical clamps to his body and throw the switch on. He wanted to see Peachfield jerk and twitch with the surging current, see his jaws clench uncontrollably, see his face contort. He wanted to see Peachfield die under his fists as he pounded that smile from his face.

'You are going to die here, Jack. That I promise you. The trouble is, once you've given us all we need, you have the same basic problem as all these others. We cannot allow you to wander off to your homeland telling all kinds of silly stories about us and what we do here. So once you have given us what we need, we will regretfully have to kill you. It's nothing personal, as the Mafia would say, it's just that we can't afford to allow witnesses to what we do down here

351

to get out into the open. You understand that? It's why it is going to be a whole lot easier on you if you just accept that we will get what we want sooner or later, and save yourself a deal of pain by telling us all you know up front. It makes much more sense.'

Peachfield turned back to the prisoner weeping around that hideous chair frame, and Jack wept with him. There was no escape, not even from this cold chair. He breathed in, tensing his muscles, trying to burst the straps that held him in place, but the leather was secure and all he achieved was to break the skin on his wrists and ankles. Rocking, he tried to damage the leather, to scrape the straps against the chair's metal, and degrade it. He attempted to move the chair itself, but the bolts to the floor were secure. He was powerless.

Another scream, more shrill this time, and André collapsed, his head hanging. Jack saw his body dangling from the German Chair like a puppet's, a long string of bloody spittle dangling from his lips. One of the guards walked to the wall and began to fill a bucket from a tap, but Peachfield shook his head. He walked to André's body and lifted his head by the hair, staring into the blank face.

'No, don't bother,' he said. 'Remove him for now, and bring Case over here instead.'

*

11.01 Whittier; 20.01 London

Frank and Debbie were set on the roadside at the far side of Whittier.

'I want to come in with you, guys,' Frank said.

'Sorry, sir. This is an HRT operation. We have control,' said the man whom Debbie assumed was the team leader. He had already kitted himself out with breathing apparatus, heavy Kevlar armour, a Glock on his thigh, and H&K MP5 hanging by its strap. There were two stun grenades on his left breast, while a torch, radio, cuffs, baton, and magazines were held on his belt, along with karabiners, rope, and items she didn't even recognise. 'You must wait back here until you get the OK. When I give you that signal, I want you to call for assistance, Frank. Got that?'

'Yeah. OK,' Frank said.

The others had already moved off among the trees and shrubs that lay about. One Jeep drove off along the roadway beyond the turnoff to the Buckner, hoping to find a way to the rear of the place. Behind them, the rest of the vehicles had parked along the road nearer Whittier town itself. Their driver walked off to chat in a low voice with two of the other drivers. The Team Leader had made it clear that no one who was not HRT was to join them in the mission.

'What now?' Debbie asked.

'You heard the man. We wait.'

*

11.04 Whittier; 20.04 London

'I think before we give you André's treatment we'll soften you up with a little wash,' Peachfield said.

Jack heard Stilson chuckle and he tensed himself, but there was little he could do.

It was clear that they were professionals from the moment Jack felt their hands on him. One gripped his wrists while the other undid the straps that held his chest and biceps, and when he was finally freed, they lifted him to his feet. There was nothing he could do to resist. All he could, he tried. He squirmed, he tried to lash out with his feet, but all he earned for himself was a heavy cuff over his ear that almost felled him.

'Be careful. Don't knock him out. I want him wide awake!' Peachfield snapped.

The blow sent ripples of nausea bubbling through his frame, and for a while he was unaware of moving, but then he came to and found himself being lifted onto a metal table. There were more straps, and he breathed in to try to make them set the straps on him loosely, but they clearly saw his attempt, and one of them jabbed an elbow into Jack's belly. The air left him, and while he was choking for breath, they tightened the straps. A strip of his flesh was pinched in the buckle on his left bicep, and he felt it puncture as the buckle's tongue stabbed the fold. It was instantly painful, a constant stabbing that made his eyes water, but just now he didn't care. He wanted only to see Peachfield suffer for what he had done, what he was about to do.

'Why were you out here?' Peachfield asked. 'We know about the journal, of course. What were you going to do with the journal if you had got it back to London?'

'I don't know what you're talking about!' Jack snarled.

His arm was on fire. He kept telling himself about the pain. He daren't look at it, because it was a part of his story to himself now, that injury. He had to convince himself that it was bleeding all over his arm, that this was a huge and debilitating injury that he may never recover from. It was a focal point for his concentration. His being was

353

focused on that particular pain, in the hope that, for a while, it would supersede all other pain.

He had a moment to think of that, before the hood was over his head, the towel was thrust over his mouth, and they began to pour the water over him.

His arm injury was not enough. Not when he was drowning.

*

11.32 Whittier; 20.32 London

They had been gone too long. That was already plain. Debbie folded her arms, unfolded them, walked up and down the rough roadway, and stared at the black concrete walls with the multiple piercings where the windows had once stood.

'What're they doing?' she demanded at last, staring up at the hideous old building.

'Preparing themselves. Acquainting themselves with the site, getting ready to blow their way in, listening to figure out where the enemy all are, making sure they don't kill a hostage – the usual. It takes time, Debbie.'

'You seem very calm about it all.'

Frank shrugged.

'It's best to get ready. Six Ps, eh? Piss poor planning prevents perfect performance, remember.'

'Meanwhile all the hostages in there are being pulled apart by some sadistic pricks. How much longer, in Christ's name!'

He shot her a look.

'You know I don't like that kind of language, Debbie. No, we wait until we hear from them. They're keeping radio silence, that is all. They've been gone a half hour or so. It's not long. Too many people die when SWAT teams go in and shoot up the whole area, and it doesn't achieve anything. Let them do…'

There was a squawk on the receiver in his pocket. Frank pulled it out and listened. Debbie leaned closer to hear the indistinct words.

'Bravo team in place. Alpha, do you copy, over?'

'Copy that.'

There was silence again, this time for at least five more minutes, and then a voice came on.

'Alpha team ready.'

'Charlie team ready.'

'Copy that. All teams in place.'

Frank looked over at Debbie, and then as the shout '*GO!*' came, they sprinted to their Jeep, sprang in, and were soon bumping over the rough roads, Debbie clinging to the grab handle with one hand, her pistol ready in her lap.

*

11.46 Whittier; 20.46 London

The first Jack knew of the attack was the rapid *boom*, *boom*, *boom* of concussion grenades. He recognised that sound from training, many years before. Then there was the staccato spitting of a 9mm submachine gun, two shots, two shots, three, and then two again. A shriek of pain and a rattle of pistol shots, all thundering in the concrete tunnels of the building. The pipes above rattled and clattered as ricochets bounced from them, and Jack, coughing, still hooded, was convinced this must be rescue.

He had been waterboarded seven times. The first had been bad and the subsequent ones had been much worse. It was drowning, in a controlled and cruel manner. The men held the water over the towel until it was filled, and immediately Jack's mouth was full of water: his nostrils filled, his mouth filled and, although he fought the urge, he had to try to breathe after a while, and the instant the fluid was in his lungs, he began to drown. Sparks and flashes of light went off in his eyes as he thrashed wildly, his lungs burning and, as he was certain he must die, they pulled the towel away and he could cough and retch up the water from deep inside his lungs. It took him an age to recover each time, and Peachfield would patiently repeat the same questions over and over as Jack heaved and swore, and then the towel was replaced and Jack was pushed back down, and the water came again.

By the fourth time, he preferred to think that they may succeed.

But as the shots rang out and a loud clanging blow struck the door of their chamber, the torture ceased for now. Jack was left, hooded, listening as the men ran to the far side of the chamber. None had weapons on them, neither pistols nor knives, in order to defend themselves against attack. The rules wouldn't allow agents like these to carry guns in among dangerous prisoners in case a firearm was mislaid or stolen. So instead of fighting, they ran. There was a rattle and clatter as another door was opened, then the echoing sound of it slamming shut against its metal frame. And then there was another detonation, and smoke filled Jack's lungs.

*

Frank took the Jeep up the entryway at full speed. The railings set up to keep the inquisitive at bay were no match for two tons of metal, and they thundered away as the Jeep rammed. Frank booted the Jeep to the middle of the building, and stopped by an open doorway.

Debbie was almost out of the Jeep before it had stopped, and she heard grenades going off, and the rapid *tap*, *tap*, *tap* of sub-machineguns firing somewhere close, although there was no way to tell where the shots were coming from. Somewhere underneath, she guessed, and she leaped over the rubbish accumulated in the doorway, her shoes crunching and crackling on shards of glass, splinters of old metal, and occasional pieces of crockery. Ceilings were coming down here and there, and she looked up at the cables spilling out like the building's nerves and intestines. It was foul.

Another fusillade, and she turned to glower at Frank, pointing down with her finger. He was right. On the way here he had said that he reckoned they would have built the main interrogation block underground, away from prying eyes and curious ears. Well, he was ASAC, as he said.

He pointed along a corridor and, when she peered round it, she saw a doorway. The door was, like all these doorways, long gone. She walked along to it, and then heard what he must have: shouts and screams. His hearing was good, she thought, as she plunged into the entryway. It gave into a small chamber, and when she reached the far side, there was a door. A keypad beside the lock spoke of security that was more recent than the dilapidated building might suggest. She stood back, and fired twice. The lock blew apart but, when she pulled the door, it remained locked. Frank pulled her away, and fired three shots rapid at the frame where the hinges should be. With the third bullet he ran at the door, kicking it high, above its centre. There was a splintering of wood, and the door gave way, rotating about the lock and remaining hinge. Frank slid over it on his backside, gun at the ready, and waited for Debbie as she followed suit. In front of them were stairs going down, but not into the dark. A new electrical system was working here. There were lighted every few feet, and their way was very clear and well illuminated.

Another shot, then a brief rattle of bullets going off, and both shrunk against the walls. There was a curve in the staircase just ahead. Frank motioned to Debbie to stay still, and made his way down the steps. He snatched a glance around the wall, beckoned, and continued out of sight. Debbie followed him, her pulse racing, standing at the point of the wall, so she could look up and down the staircase. No one coming from above, and down below her she could see Frank peering cautiously around the corner. There was a bullet going off, but it sounded flat, somehow distant. She waited until Frank turned to her, nodded, and darted out and down.

*

11.51 Whittier; 20.51 London

Debbie hurtled after him as Frank waved her on, and then they were in a long corridor. An explosion farther up the passage lit the concrete with a yellow-white flash, and then there was darkness. Lights overhead flickered and flared, and then Debbie saw smoke tumbling up ahead. She darted forward, feet pattering on the floor, aware of Frank at her side. Grey, steel doors were set into the walls with reinforcements and, when she peered into one, she saw a man cowering in the corner, naked, with dark skin marred by bruises and scars. His wide, petrified stare was seared into her memory in that one brief glimpse. She had never seen such terror.

The smoke was clearing even as they ran towards it. It made her cough, but it was only a moment before she was through it, and then she saw a man in black, submachine gun in hand. He turned and glanced at her through the smoke, whirling, his MP5 rising, and the strobe torch under his gun's barrel blinded her. She quickly held her gun up, her other hand holding out her badge. He switched his torch to plain light, studied her and Frank, then nodded at them.

Another burst of gunfire up ahead. The HRT officer waved his hand back to the wall, throwing himself flat to the floor as he did so, his MP5 up and ready again.

Debbie saw a pair of men in army fatigues pelting towards her. She was about to rise and challenge them, when there was a pair of double-taps, and she saw one of the two fall and skid on his knees, his body buckling backwards until he came to a halt; the other man was spun about, and his head snapped back under the impact of the bullet, slamming him against the wall, then sliding to the ground. The first man trembled and shook, and slowly his body eased back to the floor, his legs cocked back on either side in an ungainly mess. Without haste, the HRT officer rose, walked to the two, checked them for weapons, and moved on.

Debbie glanced at Frank. He looked as shocked as she felt. In the past Debbie had needed to draw her weapon, but she had never killed

357

anyone, and to see the almost casual manner in which the HRT despatched two unarmed men was a great shock. She holstered her Glock and carried on.

There were more doors on either side, and in them Debbie saw more men trying to hide from the violence. The rooms were little more than six feet long, perhaps three wide, and six high. A man would find it hard to lie in them. Each had a grille in the corner of the room, she saw, and assumed this was all they had for a toilet. The smell made her stomach churn. It was like living in a sewer.

Another HRT man appeared from a chamber ahead, and he nodded at them as they walked past. Up ahead she could hear someone shouting: 'Clear! Clear!', then another concussion and a blinding bright flash. A wave of heat and dust was thrown at her, and she had to lift a hand to cover her eyes as particles were scattered into her eyes. It was painful, and she blinked away the worst of it, trying not to rub her eyes in case she scratched them with the grit, and then, with an arm over her mouth and breathing slowly through the material of her blouse, she moved on again.

There was a twisted mass of metal here, steel doors that had buckled as the explosion wrenched them from the doorway, and inside she saw metal tables, metal chairs, wires, prods, chains and whips. But it was the sight of Jack Case on the steel bench, that made the breath catch in her throat.

'Hey, Jack, you OK?' she managed. She tore away the hood and then pulled her coat off and wrapped it around him, covering his modesty, but he didn't respond. His eyes were bleak, and he coughed and cleared his throat many times. 'Where's the other guy?' he asked.

'You were alone in here,' one of the HRT men said, pulling his mask off and hooking it on his equipment. 'There were five guards down the hall there, and two more outside. They're all dealt with. Four prisoners in cells and you. That's the lot.'

Jack nodded slowly, but then some colour began to return to his face as he stared about the room. 'They got out somewhere up that way,' he said, pointing.

The chamber in which they were standing had a door set into the farther end.

'We've checked that. No one out there,' the HRT officer said.

'Check again,' Jack said curtly. 'They got out that way. Peachfield, Stilson and another guy. All went up there. I heard them.'

358

The HRT team leader nodded to two of his men. They hurried to the door, slipped through, and were gone.

'Jack?' Debbie said. 'You ready to get out of here?'

'Yes,' he shivered. 'Get me away from here.'

*

14.20 Whittier; 23.20 London

Jack was glad of the large shot of rum at Suzie's.

In the complex of cells Frank had found a set of laundered clothes which he brought to Jack. They were all different sizes, but he pulled on a T and a blue striped shirt, and a pair of blue jeans. He would have to do without shoes for a while.

Chief Burns had hurried to the Buckner Building as soon as he heard about the assault, and he and two officers were helping the HRT men to shut it down and lock it. Suzie had found someone who had shoes in Jack's size, and he had at least some comfort as his feet warmed up. The cold concrete floor of the Buckner Building had been repellent to the touch.

The prisoners had been brought from the Bucky and were sitting around the fire in Suzie's, while an HRT member stood over them, arms folded. His expression adequately conveyed sympathy for their plight, and distrust in case they were terrorists. He was making no judgements, but they would be well served to behave themselves, Jack saw. It was enough to make him give a twisted grin.

'How did you know to come here?' he asked.

'You told us about the Dollar Sorensen mentioned. It made sense as soon I saw Amiss's plane heading this way, to wonder why. And then we found the Buckner building,' Frank said.

'I'm glad you did,' Jack said. 'Has anyone found Peachfield and the others?'

Debbie sipped a mug of coffee.

'That door took them out to a tunnel that brought them out behind the building, up on the hill.'

'Where'd they go?'

'There's nowhere they can go,' Frank said. 'We've a helicopter checking the hills with infrared. They can't come to town, because the railroad is guarded, the marina's secure, and if they try to get through the tunnel they'll be stopped. We have their details. There's no other way for them to get away, except through the tunnel.'

'Good,' Jack said.

359

Suzie's café was filling as people arrived from the town itself, more law-enforcement officers from the State Police, from the FBI at Anchorage, and even some BATF officers, and a group of Homeland Security officials who started leading the rescued prisoners from Suzie's out to waiting coaches.

Jack suddenly felt sick. It was the noise, the crush of people, and, most of all, the realisation that running, the fighting, and the danger was over at last.

He was safe. His part in this investigation was over, and there was no reason for him remain.

Frank and Debbie were talking with a group of Fire Department officers and a man Frank said was his boss. No one was watching him and, for once, no one was likely to care about him. Jack stood unsteadily and walked out into the coolness. Cars thronged the edge of the roadway here, and he strolled past them to get to the shoreline, sitting on a bench from where he could see the boats at their moorings. Even now, the sun had not much further to travel before it would be over the hill and throwing the area into shadow.

Jack shivered, and put his head in his hands. He had been shot at, chased and tortured… all he wanted was some peace. Even back at home, Claire was likely repelled by him. From what he'd heard when he spoke to her, she'd believed the crap Starck had told her about his phones. Didn't she realise it could be easily forged? She wouldn't care. She had given him time to mend things, and for what? So that he could fuck off again and go on a mission for the Service. The Service came first.

And she was right. It was always his first love. No matter what. Leaving the Service would be the hardest thing he'd ever done. But he knew he would soon be thrown out. He had no choice. The delicious irony was that Claire wouldn't want him back. Not now.

'Are you all right, Mister?'

He looked up to see Kasey.

'Hello. Yes. I am OK. I couldn't deal with all those people in there.'

'You were in the Bucky, weren't you?' she said, standing a little off.

He glanced up at her. 'Yes. They held me there a while.'

'Is it haunted?'

He gave a wry smile and stared out at the grey waters.

'If it wasn't,' he said, 'I think it probably is now.'

Monday 26th September

11.23 London

Sara picked up the phone on the third ring.

'Yes?'

'This is Karen Skoyles. We spoke before.'

'I remember you. You were the one who tried to tell me to keep quiet about Mo's kidnap, aren't you?'

'I tried to keep you within the regulations for your husband's good, Mrs Malik.'

'You threatened me. What do you want now?'

'You are breaking the terms of the agreement.'

'No. Those were terms imposed on my husband, not me.'

'They affect you too.'

'Fine. What have I done?'

'You have been using a computer or other electronic equipment to send messages on Twitter and...'

'No, I haven't. Someone else has, not me. It's nothing to do with me. I have no computer here, no telephone. You took them, remember? When you took everything else. And I have no money because you stopped all our accounts, so I couldn't buy them if I wanted them. You prevented me.'

'Then it's your lawyer.'

'Perhaps. You'd have to ask him.'

Karen's voice became lower.

'I could have your children taken away, Mrs Malik. You fuck around with me, and I'll have you in prison, your kids in care homes. You know what happens to children in those homes? I'll make sure yours go to the very worst ones in the country.'

Sara felt that like a punch in her belly, and she sank to the floor.

'What?'

'You heard me. I work with the Secret Service, Mrs Malik. If you don't cooperate, I'll ruin you.'

'You already have. When you took my husband from me,' Sara said, but she felt listless and worn. She wanted to sob.

'You have to call it off. This stupid campaign will cost you everything. I promise you.'

'Why? What do you have against us? Who are you?'

'Call them off,' Karen said.

'You threaten, you bully, you listen to my conversations, you stop my phone, you take my computer, you ruin my life, and now, because I want to do what I can for my...'

'We listen? What do you mean?'

Sara sniffed.

'The telephone. I can hear the noise when you are listening, the...'

But the line had died. There was that second soft click a moment later, and then the dialling tone. Sara stared at the handset, and slowly replaced it on the hook.

For some reason, she felt a little spark of hope. Karen had sounded scared, and somehow Sara was quite certain that this was a hopeful sign.

*

10.43 Whittier; 19.43 London

Jack couldn't sleep that night. He'd been given a room in the Begich Building and, while it was a delight to lie on clean sheets and feel the tension ease from his muscles, he spent a long time staring at the telephone, thinking of Claire. The anger at what Starck had done wouldn't leave him. The idea that he could have told Claire that he was suspected of murdering her lover was appalling. Jack kept feeling his fingers clench as though Starck was somewhere nearby and could be killed.

But whenever his eyes did close, it wasn't the dream of strangling Starck that came to him: it was the memory of the darkness, the feeling of the water trickling into his mouth, in through his nostrils, the sensation of water all over him, inside that hood, the dizziness of not knowing which way was up or down, the restraining straps cutting into his muscles as he strained, trying to swim to the air, to *breathe*. It was that memory that jerked him awake, his lungs bursting.

He would never find peace, not until the men responsible for his torture had been made to pay for their crimes against him, and against all the men found in that torture chamber. He wondered what would happen to the men from those cells now they had been taken away. Hopefully they'd be looked after now. The last, a tall, anxious English-speaker, had left shortly before Jack himself was led from Suzie's to the paramedics. The coach was gone before Jack was brought over to this building to sleep.

It was a relief when the sun flared over the far hill and made the room blaze with fire. He rose and showered, studying the bruises and bloody scabs all over his body with a detachment born of exhaustion.

Suzie's was as busy as it had been the night before, and Jack stood in the doorway a moment, distracted by the noise and busyness all about him until Suzie saw him and walked over to him.

'Hey,' she said.

'Hello,' he said automatically.

'You don't mind me sayin', you look like crap,' she said. 'Come over here. An old friend'll wanna see you.'

He followed her and she took him round the main bar area to the seating area where he had sat and read the journal on his first day. At a table he saw Burns.

Suzie pushed him into a chair and poured a mug of coffee before striding off.

Burns was wearing glasses again, but his face was a mass of small cuts and bruises still. He tried to grin, but the effort was too painful and made him wince.

'Hi, Mr Hansen. Or Case, I hear! Shit, you look worse'n me.'

'Actually, I doubt that,' Jack said. 'Call me Jack. Everyone else does.'

'Yeah, right.'

Jack told him about his capture, about the torture and what had been going on in the Buckner Building.

'That's sick,' Chief Burns said quietly.

'Can't have been easy to get the place changed like that,' Jack said.

'It was dead easy,' Burns said with cold certainty. 'Kasey's boyfriend was killed in there. They must have heard of that and sent their guys in to remodel the basements. They told us it was to make the building safe for other kids, so an accident like that wouldn't happen again.'

Jack thought of Kasey.

'You reckon it happened by accident?'

'No. I reckon they probably booby trapped it and killed the poor bastard so they had an excuse to keep folks away.'

'That's what I reckon,' Jack said.

'Christ! What sons of...'

The door opened and voices were bellowing. Jack turned and frowned at the disturbance, and spotted Frank and Debbie. Debbie caught sight of his face and pushed her way through the crowds.

363

'Jack, the helicopter found some guys up near the ice. They're bringing them in now.'

*

11.04 Whittier; 20.04 London

Down near the harbourside, an emergency helipad had been set up in the car park, and Jack stood with Debbie, Frank and Chief Burns as the helicopter chattered its way towards them from the Portage Glacier. It was a large machine, with the State Police signs on the sides, and on its skids were two black-wrapped parcels.

It came in towards the tunnel, then turned out to the water and came in slowly from the sea, its motor working hard in the thick, cold air, as it edged in and hovered, before settling down gently on the tarmac. While the rotor still turned, and the turbos started to quieten, men darted forward under the blades, hands on their hats.

Jack found himself led forward once the machine had stopped, and the two bodies were set down on the ground.

A trooper from the helicopter was talking to Frank beside the body bags.

'It was the bears we saw first. I didn't realise there were bodies there – whoever did it knew what he was up to.'

An orderly was already opening the bags, and Jack saw the pale features of Peachfield and, a moment later, the other man in that hideous room down in the Bucky's basement.

'Yeah, that's them,' he said.

Frank looked at him.

'Yesterday you said there was another there in the room with you and these two.'

'Just the one. The guy Debbie and I saw at Roy Sandford's place.'

'Stilson,' Debbie said.

Frank nodded.

'Well, he's done our job for us here,' he said. 'These two left the Buckner Building with him when it was assaulted. There was an escape tunnel that took the three of them into the treeline, and from there they made their way up towards the Portage Glacier. The helicopter found them at the side of the ice, under a lip. It was a miracle they were found at all, really. Bears were there and the pilot was bright enough to realise bears like their meat fresh, so he went on down for a look and found these two.'

'How'd they die?'

'Small calibre gunshot to the back of the head.'

'What now?'

'He must have hiking gear or something. We'll warn Anchorage to watch for a man matching his description, check on outward-bound flights, and see where he could have got to. Jesus, if a guy wants to get himself lost here in Alaska, he's got a lot of space to go do it.'

Frank sighed. The frustration was getting to him. He looked up at the hills behind the town.

'They went on up there, and he just killed them both as soon as they were out of sight, I'd guess. He must be a real calm bastard.'

'He's a psychopath,' Debbie said.

'What about his boss?' Jack asked. 'Amiss: where's he?'

'Being watched. He's at his home. He's been told not to go to work,' Frank said. 'He's one prick who isn't going to collect his pension. He's not arrested yet, but the prosecutors are going to have a ball with him.'

'So what now?' Jack said.

'Now, we get the helicopter refuelled and hitch a lift back to Ted Stevens International, where we take a Bureau jet back to DC,' Frank said. 'And you debrief us about the whole affair. Then, when we get back, I think I should be able to tell you more about the other guys in this business. And meet Amiss.'

*

15.25 Langley; 20.25 London

When Amiss's little jet landed at the Andrews Air Force Base, Stilson remained sitting in his seat, staring out of the window as the plane taxied across to the CIA section and halted outside one of the Lear hangars. Even when the door had opened and the steps had been extended, he remained there, his eyes fixed upon the middle distance unseeingly while the pilot went through his final shut down sequences.

'Sir?'

Stilson unbuckled his belt slowly and rose. The small bag he had beside him on the grey leather seat was all he had. It was what he had taken with him to Alaska, and now, he realised, it was perhaps all he had in the world.

As he climbed into the rental car, one thought was uppermost: Amiss must protect him. That was the key thing. Amiss knew Stilson, knew how reliable he was. The idea that he could be betrayed was unthinkable. But if Amiss himself was blown, Stilson was too. Without the protection Amiss offered, Stilson had nothing. He was just an agent without a patron, and agents without masters didn't last long. Especially if they could be connected to criminal acts.

The pistol that had ended Peachfield's and the guard's lives was already gone. He had dropped it into a crevasse in the glacier just after killing the two. And then he had set off across the waste that was the Portage Pass to the other side, where he had found an old car parked at the railroad station and hot-wired it. It was one hour to Anchorage, and he drove it slowly and carefully, his mind whirling all the way.

After all the effort and danger, the entire scheme was blown. Amiss had created the Buckner cells, he had arranged for the tripwire system that killed the kid there, so that there was a reason for the engineers to arrive and build the facility, and he had used his contacts within his Masonic group to provide the men who would be questioned. But it was Stilson who had been his enforcer, Stilson who had executed the men whom Amiss had decided must die. Stilson was the man in most danger.

He had to speak to Amiss. Hopefully Amiss could provide him with an aeroplane away from the US, and money. He'd need a lot of money. Whatever he had at his home was lost. He had been marked when those assholes appeared at his house. If Case had survived the torture at the Bucky, and when Stilson left him he didn't seem dead, then there was a witness to him being there. He was known. All his past life was lost.

His home was too dangerous. He couldn't go there, likewise, his office. He had some spare money and ID there, he reminded himself, and punched the steering wheel in bitter fury. He had to get to Amiss, get some money, and determine an exit strategy for himself.

*

16.03 Langley; 21.03 London

In his room, Peter Amiss chewed at his lower lip as he sat at his desk.

He had prayed, begging for aid and for the mental calm that would help him to see a way through this mess, but so far nothing had occurred to him.

Perhaps he ought to have bolted when he had heard from Stilson that they'd caught the Brit and taken him to Alaska, but at the time that had seemed an end to the matter. The last little item closed down. No more problems. The Brit was taken, and could be conveniently killed and ditched. That was the beauty of the Alaskan site.

He'd remembered that place as soon as the idea for the operation had first come to him. Whittier had been a place he had visited only a couple of times when he was a kid, but the site was so desolate, so far from people. It was ideal. And the fact that it was deserted now made it even better.

Amiss leaned his hands on his glass-covered desk and tried to work out a plan of action. He ought to run. That was the thing. Leave America – take a plane to a country with no extradition agreement with the US, or a place where they'd appreciate his knowledge. The problem was that he didn't want to go to a country that was America's enemy. Even if he could earn a small fortune in a place like Russia, the idea of collaborating with America's foe made his stomach turn over. No, he couldn't do that.

But there was always South America. There were plenty of places there where a man with money could hide for a long time. The Nazis proved that after the Second World War. From his previous life, he knew of a number of places to which he could run from Laos to Korea. But he was too old for that.

He studied his face in the window. It was a gloomy day and, with the trees all about his house, the windows reflected his face perfectly. And he could see the resignation in his own eyes. He wasn't going to run. This was his country. He had tried to do what he could to protect it, and his attempt had failed. Now there was a reckoning.

Tugging open the right hand drawer of his desk, he looked down into it. There was his old service Colt automatic, right where it always sat. And when he pulled harder, the drawer opened wider to display the battered, leather cover of the journal.

With that and the names of the others in the Deputies, he should be safe.

But it made him feel dirty, even as he picked up his telephone and asked for a call to be put through to Frank Rand of the FBI.

*

22.03 Langley; 03.03 London

Frank Rand drove up the driveway to Amiss's house with a feeling of grim satisfaction. There was a feeling that the last hectic days were culminating in this meeting, and that he and Debbie would soon have only the paperwork to contend with. Paper, Frank felt, was safer than bullets.

'Some house,' Debbie commented.

'Yeah,' Frank said.

He glanced in the rear-view, at the slumped figure of Jack Case in the back seat. Jack had slept almost all the way from Anchorage and, as soon as they installed him in the car, he had yawned, placed his head back on the rest, and begun to snore again.

They drew up at the colonnaded front to the house.

Debbie grunted and said 'He think he's a movie star or somethin'?'

Frank didn't respond, but turned in his seat.

'Hey, Jack? We're here.'

'OK.'

Jack was awake in an instant, and stared about him quickly. Wide driveway, house to the side here, while in front was a small circular box hedge only a foot or so high, with a pool of water enclosed within, a statue of a nymph holding a fountain aloft. But there was no spurting water today.

He climbed out of the car and walked with the other two to the front door. A moment after Frank knocked, it opened to reveal a blue-suited man with very short haircut who almost filled the width of the door with his shoulders. He glanced at Frank and Debbie's badges, stared meaningfully at Jack for a long moment, and only stood aside when Frank and Debbie squared up to him.

Frank strode over the floor and opened a door at the left.

Jack found himself inside Amiss's library. It was huge, and extravagantly decorated with memorabilia from wars all over the world. He recognised a Viet Cong flag, and beside it was a little khaki hat with a peak and a red star in the forehead; underneath there was a shirt with a ragged hole in the breast, and blackened mess all about it.

'You like my mementoes?' Amiss asked.

He had walked in from a door behind his imposing desk.

'No,' Jack said.

'Please, sit, all of you,' Amiss said. He took his own chair, fingering the crucifix at his open neck. 'You have questions for me, I assume.'

'Yes, sir,' Frank said.

Jack interrupted.

'Why?'

Amiss looked at him like he was dog mess staining his carpet.

'You're Case, of course.'

'Yes. I'm the man you ordered to be killed, and then ordered to have tortured before killing me. That's me,' Jack said.

'Yes, well, I am sorry about that. It was necessary to protect us.'

'*Us*?' Frank asked.

'That's why you are here. You see, I was invited to join a Masonic lodge some years ago. It was a good group of decent men. And it gave me the idea. The idea for a new lodge, which would be dedicated to America and protecting her.'

'You don't think the army is big enough?' Jack asked sarcastically.

'Come on, Jack,' Debbie murmured.

Jack sat back, looking away. It was hard to control his anger at this prick, sitting there so smugly.

Amiss continued, his voice soft and calm.

'No, Mr Case. I don't think her armies are strong enough, nor the air corps, nor the navy. Because they are only good for conventional warfare. Sure, we can pulverise a country, we can nuke 'em till they're scorched to cinders, we can blow their planes out of the sky, and we can destroy their ships. But when "they" are just a few half-starved individuals who hate us, our culture, our God, our films, our women – Christ save us – they even hate us giving them our money! That kind of brute individual, who is prepared to hijack a plane and fly it into a building, hoping to kill thousands by his act of terror, that guy cannot be stopped by a million troops on the ground. That kind of asshole cannot be stopped by our grunts. He needs a new form of defence. Intelligence.'

'So you decided to form a club to promote torture,' Jack said.

'We had all the systems in place, and we were getting good intel from them. Gitmo was one place, but there were others. And then Bush left office, and we got the most un-American leader this country's ever had,' Amiss said. 'We saw that the only way to keep our land safe for our children and grandchildren was to stop that fool's crusade against us all. So, as he planned to remove our sources, we worked hard to replace them with others. Then we launched our mission. We would interrogate those who our sources had told us were involved; we would find the men who had committed the crimes against us; find the men behind them, who had conceived attacks, plotted with their friends, and launched them. Our first missions were against those from al-Qaeda who had been released from custody although they were a threat. There were men all over the world who had tried to destroy us. Now it was our turn.'

Jack remembered the news of the explosion on the day he left.

'Croydon?'

369

'He was one of them. Your guys were keeping him under surveillance, but he was a threat. He had to be removed.'

'And cops, neighbours, all the others injured? That was OK, I suppose. Collateral?'

'If you want to put it like that, yes. This fight is bigger than one or two casualties, no matter how unfortunate. In war, you expect collateral damage.'

'What was next?' Frank said.

'The next stage was to isolate where the second tier of informants lay. So once we had wiped out the first line, we went after them. They were the ones you found at the Buckner Building. We got some good information from them, too.'

'In such a short time.'

At Jack's sneering tone, Amiss looked up and met his stare without flinching.

'Yes, Mr Case. In a very short time. Because we were prepared to be entirely ruthless. Like I said, this is a war to the death, between cultures and religions. If you don't realise that, you're a fool.'

'What of your Masonic friends?'

'They are senior officers who were prepared to put their lives and careers on the line for their country.'

'Who were they?' Frank said.

Amiss looked at him.

'Mr Rand, you are a good, God-fearing man. I've looked up your records. You had a bum as a brother, and your early years were… adventurous – but you still know what is right, what is wrong. You know what I did made sense.'

'Sir, you may be right,' Frank said, and Jack and Debbie exchanged a glance.

'Some people were harmed. I don't deny that. But only so that we could save lives. American lives. You see that, don't you, Rand?'

'Yes, sir.'

'So can we keep this private? I can have the—'

'But whether it was or not, you were breaking the law in doing it. I can't count all the laws you've broken just on a Federal basis, but I do know you'll be going down for them. I'll see you incarcerated for the rest of your life. That I do promise you.'

Amiss smiled thinly.

'You think so? I think I need to speak with my lawyers before I continue, then.'

'What of the Masonic lodge?' Jack interjected as Amiss stood.

'It's a private, secret matter,' Amiss said.

'I don't think so,' Jack said. 'It stopped being private when you arranged to have men kidnapped and brought here.'

'You may think so,' Amiss said. 'Good night.'

Frank stood.

'Sorry, sir. You aren't staying here. I am arresting you for...'

Amiss's face registered blank shock at first as Frank read out the list of offences and then read him his rights, but then, as Frank reached the end, his face changed. His cheeks flushed, and his mouth moved into a snarl of defiance, and he reached for the top drawer on the right.

Instantly Debbie's gun was out and pointing at his forehead.

'Stop, sir, because so help me I'll fire if you don't!'

Amiss was still, his hand only inches from his old Colt. It was tempting to grab it, and end the shame that would inevitably follow. But then, he considered, perhaps there wouldn't be any. Let these dumbass fucks arrest him now. The Lodge wouldn't allow the case to come to trial. It would be their words against his, and he was a decorated hero, a survivor.

'Fuck you,' he said, and slumped back in his chair with a sneering grin.

Frank Rand moved around the desk and saw the Colt in the drawer. He was aware of Jack at his side, and was about to tell Jack to move aside, not to attack Amiss, when he saw Jack's hand go to the drawer.

He felt as though his tongue had stuck to his palate. He couldn't move, far less speak, but only watch in horror as Jack's hand reached in, and then Frank was spinning, his hand reaching for Jack's, and he felt a swamping relief when he saw Jack pull out a battered and scuffed ledger.

'Man, don't do that to me,' he muttered.

'Eh?' Jack said. He flicked through the pages. 'What was so bloody important about this bleeding book, Amiss?'

'Didn't you realise? Nothing to do with me personally,' Amiss smiled feebly. 'You should ask your friends back at home about that.'

*

22.56 Langley; 03.56 London

Jack sat on Amiss's desk and cradled the phone on his shoulder as he leafed through the ledger again.

'Hello. Did I wake you?'

371

Starck's voice on the other end was thick and fuddled with sleep as he demanded 'What?' Jesus, do you know what fucking time it is? Who is this?' before dissolving into a hacking cough.

'Light one and shut up,' Jack said. 'You know who this is? I know what's been going on, Paul. I know who's been ordering my execution.'

'Don't be melodramatic, Jacky. You were a player and it went horribly wrong. You fucked up. That's all.'

'How did I fuck up?'

'When you killed Jimmy O'Neill.'

'No, Paul. It went wrong because someone wanted to be rid of me. She wanted to keep things quiet,' Jack said. He carried on turning the pages, and then he found the piece about his interrogation of Lewin, and read more slowly. It didn't take long. Immediately after that was a short item about Karen. The piece he had noticed all those days ago when he first picked up this ledger: something about Karen and interrogation. 'You still there?'

'This had better be good.'

'Good enough for you to stop trying to have me killed, Paul. I have the ledger. Lewin wrote that his first introduction to the group over here came from Karen. She was recruiting for them. And I think she was telling the Americans all about European suspects too. Which is why she wanted me out of the way.'

'Because you had read the ledger?'

'She thought I had. That's why she raised Jimmy's death again. Originally she put the finger on me about Jimmy so that I'd lose credibility in the Service. Now she's done it again so the Americans would find me and kill me. Just to keep me silenced. Don't you love loyalty?'

Starck gave a hacking cough and reached for a Rothman's.

'There's not enough loyalty around.'

'Don't believe her propaganda, Paul. I didn't kill Jimmy.'

'Sure.'

'Look, this is what Lewin's ledger is all about. I have it and I'll bring it back with me. I suggest you tell Karen at the earliest opportunity.'

'Why?'

'Because it says she was asking Lewin to join a team of interrogators. She was part of this whole mess, Peter. She was working to bring suspects to America so they could be tortured,' Jack said. 'I have the proof.'

'Give me names,' Starck said.

Jack glanced at the list in his hand.

'The English one here was a guy called Mohammed al Malik.'

Starck lay back on his pillow.

'Now that name is interesting,' he murmured.

*

23.01 Langley; 04.01 London

Outside the gates, Stilson watched in horror as the four cars rolled down the driveway and then took off at speed in the direction of Washington. It was a glimpse, no more, but it was enough. As the third car came out and accelerated away, he recognised Amiss's white face in the window.

When the last of the cars had disappeared, Stilson crept back through the trees to his car, which was parked at the far edge of the woodland. He climbed inside and sat there a long while, deep in thought.

Amiss was gone, that was certain. The man who had served as Stilson's patron and protector had been arrested. So from now on, he would have to look to his own safety. He must now assume that the men who had stood over him were gone. Peachfield he had killed, Sorensen too. Gutterson was still there, as were Keen, Tullman and Barbard, but since Amiss was under arrest there was a good bet that the others would soon be blown too.

He turned on the engine. In the days when the recession had started to hit really hard, whole districts which had relied on the same savings and loans companies had suddenly found that their mortgages were called in. He knew a little suburb of McLean which had almost an entire street repossessed, and there was a little house there he had bought for a few thousand. It also had the attraction that it was close to the Chapel.

It would be a good safe house for now.

Tuesday 27th September

07.22 London

Starck was in his office at Vauxhall Cross before seven that morning, and he sat typing at his desk for two hours, revising and editing, until he was happy.

Taking a pencil with him, he went down to the rear of the building, where he sat on a concrete bench, sipped a cup of strong tea, and read all six pages. Setting his cup down, he inhaled deeply with a sense of deep satisfaction. He lit a Rothman's and enjoyed the clean, sweet aromatic flavour at the back of his throat, catching his breath momentarily, and let out a long feather of smoke.

Life was good, he thought.

Finishing his cigarette, he took his papers back indoors and made his way to the sixth floor.

'I need to see the deputy DG.'

Jessica Stewart looked at him without enthusiasm.

'He is busy.'

'He will want to see me.'

She sighed, shaking her head, and picked up the telephone. A few moments later there was a buzz and Starck was allowed into the office.

'Sir,' he said. 'I've had disturbing news.'

'What sort of news?'

'Karen Skoyles has compromised the Service and colluded with a small group of disaffected American CIA and NSA officers to kidnap British and other nationalities for the purposes of torture. She has provided these individuals with assistance in Britain and abroad so that the Americans could conduct operations. She has also provided them with the details of British subjects who could be captured and rendered to foreign locations, and conspired to prevent us from knowing about their fates. Finally, I have evidence that she concocted false evidence against one of our own agents in order to discredit him so she could take his job.'

Richard Gorman gave him a shrewd glance.

'I suppose you have proof of at least some of this?'

'Jack Case is alive and well. He was captured as a result of Karen's schemes and tortured by this group. He has shown what the group was involved in, and is being debriefed. He has the ledger that Lewin took with him to Alaska.'

'I see,' the DDG said and waved his hand. 'Tell me the worst.'

'Karen herself put him back on the active list,' Paul said, and as the DDG leaned back, he began to tell the whole story of Lewin's death, the ledger, and the Deputies of East and West.

When he left the room two hours later, he had the warm feeling that his career was about to move upwards again. He smiled, and as he reached his desk he gave a wolfish smile, took his packet of Rothman's, and went out to the terrace to smoke a victory cigarette.

*

07.17 Langley; 12.17 London

Stilson walked in through the doors in his suit, carrying a laptop bag over his shoulder, same as he would any other day. Langley was a huge site, and the reception area was always full, even this early in the morning. He was counting on the fact.

As he lifted his card to swipe it at the turnstile, he felt a frisson of anxiety but, to his relief, there was only the soft click of the mechanism operating, and he was inside. No one had yet told Human Resources to cancel his cards or passes. Good.

He crossed the marble floor to the elevator lobby, where he waited with thirty or more agents, all of them staring up at the floor indicators or murmuring in low, early morning tones. It was reassuring. No one remarked upon him standing there, no one spoke to him or even appeared to look at him over-long. It was just an ordinary morning.

Except it was a vitally important morning for him. He had to clear out the safe in Amiss's room. Amiss had too much information on him and on the Deputies for him to be safe. His personnel files in HR would hold very little, but his files in Amiss's safe could break him. He knew that. He had to clear out Amiss's room of everything to do with the Deputies.

The doors opened and he stepped into it, pressing the button for Amiss's floor. He knew he had to move fast, before Amiss's arrest became common knowledge and his passes and clearances were revoked. The elevator stopped, he stepped out and walked along the corridor. Two people passed by in the other direction, talking about 'Poor Roy', and he realised they were talking about Sandford. It made him wonder whether the agent had died. Certainly should have,

375

after the crash. Everyone had heard about that, presumably. That was the day that the Deputies had begun to collapse.

He was at Amiss's door, and he used his card to validate the sequence of keys, sliding his ID card into the slot after pressing the buttons. Amiss had always had a pathological dislike of the use of more modern technology. He preferred the systems that were known and proven. A fingerprint was fine, but could be copied. There were too many cases of migrants in the Far East who were forging fingerprints for him to trust them, and iris scanners could be thrown by a cleverly designed and etched contact lens. Amiss liked key codes and proof of ID. The lock snapped back and he was in.

Knowing Amiss's reluctance to use a computer for any data that was intended to be kept secret, he ignored it. The safe was where Amiss would keep the important files, and it was easy to open. He knew Amiss's codes and, in a moment, he was in and leafing through all the files relating to his own work. He was pleased to see that Amiss had kept them all together, and soon he had the papers stored in his laptop case. Picking it up, he slung it over his shoulder, and was on his way. He had reached the corner that led out to the elevators, when the lift opened, and he saw Jack and Frank Rand being led by a pair of CIA operatives, all making their way towards him.

He faltered, then turned on his heels and strode back the way he'd come. There was a staircase at the far end of this level, which would take him down to the reception area. He'd take that.

*

07.43 Langley; 12.43 London

Jack reacted first.

'That was him,' he blurted, and sprinted for the corner of the corridor.

Debbie blinked. She hadn't been looking up the corridor when Stilson appeared.

'Who?' she demanded before setting off after Jack, the two CIA agents hurrying after them both.

'Sir, you cannot run off here,' one bellowed at Frank.

'It was the man we saw at Sandford's house,' Jack explained.

'Sir, you cannot run off,' the agent said again. 'This is a restricted zone!'

'It's not restricted well enough!' Debbie shouted over his shoulder. 'You have a rogue agent in here. He should have had his clearances shut down!'

'He went up there,' Jack said, not stopping.

Debbie could see the door closing.

'Stairwell,' she said. She took her phone and punched the speed dial for Frank Rand, who had agreed to fetch coffee and doughnuts from the canteen.

'Yeah?' he responded.

'Stilson's here,' Debbie said.

She was at the door now, her hand on her Glock.

She looked at Jack, pocketing her phone, and Jack kicked the door wide, fearing shots. Nothing happened. He darted in, low, looking to keep to the wall so that no shots could come at him from the lower stairwell. It was an open, concrete construction, and he could see down to the next level of stairs. No sign of Stilson. Had he gone up or down? Guessing, Jack reckoned down. He listened, and could hear steps pattering off down the stairs in a hurry.

'Come on!'

He took the first flight in a single leap, and then hurtled off down the next and a third. It was only there that he felt the soft puff of air as a bullet passed by his face. He threw himself down. Stilson had a silencer. An explosion of dust from the wall threw gritty plaster in his face, and he heard steps moving again, but now he was more circumspect. He glanced around and saw Debbie and the two agents, who looked shocked while Debbie looked merely resolute. She put a hand out as though to stop Jack, but he ignored her and took the steps quickly, rushing down, and keeping an eye on the open space that gave him a view of the lower section.

A second puff of wind felt like the kiss of death, and this time he felt a sharp burn on his left cheek as it went past his cheekbone. Jack carried on as the wall shattered behind him, a bullet punching a neat dimple.

He saw Stilson now, a blue-suited figure at a doorway. Jack sprang down the last steps and as he did Stilson fired. Jack felt it in his flank, but then there was a shot from above, a crashingly loud report, and he saw Stilson's shoulder jerk as he reached him, but then Stilson moved forward, so Jack was blocking Debbie's sight picture, and Stilson took Jack by the throat, his stubby silencer at Jack's throat, behind his jaw.

377

'Don't shoot, Deborah,' he shouted sarcastically. 'You might hit *me*!'

'Put the gun down. You can't escape from here,' Debbie called. 'Christ, man, there are a thousand agents in shouting distance!'

Stilson was breathing heavily, and Jack only prayed that his gun didn't have a hair trigger. He had a sickly feeling in his belly that this could all end unpleasantly, and his flank was stinging like someone had stabbed him.

'I think I'm going to fall soon,' he said.

'Do that, Case, and I'll put a bullet in your fucking head,' Stilson snarled. 'Right, Deborah, this is what we're going to do. I'm walking out of here by this door, and you're waiting here while I go. You come out, or I get stopped, and first thing that happens is, you have yourself a nice diplomatic incident. You get me?'

'Stilson, you aren't going to get out of here,' Debbie said. Her finger was on the trigger, Jack saw. Vaguely he recalled Frank telling him that she was a marksman, but Jack didn't like the thought of her testing her skills by trying to shoot around him.

'We're walking now,' Stilson said. 'You shoot if you want to, but just remember this Brit could be an embarrassment if you hit him.'

Jack had no idea how to escape from Stilson's iron grip, especially since he felt as though he was losing his strength by the minute.

But then he thought about Mohammed, and he thought about Claire, and he thought about all the people who had been hurt by this man and his associates, and he resolved that he would not be another man injured by the Deputies. He stumbled along crabways with Stilson hiding behind him, wondering how to break free. The door was at Stilson's right shoulder now, and Jack and Stilson stood still a moment, while Stilson tried to work out how best to open it.

'Pull the door open,' Stilson snarled in Jack's ear.

Jack cocked his eyebrow as he tried to see where the door handle was. Stilson's silencer cut into his neck as he reached over with his left hand across his body to grab the handle and tug on it. The door opened, Stilson edged to it and, as his shoulder and Jack's were through the door, Jack moved.

He jerked his head forward, turning slightly, and rammed the door back hard. The door's edge caught Stilson's gun hand, and the barrel was knocked back. There was a waft of gun smoke, a *phutt* that sounded oddly loud in the still air, and a bullet washed past Jack's ear. He kneed Stilson in the balls and slammed the door hard,

378

catching Stilson's chin and nose, before grabbing the gun and wrestling it from Stilson's fist. He felt a slamming blow on his brow as Stilson punched him, and then he head-butted him, feeling Stilson's nose crunch against his forehead. Grabbing the silencer and the gun, Jack shoved them against Stilson's throat to throttle him, but Stilson was stronger, and the gun was pushed away, and began to turn to face Jack again.

Jack turned, twisted, and threw Stilson over his shoulder, still holding the gun. Stilson's back was hurled against the concrete edge of the lowest step. The shock made him give a roar of pain, and the gun went off again, with that strange, peaceful sound of a bullet ricocheting off concrete. Jack jumped and, using all the weight in his body, came down on one knee on Stilson's belly, twisting his hands as he did.

Stilson convulsed as Jack's weight landed on his stomach, his body jackknifing, and as he moved up, Jack's twisting pushed the barrel of the gun down towards him again. Jack felt the gun jump in his hands as it fired once more, and a spray of blood misted up before him as Stilson's face exploded.

Monday 3rd October

06.43 London

Jack was jetlagged, sore from gunshot wounds, and miserable when he landed at Heathrow Airport. The flight had been bumpy, and he was not a good passenger at the best of times. A friend, Clive, had once told him that he found aeroplanes terrifying, because when he looked out the window, he couldn't see any strings. It was a thought that had never occurred to Jack before, but now every time he flew, that throw-away comment came back to haunt him with renewed vigour.

The hand luggage restrictions meant he had little else besides his book in his carry-on bag. He felt filthy, his teeth caked with muck from the airline meals, and his mood was complemented by the two phone calls he had managed to secure with Claire before he left. Neither gave him cause for hope. As far as he could tell, she wasn't sure whether she was more angry that he had been accused of killing her lover, or that she was afraid he was a full-time murderer for Her Majesty. He never had been, but that didn't sway her. She trusted nothing he said about his work now. He didn't blame her.

379

But for his part, he ached. His body was not built for the punishment it had absorbed in the last weeks, and the final battle with Stilson had savaged a frame that was already weakened from stress and exhaustion. He wanted only to go to Dartmoor now with the dogs, take a basha, and camp out in the wilds for a few days. To get away from politics, from cities, and especially from Karen.

He had liked her. He had wanted to support and promote her. And in return she had tried to have him killed.

At Customs, he met the gaze of the officers with resentment in his eyes. One tried to have him open his bags, and he stiffened his back before agreeing. He had nothing to declare. Although the clothes were all new in the last fortnight, the officer saw nothing to make him think that Jack had gone over his allowance, and Jack was soon through and walking down the corridor of humiliation – that was what he called the exit. On either side were smiling, happy people, welcoming home their loved ones, greeting lovers with hugs and kisses. But for Jack there was only the slow walk without looking from one side to another. Ahead of him were two policemen with their Heckler & Koch submachineguns held negligently across their chests, and behind them, a huddle of scruffy men and women clutching cameras or voice recorders.

And then there came a roar and the flashes of many cameras as the press hurried forward. Jack was shoved aside as Mohammed al Malik appeared, blinking, pale, confused, and flanked by two Special Branch officers. He covered his eyes from the flashes, and the two officers tried to hustle him away, but before they could, Sara beat her way through the crowds and cried out to him. Although the officers tried to keep her from their charge, she threw her arms around her husband.

Jack stared at them, then turned and was about to stride away when he saw a familiar face outside, peering in through the glass door. There was a studied calmness about him as Starck inhaled on a cigarette, then stubbed it out and beckoned.

He had little choice. He complied.

'So, Jacky, my boy. How are we this fine morning?'

'Shit.'

'I can imagine it. I feel repulsive myself. Not used to such early mornings, you see. Anyway, come with me, dear heart. You have a debriefing.'

'No. I'm going home. You can sort something next week, if you pay my fares.'

'Jacky, old cock, I'm afraid you don't quite understand. This isn't an invitation to a pub lunch with a riotous game of darts to follow: this is an order from the DDG himself. He wants to know exactly what has been happening between you and the Brothers over the pond. And you will be coming if you value your pension.'

Jack followed him out to the car, which was double parked and protected by a scowling police officer. He cast disdainful look at Jack and ignored Starck's patronising gratitude, turning on his heel as Starck opened the boot and threw in Jack's case.

'What's it all about?' Jack asked as they left the terminal and drove slowly over the road following the exit signs.

'Well, me old darling, it's like this. I think people are a little resentful about your last manager so, from now on, I am in charge of Scavengers, and you will be in charge of team one.'

'Haven't you forgotten something?' Jack demanded.

'No. Don't think so.'

'The bit where you say, "Your mission, should you choose to accept it". That bit.'

'Ah, that is so 1970s, Jacky. This is the new century, and we prefer to think in terms of the immediate obedience of all staff. So no, there is no "If you wish to" about it. It's there, this is your job, and you will be starting next week.'

'Fuck off.'

'Not the best start to a professional relationship.'

'I mean it. No. I'll think about it and give you an answer next week.'

'End of this week.'

'Next week.'

'Saturday?'

'Next week.'

Starck gave an elaborate sigh.

'If you think you have so much more to do: better DIY jobs about your house, I suppose? Very well. Next week.'

Wednesday 12th October

04.32

It was early in the morning when Jack left the house.

He had not been sleeping well since his return. Claire was civil, just, but they had lost any spark of intimacy that had once existed. He slept in the second bedroom, an unspoiled room which gave out directly to the thatch. All night he could hear the scurrying and pattering of small feet – rodents or birds, it didn't matter to him. Not any more. He was here, and he was soon to be thrown out if Claire didn't come to some kind of arrangement with him. The way things were, he didn't think that was going to happen any time soon.

It was still dark as he pulled the door to behind him. He had a driving mug of coffee with 'FBI, Fabulous Bloody Infantry' emblazoned on the side, a gift from Debbie, and he set it in the mug holder as he started the Subaru's engine. While it warmed, he wandered to the front and back. He had spent an age at an internet café looking for cars of the right age and style before finding one with number plates that suited him. When he was done, it had taken him a while to go up the potholed driveway to the road, and on to the A30, heading up towards Exeter. With his new number plates, it was tempting to wave at the ANPR cameras. Automatic Number Plate Recognition was rapidly becoming standard software throughout the UK, but he didn't care today.

He didn't care at all. In his mind, he saw that Munch picture Lewin had sketched. The horror of Lewin's end was there still: the self-loathing at what he had done. And Jack now had it, too, ever since his torture of Sorensen.

It would take Jack a good four hours to get to where he wanted, and then another couple of hours to do what he needed.

No problem. He had all day.

*

19.34 London

Karen Skoyles left work early that evening. She had lost much of her motivation since the catastrophic end to Jack Case's mission in America. At first she had been placed on gardening leave, a polite euphemism for the condemned civil servant before execution, but more recently she had been permitted to return, on the understanding that she would not be permitted to have an executive position, nor even managerial responsibility for staff.

That meeting had been intolerable. She had been called to HR and, when she entered, Starck was sitting in the corner, arms folded over his waistcoated belly, eyeing her without feeling.

'I am entitled to my line manager being present at a disciplinary meeting,' she pointed out.

'Yes,' the HR officer agreed, and he waved a hand towards Starck. 'You know Peter, of course? He has been promoted in your absence, Karen. Now, please take a seat. We shall try to keep this as civilised as possible.'

She sat.

First she was passed a file. In it were the transcriptions of her telephone calls to her American handler in the US embassy, as well as others, including the call to Sara al Malik. Karen stared at her words, then threw the papers aside. They dangled from the treasury tag as she read the next pages. *Deliberate deception*; *misleading senior officers*; *planning to subvert the career of a fellow officer*; *conspiracy to aid a foreign power at the expense of the Service…* and so it ran on for several pages.

'Well?' she said, pushing the folder onto the desk.

She was informed that her post no longer existed, her liaison duties were properly being taken up by a new liaison division, and her management of Scavengers was ended. In future, only those with operational experience would have control of such units. The Bullies were to be returned to their former home, and her ops and tech and analysis groups were all returning to their home teams in the normal organisational structure.

'So you're making me redundant?' she said with a sneer.

'No, Karen,' Starck said, and levered himself up heavily from his corner. 'You are being saved, my dear. You will spend the rest of your career with us. You are fortunate. You will, however, have to accept a lower salary and reduced pension concomitant with your new position. Obviously you will be expected to aid us when we ask for details of your contacts with the Americans. And if there is ever any suggestion that you are not dealing fairly with us, there will be consequences.'

And that was that. Her humiliation was complete.

She had left today to go shopping after work – a week's food for her apartment. She stowed the bags on the back seat, climbed in, and drove the short distance back to her home in the Barbican. Driving into the apartment, she went down the ramp to her parking bay, and reversed into it.

Opening the car door, she reached inside for the bags and, as she came back out, hip swinging the door closed, she heard the step behind her. It made her freeze. She recognised that step instantly.

'Hello, Jack.'

'I don't suppose you expected to see me again, once you'd sent me off to America,' he said.

'No,' she sighed.

He was behind her, and she would have turned to face him. She began to bend, to put the bags down.

'No,' he said sharply. 'Hold them where I can see your hands, Karen.'

'What, you think I've got a gun? Remember Lewin? We're not allowed guns when we get beyond a certain pay grade, Jack.'

'I wouldn't put it past you to buy a black market one. Or to steal one from the armoury,' he said. 'So keep them up, and don't drop the bags.'

'Why?' she said.

'I don't want to have to stab you,' he said. 'You ruined my life. You realise that?'

'I was just trying to get on.'

'So you had Jimmy McNeill stalk my wife, force her into his bed. Just to ruin me, so you could get me out and take over my teams'? That's not nice.'

'No. But it's how to get on.'

'You could have tried it by simple merit, Karen. I liked you. I tried to help you. Christ, I even *hired* you!'

'Oh, right. So you'd have given up your job for me? I don't think so.'

'Karen, even if it meant you went above me, I'd have done that, yes. Because I liked you, and you were very good.'

'Well, it's academic now. I'm finished. Washed up, and I'm not forty yet! I thought I'd be retiring at fifty, and as it is, I'll be lucky to get out at sixty with a clerical pension.'

'You want sympathy?'

'Not from you.'

'Your story about me was an insult. I've seen the reports you concocted about my phone on the day Jimmy died. What a load of bollocks. How did you do that?'

'I just copied a report on my scanner, removed the bits that didn't agree, inserted your phone details, and bingo. It was Jimmy's report, actually. So it went exactly where he was.'

'And you thought you could make it seem like me? Jesus.'

'I know. It was persuasive, though. Persuasive enough for the DDG.'

'Yes,' Jack said. 'But I wasn't stupid enough to take my phone. I'm bright enough to leave that behind when I commit murder, Karen.'

'But you…'

There was a hideous realisation even as she stammered, and then she felt the cord go about her neck. She tried to reach up to pull it away as the pressure about her throat tightened, the two bags fell to the ground, and a bottle smashed. The last odour she could discern as her sight blackened, and her lungs seemed to fill with concrete, was the smell of good Bordeaux as it flooded the concrete parking floor.

Jack waited a while longer, the cord taut in his hand, and felt for a pulse. It was there, a fluttering little feather of movement, and then… gone.

He removed the rope from her, and went to the edge of the parking bay. There was a four-inch pipe up there. He climbed on the car's bonnet, threw one end of rope over the pipe and made a noose of the other end. He pulled her up to the car, put the rope over her head, then grabbed the other end, pulling her up until her feet swung some six inches from the ground. He took both her shoes, and placed them heavily on the car's bonnet to make it appear she had stepped from it, then released her so that the shoes scraped over the paintwork. Finally, he stood back and began to walk away. He pulled the latex gloves from his hands as he went, putting them into his pocket, and then shoved his hands into his trousers, whistling, as he made his way up the stairs.

Half an hour later he was at a bus stop when the police cars came hurtling past, sirens blaring and lights flashing.

He watched them for a moment. There was no guilt or sadness. He had just killed a woman he had known for over a decade, and there was nothing in his heart – only an emptiness. Her death was irrelevant. It achieved nothing.

'But at least she didn't get away with it, Danny,' he muttered. She had tried to keep the torture going, helping Amiss and his fundamentalist supporters and ignoring the fact that their victims were mostly innocent.

Yes. Jack felt no guilt, but there was just a small tingle in his heart, a small sense of satisfaction – a feeling that Danny Lewin and Stephen Orme and the others were avenged.

Acknowledgements

This book would have been enormously difficult to write without the active help of many people all over America and England. It would be impossible to list them all, but there are some who helped a great deal.

I am very grateful to Sergeant Sean Whitcomb of the Seattle Police Media Response Unit for his advice on firearms laws in Seattle;

To James H. Frounfelter of the Benaroya Hall, Seattle, for his help identifying certain plaques outside his hall;

To Mary Burke of Conway Stewart USA for her help in checking details of shops in Seattle;

To Gordon S. Burton of the Anton Anderson Memorial Tunnel for helping me with the location and equipment in the tunnel's safe houses;

To the delightful staff of the Seattle Mystery Bookstore for their great support and kindness to this wandering author;

To Dana Stabenow and Karen J. Laubenstein for their help during my all too fleeting visit to Anchorage in 2007, especially for their advice on where to go to play with handguns;

To Ruth Dudley Edwards and Jane Conway Gordon for their acerbic wit during the Bouchercon trip in 2007, during which this story first came to my mind;

To Keith, my brother, for making some excellent suggestions about cuts from the original manuscript. I never thought I'd have to thank an actuary for his literary skills. And neither did he;

To my agent, for having the faith to see the potential of this story and for his unswerving support during the writing.

But most of all to my wife and family for their patience during a very tough few months while I locked myself away and wrote this tale.

20010471R00229

Printed in Great Britain
by Amazon